HIS LAST MISTRESS

I struck the little brass cymbals again and again, faster and more surely, until my hips and belly began to respond to the rhythm my fingers coaxed from the *zil*. The room grew oppressively hot as I danced on. I shed my restrictive garments one by one and flung them into the cavernous wardrobe. My prim highbuttoned shirtwaist was followed by my brown flannel skirt, neat kid boots, even the pins that tamed my hair. How lovely to feel its saffron waves slide free around my shoulders!

I threw back my head and laughed. Then, urging my cymbal-bedecked fingers to an even faster pace, I abandoned what was left of my usual reserve.

I did not hear Thorn Ramsay enter the room, nor did I know how long he had been standing there watching me, his image wavering ghostlike behind mine in the mirror. He advanced slowly toward me, his intense falcon-eyed gaze fixed upon my astonished reflection.

"I heard the cymbals," he said. "I couldn't . . . I thought . . ." He shook his dark, shaggy head as if in denial of unimaginable suspicions. "It was as if she had crept back from some shrouded netherworld to plague us all."

I had no need to ask to whom he referred. As his searching green eyes captured mine, his hands drifted down to rest upon my naked shoulders. The sensation of scorching heat scattered my thoughts into the rose-scented air. I swayed unresistingly into his demanding arms, nuzzled against his broad chest, delighting in the male smell of him, of leather and wood smoke and cigars. I raised my mouth toward his as eagerly as a dungeoned prisoner seeking light and air.

GOTHICS A LA MOOR—FROM ZEBRA

ISLAND OF LOST RUBIES
by Patricia Werner   (2603, $3.95)

Heartbroken by her father's death and the loss of her great love, Eileen returns to her island home to claim her inheritance. But eerie things begin happening the minute she steps off the boat, and it isn't long before Eileen realizes that there's no escape from *THE ISLAND OF LOST RUBIES*.

DARK CRIES OF GRAY OAKS
by Lee Karr   (2736, $3.95)

When orphaned Brianna Anderson was offered a job as companion to the mentally ill seventeen-year-old girl, Cassie, she was grateful for the non-troublesome employment. Soon she began to wonder why the girl's family insisted that Cassie be given hydro-electrical therapy and increased doses of laudanum. What was the shocking secret that Cassie held in her dark tormented mind? And was she herself in danger?

CRYSTAL SHADOWS
by Michele Y. Thomas   (2819, $3.95)

When Teresa Hawthorne accepted a post as tutor to the wealthy Curtis family, she didn't believe the scandal surrounding them would be any concern of hers. However, it soon began to seem as if someone was trying to ruin the Curtises and Theresa was becoming the unwitting target of a deadly conspiracy . . .

CASTLE OF CRUSHED SHAMROCKS
by Lee Carr   (2843, $3.95)

Penniless and alone, eighteen-year-old Aileen O'Conner traveled to the coast of Ireland to be recognized as daughter and heir to Lord Edwin Lynhurst. Upon her arrival, she was horrified to find her long lost father had been murdered. And slowly, the extent of the danger dawned upon her: her father's killer was still at large. And her name was next on the list.

BRIDE OF HATFIELD CASTLE
by Beverly G. Warren   (2517, $3.95)

Left a widow on her wedding night and the sole inheritor of Hatfield's fortune, Eden Lane was convinced that someone wanted her out of the castle, preferably dead. Her failing health, the whispering voices of death, and the phantoms who roamed the keep were driving her mad. And although she came to the castle as a bride, she needed to discover who was trying to kill her, or leave as a corpse!

Available wherever paperbacks are sold, or order direct from the Publisher. Send cover price plus 50¢ per copy for mailing and handling to Zebra Books, Dept. 2896, 475 Park Avenue South, New York, N.Y. 10016. Residents of New York, New Jersey and Pennsylvania must include sales tax. DO NOT SEND CASH.

THE LOST HEIRESS OF HAWKSCLIFFE

JOYCE C. WARE

ZEBRA BOOKS
KENSINGTON PUBLISHING CORP.

ZEBRA BOOKS

are published by

Kensington Publishing Corp.
475 Park Avenue South
New York, NY 10016

First printing: February, 1990

Printed in the United States of America

For Wilson

PROLOGUE

There it is, Kate . . . do you see it? Hawkscliffe!

I can still feel the warm pressure of Uncle Vartan's arm
around my slight shoulders as I stood snuggled against
him on the deck of the *Mary Powell*, my eyes straining
to follow his pointing finger.

It was my first trip on a Hudson River steamer, an
outing planned to celebrate my thirteenth birthday. What
made it memorable—unique, in fact—was that Uncle
Vartan had decided to close his shop. He even paid his
astonished helpers the day's wage they could ill afford to
lose.

"Let the Hagopians sell a rug for a change," he said as
he locked the door, pocketing the key with a flourish.
"Come, dear child, the river awaits us!"

Oh, what a day it was! There was so much to see, I
wished for eyes in the back of my head. Suddenly, Uncle
Vartan's arm tightened around me.

Hawkscliffe?

The name meant nothing to me then; confused, I looked

downstream across the churning wake of the paddlewheel.

"No, dear child, up there! Higher than high!"

I pressed hard against him, my hands gripping the glossy mahogany rail, the better to trace the path of his finger across the swirling water and up the craggy cliff face to the very top.

"Where, Uncle Vartan? I don't see. . . ."

Then, all at once, gleaming gold against a phalanx of dark, jagged spruce, I spied soaring minarets and a glitter of mosaics more brilliantly blue than the June sky above us. A moment later, the steamer rounded a bend, and the delicate lofty spires were veiled by billowing verdancy.

In later years, as I helped him roll up a glorious antique rug he had just sold, Uncle Vartan would sometimes whisper that there was an even finer one of its type at Hawkscliffe.

"If only we might visit there someday," I would murmur longingly, for by then I knew that the estate's owner, the famous artist Charles Quintus Ramsay, had once been my uncle's most valued customer. "Please do say we may, Uncle Vartan."

But no matter how artful my plea, his response never varied. "We'll see, dear girl, we'll see," he would say, but a troubled look in his deep-set eyes belied the tender smile meant to ease my disappointment. By the time I was eighteen, I knew that what he really meant was no.

CHAPTER ONE

The day I finally journeyed to Hawkscliffe it must have been raining in New York, for as the train chugged north I recall spatters of sleet starring the fogged windows. I remember, too, wiping the soot-streaked glass with my handkerchief, but all I gained for my scrap of soiled linen was a dismal view. The gaudy dress of fall had given way to the mourning cloak of early November, and even that month's subtle hues were washed to gray that drear afternoon.

I tried to glimpse the long-remembered fabled aerie as the train slowed for Hendryk, my destination, but this time clouds masked the towers soaring above the rocky eminence that dominated the old riverside town. *Hawkscliffe!* A romantic conceit, some called it; a folly, said others. Uncle Vartan had pronounced it more suitable for Constantinople's Bosphorus than the wilder shores of the Hudson.

Dear Uncle Vartan! I sniffed back the tears that had reddened my eyes so often during the six months since his death. I opened my purse, and as my fingers blindly sought a clean handkerchief, the rustle of the creased letter within reminded me that the time for weeping was past. If my bold plan was to succeed, I needed a stiff spine, not sobs.

The entrance to Hawkscliffe was closer to the town than I had expected. Layered masses of rhododendron masked it from curious exploration by casual passersby, and beyond the curtain of gray-green leaves a narrow drive wound steeply up. I feared the small horse harnessed to my hired runabout would be hard taxed to accomplish the task set for him, but my fears proved groundless. The lane curved this way and that, softening the grade, and at every bend a rustic pond, a glade, or a towering stand of evergreens diverted the eye. The distant views were shrouded still by clouds, and perforce my attention was claimed by the fairytale spires playing peekaboo among the hemlocks and spruces.

The small wagon rolled to a halt. The driver wordlessly deposited my bags in a wide recess set into a head-high stone wall, a massive bulwark of roughly quarried granite cubes, backed with shrubbery and matted with vines, which effectively shielded the mansion from view. I stared at the stout wooden door barring my entrance. Its only ornamentation was a series of spear-shaped iron hinges pocked with rust and the swags of abandoned spiderwebs whose dusty strands still clutched the husks of hapless victims. I could find no latch or any means by which to announce my arrival, and as I huddled under the meager overhang to escape the raw wind, fitful eddys swirled dry leaves from neglected nooks to pluck at my ankles like inquisitive, bony fingers.

As the clip-clop of the descending pony's hooves faded into silence, I became aware of a shrill cry above me. *Kee-er-r-r. . . . Kee-er-r-r. . . .* It trailed breathily into stillness, like the wail of a lost child who has given up all hope of being found. *Kee-er-r-r. . . .* I peered up, hoping to distinguish the source of the keening, and all at once there they were: birds—large birds—circling low above the cliffs, the hawks that gave this windswept fastness its name.

Then another sound nudged at my ears . . . it was low, but strangely disquieting. In front of me an overgrown thicket shivered. A moment later a massive lop-eared head pierced the tangled branches, its teeth bared in a dreadful grin. The rumbling growl became a snarl as the dog's heavy, rough-coated body emerged, and startled recognition sent me scrambling up the wall faster than the dog's uncoiling muscles could hurl it toward the spot I had just abandoned.

"Zuleika!"

The voice was as deep as the dog's growl; its commanding tone turned the animal's menacing attack into slinking retreat. Whining piteously, the dog sat back on its haunches and cast an imploring look at the man who crashed from the thicket, then pulled up short at the sight of me.

"Well, Zulu, not your usual prey, eh? Prettier than a sheep, but not as edible—unless, of course, you could first unwrap her from all that serge."

He was a tall man. Cleanshaven and hatless, with dark hair ruffled by the wind, he wore his rough, leather-patched shooting coat with the easy grace of an outdoorsman. The groundskeeper, I guessed: those oiled, high-laced boots were too well worn to be those of a weekend sportsman. He talked soothingly to the dog, snapped a heavy leash to her wide, hobnailed collar, skewered his walking stick through its loop as a makeshift stake, then turned his attention to me.

"She's really quite harmless. Now if it had been her brother, Pasha. . . ." He grimaced expressively, intimating that I would be in bloody shreds by now if that had

11

been the case.

"Hardly harmless," I retorted heatedly, "if her usual prey is sheep. In her native land that would not be tolerated."

The man looked startled. His eyes were the clear water-green of mountain tarns. "You know the breed, then?"

"Yes, I do." Once seen guarding sheep in its native Anatolia, the fierce, single-minded Akbash was not easily forgotten. "Why else would I be up here, playing at Humpty-Dumpty?"

"Why else, indeed?" He cocked his head to one side and placed his brown fists on his hips. "A lady alpinist, perhaps? Not another claimant to the estate, I trust—a long-lost cousin? Or maybe a bastard daughter! Now *that* would be a capital jest!"

His choice of words was, I was sure, as deliberate as his concluding, mirthless snort of laughter, but the disdainful curl of lip? Habitual, I decided.

"Your language, sir, is exceeded only by your impertinence! I am here at the invitation of Mr. Philo Ramsay, and if your manners were not in as sorry a state as the grounds entrusted to your care—"

"Invited by Philo? The devil you say!"

I was startled by his familiar reference to the person who, judging from the letter in my purse, would soon be master of Hawkscliffe. We stared at each other. The man made no move to assist me from the stony ledge. He crossed his arms and adopted an easy stance, prepared to wait me out. His lazy, confident smile was that of a man accustomed to treating women with the same light-handed, careless mastery as he would a mettlesome horse. Uncle Vartan had warned me about men of his ilk.

I gathered my forces. "My purse, if you please."

"I beg your pardon?"

"My purse!" I commanded. "There! On top of my bags."

12

The man looked at my purse and then at me. He smiled again. Obviously, he was not mine to command—at least not without a reason that suited him. Very well, then . . . two could play at this game.

"The invitation you appear to question, my good man, is in that purse."

"*'My good man'?*" He repeated the words under his breath, shaking his head. He handed the black pouch up to me. "At yer service, milady," he said with a servile bow.

He was making fun of me! My fingers trembled with indignation as I extracted the creased letter. What was it Uncle Vartan used to say? *Let no one rob you of your dignity, dear girl.* I drew a deep breath and thrust the paper at him. "There! Read it yourself. Assuming you know how," I added in a mutter.

A twitch of his wide mobile mouth was the only indication he had heard my aside. His eyes scanned the paragraphs rapidly.

"It must be a miracle," he said at length, eyeing me solemnly. "The last time I saw Vartan Avakian he was a middle-aged Armenian."

I could feel the hot blood rise into my cheeks as I snatched the letter from his outstretched hand. Why should I have to pass muster with a groundskeeper? I was tempted to make my way off the wall as best I could, march down to the town, and take the first train back to New York City. The modest brownstone Uncle Vartan had left me had never seemed more appealing. But there were my bags—much too heavy to carry that long distance—and above all, my mission. I could not allow pique to deflect me. A few ruffled feathers were a small price to pay for all I planned for my future.

"I am Vartan Avakian's niece, Katherine Mackenzie," I began, in as dignified a manner as it is possible to muster while sitting, legs adangle, on top of a stone wall. "My uncle died six months ago; I have come to accept in his

13

stead the commission offered him." Exasperation clipped my words short. "Now will you please conduct me to Mr. Ramsay?"

The man stepped back, folded his arms again, and regarded me speculatively through narrowed eyes. The piercing intelligence in their green depths arrested me. Whatever else this fellow was, he was no fool.

"And what does a little saffron-haired girl like you know about appraising oriental rugs? Since when have Scots taken to trading in carpets?"

"It is true, my father was a Scot—"

The man nodded. "Strong blood, that. I can see it in the hair and the set of the jaw." He chuckled. "And in that splash of freckles across your nose."

"—But my mother, Uncle Vartan's sister, was Armenian," I continued, ignoring his personal remarks.

He stepped closer. He placed his long hands on the wall, one on either side of me. "Of course," he murmured, searching my face, "that explains the dark eyes: those liquid, eastern eyes. . . ."

His voice drifted off. I could feel the blood pounding in my ears. His eyes seemed to draw me in until I was drowning in the clear water-green of them. I heard a sigh—my own—and than an indignant yelp.

The man turned, releasing me from his gaze. "Hush, Zulu!"

By the time he turned back I had recovered my self-possession, but the inactivity forced by my precarious perch had taken its toll. My kid walking boots offered scant protection from the numbing cold, and sleet had once again begun to needle my cheeks. At length, discomfort conquered my distaste.

"Please, sir, I fear I require your assistance."

I leaned down to grasp the hands he reached up to me. Their strength was reassuring, but as I inched myself uncertainly off the rough granite, the warm pressure of those hands, transferred to my waist to support me, made me tremble. Fearing I would fall, he held me even closer, and as I eased down along the warm, strong length of him I inhaled a heady aroma of tweed, oiled leather, and healthy male skin.

"Violets," he murmured, his lips grazing my ear. "You have the scent of violets. . . ."

My toes touched the ground. Breaking free from his embrace, I busily began to assemble my few belongings.

He strolled over and relieved me of my bags, brushing me aside as unconcernedly as one might a small, ill-tempered terrier. "We go through the gap." Both hands now occupied with my belongings, he motioned with his head. "Just there, up ahead." The dog yelped again. "Would you mind?"

I removed his walking stick from the loop in Zuleika's leash. She favored me with a brief wag and moved on at a sedate pace, the leash trailing behind her.

He led the way through the rock-bound passage, then stopped to let me precede him into the rough-mown clearing beyond. My clasped hands flew to my breast as my eyes opened wide. I couldn't decide whether to be amazed, amused, or dreadfully homesick . . . perhaps all three.

The extraordinary building that dominated the hilltop above me was a pastiche, a veritable Turkish stew of the architectural styles of my birthplace: mosque and *medrese*, castle and *yali*. It combined stone and wood, mosaic and gilt in a dizzying, dazzling array of Ottoman-Byzantine-Arabic ornamentation. Both foolish and fine, it was as grand an expression of the brashly romantic spirit of my adopted land as I could ever hope to see.

"But it's so . . . it's so *American!*" I exclaimed.

My companion stared at me thunderstruck, then threw back his dark head and laughed wholeheartedly. "My dear Miss Mackenzie," he finally said, "I am forever in your debt. I had given up hope of ever being surprised by

15

anything again. Come, let me introduce you to Philo. Sometimes I think he's even less susceptible to surprise than I—though for very different reasons."

As I climbed the wide steps to the broad terrace surrounding the mansion, I became aware that the neglect I had already noted in the encroaching thickets extended to the building as well. Sculptured timber arches, splintered along the edges, were soft with dark decay at their centers. Eroding mortar betrayed a crumbling buttress's lack of useful function. Spires discolored by tarnish proved the gilding counterfeit, and the tulips and carnations swirling over the glazed wall tiles had sacrificed petals and leaves to a score of frosts and heaving thaws.

How sad, I thought. Suddenly I was reminded of the woman I had once seen by chance on my uncle's arm. I was hurrying through a neighborhood I seldom frequented, on an errand I no longer recall, when all at once there they were, strolling out from under the gaily striped canvas awning of a small hotel. When I recovered from my mild surprise—for in my innocence I assumed he had taken the lady to tea—I remember thinking how pretty she was. Blond and pink-cheeked, she was dressed in the latest fashion, and a flirtatious smile curved her lips as she listened to what my uncle was saying. As they drew closer, however, I realized that her clothing was garish, her lips and aging cheeks were painted, and the gold of her hair was as false as the gilt on Hawkscliffe's spires. Shocked, I stopped and stared, and then my uncle saw me. I can still see the guilt and shame in his eyes.

We never spoke of the incident, but it was soon after that Uncle Vartan began my apprenticeship in earnest. He said he did not wish to see me forced either to marry for my keep, or, because of what he was pleased to term my superior intelligence, to settle for ordinary employment.

In time, of course, I became aware of yet another alternative for young women with no prospects, and if Uncle Vartan had known how often the memory of that raddled, painted face served to spur my studies of carpet structure and repair, he might have been more grateful than sorry for the encounter.

"Come along, Miss Mackenzie! Let's get you settled. You'll have time enough to gawk tomorrow."

Gawk, indeed! I looked up once more at the facade's shabby grandeur. Even wasted faces have their uses, I reminded myself. I then hastened obediently across the leaf-littered terrace in the wake of my long-legged guide, disconcerted to find myself traveling in tandem with the ambling sheepdog. Docile and silent—for the moment, at least—the pair of us no doubt fulfilled his requirements for females of whatever species. It was, after all, what my father had required of my mother and would, if he had lived, have demanded of me. As it was, I was expected at a very young age to attend as raptly to Papa's lectures on Eastern art as his converts did to his parables.

My poor father! How my stifled yawns pained him! He never realized how much more compelling his sermons on sin were than his dry discourse on architraves. When John Mackenzie preached, one could almost feel the searing heat of hellfire and hear the screams of the damned. An odd talent, I've often thought since.

I truly mourned my parents' untimely deaths, but after the weeping, after the voyage to New York, after I made a new life with Uncle Vartan—who found my childish prattle charming—I vowed I would never accept a man who could not accept me as his equal.

To be sure, romantic love had its charms—at twenty-three I had experienced infatuation's fleeting magic more than once—but I was firmly convinced that only friendship, the noblest of human ties, would allow me to remain captain of my own soul whilst navigating life's stormy

17

passages to the calm harbor of my golden years.

I reminded myself of this conviction as I hurried along after the dark-haired man whose rough, careless dress could not disguise his lithe grace and erect, confident carriage. Surely the heat in my cheeks was due only to my effort to keep up with him, and the heightened beat of my heart merely anticipated my meeting with Philo Ramsay. I was a businesswoman with a mission; what could I possibly find of interest in the kind of bold masculinity that provokes sighs from shopgirls?

He stopped before a bank of French windows and turned. His saturnine face remained unsmiling, but a glint in his eyes—perhaps a mere reflection of the warm light spilling out from within—seemed to mock my earnest thoughts. I swept by him, under the arch of his tweedy arm, through the pair of windows he opened for me. As I did so, a slight exhalation escaped my lips that, I must confess, sounded uncommonly like a sigh.

CHAPTER TWO

"I understand you have come to catalog my late uncle's rugs in *your* late uncle's place, Miss Mackenzie."

Despite his dry tone and faintly skeptical expression, Philo Ramsay extended his hand in greeting. It was a simple, friendly gesture, one that under the circumstances I had not expected. He was a tall man, slim, fair, and elegantly turned out, but although the gaze he bent upon me was kindly, there was a hooded watchfulness in his gray eyes.

"My cousin tells me you brought my letter to Mr. Avakian with you. May I see it?" Then, as if to soften the implied challenge, "To refresh my memory?"

"Your *cousin?*"

Covered with confusion, I turned my eyes uncertainly from one man to the other. Aside from their commanding height, there was no family resemblance whatsoever. The clean, classic lines of Philo Ramsay's face contrasted markedly with his darker cousin's rugged features. At first he seemed little more than twenty-five, but a slight pouching of his jowls—apparent only when he turned in profile against the light—caused me to amend my estimate. Late thirties was more like it, I decided; and a gentleman, unlike his hawk-nosed gypsyish cousin, nameless still, who appeared to relish my embarrassment.

"Miss Mackenzie took me for a gatekeeper," he said with evident amusement.

"And you, of course, said nothing to enlighten her," Philo Ramsay said, all but wagging an admonishing finger at his cousin. "Really, Thorn!"

"She's a ready jumper to conclusions, I fear."

"Not gatekeeper," I corrected perversely, as I handed the requested letter to Philo Ramsay. "*Grounds*keeper."

Both men laughed at that.

"Would that he were!" Philo Ramsay exclaimed. "Allow me to introduce you, Miss Mackenzie. Thornton Ramsay is also a nephew of my late—"

"But unlamented—"

"Lamented by some," Philo corrected sharply. "As I was saying," he continued, "Thorn is my late uncle's other nephew, the stepson of my uncle's next-to-oldest brother—"

"Who was also your uncle, as were the other two—"

"Yes, yes, but do stop interrupting, Thorn; our family is confusing enough as it is."

"Which is good reason to spare Miss Mackenzie the tedious details. Suffice it to say, thanks to mortality's fearful toll of C.Q.'s siblings and their offspring, Philo appears to be the only surviving heir to Charles Quintus's estate, and I am the executor."

Appears to be? As executor, surely he must know, I thought; and, just as surely, the conservation of the estate until its distribution was his responsibility. "Am I to understand, then," I blurted, "that you are responsible for the sorry state of Hawkscliffe?"

20

Philo smiled. "Ah! What a clever girl! She's only just arrived and has already put her dainty finger right on it."

Thornton Ramsay's answering scowl was gratifying proof that I had drawn blood at last. "My dear young lady, since Hawkscliffe is none of your business, there is nothing for you to understand. You would have done well to absorb some of your uncle's tact along with his rug lore. Now, if you will excuse me, I'll leave you to discuss what *is* your business while I acquaint Cora with the news of Miss Mackenzie's unheralded arrival."

"And put Zuleika out," Philo called after him. "You know how Cora feels about those dogs in the house."

The big dog lumbered to her feet in response to Thorn Ramsay's whistle. Just before leaving the room, he turned back to tip me a wink as if to prove he had recovered his balance sooner than I.

Suppressing a very strong, very childish urge to stick out my tongue at the closing door, I turned back to make my apologies as best I could.

"I *am* sorry, Mr. Ramsay, I know I should have acquainted you with my intention to assume my uncle's mantle, as it were, but . . ." My words trailed off. I was uncertain how to continue without sounding either accusatory or self-pitying.

"You thought I would reject you either because of your sex or your unlikely name," he completed for me.

"Good heavens! How did you ever guess?"

"I've had my own experiences with unwarranted judgments," he said dryly. "Actually, if anything would put me off, it is your youthful appearance. How can anyone so young be knowledgeable enough to assess what is considered to be the finest collection of oriental carpets in America?" He tapped the letter with long, well-cared-for fingers.

It was a fair question, one that deserved a considered

21

answer. As I gathered my thoughts, he spoke again.

"I should tell you that my present position as director of the Pennsylvania Academy of Fine Arts affords me a certain, ah, sophistication in matters of this sort. What that means is that I am rather good at spotting weaknesses in claims of expertise—including my own," he added disarmingly. "My field happens to be European art, and I'm considered to have a good eye—but carpets?" He opened his arms wide, as if to expose himself to my scorn. "I am a Philistine, a veritable Caliban—in short, Miss Mackenzie, I know nothing about carpets, but I can soon tell whether or not *you* know something. Do I make myself clear?"

I nodded briskly. "Very. It is refreshing to know at the outset where I stand, unlike—" I paused. Thornton Ramsay was his cousin, after all.

He raised his fine eyebrows. A fleeting smile curved his lips, which were pleasantly accentuated by a mustache so blond it seemed more a suggestion than a reality. How handsome he was!

"Thorn can be trying," he admitted, "but he is very good at what he does—although we do not always agree on what it is he should do," he added, more to himself than to me. He cleared his throat. "Please be seated, Miss Mackenzie, and think of this not as an interview, but a conversation between friends." He returned to the large, ornately carved desk from which he had risen to greet me. He sat, neatly aligned the papers on the embossed leather top, then leaned back and crossed his legs. His gray eyes regarded me with keen interest.

"My earliest qualification," I began, "was an accident of birth. I was born in Constantinople, and I traveled the length and breadth of Anatolia during the first twelve years of my life. My father, a Scot, was a lay Catholic missionary, and although converting the Muslim and adherents of the Oriental Catholic churches to Rome was his passion, Eastern art was his avocation. I absorbed it—and Latin and Greek—in spite of myself. My father was nothing if not determined."

"Latin and Greek, eh?" Philo Ramsay nodded approvingly. "Impossible to be a genuine scholar without them. I am impressed, Miss Mackenzie, please go on."

Hastily, I mentally reviewed my biography. Surely Mr. Ramsay was not interested in the conflicts that warred within a girl torn between East and West—conflicts I was only now beginning to recognize myself, and that men like Thornton Ramsay seemed, inexplicably, to fan into flame. I continued with an edited version.

"My mother was Armenian. Her family had for generations been carpet weavers and sellers, as well as leaders in whatever community they found themselves—you see, the Armenians in Turkey, the passionate ones at least, are always on the move. It is not wise to be a nationalist under Ottoman rule."

I paused. "That is what killed my parents. We were staying for a few days in a village with relatives, some of whom were suspected of fomenting rebellion. One afternoon, while I was taking bread and cheese up to the shepherds, soldiers came. The village was torched—we could see the smoke from the high pastures—and my parents died in the flames. My Uncle Vartan, who had emigrated to America to escape persecution, was at home in New York between rug-buying trips, and as soon as the sad news reached him he arranged for my passage. It was not safe for him to return to Turkey while feelings still ran high.

"So there I was, a little girl with an inquiring mind in the home of an aging, childless widower who yearned to pass on the knowledge he had acquired over so many years. 'This is my legacy to you, dear child,' he would tell

23

me, for although his business was profitable, much of the profit went back into more rugs, finer rugs. In truth, his livelihood was in his hands, his eyes, and above all, his heart."

"And that man was your teacher," Philo Ramsay mused.

I nodded. "For ten wonderful years." I fell silent for a moment, remembering; then I laughed. "Uncle Vartan had all these sayings! 'See with your hands, dear child,' he would admonish me, or 'the front is the glory, but the back tells the story.' That one was his favorite; I must have heard it a hundred—no, two hundred times."

"What does it mean?"

I stared at the blond man. His gaze was guileless. He wasn't testing me; he really was ignorant about rugs. "Simply that anyone can copy a design, but a weaving style learned in childhood flows through the fingertips onto the loom as naturally as breathing. The design tells us something; the colors and wool tell us something more, but if we want to know for sure where a carpet was woven we look at the pattern of the weave on the back."

"Like brush strokes in painting."

"Exactly!"

We smiled at each other, and I sensed a kinship that eluded words. It wasn't friendship—we didn't know each other well enough yet for that—but whatever it was, his lack of condescension, the attention paid to what I had to say, was cheering. For the first time in months I no longer felt completely alone.

I rose to my feet, the better to take in my surroundings. The room was dominated by tall windows whose borders were painted representations of the arched, columned mihrab found on Ottoman prayer rugs. A majestic, beautifully crafted mahogany easel, angled to catch the north light, defined the room's function.

"So this was Charles Quintus Ramsay's studio," I said in an awed tone. I stepped closer to the easel. On it, a large luminous oil depicting a grand and romantic view of the Hudson commanded my attention. The river, winding sinuously below tree-crested, craggy heights, was divided by small islands into glittering ribbons that met and parted in a coruscating dance of sunlight and water. In the lower righthand corner, C. Q. Ramsay had signed and dated it in a bold slash of black.

"1862!" I exclaimed. "That's the year I was born."

"Uncle Charles's fame was at its height then." Philo Ramsay shook his fair head regretfully. "Before long, the critics' taste began to turn toward the moody Impressionist works which are now all the rage."

As I studied the impressive landscape I wondered if Uncle Vartan had seen it in progress. I knew that it was during the sixties and early seventies that he must have sold C. Q. Ramsay the rugs that constituted his collection, some of which were scattered here beneath my feet like a splash of jewels.

"What a wonderful room!" I exclaimed.

"Isn't it, though?" Philo Ramsay agreed. "I've appropriated it as my own," he added with a smile, indicating a low sleeping couch covered with a fine Kirman shawl and flanked by a large wardrobe in the Dutch style. "C.Q. was at his best here; he was, as my cousin intimated, a difficult man in many respects: arrogant, selfish and insensitive. But when he crossed this threshold," he said, pointing toward the iron-strapped door which had barricaded the artist from the prosaic world of his household, "he was a different person altogether, serious and dedicated.

"Before my uncle built Hawkscliffe, I was the only one permitted in his Manhattan studio while he worked, much to my Aunt Louise's very vocal annoyance. I suppose it was because of my ability to maintain silence for long

25

periods even at a young age. How I treasured those visits! He was a superb craftsman as well as an inspired artist, you know. Just watching C.Q. work taught me more than thousands of words from a lesser teacher. It was like being allowed into the presence of a high priest."

"With you as the worshipping acolyte."

It was Thornton Ramsay, returned to plague us. His sardonic tone caused my insides to roil.

"A willing servant, Thorn."

"Because you were never a threat, Philo. Charles Quintus saw to that early on. What is it the Jesuits say?"

Ah! I knew that one well. "Give me the child before he is seven—"

"And he's mine the rest of his life," Philo finished in my stead. "I don't see how it applies, cousin."

"Have you forgotten what he said about your boyhood sketches? 'There's no fire, no muscle in your hand, boy. Try again when you no longer sing soprano.' Considering your voice had already changed to tenor by then, I would hardly call that encouragement."

Philo Ramsay colored deeply. "He merely meant my work lacked maturity. Besides, I was never serious about becoming an artist. Early on, I decided my mission was to preserve art, not create it. It's not as if I were Cora . . ."

His voice trailed off, but whatever he meant was fully understood by his dark-haired cousin, whose curl of lip tightened into a grim line. "Yes, Cora. But here we are, burdening Miss Mackenzie with bits and pieces of the family skeletons again. I'm sure she would much rather go to her room to unpack and change out of that fusty serge in time for dinner, which Cora tells me will be at eight o'clock, or," he extracted a large gold watch from the pocket of his breeches, "about an hour from now."

Good heavens, I thought, I haven't even seen my room yet. My expression must have betrayed my dismay.

"No need to primp for a family dinner, Miss Mackenzie. Just brush out that pretty hair and pinch your cheeks and we won't even notice the serge."

"Mr. Ramsay!"

"And do call me Thorn, Miss Mackenzie, otherwise we won't know to which Mr. Ramsay you're referring—except, of course, when you employ that indignant tone of voice." He smiled and winked, and the calculated charm of it vexed me even more. "Come along, then. Time's a-wasting."

I glanced imploringly at Philo, but he merely smiled resignedly and waved me on. "At dinner, then, Miss Mackenzie."

"Harry has already taken your bags to your room," Thorn Ramsay offered as we walked side by side down the long corridor hung with stunning examples of Charles Quintus Ramsay's work, and wide enough to accommodate two very beautiful old Caucasian main carpets laid end to end.

"Harry Braunfels is the genuine Hawkscliffe groundsman," he added. "He is also the gatekeeper I thought you had mistaken me for, as well as kennelman, head groom—the only groom now, for that matter—and falconer. Vicious creatures, those hawks. I would have gotten rid of them long ago, but Harry said, 'They go; I go.' A man of few words is our Harry, and he never minces them. He was the model for the few figures C.Q. put in his landscapes. They got on very well, those two. He was the natural man that C.Q. could only play at being. Poor Charles Quintus! All bluff and boast and swagger. Harry's the real thing. You'll see when you meet him."

Despite myself, I was interested. Thornton Ramsay's breezy, anecdotal style had a perceptive quality that lifted it out of gossip into the realm of wry comment on the human condition. As we came to the end of the corridor,

27

however, the scene that greeted me as we turned into the main entrance hall captured my entire attention.

"Good heavens!" I hardly knew where to look first. Even at a time when a Turkish corner was de rigueur in fashionable homes, the effect was so calculatedly exotic as to be bizarre.

A pair of Persian bronze peacocks, larger than life, stood in front of a pair of intricately patterned Anatolian tribal kilims which served as portieres. In their beaks they clutched tall, flaring candleholders which in real life would surely have broken their slender necks. Beyond lay a central hall chockablock with small inlaid tables, carved stands, and wrought-iron racks upon which tribal artifacts, finely woven bags, and trappings of all kinds lay carelessly strewn. I half-expected the arrival, in a flurry of dust and curvetting hooves, of a horde of tribal chieftains come from Turkey and Persia and even far Turkestan to lay claim to their belongings.

At the end of the hall, a short, broad flight of brightly colored, kilim-carpeted steps directed the eye to the main staircase, an impressive amalgam of gleaming mahogany and brass-fitted balusters, each of a different design. A glossy Kurdish rug flowed up the shallow risers to the first landing. Displayed upon it, below an arched, elaborately shuttered, amber-painted window, was the pièce de résistance: a dramatic composition of crossed spears and shields whose unblemished surfaces betrayed them as unlikely to be genuine trophies of tribal clashes or bloody border skirmishes.

"Cat got your tongue, Miss Mackenzie?"

Despite my determination not to react to his mocking tone, I could feel my shoulders tighten and my nose elevate to a haughty tilt. "I beg your pardon?"

"You readily voiced your opinion of Hawkscliffe's exterior—have you nothing to say about this?" He gave a grand sweep of his hand denoting the motley array of furnishings. His green eyes glinted challengingly.

"For an artist, your late uncle had a remarkably . . . catholic taste in decoration," I ventured cautiously. There was scarce a style of Eastern art, ancient or modern, which was not represented. "Draping an ancient Hittite stone lion with strings of the blue-and-white glass eyes hawked in every market in Anatolia is a very . . . *original* concept."

He laughed. The flash of strong white teeth against nutbrown skin was, I admit, attractive. "Your talent at faintly praised damnations rivals that of the great C.Q. himself."

"Surely not, Mr. Ramsay!" It was a talent I did not covet.

"Perhaps not." His smile was softer now, and to my surprise he did not call me to task for ignoring his request to address him by his given name. "Perhaps you are merely employing the tact I accused you earlier of lacking. But tell me, just what *are* those glass eyes? I find them rather repellent."

"I hope not with good reason," I retorted. "They are amulets to ward off the evil eye. Versions of them are to be found throughout the Middle East. These are contemporary, but I have seen some too old to date."

"Religions come and go, but evil is never vanquished, eh?"

I nodded. I had a small collection, both old and new, bought covertly during my childhood. My father, who fervently believed evil would one day be vanquished by the church that commanded his heart and soul, would not have tolerated the heathen objects under his roof. I hid them in an ingeniously crafted cedar box I found one day in a dusty Stamboul shop, and they lay there still. Once, shortly after my parents' fiery deaths, and troubled by any

29

sins on my part that might have accounted for such a horror, I confided in Uncle Vartan. He had looked at me searchingly in a way I had found unsettling.

"It was no fault of yours, dear child, or of your pretty keepsakes. The evil lay elsewhere, in the minds and hearts of people bent on destruction. Only faith and courage can ward off evil such as that." Then, sensing my childish dismay—for I had been thinking in terms of guarding against evil imps and fairies, not people—he advised me to keep my amulets. "Because," he added in a reassuring whisper, "one never knows!"

I stepped forward to examine the amulets more closely—cheap bazaar trinkets, as I suspected—and noticed, for the first time, a striking portrait hanging on the wall to my right. It was of a woman: young, but without a trace of girlishness; and although she was no beauty, with looks so compelling as to render prettiness, even beauty, trivial.

Her white dress was high-waisted and flowing, conveying an impression of virginal sweetness mocked by the wearer's bold, fleshy face. Her slightly protuberant dark eyes were very large; her nose, aquiline; her skin, dusky. Sculptured, sensual lips curved in a smile which the smoldering challenge in the heavy-lidded eyes invested with seductive promise. Abundant dark hair fell in ringlets on shoulders carelessly swathed in a length of fine muslin gorgeously embellished with tulips and carnations embroidered in silk.

One of her hands clasped the finely worked shawl to her full breasts, and on her gently curved index finger she wore a ring striking because of its size and simplicity. It was a flat disk of gold about the diameter of a silver dollar, engraved with archaic calligraphy in a style which, like the embroidered floral motifs, was unmistakably Ottoman. Perhaps that explained the curious, haunting familiarity of this face I had never before seen.

"'That's his last mistress painted on the wall,'" Thorn Ramsay intoned, "'looking as if she were alive. . . .'"

It was a line of poetry, of that I was sure, but there was something not quite right about it. . . .

Ah! Of course! "'I call that piece a wonder. . . .'" I quoted in turn, "and it *is* wonderful, but who is she? I didn't realize Charles Quintus Ramsay did portraiture."

"He didn't—unless, of course, you count Harry Braunfels inserted into landscapes to lend scale to the elms. Roxelana was unique. In more ways than one," he added wryly.

"Roxelana," I repeated in a musing tone. "Seems an unlikely name for either a duchess or an Americn mistress," I said pertly, referring to his misquotation of Browning.

"As well as too humble a rank by far. Roxelana was neither American nor a duchess: she *claimed* to be an Ottoman princess. Be that as it may, they met in Constantinople near the end of C.Q.'s pilgrimage in search of exotic scenes to capture with his brush and recapture the attention of the art world, and for the first time in his life C.Q. was too smitten to be wary of a woman's wiles. In addition to her exalted rank, Roxelana further claimed to have been warned by persons loyal to her royal self that the sultan—or was it the sultan's chief wife?—was planning to tie her up in a sack and drop her in the Bosphorus.

"So Charles Quintus Ramsay, according to his often repeated and variously embellished account of it, proceeded to smuggle the doomed princess out of the Dolmabahce Palace and into his cabin on his homeward-bound ship just before it weighed anchor. Quite a feat of derring-do for an aging Lothario and a co-conspirator, rumored at the time to be a certain Vartan Avakian."

I smiled. Roxelana was the Western name for the scheming, influential favorite wife of Suleiman the Magnificent, who ruled the Ottoman Empire at the fifteenth-century peak of its fortunes. It was the perfect choice of a name for an ambitious imposter. The notion of Uncle Vartan being a party to such a scheme was preposterous.

"Smuggled her out how?" I asked. "Rolled up in a carpet, like Cleopatra?"

He shrugged and smiled. "I said it was rumored; I didn't say I believed it." His smile faded. He looked at me intently for a long moment, as if searching for words. When he finally spoke he did so hesitantly, with his face angled away. "I meant to say earlier that I'm sorry about your uncle. He was a good man."

I was touched by his awkward sincerity. It was difficult for this man to sheathe his verbal knives.

"You knew him, then?"

"Not well. His last visit here coincided with the house-warming. All the Ramsays were here; Roxelana was queening it even more than usual, and Cora was beside herself. As was your uncle, now that I think of it—in a much more subdued fashion, but something was definitely amiss."

Thorn Ramsay gave what I was beginning to think of as a characteristic shrug. "We clung together during those few days. Maybe it was just that he felt an outsider here, as I always did. He and C.Q. had a falling out soon after that. I never knew why, but I had the feeling your uncle disapproved of Roxelana. Curious . . . you would have thought they might find something in common."

I raised my eyebrows. "An old Armenian and a young Turkish woman? Not likely! Especially if she was highborn, as she claimed." I looked again at the arresting likeness. "She has a certain . . . appeal," I admitted grudgingly.

Thorn Ramsay smiled knowingly. "Yes, I guess you could say that," he said in an amused drawl. "Lord knows she affected everyone at Hawkscliffe in one way or another. Sometimes I fancy I can hear her still—that distinctive husky laugh, late at night, from behind closed doors."

Thornton Ramsay paused. The amused smile on his wide, mobile mouth faded, and he turned his dark, shaggy head back toward the portrait. The silence lengthened. When he turned back to stare at me broodingly from under lowered brows, his shadowed eyes seemed more black than green, as darkly somber as the firs of northern forests.

"Oh, yes, Miss Mackenzie, my uncle's last and long-lost mistress did indeed have a certain appeal."

CHAPTER THREE

"I trust your room is satisfactory."

It was not a question. Cora Banks's bright brown eyes as they met mine across the massive dining table held neither challenge nor inquiry. Her gray-streaked brown hair was pulled back into a bun in a severe style which emphasized the housekeeper's high forehead and narrow beak of a nose . . . a small beak, like that of a small, neat bird—a sparrow, perhaps. Her old-fashioned, trim-fitting brown woolen dress and alert, emotionless gaze underscored the comparison, and for the merest fraction of a moment I felt uncomfortably like a plump worm about to be skewered and gobbled down without the slightest remorse. Then she smiled, and the image skittered away.

"Perfectly satisfactory, Miss Banks," I replied. It was, in fact, a rather cheerless room—the colorful Orient appeared to have stopped at its threshold—but it was neat and clean and, to my surprised delight, had access to a modern water closet.

"Roxelana's personal maid occupied that room," she

amplified unnecessarily. "That was some time ago, though; you can rest assured the linen has been changed since."

Well! That certainly put me in my place. I smiled, nodded, and silently addressed the consommé. Although a wisp of a woman in comparison with the tall Ramsay men, Miss Banks's presentation of herself as more doyenne than housekeeper went unchallenged. I gazed covertly through my lashes at the Ramsay men: Philo looked embarrassed by her slighting remarks, which were veiled thinly by an insincere smile; Thornton seemed amused.

"I changed it myself, miss . . . just last week I did."

Startled by the sibilant whisper in my ear, I turned my head, nearly bumping the brow of the harried young girl serving us. She offered a basket of warm rolls redolent of yeast and butter. Her guileless blue eyes met mine in earnest apology; her cheeks flamed with color. The well-meant protestation touched me, confirming my opinion that the best manners were instinctive.

"I'll help you unpack after dinner," she offered impulsively, encouraged by my grateful smile.

"Mary Rose," Miss Banks said sharply, "I believe the rest of us would also enjoy Agnes's rolls with our first course."

"I've already unpacked, Mary Rose," I returned softly, "but I do appreciate your offer."

"Mary Rose!"

"The fault is mine, Miss Banks," I protested, "and I *am* sorry, for the rolls are very good indeed."

As she turned away, the chastised girl's bob of a curtsy in acknowledgment of my defense rustled her long, starched white apron. Her eyes sought mine conspiratorily as Philo's hands, slim and as elegantly attenuated as an El Greco saint's, paused uncertainly above the rolls she offered him.

Mary Rose's quiet sigh as she awaited Philo Ramsay's choice caused the streamers of her little white cap to flutter. Her somber black and white garb contrasted interestingly with the rich olive green of walls ringed by an intricately detailed dado of pseudo-Arabic calligraphy traced in copper and gold. Dark canvases framed ornately in carved and gilded wood punctuated the long, narrow room like portholes in a ship; the flames in the fireplace cast shifting shadows over all. It was a scene Rembrandt might have painted.

"Tell me, Philo, are you planning to eat a roll or acquire one for that museum of yours? They look as alike as peas in a pod to me, but then I don't pretend any connoisseurship of the culinary arts."

As Thornton Ramsay's teasing darts reached their unsuspecting target, Philo colored, Mary Rose tittered, and Cora Banks's mouth tightened.

"Nor I, Thorn," Philo said, "but I was unwilling to settle for something half-baked," he added lightly.

The two men were even more of a contrast at dinner, now that Thornton Ramsay was dressed in more conventional attire. Both wore well-tailored suits of a rather similar gray-shaded tweed, but Philo had chosen to augment his with an elegant paisley waistcoat enhanced by a gold swag of watch chain and fob. Thornton wore a waistcoat of the same conservative tweed as his suit, but his gleaming white collar was softened by a length of dark red silk tied in a soft, careless bow. The one effect seemed calculated; the other, the first thing that came to hand, yet the more I thought about it, the less sure I became about which was which.

"Thornton tells me you are Vartan Avakian's niece, Miss Mackenzie." Cora Banks arched her thin eyebrows. "I must say you don't look like one of them."

"I beg your pardon, Miss Banks?" I was honestly perplexed: aside from being female, what quality was necessary to earmark one as a niece?

"One of *them*, like your uncle." Then, as I continued

to stare at her uncomprehendingly, she finally got to the point. "An Armenian rug merchant, my dear. But, I suppose with a name like Mackenzie—"

"Miss Mackenzie has already been put through this once today, Cora," Thorn interjected in a tone of mild reproach.

Put through by *you*, I accused silently. "I'm willing to go through it again, if necesary," I said evenly, hoping my annoyance wasn't as apparent as it felt. "In Turkey, my birthplace, and throughout the East, the making and selling of rugs is an honorable profession, Miss Banks. I am proud to be following in my late uncle's footsteps."

"And are you clever at bargaining, my dear?"

Her sweet tone, no doubt intended to sugar-coat the implied snub, failed to make it more palatable.

"I do not know. Uncle Vartan advised me against it. He told me Americans were not very good at the game— except, of course, for Charles Quintus Ramsay, who, he said, sometimes got the better of the deal."

Philo hid a smile, but Thornton threw back his shaggy dark head and hooted with delight. "He would, the old reprobate!"

Spots of red burned in Cora Banks's cheeks. "Do I gather, then, that he usually got the worst of it?"

"Not at all," I retorted defensively. "All I meant was that Easterners assume that people who wish to buy know the value of the item sought, in which case the bargaining process assures a fair price for the buyer and a reasonable profit for the seller. Mr. Ramsay knew well the value of all the goods he bought."

Cora Banks rose abruptly, toppling her bentwood chair off the carpet to clatter on the parquet floor beyond.

"How dare you, Miss Mackenzie!" The crystal prisms on the huge brass lamp suspended above the table tinkled in seeming protest of her shrill outburst. Her small hands, fisted with agitation, swung wildly. The cut-glass water pitcher overturned, loosing a gush of icy rivulets among the place settings.

What had I said to provoke such fury? I looked from one cousin to the other, hoping for enlightenment, but they sat transfixed. For a brief, frozen moment the only sound was Miss Banks's labored breathing accompanied by the muffled dripping of water from the damask cloth to the Heriz carpet below.

"Charles Quintus never saw through that woman's self-inflated value to the base metal below," she hissed, fixing me with a baleful stare. "He saw gold where there was only lead—dark, cold, and poisonous. He was bewitched by that Turkish harlot in the stews of Stamboul—*and Vartan Avakian was the go-between!*"

Philo retrieved Cora's chair, but although she made a conscious effort to compose herself, she resisted his effort to reseat her. "Tell me, Miss Mackenzie, what 'reasonable profit' did your precious uncle make on *that* transaction, I wonder? And what is your real purpose in being here?" Her false smile transformed the open challenge into an insinuating taunt.

"You go too far, Cora!" It was Thornton Ramsay, his voice a low rumble of reproving thunder. "Miss Mackenzie is a guest in this house. Until she and Philo accomplish what he has commissioned her to do, kindly keep your reservations about her, her uncle, and her heritage to yourself." He then turned to me, his green eyes shadowed and haunting under darkly frowning brows. "I apologize for Cora, Miss Mackenzie. She sometimes forgets her place."

Miss Banks's sharp gasp made me tear my gaze from those mesmerizing eyes. With one hand clasped to her pale, thin lips, which had rounded into a quivering circle of anguish by Thornton's harsh reproof, she whirled from the table and out of the room.

Philo sighed. "Cora's not the only one who goes too far, Thorn," he said in a weary tone. He passed a long, slender hand over his blond head as if attempting to erase the unpleasant exchange from his mind. "I had better go see if I can mend fences. I *am* sorry, Miss Mackenzie . . . I'm afraid you've been offered little in the way of welcome."

I wordlessly inclined my head, both in acknowledgment of his statement and to convey my indecision about the advisability of my continued presence in this troubled house.

We sat in silence, Thornton Ramsay and I, at a table that seemed too long in a room too big for two diners paired by chance rather than choice. Reluctant to meet his penetrating gaze, I looked above the centerpiece between us, an elaborately chased silver epergne filled with ferns and orange-berried bittersweet, as if fascinated by the artworks hanging on the wall beyond him.

Out of the corner of my eye I saw him smile, for it was a pointless ruse. I could not tell if the gilt-framed oils on the green leather-textured walls were landscapes, portraits, or scenes of conquest: the shadows beyond the circle of lamplight lent them all an air of brooding mystery.

A shudder of wind rattled the high windows and sent sleet slithering across the painted panes. I shivered. The only sources of warmth were the flames flickering in the brass-framed Mooresque fireplace and the flush which washed over my cheeks as Thornton Ramsay continued to assess me. The orange tongues of fire lighting his craggy features from below lent his face a wolfish aspect. His strong, even teeth gleamed white as his mouth curved in a slow, insinuating smile which aroused in me an unfamiliar swirl of emotions. Fright? Yes, that I recognized, but excitement? Even as I denied the possibility, I was forced, to my shame, to admit the truth of it.

"You were right to change, Miss Mackenzie," he said at length. "Russet velvet becomes you."

The unexpected compliment unsettled me. "I fear it is sadly out of fashion, and I appear to have lost a button—"

"A simple thank-you would have sufficed."

Although his tone indicated a gentle tease rather than a rebuke, I bent my head to hide my confusion and gain time to gather my scattered wits. When I looked up, I was able to speak without a betraying tremor. "Might it be possible, please, for me to be driven down to Hendryk tomorrow to take an early train back to New York?"

My stiffly phrased question surprised him. "Giving up so soon, Miss Mackenzie?"

I rose angrily. "My business here is—was—straightforward, and my conduct has, I think, been professional. I do not understand why I should be subject to insult and innuendo, Mr. Ramsay—truly I do not! I grant you my notion to arrive without proper notice was ill conceived, but—"

"Hush, Miss Mackenzie, and do sit down. You are quite right, of course, I have behaved churlishly—expecting, I guess, that those soulful Eastern brown eyes of yours would penetrate our hearts and read all our secrets, when all you are, really, is the person from Porlock, come on business."

I couldn't help but smile at his reference to the commercial visitor who arrived unannounced on Samuel Taylor Coleridge's doorstep, fatally interrupting the poet's flow of poetic fancy.

"Ah, but Charles Quintus's pleasure dome, unlike Coleridge's creation for Kubla Khan, has endured. A little the worse for wear, of course," I added slyly. "I wish I had seen it in its heyday."

"Do you?" He shrugged. "Perhaps if you knew more of its history—"

Whatever he meant to say was interrupted by a hurried click of heels. "Oh! Are you all that's left, then?" It was Mary Rose, entering with a platter of roast lamb surrounded by succulent, crisp brown potatoes and buttered carrot spears. She eyed the two of us, seated

41

diagonally across the wide table, with consternation. After serving us in silence, she was clearly unable to determine how to place the platter within reach of us both, a puzzle Thornton Ramsay readily solved by moving his place setting to one end and mine directly to his right.

"There you are, Mary Rose. Accomplished faster than you can say *prestidigitation!*"

Unused to being teased by a man she considered her better, she colored prettily. "Aren't Miss Cora and Mr. Philo expected back then, sir? Cook will be that upset, she will!"

"Tell Agnes I said to let them fend for themselves."

Mary Rose was obviously horrified at the thought of the gentry lifting a finger to help themselves. At times like these I had considerable sympathy for the bomb-throwing anarchists bent on sweeping away monied privilege; on the other hand, I reminded myself, only the privileged buy Oriental rugs.

"You were about to tell me something about Hawks-cliffe's history," I said as Thornton Ramsay filled my glass with wine.

He took a sip, then nodded approvingly. "Good wine, this. C.Q. had better taste in wine than he did in interior decoration—or women." He rubbed his clean-shaven jut of chin reflectively. "How much did your uncle tell you—about Hawkscliffe, I mean?"

"Almost nothing. A glimpse of its towers pointed out from a steamer one day; an occasional mention of rugs he had sold Charles Quintus. Odd, now that I think of it. They must have had a close association—I know they had a shared passion."

Thornton looked at me sharply. "Concerning rugs, you mean."

"Of course," I agreed. What else could I have meant?

"Let me see," he murmured absently, almost to himself, "where to begin unwinding this tangled tale?" He raised his eyes to mine again. "You are aware of C.Q.'s extraordinary artistic success?"

I nodded. "I know something of it. Having seen his paintings, I know the why of it, of course."

"Yes. An amazing talent accompanied by an equally amazing skill at peddling it."

I opened my mouth to protest, but he waved my words impatiently away. "I assure you, Miss Mackenzie, that for every hour my uncle spent invoking the divine spirit of nature with his brush, he spent at least another on schemes to win both critical and public esteem.

"At the crest of the God-in-nature wave in the mid-fifties, the exhibitions at the National Academy were highlights of the social season. Why, at the openings the painted sunsets and storms were hard put to hold their own amidst the crowd of crinolines and silk hats! I'm told that when C.Q. exhibited his latest masterpiece in his own studio, he would hang it against black crepe curtains, then light it brilliantly with clusters of gas jets concealed behind silver reflectors. To the awed spectators it must have seemed as if they were looking at the magnificent scene through a window. In short, Miss Mackenzie, Uncle Charles was a high-class snake-oil salesman."

"Except that his paintings were genuine, Mr. Ramsay," I admonished.

"Genuine, yes, but their size and prices inflated along with his ego until only museums, which were then springing up in every town that aspired to being cosmopolitan, had space enough to display them. But since all of them vied for a Charles Quintus Ramsay to give their fledgling collections the required cachet, C.Q.'s demands were met unquestioningly by a seemingly endless supply of patrons with bottomless pockets."

I shook my head. "It all sounds larger than life."

Thornton Ramsay raised his dark eyebrows. "But that's exactly how it was, and the cock o' the heap was Charles

Quintus himself. He had fame, money, women—oh yes, Miss Mackenzie," he added, obviously amused by the involuntary tightening of my expression, "many a starched petticoat wilted in his—how did you put it?—larger-than-life presence."

Suddenly his countenance darkened. "And many a young girl was ruined. A monstrous man, really. I never did understand how Roxelana curbed his appetites. Louise never managed it." He gave a bark of mirthless laughter.

Philo had mentioned someone named Louise . . . yes, Aunt Louise. "Charles Quintus's wife? Is she still alive?"

Again that mirthless laugh. "Very much so." He paused and looked beyond me into the dark shadows. "A dazzling woman in her prime. Classic features, and a full figure whose promise—" He stopped abruptly, literally biting off his words. His mouth twisted bitterly.

Discomfited, I dropped my eyes to my plate. During the silence that ensued, I toyed with the remaining carrot spears. When he resumed his narrative, it was in the same impersonal, ironic tone with which he had begun it.

"You see, C.Q. married Louise because she was a bona fide member of New York society, the coveted world his comfortable but bourgeois background denied him; she married him because she thought him artistic. It never occurred to Louise that the true artist is more apt to be egotistic and boorish than chivalrous and romantic. Poor old Lulu," he added in a derisive drawl. "C.Q. would have strayed even if she had been Helen of Troy."

I wondered at his lack of charity. "I assume she divorced him, then?"

He shifted uncomfortably. "I guess you could say that."

At that moment, Mary Rose's entrance with a raisin-and-citron–studded rice pudding effectively ended further discussion of a subject he was obviously unwilling to have me pursue. We ate the creamy custard in silence, lost in our separate lines of thought.

My curiosity was piqued. Although Thornton Ramsay made no secret of his dislike for both his uncle's former wife and his last mistress, he was obviously unwilling to share with me the reasons for it. I glanced up at him through my lashes. Perhaps if I caught him unawares. . . .

My eyes met the compelling green magic of his steadfast gaze. As if he had been reading my thoughts, instead of the other way around, he began to laugh; but his cousin's unexpected return made it unlikely I would ever learn why.

"Do you suppose there is enough of Agnes's pudding for me?" Philo asked.

"I'm sure there is enough of everything, Mr. Ramsay," I volunteered.

"No, no," he said, frowning and waving his hand. "Thank you for the thought, Miss Mackenzie, but I really haven't the stomach for it." He turned to the sideboard for a Canton bowl and plate.

"There you are, Philo!" Thornton spooned a generous dollop into the proffered bowl. "Something as soothing to your palate as I'm sure your words were for Cora. You were right, of course, but one of these days she and Harry really will go too far. They're simply taking advantage of the fact that I have neither the time nor financial resources it would take to find suitable replacements."

Philo looked at his dark cousin in disbelief. "How can you say that, Thorn? Cora has spent her entire adult life with the Ramsays, first in New York and then here at Hawkscliffe. This is the only home she has, and except for her nephew, the only family."

"The same could be said of Harry, Philo, yet I don't hear any stirring words from you in *his* defense. No one asked Cora to become C.Q.'s slavey, stretching his canvases, cleaning his brushes, meekly accepting his poor opinion of her own talent."

Thornton Ramsay turned to me. His uncharacteristically earnest expression made me uneasy. "You see, Miss Mackenzie, Cora is an artist too. Her forte was botanical watercolors, and she was very good indeed." He turned back to his unhappy cousin. "Has that portfolio she gave C.Q. ever turned up in the library, Philo? It was just like him to 'misplace' it. But, as I was saying, hers was an entirely different talent from C.Q.'s, and of course he sneered at it—told her it was suitable for painting posies on teacups—and before long she didn't think much of it either." His sardonic quirk confirmed the mockery I had suspected earlier. "The master had spoken, don't you know. I doubt if Cora has drawn a line in years, eh, Philo?"

"Everything is a joke to you, isn't it, Thorn? Cora, Hawkscliffe, me—even that poor girl who enjoyed a brief, shining hour as the apple of your eye before you made it clear you preferred a worm—or should I say snake?—to her sweet young innocence! Or perhaps you think every woman is an odalisque at heart? That Miss Meriwether merely got what she would have deserved sooner or later?"

The merry light in Thornton's green eyes vanished. "What occurred between Eloise Meriwether and me is no concern of yours! I did not break our engagement, nor did I give her sufficient cause to break it, on my word I did not!"

I was unsettled by his failure to refute Philo's provocative questions. Apparently Philo interpreted this as agreement. Realizing he had wrested the upper hand from his cousin, he pressed his advantage. The very model of gentlemanly assurance and rectitude, he raised his blond eyebrows. "Come now, Thorn, I was there! I saw you and Roxelana twined around each other—"

"*She* was dancing, not I! I . . . it lasted such a short time. . . ." Despite his dark scowl he seemed almost to be pleading.

"It lasted long enough for Eloise, and for everyone else who saw you that night, including Uncle Charles. That woman of his mesmerized you, Thorn! It's a wonder he ever made you executor of his estate."

"And as such, I have a monumentally time-consuming task you are not making any easier! By God, if there were any way—"

"Any way you could prevent me from inheriting Hawkscliffe?"

"You have no reason to think that, Philo!"

"No? You and your pinch-penny ways will leave me nothing to inherit. Why do you suppose I didn't ask your permission to have the Hawkscliffe rug collection catalogued? I knew they were the finest things in the house; I didn't want to run the risk of you selling them to some itinerant Armenian—sorry, Miss Mackenzie!—for a few dollars to pay the butcher and fill the coal bin."

"C.Q.'s will tied my hands, you know that!"

The two men fell silent, the only sound their heavy breathing. I pushed back my chair to escape.

"Please, Miss Mackenzie, stay," Philo said, moving his untouched bowl of pudding to one side. "My appetite has quite deserted me. If you decide you do not wish to remain at Hawkscliffe I will of course understand; if you do, I will meet you in the library tomorrow after breakfast." He bowed stiffly and departed.

Unsure of what to do, I looked up at Thornton Ramsay, who had also risen to his feet. He looked down at me with eyes still glittering with the emotion stirred by the clash I had just witnessed. Pacing restlessly, he grabbed the poker and jabbed at the slumbering embers in the grate behind me. The taut vitality of his movements both frightened and exhilarated me, and although he failed to arouse more than a dull red glow in the burned-out logs, I felt scorched as if by leaping flames. When he sat down again I felt a twinge of regret. The tiger was back in his cage.

47

CHAPTER FOUR

Thornton reached for the decanter.

"Welcome to Hawkscliffe," he said with a twisted smile devoid of amusement. "Here, have some more wine."

A few sips steadied my nerves, and I found myself reconsidering my impulse to flee. The Hawkscliffe rug catalog would establish me in a highly competitive trade in my own right, I rationalized; it would be foolish to abandon it. Henceforth I would pretend I was watching a play whose conflicts I could walk away from any time I chose, despite Cora Banks's attempt to assign me an unfair and unwanted role in this unfolding drama. I cleared my throat.

"I have decided to stay on after all, Mr. Ramsay. Your cousin has accepted my professional qualifications; the least I can do is respect his trust in me. But it would be more pleasant if I could initiate a truce between Miss Banks and me for the remainder of my stay. Perhaps if I had a clearer understanding of her position here I would be better able to avoid displeasing her."

My companion's mood brightened as I made my earnest little speech; at its conclusion, he threw back his head and laughed.

"Good girl! As you know, I do not think Philo's decision to have the rug collection catalogued was his to make, but now that you're here . . . well, I'll admit I hoped the starch in your pretty spine would stiffen up again."

Although I wasn't sure I cared for his familiarity, Thornton Ramsay's approval pleased me more than I cared to allow.

He leaned toward me, slowly turning his wineglass in his long fingers. "So, now that you've chosen to cast your lot with us here, there is all the more reason for you to know what you're getting into. The truth is, Miss Mackenzie, I doubt if it ever occurred to Cora that C.Q. had little use for a handmaiden distracted by her own talent. By the time C.Q. departed with your uncle for Constantinople, no fabled sovereign could have wished for a more loyal retainer than Cora."

"His wife had left by then?"

"Oh, yes. Cora had become quite adept at fending off Louise's intrusions into C.Q.'s studio, and when Lulu departed with the housekeeper in tow, Cora promptly extended her domain to the entire house."

I suspected not many people addressed as 'Lulu' the aristocratic woman he had described earlier, yet Thornton, who could have been hardly more than a boy at the time, had twice referred to her thus. But, deciding it would be imprudent to pry, I prodded instead.

"I guess, then, that despite C.Q.'s notorious . . . philandering, his return home accompanied by Roxelana came as a bit of a surprise?"

Thornton laughed. "Surprise? Oh, yes." His eyes crinkled appealingly at the corners, softening the somber effect of the deeper grooves that bracketed his wide mouth. "Roxelana rocked the boat to a fare-thee-well. She was no giddy girl or common adventuress to be discouraged by Cora's snapping at her heels. You see, the Hudson River School's tide in the art world had turned, and I suspect C.Q. welcomed the distraction provided by building a palace for his lady love with the fortune his talents had earned him. During that period she never left his side. She was like a vine around an aging pillar, clinging yet sustaining its eroding host."

He paused for a long, brooding moment. Perhaps it was the wine, but I found myself fascinated by every nuance of his expression, every inclination of his dark head and the play of his strong hands as they curved gently around the stem of his glass or cut the air to emphasize his words.

"Most of the excesses you have observed here at Hawkscliffe are Roxelana's," he continued, encompassing the room with a scimitar sweep of his long fingers. "I imagine she expected C.Q. to marry her, but he made it very clear one marriage had been more than enough for him. Besides, he was the type of man for whom a wife isn't nearly as exciting as a mistress. So she made sure, somehow, she would be his last mistress, and in the end she mastered him." Thornton Ramsay's lip curled. "C.Q. had ridden roughshod over everyone his entire adult life; it seems only fitting he end his days with the imprint of her dainty hooves on his back."

"I'm surprised Roxelana didn't get rid of Cora."

"Oh, she tried, but Cora knew C.Q.'s needs and habits too well. So Roxelana shrewdly decided that if she couldn't replace Cora she could at least *dis*place her, by physically removing her to the cottage, a remnant of the former estate, where she now lives. She was still the housekeeper, mind you, but from dinner until dawn Roxelana had C.Q. and the house to herself."

He burst out laughing. "Cora vented her rage on the shrubbery. I remember seeing her scurrying about, grubbing out overgrown forsythia and rhododendron plantings with her bare hands. Time and events have tamed her frustration, Miss Mackenzie; it readily comes to heel now except when she is reminded of Roxelana by anything she associates, rightly or wrongly, with her: your uncle, for example, and the dogs. You attracted the lightning merely by association. Part of it, of course, is due to her worry. Especially now. If only C.Q. had had time to change his will. . . ."

The wine made me bold. "I know it is none of my business, but hasn't his estate taken an unusually long time to settle? It must be five or six years since your uncle died—I recall how very depressed Uncle Vartan became when he read the long obituary. No! Now I remember, it was seven years ago, because it was only about a week later that he announced his intention to adopt me—as a safeguard, he said." I paused, wondering for the first time why he had thought a safeguard necessary; at the time, I was too thrilled to give it much thought.

Thornton Ramsay stared at me. The intensity of his green eyes as he gazed deep into mine shallowed my breathing. My hair seemed suddenly too thick and warm to bear, and as I reached up to sweep the weight of it from my neck I could feel the thudding swell of the pulse in my throat under my trembling fingers.

"You really *don't* know, do you?" His expression conveyed, oddly, relief as well as surprise. "Seven years ago, C.Q. learned Roxelana had a lover. It was the one transgression he would not, could not, countenance.

"According to Cora, Uncle Charles and Roxelana had a flaming row. Roxelana then fled Hawkscliffe—to join her lover presumably—and a week later C.Q died before he had a chance to change the will that left everything to her. This estate, his paintings, his New York property—everything.

"Roxelana hasn't been seen or heard of since, and in ten days she will have been missing exactly seven years. That's why Philo and I are here, Miss Mackenzie; that's why I thought *you* were here. In ten blissfully short days, in the courthouse in Hendryk, Roxelana will be declared legally dead, and the disposition of the estate finally determined." He raised his eyes to heaven and lifted his glass in a mockery of gratitude. "Hallelujah!"

"What a heartless thing to say!"

"You never knew her, Miss Mackenzie," he returned, frowning darkly.

"She was a human being, that's all I need to know." I could feel the blood drain from my cheeks. I pushed my chair back angrily, but before I could rise, Thornton's strong brown hand reached across to grasp my wrist. His fingers tightened on it like bands of iron.

"Hear me out, Katherine Mackenzie! That greedy parasite has cost me seven years of my life! Seven years of trying to maintain this absurd folly; seven years of fending off preposterous claimants—why, I've been petitioned by enough so-called long-lost relatives to populate a small Turkish village! Heartless, am I? I'm sick to death of Hawkscliffe, of Cora's pinched face, of Philo's suffering in not-quite-silence, and of Harry's swaggering bluster, and if that blasted woman *dares* to turn up at the hearing to claim her inheritance after seven long years of silence, I swear I'll strangle her with my bare hands."

Not only was I aghast at this outpouring of enraged frustration, it seemed to me he was venting it on the wrong target. "No one forced you to be the executor of the estate, Mr. Ramsay. If anyone is to blame, perhaps it is yourself."

He rose from his chair. His fingers bit deeper into my wrist, and I whimpered with the pain of it. Abruptly he loosed me. He stared at the darkening imprint of his grip on my white skin and then into my eyes. I could see no trace of remorse in the smouldering depths of his.

"Go to bed, Miss Mackenzie," he commanded in a sneering tone of dismissal. "Go to bed, and try to restrain yourself from meddling further in affairs that are no concern of yours."

At that, he turned on his heel and strode out of the room. I waited, holding onto the back of my chair for support, my wrist throbbing dully, as his steps retreated upstairs. Mary Rose, who came in to clear away the dishes, hastened to my side.

"Oh, miss! Are you ill? It's that pale you are!"

"No, Mary Rose, I just . . . I've had a very tiring day, and I believe I drank a bit too much wine. But thank you . . . thank you for your kind concern."

I walked into the court hall and slowly climbed the stairs, my way feebly lit by long tapers that guttered and smoked in the peacocks' beaks. As I passed Roxelana's portrait, a rivulet of wax flared up briefly. A gleam of malicious glee appeared to flicker in the varnished, heavy-lidded dark eyes, and the full lips seemed to quiver with imminent speech. A moment later, the flame died and the painted face retreated into the shadows.

The corridor was very still. The wintry sound of wind-driven sleet was muffled by the rooms which opened off it, and as I walked down the long carpeted hall toward my room, I heard only the heavy sibilant whisper of my velvet skirt. I paused with my hand on the glass knob of my door and stared at the elaborately carved double doors facing me at the end of the corridor. The intricate interlaced pattern was Ottoman workmanship, more suited to a sultan's seraglio than a bedroom in a country house on the Hudson, but then this room, Roxelana's room, was unlikely to be in any way usual.

I stepped closer and slowly traced the incised patterns with my hands. *His last mistress* . . . I wondered what it was like, to be a man's mistress. I curled my fingers around the curved brass handles. My hands tightened, and then, without conscious direction, pulled down. . . .

No!

I was, I sternly reminded myself, only a passing and reluctant player in this drama. I was no heroine, and surely there was no hero here for me. Yet I sensed that Roxelana's role was not yet played out, and in my heart of hearts I found her as fascinating as the forbidden amulets I had long ago secretly bought, one by sinful one, and hidden away in my little cedar box.

Secrets. We all have them. I could sense them rustling in the shadows of this strange, exotic house; I could hear them whispering to me behind these closed doors. Who was she, really, this woman who called herself Roxelana? How had the mistress become the master, and where had she gone?

My musings followed me into my dreams. I found myself again in the corridor outside Roxelana's room with my hands once more on the engraved brass handles. It was very hot, and as I pulled at the satin bows which modestly secured my nightdress across my throat and breast, I heard a woman's throaty chuckle. *Roxelana!* The handles twisted in my fingers, and the doors swung open. I seemed to float across the threshold into a saffron-colored mist scented with cedarwood and roses.

At first I could see nothing else. Then, impelled by the illogic of dreams, I slowly revolved, like a music box ballerina, and when I had completed the turn I saw in front of me a low couch draped in fine shawls and silk embroideries. Next to it stood a man, standing at ease, one knee slightly bent, as if he had all the time in the world. He was turned away from me, clad only in pale, skin-tight breeches that molded his firm buttocks and muscular calves. He wore soft, lustrous black leather boots, and in his hand he carried a small, intricately braided whip. His back was long and strongly tapered from breadth of shoulder to trim waist. His skin had the satiny glow of virile good health, and the elegant curve of his spine invited the touch of my fingers.

As I glided slowly forward, my eager hands out-stretched, the man turned, and as he waited, he impatiently tapped the little whip into the palm of his hand. The mists swirled and cleared, and I met his provocative smile and heated eyes . . . green eyes . . . Thorn Ramsay's eyes.

"Harlot!" he thundered. But it was my father's voice, and the smile became my father's disapproving glare. Icy blue eyes replaced the glinting green, and I gasped with horror and shame *and it was so hot. . . .*

I woke trembling and breathless, and as I clawed at the bedding which threatened to suffocate me I could still hear that low, mocking laughter. Pushing damp tendrils of hair from my forehead, I rose to fling open the window. As the fresh breeze poured in to cool my brow, I realized the temperature had risen sharply, melting the sleet and sending water spiraling through the gutters and down the leaders in an erratic chuckling flow that mocked my fevered dreams and the altogether unsuspected self, the secret me, that inhabited them.

CHAPTER FIVE

I awoke reluctantly, wrenched from a deep and dreamless second sleep by a muffled thudding sound, erratic in nature, as if a giant woodpecker were prying a meal out of the masonry with a beak wrought of iron. I raised my aching head—a memento of too much wine and too little sleep—and shielded my eyes against the light that streamed through my window, alternating inexplicably with shadow.

It was the shutter! Unable to find the hook for its eye when I flung it open during the night, I had abandoned it to the wayward wind. As I rose now to rescue it from the fresh breeze that had chased the rainclouds east to the sea, I breathed in the air that tumbled in over the sill. It was as fragrant as linen laid out to dry in a summer meadow. I leaned out and sniffed appreciatively; as I did so, the night vision that had possessed me seemed to melt away like hoarfrost, its chilling grip no match for the sun's warming rays.

Below me was a courtyard, enclosed on three sides,

banded by espaliered fruit trees and crisscrossed with an elaborately knotted pattern of clipped boxwood, each knot tufted with the stalks of frost-blanched herbs. The garden's centerpiece was a graceful tiered fountain of pink, white-veined marble bordered by roses from whose thorny stems still fluttered brave remnants of pink and crimson and coral. They reminded me of my childhood home.

Resting against the sill, I cupped my chin in my palms, closed my eyes, and allowed full reign to the memories conjured up by rose petals and fountains and the unseasonable, welcome warmth of Indian summer.

When I next looked down I saw Cora in the garden, bending over the rose bushes, cradling a tattered blossom in her hand. The tenderness of her gesture moved me. I remembered what Thornton Ramsay had said of her talent as a botanical artist—was this her garden, then? Somehow, I doubted that the exotic woman Charles Quintus Ramsay had painted ever risked blemishing those smooth, plump arms with thorns.

The errant shutter, which I had not yet secured, thumped smartly against the stuccoed wall, attracting the attention of the woman below. She peered up at me, her hand tented above her eyes, and on impulse I waved. Cora stiffened, then nodded her head in recognition of my greeting. I smiled. To be sure, her response was grudging, but victory is often won through a series of small, patiently achieved successes. I watched as she turned and walked briskly out of the courtyard and down a gentle slope where a steep little mansard roof peeked above a high yew hedge. That must be the cottage to which Roxelana had banished her. I could think of worse fates.

Walking *down* . . . good heavens! Cora was returning to her cottage, and I was due to meet Philo Ramsay after a breakfast I feared was long since past. My face burned and my fingers seemed as clumsy as thumbs as I hastened to dress. To be late on my very first day!

I snatched up the small carpetbag that held the few tools of my trade, and as I opened the door I heard another door opening nearby. I peered out cautiously and saw a tall, lithe figure enter the room at the far end of the corridor. It was Thornton Ramsay. My hand flew to my throat as I recalled my dreams. Flustered by my recollection, and unwilling to risk crossing Thorn Ramsay's path so soon after our dinner-table crossing of swords, I tiptoed down the carpeted hall and stairs as if I were a truant eluding a stern schoolmaster.

As I descended into the court hall, my eye was drawn across it to an airy tile-floored room filled with a variety of conservatory plants. The closely arrayed mass of windows, virtually a wall of glass, commanded a view of the river winding through the valley far below and the hills which rolled grandly beyond it to the western horizon.

"Splendid, isn't it?" It was Philo Ramsay. He looked chipper, as befitted the bright morning, and well fed. Last night's confrontation with his cousin was apparently the last thing on his mind. I decided to follow his lead.

"Oh, yes!" I exclaimed. I smiled up into his gray eyes. "It's the scene in the painting on the studio easel, isn't it?"

"Right you are, Miss Mackenzie." He dabbed a crumb from the corner of his trim blond mustache, confirming my guess, then rubbed his hands briskly. "Ready to begin, I see. I'm glad to find that punctuality is another trait we share."

My heart sank. Then, putting the thought of breakfast firmly behind me, I told myself that if I could survive my father's obligatory fasts in my childhood, surely I could last until lunch.

"I'm at your service, Miss Mackenzie—where do you suggest we start?"

"With a listing of all the carpets in the house, I think, then their measurements and an examination of the

59

weaving hallmarks—the knotting and the finishing of the edges and ends. The colors, too, contribute to the determination of age and provenance, so unless natural light is available wherever there are carpets—"

"Well, now, we may have to organize an expedition to explore the unknown territories."

I laughed. "Then we may be forced to hire native bearers to carry rugs to the light. A large carpet is a heavy load, Mr. Ramsay."

"Harry Braunfels will be more than equal to the task. He would like nothing better than to demonstrate how much stronger he is than I."

I was startled by the bitterness of his tone.

"Perhaps even Thorn could be persuaded to lend a hand," he continued, "although I suspect that since I failed to consult him about this commission, he would decline to help me solve any problems arising from it."

"That seems rather mean-spirited!"

My heated tone made him smile wryly. "I'm sometimes tempted to come to the same conclusion, but seven years is a long time to wait for a resolution to an impossible . . ." He stopped abruptly. "It's been hard on all of us," he concluded simply.

"Maybe it won't be necessary to move the carpets at all," I offered soothingly. "The cheap chemical dyes that are causing such havoc in the market now have only been available in the East since the seventies, and the carpets chosen by your uncle and mine were woven long before that. . . ."

The morning sped by, its passage spurred by the discovery of marvelous rugs partly hidden under tables and chairs and unearthed in dim corners. It was like opening a treasure chest. Part of the pleasure was due to Philo Ramsay's presence: he was a conscientious helper and a charming companion.

"What a clever notion, Miss Mackenzie," he said, as I

inserted large pearl-headed hat pins to mark the measurements along the edge of a carpet several times the length of my little folding yardstick. "One that no man would have thought of, I reckon."

I turned my head to smile at him as we knelt side by side on the elegant multiple-niched prayer rug, for all the world like two Muslims at prayer. I was proud of my ingenuity and pleased he had noticed.

"And what a handsome satchel to keep your pins in!" He picked up my leather-trimmed carpetbag and stroked the velvety pile. "Surprisingly light in weight, too."

"My uncle gave it to me on my twenty-first birthday to mark the official beginning of our partnership."

Philo Ramsay sat back on his heels and regarded me gravely. "I have a dear friend who is quite ill and, as a consequence, lacking in strength—something like this would be the very thing for a shawl and a book. . . . Do you suppose . . . I mean, I wonder where . . ."

I decided to rescue him. "I could have something similar made for you by one of my carpet repairers—we always have suitable fragments on hand—but the workmanship . . . it might be rather expensive."

"Hang the expense, Miss Mackenzie!"

His high spirits were infectious. I wondered who the friend was—a favored lady, perhaps? I masked a twinge of regret with a smile and held out my hand. "Please. Do call me Kate."

He grasped my hand in one of his and covered it with the other. "Done and done, Kate!"

"Well, well, well . . . isn't this a cozy scene?" a lazily mocking voice broke in. "If Philo alone were on his knees, I might suspect him of proposing."

It was Thornton Ramsay, standing above us, legs astride the carpetbag Philo had just relinquished, hands thrust into the pockets of his tweed shooting jacket. "But if I were you, Kate," he confided in a loud aside, "I wouldn't expect him to kiss me."

So! Was I to infer I was a shrew in need of taming? *How dare he . . .* I turned toward Philo, but the words I might have said died aborning. His pallor was alarming, reminding me of the waxwork figures Uncle Vartan had taken me to see at the Eden Musée in New York, mistakenly thinking they would amuse me.

I rose to my feet in the smooth flow of movement that years of plying my trade had perfected. "Miss Mackenzie, please," I corrected quietly, determined to display no outward sign of my anger.

Thornton Ramsay's eyes as they looked searchingly into mine were as cool and green as moss. I found myself snared in the web of his penetrating gaze which, as it widened, brushed across my face as softly, as warmly, as a caress. When I lowered my head to break the spell—and hide the sudden tremble of my lips—he stepped back, forearms up, palms out, in a gesture of silent surrender.

"Philo . . ." He paused, for once at a loss for words; then, in a voice so low it was almost a whisper, he added, "I'm sorry. That was quite uncalled for." He nodded his head toward me in a gesture of leavetaking, and then, in a few swift, long strides, he was gone.

I turned to Philo Ramsay. He too had risen to his feet, and averting his eyes from mine, sought to hide his discomfiture by brushing the dust from the knees of his impeccably cut trousers.

"Let it go, Miss Mackenzie," he said at length. "As you have gathered by now, Thorn has a way of bulling himself through my china shop. I don't think he means any real harm by it."

What an odd way to put it, I thought. It was clear to me that no matter what the intent, harm had indeed been done. My companion's gaiety had been driven into hiding, dulling his fine gray eyes and robbing his smile of its warmth. I was even Miss Mackenzie again, but as I opened my lips to protest his return to formality, I realized it was probably for the best.

The clock in the great hall bonged sonorously. Twelve-thirty. "Lunch is served promptly at one, Miss Mackenzie; what would you say to calling a halt?"

I assented eagerly. My poor stomach was beginning to protest the lack of anything to digest. "We've done more than enough groundwork to keep me out of mischief for the rest of the afternoon. Thank you for your help." I smiled. "If ever you need a position, Avakian's is at your service," I added lightly.

Thoroughly bewildered by the morning's recent events, I prayed that lunch would involve me in nothing more controversial than an exchange of comments about the weather and an occasional request to pass the butter.

In fact, lunch was an unexceptional event. Thornton Ramsay had gone to New York to attend to an urgent matter regarding his law practice, and Cora, who was engaged in totting up household accounts, took lunch in her cottage. This left only Philo and me to invent innocuous topics for conversation, so I was unprepared for his surprising reply to my last in a series of bland questions.

The subject was the decoration of the dining room. The paintings were revealed by daylight to be densely populated allegoricals of a religious or historical nature, like the old masters in style. I found the themes trite.

"There are so many of them," I exclaimed. "Why, there must be a small fortune hanging on these walls."

"A very small fortune," Philo said, "because every last one of them is a forgery."

At first I thought he must be joking, but the wry twist of his mouth alerted me to the fact that although his tone was light, he found no humor in the situation.

I decided to take a bold line. "Will it shock you very much if I say I'm not surprised? I really don't care for them very much."

To my relief, Philo laughed. "My dear Miss Mackenzie, that is something very few visitors to Hawkscliffe admitted to during my uncle's lifetime. You see, it was by way of being a leg pull: Uncle Charles knew that most people would assume that a famous artist would be unlikely to surround himself with anything but the best. He found their awed praise of this trash very amusing." He sighed, "Nevertheless, I hoped against hope; even a third-rate old master has some value after all, but these?" He surveyed them contemptuously. "These are hardly worth the canvas they're painted on. The frames alone would fetch more at auction. . . ."

As his voice trailed off into thoughtful silence I realized it wasn't just the fact of the paintings being bad art that bothered Philo. The monetary value, too, was important to him. I wondered why . . . surely his position at the Philadelphia Museum must be well remunerated, and Hawkscliffe itself should bring him a tidy sum despite its neglect.

"I have some letters to write this afternoon, Miss Mackenzie, so the library will be at your disposal. I believe that's the only room on the ground floor we did not inspect this morning. It has some handsome Bokharas that may please you."

The four library rugs did indeed please me. All were red—each shade was characteristic of a particular tribe, all displayed rows of distinctive medallions, elegantly spaced, and all had the desirable patina bestowed by the to-and-fro of slippered feet over many years. They glowed like rubies in the light of the shaded lamps. My uncle had served Charles Quintus Ramsay well.

By mid-afternoon, the neatly filled pages in my notebook convinced me I was entitled to a pause in my day's occupations. I had yet to set a foot outdoors on this bright, blustery day—only my nose had ventured out beyond the windowsill this morning—and the memory of the grand prospect I had viewed through the conservatory windows kept returning to distract me.

Revisiting my room just long enough to stow my carpetbag and snatch up a light shawl, I hastened downstairs, through the silent corridors, and out onto the front terrace, for all the world like a child released from school.

I wrapped the shawl closer as the breeze tugged at my skirt and loosed strands of my hair to tickle my ears and dance before my eyes. Invigorated, I scuffed through drifts of bronze and crimson leaves abandoned to the quixotic winds of autumn. Loosened by my toes, they sailed up like small, bright kites to shower down about my shoulders. It was a day to ramble!

My eager feet led me down a path curving sharply into a dense, mazelike stand of Norway spruce. My footsteps slowed, then halted. It was very still inside. The low sweeping branches, so dark as to be almost black, kept both the sun and the wind at bay. I could hear only a sighing chuff as the tall crowns swaying above me divided the light into uneasy flickers. Smothered by the shadowed, stagnant air, I turned and turned again, breathlessly seeking an exit. Then, spying a few slender rays of sun fingering in from the western end of the long green tunnel, I made my escape.

My relief was short lived. Though once again under blue skies and full sun, the path I had chosen rose steeply, narrowing as it skirted rocky crags on the uphill side, falling off abruptly on the other in a descent to the river broken only by precariously balanced boulders and sparse clumps of scrub oaks.

I clung to the cliff as I inched along the ledge, seeking grassy strips to avoid the loose pebbles which rolled beneath my shoes like tiny marbles, threatening to catapult me into the sparkling water below.

As I paused to catch my breath and pluck burrs from my green tweed skirt, I was startled by a keening cry close over my head. I looked up to see a bird—a hawk, actually, very large and fierce-looking—glide down to land on the outstretched, leather-gauntleted wrist of a man so rough-hewn in appearance he looked carved from the trunk of an ancient storm-battered oak. He stood on a crudely cobbled narrow wooden platform which overhung, somewhat atilt, the broken edge of the cliff top. One arm lay carelessly along a rustic cedar railing that was all that stood between him and a plunge into the valley far below.

Seated by his side, equally oblivious to the danger so terrifyingly apparent to me, was a sheepdog, but I doubted it was Zuleika. The head was more massive, the muzzle blunter, and the intensity in its gold eyes unnerved me even more than Zulu's rackety greeting had. The dog's unrelenting scrutiny was shared by the bird and the man. As the silence lengthened, my vexation grew.

"You must be Harry Braunfels," I finally said, my dry mouth transforming my words into a hoarse croak.

"You're Avakian's girl, then." His expression was unreadable. His small eyes, bright blue under a bushy overhang of grizzled eyebrows, held the shrewd knowing-ness of unschooled intelligence. It was hard to tell how old he was . . . no less than fifty, I guessed, but his gnarled and knotty look could be the result of either age or a hard life, most likely both.

"I'm his niece. I've come—"

"I know what you come for. Cora told me."

I couldn't help wondering what Cora had said, but I had no wish to betray my uncertainty.

"Afraid of high places, are you?"

It was true enough, but I didn't care for his contemptu-ous tone. "I didn't expect—"

"Most females are. 'Cept Cora, of course."

"And Roxelana," I said firmly, not knowing why. I certainly had nothing to base my opinion on, other than that painted face. Somehow she didn't look like a woman afraid of many things—of anything.

Harry shrugged. If he was surprised by my comment, he hid it well. "She never came this way."

"You mean there's another way back?" I was relieved at the prospect. I had no wish to retrace that precarious route in the fading light of approaching dark.

He laughed. "O' course. Can you see Master Philo eelin' his way up along those rocks? Thorn and me're the only ones who choose it."

Thorn and he? Were the two men friends? I found the thought disquieting. Thornton Ramsay's forceful, virile nature held no trace of coarseness; this man, approaching me as though he walked thickly on hooves, seemed almost . . . goatish.

He reached out grimy fingers to snare a lock of my hair. "Nice stuff," he said, the fine strands seeming more gold than red as he drew them across his creased, work-blackened palm.

Involuntarily, I inhaled sharply and stepped back. As I did so, he tightened his callused grip, laughing as I cried out shrilly.

"'Squeak, squeak,'" he mocked, "like a little mouse in a trap. Pretty little mouse . . . come little mouse. . . .'"

He tugged cruelly at my imprisoned hair, and to ease the sharp pain of it I surrendered to the pressure. More humiliated than frightened—although the nearness of the hook-beaked bird on his other wrist unnerved me—I could feel tears well up in my eyes.

Sensing his little game had gone too far, the man abruptly loosed me. "Harry Braunfels has no need for unwilling playmates, missy," he said in a contemptuous tone, as though I were the one at fault. "I've enjoyed tastier sport with your betters. When you change your mind—"

I cut in sharply. "The only thing I intend to change is my present company, so please be good enough to point out the alternate route to Hawkscliffe. These lower animals seem more suited to you than civilized human beings."

After a startled moment, Harry threw back his head and guffawed. The sudden movement of his body unbalanced the bird on his wrist. Squawking a surly protest, it unfurled its great dark wings and lunged forward.

"Now, now, Jessie, I never said you was a lower animal, milady here did. And you, Pasha," he continued, addressing the huge dog who, disturbed by the hawk's excitement, had risen restlessly to its feet, "are you, too, a lesser beast?"

The dog, as if sensing the man's sly hostility toward me, fixed me with an unblinking stare and growled softly. It was a sound hardly worth remarking unless, like me, one had been raised in an uneasy landscape where quaking shifts of the earth's crust were foretold by no less gentle rumbles, hardly more than murmurs, that whispered of menace.

Sensing my fear, Harry knitted his shaggy eyebrows and eyed me balefully. "Harsh words turneth on wrath," he intoned, mocking my distress. He guffawed again, then pointed out the direction I should take. As I scurried by him in the gathering dusk, he warned me to hurry. "The dogs are set loose after dark, miss, and Pasha here tends to nurse a grudge, he does."

His taunting laughter followed me down the wide, grassy slope, booming and echoing like a strike of ninepins. Three enemies in two days—first Cora, then Thornton Ramsay, and now Harry Braunfels. I didn't know how I could have avoided this unhappy state of affairs; I wasn't even quite sure what I had done to bring it about. It was certainly not deliberate.

I am not a difficult person; I have no more odd quirks or chips on my shoulder than most. Until now, most people I've met have liked me; the worst I have had to contend with is indifference. I have never before been the cause of scenes at dinner tables nor provoked men to abuse me physically.

I could see the lights in the great house as I flew down to meet it, aware of the irony in seeking shelter in a household that would be better pleased to speed me on my way. What was it about Hawkscliffe that brought out the worst in its inhabitants? At least Philo had not turned on me.

Alas, his exception was short-lived.

Chapter Six

It is my habit, when preoccupied, to follow the lead of my restless feet, an inclination which occasionally leads to unexpected consequences. My unsettling encounter with Harry Braunfels was proof enough of that.

The next afternoon, confined to the house by a change in the weather, I adjusted my stride to the dimensions of Hawkscliffe's library. Yesterday's fresh breeze had strenthened to a gusting wind that wailed through the chimney pots and rattled the painted windowpanes in their frames, but my conscious mind took only intermittent notice of it, taken up as it was with the puzzle presented by the so-called Damascus Gothic carpet upstairs in Charles Quintus's Napoleonic suite, with its ponderously graceful black-laquered, gilt-lined furnishings set against dark red walls relieved only by an ivory band embellished with gold fleurs-de-lis. Thorn Ramsay thought its imperial ostentation amusing; I found it oppressive, except for the carpet, which I coveted. The iridescent blues, greens, and reds seemed to float above the floor . . . a curious, almost mesmerizing effect. . . .

I paced aimlessly, occasionally pausing to riffle through a book or periodical that caught my eye, if not my entire attention. I stooped to pluck out a portfolio whose gorgeously marbled cover winked at me from an assortment of papers piled askew and forgotten on a shelf largely hidden by an elaborately mounted antique globe. I blew off the dust, revealing a faded label identifying it as a gift "to the master artist Charles Quintus Ramsay, who has allowed me to bask in the light of his presence, and who inspired these modest sketches." It was signed "Cora Banks."

This must be the portfolio Thornton Ramsay had mentioned. As I turned the pages, my sympathy turned to indignation. Thorn Ramsay's high opinion of Cora's botanical drawings was justified: her composition was unerring, the detail sensitively rendered, and the application of watercolor proved her mastery of a demanding technique. To dismiss this talent as no more than a knack for painting pretty posies had been an act of deliberate cruelty, just the ticket to undermine a fragile ego. Cora had indeed been badly used by the man she'd served so loyally.

I wondered, not for the first time, why women were expected to accept such treatment without complaint. Was it because we had so few choices? I frowned. More likely it was because so few choices were actually permitted us. More than one of Uncle Vartan's competitors had, after all, expressed astonishment at my determination to carry on the business by myself.

I lost count of the number of eligible sons paraded before me after my uncle's death in an unsuccessful effort to persuade me to settle for having babies and making shish kebab. I was told that I was unrealistic, unknowing, and unfeminine. I may have been unrealistic, but I knew more about carpets than most of the sons, and being accused of a lack of femininity made the prospect of sharing a marriage bed with those patronizing young predators even less appealing. Never had I appreciated Uncle Vartan more. Had it been our unusual closeness or my eager response to his teaching that had influenced him? I would never know for sure, but he had encouraged me to set my own course, and I was not about to defame his memory by departing from it.

All in all, it was a wonder Cora Banks wasn't even more pinched and sour than she was. She was fast approaching the end of her work life with nothing to show for it. And then it came to me: Although the prestige associated with cataloging the Hawkscliffe collection was assured within a small circle of collectors and dealers, what if that catalog were illustrated and published by a commercial firm? Cora's talent was eminently suited to such a project, and Philo and I between us could accomplish the historical, artistic, and structural analyses. Oh, what a coup it would be!

"Miss Cora always takes tea in her cottage," Mary Rose informed me when I invaded the kitchen in search of the housekeeper. "And she doesn't much like being disturbed," she added. "Isn't that so, Aggie?"

The cook, who was up to her plump elbows in flour, nodded her agreement. "Especially by outsiders," she threw in over her shoulder. "No offense meant, miss," she added, turning to me apologetically. "It's just that . . . what I mean to say is . . . ." Unable to find a tactful way to express her thought, the cook eyed me helplessly.

"Miss Cora has her ways?" I suggested. "Nevertheless, I think I'll chance bearding the lioness in her den, but if I'm not back within the hour, perhaps you'd better send in the cavalry—I wouldn't want to miss dinner if that's a batch of your delicious rolls in the making."

Agnes and Mary Rose promised that they would save

out a generous portion for me.

"For bravery," Mary Rose said.

Cora Banks's reception of me at the door of her pretty little cottage was less than welcoming. "Even housekeepers are entitled to some privacy, Miss Mackenzie. If you have a complaint, I will be glad to meet with you in the library at half past four to discuss it."

"I have no complaints, Miss Banks. My errand is of a private nature, one that may prove of advantage to you; but if you prefer . . ."

I began to turn away, but as I hoped, I had succeeded in arousing her curiosity.

"Oh, very well. Come in, come in. . . ."

As I squeezed by her rigid figure—her invitation was halfhearted at best—I was struck by how worn she looked. Her sparrowlike alertness had temporarily deserted her, leaving in its place just a tired old bird, her grayed-blue dress no less drab than the dusty brown she usually wore. But, oh my, what a charming nest this bird had made for herself! The furniture was of an earlier, simpler, more graceful design than the dark, ornately carved pieces that overburdened many fashionable parlors, and the flowered chintzes at the windows invested the crisp November day with the warmth and light of spring.

"May I offer you some tea, Miss Mackenzie?" Her voice was sharply edged, challenging me to accept.

"How kind," I murmured, smiling blandly as she rose grudgingly to prepare a fresh pot.

She disappeared into a curtained alcove whence the clink of silver and porcelain told of the setting of a tray. As I waited for the hiss of escaping steam from a kettle, I idly explored the pleasing room, pausing at a half-opened door. Her bedroom? Curiosity impelled me to widen the opening with a gentle push of my fingertips. It was a small room. Ahead of me, between two simply curtained windows, was a painted bureau charmingly decorated with flowers and butterflies—Cora's handiwork? A narrow, blue-and-white homespun-covered bed stood against the wall; across from it was a rush-seated cherrywood rocker and a low cupboard on top of which, along with a serviceable lamp, stood three framed photographs. Did this prim, bloodless little person actually have a family?

I moved a step closer. In the first photograph, a uniformed young man, a Union soldier, postured jauntily against a huge tree, his elbow resting on the butt of his long rifle, his chin on the knuckles of his hand. His faded features radiated mischief. A brother, perhaps? In the second stood a solemn young couple stiffly posed for their wedding picture, and in the third a slim woman, hardly more than a girl, smiled down at the sailor-suited blond boy whose hand she was holding.

"Miss Mackenzie! If you please!"

I whirled guiltily to find Cora standing behind me, the tea tray in her hands.

"I'm very sorry if I have offended you, Miss Banks, but having lost my own family, I am always drawn to those of others. Your parents?" I said, pointing to the bride and groom.

She shook her head as she conducted me back into her parlor. "My sister and her husband. Lost in a fire. That is their boy with me," she volunteered.

"Oh, Miss Banks," I cried, reaching out for the cup she offered. "What a tragedy! And how sad for the boy . . . I know how he must have felt. You see, my parents too were lost in a fire—"

"You seem to have landed on your feet," she interrupted coldly, "whereas my poor . . ."

Her face seemed to collapse. What little color she

possessed fled, leaving mottled whitish-gray patches. Alarmed, I decided a change of subject was in order.

"What a lovely home you have, Miss Banks," I burbled. "You certainly have an artist's eye for style and color."

Startled out of her dazed state by my non sequitur, Cora rattled her fragile porcelain cup on its saucer. She looked at me penetratingly. "What on earth would make you say that?"

"Your choice of furnishings—"

"Leftovers from the New York house."

"These fabrics—"

"Discarded by Roxelana. *She* had the taste of a pack rat," she added in a mutter, her mouth twisting with disdain. "All gauze and glitter."

"—and these beautiful watercolors, which of course are yours."

"Those watercolors were done many years ago, Miss Mackenzie. They are the artless dabblings of a silly girl, nothing more. Now, if you don't mind . . ."

Ignoring the cup I held out to be refilled, Cora returned the teapot to its tray. Politesse had its limits after all.

"But they are the reason for my visit, Miss Banks. I found a porfolio of yours in the library, and it gave me the most wonderful idea. . . ."

As I outlined my proposition, I could see her becoming interested in spite of herself.

"I lack the talent—"

"I beg to differ, Miss Banks. Your talent is exactly suited to the fine detail the project requires."

"I know nothing about rugs—"

"It is not necessary that you do. What you *do* know is which rugs Charles Quintus liked best and why, am I correct?"

"Yes . . . yes, with a little thought I could . . . but I cannot give you an answer yet. Please tell Philo that . . .

it's been so long. My hands . . ."

As she held them out consideringly, my heart ached for her. The knuckles were enlarged, and her fingers had begun to assume the ugly twist characteristic of rheumatism. What a cruel affliction for an artist!

"I have not yet discussed my idea with Mr. Ramsay," I confessed. "Our contribution would be secondary to yours, you see." Admittedly, I was shading the truth a bit, but it was all in a worthy cause, and she was clearly flattered to have been the first to be informed of the project.

"I'm sure dear Philo will approve." Cora nodded absently, her gaze settling somewhere, unseeingly, beyond me. I had to strain to hear her next words, which I sensed were as much to reassure herself as to inform me. "We could work together here at Hawkscliffe, once his inheritance is assured. He has promised me this will always be my home, you know. . . ."

She chattered on, not because she considered me a confidante, I was sure of that, but because the relief associated with the imminent end of seven years of uncertainty was too great to suppress.

"You feel there is no chance Roxelana will be found, then?" I queried gently.

She turned on me a look of purest dread so stark and undisguised I had all I could to keep from gasping aloud.

"Found? Found, you say? Who would be looking for that . . . that *creature* at this late date? Answer me that!"

Oh dear. I seemed to have revived all her suspicions. Walk softly, I warned myself. "All I meant was that usually there are published notices, are there not? I seem to remember reading something of the sort in the New York papers when my uncle died: legal advertisements to notify possible claimants—tradesmen, distant or unknown relatives, that sort of thing."

Cora visibly relaxed. "Oh, but that was done years ago,

77

Miss Mackenzie. All that is behind us now. This is my home, you see," she repeated firmly. "And now, if you will excuse me, I must return to my duties."

This time, I welcomed my dismissal. Conversation with Cora Banks was, like traversing a glacier, laced with crevasses ready to claim the unwary. However, as I trotted up to the house by way of the walled garden, my mental fatigue surrendered to the pleasant anticipation of my conversation with Philo Ramsay.

I rapped smartly on the door to the studio and entered before Philo had quite completed his invitation for me to do so.

He looked up from a desk heaped with papers and regarded me frowningly. "Well, Miss Mackenzie, been running a footrace, have you? You look at sixes and sevens and more than a little out of breath. May I relieve you of your wrap?"

Disconcerted, I realized I should have gone to my room to change, or at least refresh myself, before meeting with my meticulously groomed employer. I smoothed back errant wisps of hair and surreptitiously dusted the toes of my shoes across the backs of my stockings before seating myself in the chair he drew up for me.

"I have just come from tea with Cora Banks," I announced. My initial statement elicited a raised eyebow of surprise; then, as my eager words describing my proposal for the Hawkscliffe catalog tumbled out, the sparking glint in Philo Ramsay's eyes, which I assumed was struck by interest, was succeeded by a controlled expression I found impossible to read. It left me woefully unprepared for his reaction.

"No, Miss Mackenzie."

I gaped at him, unwilling to believe my ears. Perhaps he

felt the result would not be worth the effort? I searched the set lines of his face, hoping to detect uncertainty, or at least a hint of his usual gentleness, but even the soft blond hairs of his moutache seemed to bristle with resolve.

"There is nothing else like it, that I know," I persisted doggedly, "and I'm sure an illustrated volume of Charles Quintus Ramsay's celebrated carpet collection would be both prestigious and profitable."

"I have no doubt of it."

"Then I . . . I don't understand. . . ."

"You accepted the fee I suggested in my letter, did you not?"

"Why yes, it was quite generous, but—"

"Then any prestige or profit that may accrue to the Hawkscliffe collection once you have completed your commission is no concern of yours."

No concern of yours . . . a popular phrase with the Ramsay men. I continued to sit numbly. *Et tu, Philo.* The hurt I felt must have shown in my eyes, for he avoided meeting them.

"Miss Mackenzie?" His manner remained stiff and unyielding. "If you don't mind? I have business to attend to here."

"Of course." I rose abruptly. "I'm sorry to have intruded." I reached for my wrap, and in my awkward haste I nudged a pile of papers on his desk, loosing the top few to float to the floor. As I stooped to retrieve them, ignoring Philo's plea to leave them be, I couldn't help noticing that the sheaf I collected were bills, medical bills—and sizeable ones at that. I had seen no evidence of ill health among those residing at Hawkscliffe—were these for the ailing friend he had mentioned? *No concern of yours*, I reminded myself.

I retreated to the library to lick my wounds, pacing restlessly in the gathering darkness as I sought to come to terms with what had happened. Perhaps, as Philo Ramsay had hinted, I had overextended myself. The Hawkscliffe collection was literally no concern of mine. Perhaps the payment of my fee was all I had a right to receive, but was a simple thank-you too much to expect? Had Philo's earlier expression of camaraderie been for him merely a passing amusement? I caught my lip between my teeth, hating to be so suspicious, but a young woman in my position could not afford to be otherwise.

In the East, my uncle had often told me, business agreements were sealed with a handshake, "but in America," he once added with a regretful sigh, "it is more complicated than that. And for you, dear child, it will be even more so, as it is for any woman. Much more." Then his shoulders hunched in that characteristic, dismissive shrug of his. "But if you put into practice everything I have taught you, and remember to look over your shoulder every step of the way, it will be good to you, this business."

I already knew and accepted the fact that the antique carpet trade was demanding, but good to me? For the first time I doubted Uncle Vartan's wisdom. The disloyal thought brought sudden tears to my eyes, blurring the light which suddenly spread across the leather bindings on the facing bookcases.

"Communing with the shadows, Miss Mackenzie, or are you a creature of them?"

Stooping over the newly lit lamp, adjusting the mantle's glow, was Thornton Ramsay. His deep voice seemed to penetrate my skin, my nerves, my very bones. I was appalled to discover how much his presence thrilled me. I dabbed at my moist eyes with the heels of my hands and turned to face him.

"Neither, Mr. Ramsay. I was merely absorbed by the puzzle presented me by one of the Hawkscliffe carpets," I fibbed. "My mind's eye functions as well in darkness as in the light, you see."

"What I see is a very pretty young woman more suited to raising rosy-cheeked cherubs than losing track of time among heaps of dusty floor coverings."

I closed my eyes and took a deep breath. Losing my temper would solve nothing. *"Chacun à son goût,"* I said evenly.

Thornton Ramsay regarded me in silence.

"Each to his own taste," I translated.

"I know what it means."

"But you're surprised I do? What a snob you are, Mr. Ramsay."

"I may be many things, Miss Mackenzie," he retorted hotly, "but snobbish is not one of them. And surely I'm not the first person—man or woman—who suggested that being a mother—"

"And a housekeeper and obedient wife? No indeed, you are not the first. Another man, who also thought me willful and unnatural, well preceded you. If my father had lived, he would have seen to it that my learning and my capacity for it was imprisoned in domesticity."

"A home is hardly comparable to stone walls and iron bars!"

"Do you think a prison cell pleasanter if softly padded, Mr. Ramsay?"

"I think your uncle has a lot to answer for if he encouraged your narrow view of life."

"My uncle valued my intellectual curiosity and, because of it, my company. My father was a domestic tyrant; Uncle Vartan was my mentor. I will never exchange the freedom I enjoyed with him for the domestic chains my mother wore."

We stood staring at each other, Thornton Ramsay and I, the very air seeming to vibrate between us. His next words erased my self-satisfaction.

"And has love no place in your scheme of things, Miss Mackenzie?" His voice was low and soft. Its careless tone was matched by the lazy smile that curved his wide mouth, but challenge glinted in the depths of those green eyes.

For a long moment I was at a loss for words. Love? What did I know of love? An exchange of soulful glances at a party, a sigh, at most a fluttering of the heart, soon eased. But the love to which I sensed he referred—the love of a man for a woman . . . *carnal* love—the very thought of it dizzied me. Then, from out of the whirl of my confusion, the perfect retort presented itself.

"That, Mr. Ramsay," I pronounced triumphantly, "is no concern of yours."

As I moved forward to sweep by him, Thornton Ramsay reached out to grasp my arm above the elbow. The hard, rough, unfamiliar touch of strong masculine fingers, *his* fingers, seemed to burn through my sleeve to brand the soft flesh beneath it, unleashing a wave of sensation—electric, frightening, and so overwhelming that my proud steps faltered. I stumbled against him. His chin grazed the top of my head, and his warm breath stirred the tendrils of hair on my brow.

"I'm not so sure of that, Kate," he whispered, "are you?"

Hardly able to draw a steady breath, I shrugged off his encircling arm and walked away without another word. As usual, Thorn Ramsay had the last one.

CHAPTER SEVEN

In the days that followed, I felt like a boat adrift on a tropical sea beneath whose calm surface an alien life swirls unseen through secret coralline paths and mysterious shadowy caverns.

Polite inattention became the order of those days. Cora substituted vague smiles for her former suspicious scrutiny of me. Whether she was distracted by the book proposal I had discussed with her or by the approaching legal proceedings to determine the disposition of Hawkscliffe I could not say, but it was a change of attitude with which I had no quarrel, as I preferred being overlooked to being made to feel unwelcome.

Philo observed the forms punctiliously, inquiring after my health with a solicitude belied by an obvious lack of interest in my answer. If I had told him I was at death's door, his expression would have been no less agreeable.

Thornton Ramsay appeared to be biding his time, but to what purpose I could not imagine. At meals, when Philo and I exchanged surmises about the origin of a carpet motif—for he was indeed well versed in art history—I could sense those green eyes contemplating me; and once when Cora's tongue sharpened long enough to dismiss as rubbish the Ottoman textiles I had been extolling, he laughed and suggested that perhaps her concern about Roxelana had adversely affected her aesthetic judgment.

As might be imagined, that comment did not sit at all well with Cora Ramsay. The murderous look she aimed at Thornton was, though quickly controlled, like seeing a shark's fin knifing through my placid metaphorical sea.

Roxelana. She was always lurking at the core of it, wasn't she? What was it like, I wondered, to have the power this woman, lost these seven years, still possessed? Cora hated her, Philo feared her return, and Thornton bitterly resented the toll taken on his personal and professional life as a result of C.Q. Ramsay's indulgence of her demands. They were strong emotions, and perhaps not the nicest way to be remembered, but I was sure no one ever thought of Roxelana in terms of niceness. She was an elemental force that carried all before her, and I was horrified to realize that I envied her.

Gentle persuasion and good sense had always been my stock-in-trade, but, oh, how I coveted the ability to snare admirers with a single sidelong glance, or, as Roxelana had, to gain a palace on a hilltop by the shrewd exercise of a seductive smile! Alas, I was unlikely ever to fathom her secret; even if I did, I doubted my willingness to pay the price that putting it into practice would exact.

Three days before the hearing which would declare Roxelana legally dead, my foolish longings and discontents were routed by a veritable maelstrom of emotion that whirled Thornton, Philo, and Cora into its vortex, leaving me teetering uncertainly on its perimeter.

It began unremarkably enough with a telegraph message brought up from Hendryk by Harry Braunfels and delivered to Thornton by Mary Rose as she prepared to serve us our noonday meal. Assuming it to be of a private nature, Cora, Philo, and I exchanged banal comments about the weather—it had remained brisk and bright, as I remember—when a loud oath from Thorn startled us into silence.

"Not bad news, I trust, Thorn," Philo said, observant of the niceties as always, although I sensed a lack of genuine concern in his dulcet voice.

"It is too soon to say if it is bad news, but at the very least it is bothersome. A damned nuisance, in fact."

We all stared at him expectantly as he folded the telegram and placed it alongside his place setting. "It's from Louise Ramsay," he finally said. "She is arriving tomorrow afternoon with her son, Lance, in tow."

C.Q.'s ex-wife arriving with her *son?* Good heavens, I thought, is there no end to the complications here? I turned to Philo, curious about his reaction to this surprising news, and found him almost as pale as the ivory damask cloth.

"Louise and her son . . ." His voice echoed Thorn's words in a whispery, strangled sort of way. "Why now? Whatever can she want?"

"Well might you ask, coz," Thornton returned with a sardonic lift of one eyebrow. "Well might you ask indeed."

"But she can't!" Cora said, frantically eyeing the cousins in turn. "She *mustn't!* Thornton, you can't allow this, you must tell her—"

"Tell her what, Cora?" he broke in sharply. "That there's no room at the inn? She's still our aunt, Philo's and mine, and the boy—" Thornton broke off, scowling, and drew his finger back and forth along the fold of the telegram.

"No longer a boy, I warrant," Philo said bleakly. "He must be sixteen or seventeen by now."

"Eighteen," Thornton muttered. The cousins exchanged wary glances.

"Whatever his age, that boy is her bastard," Cora announced flatly.

"We don't know that, Cora. Not for sure," Thornton cautioned her.

"He is! I know he is . . . Philo?" Twisting her napkin in her hands, she turned to the blond cousin for reassurance, but Philo Ramsay had slumped in his seat, his face puckered with anguish.

"She's here to put in a claim, isn't she, Thorn? After seven long years that harpy—"

"They were divorced, Philo, there's no doubt about that. She has no grounds for a claim."

"Not for herself, for the boy!"

"For the boy," Cora echoed.

"You put her up to this, Thorn," Philo accused, his long, nervous fingers tracing aimless patterns on the tablecloth. "That's why you went to New York last week, isn't it? Admit it! It offends you to think of Hawkscliffe in the hands of someone like me."

Thornton looked at him in alarm. "Hold on, old man! I grant you I'm concerned about the commitments in both time and money that ownership of Hawkscliffe will demand of you, but believe me, Philo, my trip to New York had nothing to do with Lulu—in fact, I haven't seen her, except in passing, in years. Why, I would as soon face down a speeding locomotive as conspire with Louise Ramsay!"

The last, delivered in a tone of jocular exaggeration, eased the tension in Philo's face, like a hand smoothing out a sheet of crumpled paper. I couldn't help marveling at Thornton's pains to soothe him, and I was, of course, agog with curiosity about this interesting turn of events, as was Mary Rose, who served us in a carefully maintained silence, absorbing juicy tidbits to chew over later in the pantry with Agnes.

"Where shall we put dear Aunt Louise, then? In fair Roxelana's suite?" I was sure Philo's question was deliberately provocative.

"No!" Cora said. "I suggest we move Miss Mackenzie into the suite. Then, since we can be sure Louise Ramsay would turn up her aristocratic nose at the maid's room Miss Mackenzie will be vacating, we can put both her and her son on the top floor, out from underfoot."

"But those rooms haven't been used in years!" Philo cried. "Louise will raise a fearful fuss, I just know she will."

"Then let her, Philo. It's more than she deserves on such short notice," Cora added with a meaningful look at me. "Mary Rose and I will make sure the rooms are clean, although with all there is to do . . ."

"I'll be happy to help, Miss Banks," I offered. "The carpet inventory is largely complete except for those on the top floor; this way, I could kill two birds with one stone."

"But will that give you sufficient time to settle into your new quarters before Mrs. Ramsay arrives?"

"It is important that your tenure appear to be well established," Thorn Ramsay added. "The thought of Lulu in Roxelana's suite. . . ." His proud face wore, for a moment, an expression I can only describe as desperate.

Why, I'm being asked to participate in a conspiracy, I realized, not knowing whether to feel uneasy or amused.

"I brought so little with me, I can easily accomplish that after supper this evening." Once said, the die was cast, and my willingness to take part in what seemed a harmless enough deception was so eagerly seized upon I experienced an uneasy tremor of doubt.

"Thank you, Miss Mackenzie," Thornton Ramsay said with heartfelt sincerity. "I'm just sorry to involve you in this tedious family affair."

"No more than I, Mr. Ramsay. Shall we pretend I have heard not a word of it?"

"You are a very unusual young woman," he remarked in a voice pitched low for my ears alone. "Very unusual indeed."

"If I am, sir, it is because my uncle encouraged me to be so," I replied with a demure smile.

He grinned in recognition of my sly reference to our lively exchange in the library several days earlier; then, to the mystification of our companions, he raised his water goblet to salute me. As I met his admiring glance, I reflected that gentle persuasion did, after all, have its advantages.

Mary Rose and I made short work of preparing the top floor rooms for guests. Feather dusters and the crisp November air invited in through the opened windows soon routed the dust and mustiness. There was nothing exotic about the furnishings. In fact, the only Eastern touches were the rugs that lay overlapped on the floors and piled carelessly in a large unfinished space given over to the storage of miscellaneous furnishings that had fallen out of favor.

Mary Rose crinkled her nose at the sight of them. "Horrid, dusty things," she declared. "Just look at this," she added, curling back one of the rugs with her toe. "These edges are coming apart, and this hole . . . why, it's almost in tatters, miss." She looked around the room disdainfully. "They all are, more or less. Shall we bundle them into the dust bin, then?"

"No!"

My cry of alarm made Mary Rose blink in astonishment. I smiled reassuringly. "That's not our decision to make, Mary Rose. Let's just choose the least disreputable for the guest rooms and store the rest. I'll take the matter up with Mr. Ramsay myself, after I've had a chance to add them to my inventory."

I yearned to wash away the clouding film of dust that clung to the rugs' neglected pile. Waiting there to be revealed were rich indigo blues, warm madder reds, and a distinctive shade of yellow found only in antique rugs.

These forgotten rugs were very old, by far the oldest in the Hawkscliffe collection. They looked rather like . . .

I surveyed them more closely, then realized excitedly that they were, in fact, the very rugs whose distinctive, archaic designs my uncle had roughly sketched many years before. I recalled his telling me he had collected them one by one from mosques in remote Anatolian villages where the modest sum he offered for them was eagerly accepted.

Those sketches and his incomplete notes still languished in a drawer of my uncle's desk. I had often wondered why he had abandoned the study he had planned of the rugs, and now I knew; he had neither set foot in this house nor had access to these wonderful rugs for fifteen years or more. But by whose choice? Had Uncle Vartan turned his back on Hawkscliffe, or had Charles Quintus Ramsay refused him entry? And, whichever the case, *why?*

I smoothed my dully aching temples with my fingers, no nearer an answer now than I had been when I first asked to visit the splendidly spired castle I had viewed longingly from that Hudson River steamer so many years before. One thing I did know was that I would keep my discovery to myself for the time being, lest Philo Ramsay snatch another opportunity from me.

After Mary Rose returned to the kitchen to assist with preparations for supper, I decided the rooms needed a personal touch, something to make the uninvited guests feel welcome, even if they weren't. Accordingly, I hastened downstairs and applied to Agnes and Mary Rose for a stout knife to cut a few branches of autumn leaves to arrange on the bureau tops. As I had expected, the usual chatter over the pots and pans was considerably enlivened by what Mary Rose had heard while serving the noonday meal.

After the brief pause my unexpected arrival occasioned, Mary Rose turned to me breathlessly. "Do *you* think he is, Miss? Do you think Mrs. Ramsay's son could really be a . . . a . . . ?" She was unable to force the offending word past her lips.

"A bastard? I don't know, Mary Rose, and I won't know any better tomorrow. One can hardly tell by looking at a person, can one?"

Mary Rose blushed redder than I thought humanly possible. Poor girl, apparently she mistook my teasing for chastisement.

"I told you I overheard them carrying on about it, Mary Rose," Agnes said crossly. "It's not the sort of thing a person forgets, not even after all these years. They were in their bedroom on the second floor of the New York house, miss," she said, turning to me, obviously pleased to have new ears for her tale. "I was passing through the hall, collecting the morning tea trays—I was only cook's helper in those days—and their door was open just a crack. They was all but shouting, so unless I stopped up my ears, which I couldn't very well do with my hands full and all, I couldn't help but overhear. She even boasted of it at first;

told the mister it was the one thing he couldn't do for any woman."

"She never did!" Mary Rose was shocked, but not so much as to neglect asking the obvious next question. "Who was it then, Cook?"

I was as curious to hear the answer to that as Mary Rose, but Agnes was unable to supply it.

"Don't know," she replied, sounding quite put out about it. "I have me guesses, though," she added with a smirk, "and none of 'em's farther than the highroad to Hendryk. But to tell you the truth, I don't think Mr. Charles Quintus Ramsay cared much *who* it was."

"Saints preserve us, why ever not?" Mary Rose was astounded. In her world, being cuckolded was not the sort of thing husbands took lightly.

Agnes's plump mouth described a grim downward arc. "Why? Because he was glad of an excuse to rid himself of that stuck-up thing, that's why! You'll see when you meet Missus High-and-Mighty yourself."

I was already beginning to regret my involvement in the family conspiracy.

"But if you ask me," Agnes added, "he jumped out of the frying pan smack-bang into the fire."

Anticipating yet another denunciation of Roxelana and her foreign ways, I slipped out the back door with the knife I had borrowed and a basket to put my cuttings in.

The trees near the house had largely shed their autumn dress, so I had to wander farther afield than I had planned. My first stop was in a grove of young beech where leaves the color of parchment still fluttered. Next, I spied orange bittersweet twining through a thicket of barberry, and beyond, the frosty blue-green of field juniper berries beckoned. It was while I was gathering their pungent, densely fruited stems that I heard a menacing growl close by.

I froze. Not daring to move my body, I turned my head slowly and saw Harry Braunfels above me on the path. Two large dogs, both of the Turkish Akbash breed, accompanied him, one on either side. Although only one was growling, neither dog was leashed, and the light had grown too dim to allow me easily to distinguish which was which. Long moments passed. Exasperated, finally, by my unwilling participation in this impromptu tableau of intimidation, I stuffed the juniper in my basket and advanced up the hill, intent on calling Harry's bluff. The growl grew louder as I approached, but I noticed that the ears of the dog on the left had relaxed ever so slightly, and I was sure I could see the white tip of its tail vibrating against the dusty path. Mentally crossing the fingers on both my hands, I strode forward without a pause, patted the chosen beast on the head, and addressed it in the most cheerful tone I could muster.

"Good girl, Zulu! Out for a walk, are you?"

The big dog, bless her, ambled forward and nuzzled my hand amiably. The snarler on the right—Pasha, I assumed, or were there more than one of his hostile nature in the kennels?—was quickly silenced by a gruff command and tethered with a hastily produced stout leather lead.

"Why, it's you, missy!" Harry said in an exaggerated tone of surprise. "I didn't recognize you at first."

"Does Mr. Ramsay know you're in the habit of allowing the dogs to threaten unidentified young women?"

"I'm in the habit of doing mostly whatever I please because they can't get no one else to do what I do."

We stared each other down for a long moment—he wasn't the kind of man to admit defeat easily, especially to a woman—and as I prepared to return to the big house, where I could see the swelling glow of lamps being lit, he tried another gambit.

"Louise and her pup are expected tomorrow, then?"

I was startled as much by the familiar tone of his reference to Mrs. Ramsay as by his question. Either Mary Rose or Cora must have told him of the expected guests, or he had read Thornton Ramsay's telegram before delivering it.

"You know Mrs. Ramsay?" I had assumed that his employment went no further back than the construction of Hawkscliffe, but now that I thought of it, those landscapes he appeared in—to lend scale to the elms, as Thornton Ramsay had put it—must have been painted considerably earlier.

"We've had a go-round or two," Harry said enigmatically. He gave a bark of laughter. "Should liven things up around here, having Louise and her by-blow in residence."

I refused to rise to his bait. "Hardly in residence, Mr. Braunfels," I replied calmly, ignoring his coarse reference to Louise Ramsay's son. "For a few days at most, I understand."

"No matter how short, it won't be sweet, miss. But if she gets to be too much for you, you can always come to Harry for comfort, that you can, but leave your airs at home."

I spun on my heel with an indignant huff, immediately regretting I had allowed him the pleasure of knowing he had finally succeeded in ruffling my feathers. His self-satisfied chuckle echoed in my ears long after he set off with the dogs for his quarters above the kennels.

"A bit late for an afternoon walk, isn't it, Miss Mackenzie?"

"I have no foolish fears of things that go bump in the night, if that's what you're suggesting," I said more sharply than I intended. Thornton Ramsay's tall figure looming up unexpectedly on the dark terrace had, in fact, given me quite a start.

"Not a bit of it," he replied in a surprised tone. "It's just that it has grown colder since the sun went down, and you seem to be without a wrap. We can't have you sneezing and coughing among the prayer rugs, can we?"

"Should that be the case, I shall be well positioned to petition Allah for a rapid recovery, won't I?"

He slowed his restless pacing, and even though I could not see his green eyes, I sensed their curious regard of me.

"A bit snappish this evening, Miss Mackenzie?"

"If so, I am merely following the example set for me here!" My hand flew to my mouth as I realized I had crossed the thin line between defensiveness and impertinence. "Forgive me, Mr. Ramsay, it's just that I've had an unpleasant . . . encounter with your friend Harry Braunfels."

"My *friend*? Whatever gave you that idea? And what do you mean by 'encounter'? Is that a ladylike way of saying he made improper advances?"

"Please do not patronize me, Mr. Ramsay. Harry Braunfels gave me the distinct impression that you and he were comrades or chums or something of the sort, so I was trying to put the best face on it. Yes, he made advances, on more than one occasion I might add, and I did not like it one bit. He theatened me."

"*Threatened* you?"

I did not have to see his face to recognize disbelief. "Must you repeat everything I say in that tone? Yes, he threatened me, or implied as much. He said the dogs sometimes ran loose after dark, and he suggested they might attack me."

Even to my own ears that didn't sound much of threat. "It was the way he said it," I continued lamely, "and one of the dogs—it may have been Pasha—growled very . . . very . . ."

94

"Threateningly," Thornton completely gently. "Miss Mackenzie, Harry's bark is, or at least always has been, worse than his bite; I can't say the same for Pasha and his kennel mates."

There *were* others, then.

"Zulu is a bit of a fraud, as you already know, but the other dogs—well, you'd do well to heed Harry's warning."

I knew there was no point in pursuing the subject. Experience had taught me that intuition was not infallible, and no man took a woman's intuition very seriously anyway.

"Am I at least correct in my assumption that Harry worked for Mr. Ramsay before Hawkscliffe was built?"

"Oh, yes. He was the caretaker of Charles Quintus's lodge in the Catskills, long since sold. Harry was raised in those parts. When I needed practice scrambling up rocks preparatory to more serious climbs in the Alps, he always knew the best places to go."

Thornton Ramsay was an alpinist? The very thought made me shudder, as heights always did.

"Feeling the chill are you, Miss Mackenzie? I suggest we continue our conversation indoors."

Once inside, I placed my basket of cuttings on the stair landing, then followed in his long stride to the library, where a cheery fire blazed and crackled with a warm invitation to draw near. The fireplace in the Ramsay Catskill lodge would have been three times as big, probably, fashioned roughly of lumpy stones and supplied with a rustic mantel of native oak. It was hard to imagine an aristocratic woman like Louise Ramsay in such a setting.

"Did Mrs. Ramsay ever go to the lodge? Harry said he knew her."

"As a matter of fact, she did. Harry's hawks fascinated her. They used to go off after pheasant together, and I believe he trained a peregrine for her. Lord knows they didn't have much in common otherwise," he concluded with a chuckle.

"Extraordinary," I murmured. I was sure Harry's use of the term *go-round* in reference to his employer's wife meant more than hawking, but perhaps my imagination was overactive in this regard, too.

"Harry's the kind of man who would be challenged by the seemingly unobtainable," Thornton said, as if he had read my mind.

"And no doubt boast of nonexistent victories," I declared.

"Don't be too sure. He wasn't always as grizzled as he is now, you know, and many women are attracted to roughhewn men with a swagger in their walk. Ask Mary Rose."

Mary Rose! I was as astounded as he intended me to be. "Good heavens, the man's old enough to be her father!"

Thornton Ramsay smiled at me. The firelight glanced off the smooth planes of his face and reflected in the deep green of his eyes. I could feel a warm spark spiral from them into my own.

"May-to-December liaisons are hardly unheard of, Miss Mackenzie . . . look at C.Q. and Roxelana. And no one would find it at all remarkable if you and I . . . yet I'm almost old enough to be *your* father, you know."

"Hardly likely!"

"I'm thirty-six, Miss Mackenzie."

"I repeat, hardly likely—unless you were in the habit of fathering children at the age of thirteen."

"No, not at thirteen." His voice was very low, and as he turned away the light left his face as the lightness had his voice.

We stood a moment longer in a silence that threatened to become uncomfortable, and when I excused myself to

96

arrange the branches I had cut for the guest rooms, he nodded wordlessly and turned back to the fire. I sensed he was as relieved as I to abandon a conversation which seemed to be leading into thickets best left unexplored.

Basket in hand, I made my way slowly up to the third floor, trying to make sense of what I had learned that afternoon. Thornton Ramsay had confirmed the existence of a relationship between Harry and Louise Ramsay, but I told myself again that what had actually happened between them might be quite different from what I inferred Harry had meant by his use of the term *go-around.*

Harry Braunfels and Thornton Ramsay, both presently in resident above the highroad to Hendryk, met Agnes's test. And then there was Philo, also younger than his aunt, but elegant and refined. . . .

I must have made arrangements of those leaves and berries for the guest rooms, but I have no memory of doing it, or of how they looked afterward. All I could think of were Harry, Thornton, and Philo, and by the time I joined the Ramsays in the dining room I was convinced that of the three, Philo was the only logical candidate.

Supper was an uneasy affair. Conversation was conducted in fits and starts and peppered with non sequiturs. Apparently the time for protesting the approaching visitation was past; Cora, Thorn, and Philo were now trying to come to terms with it, each in his or her own way.

Cora excused herself immediately after the meal, leaving Thornton, Philo, and me to have coffee in the library. Thornton was even more restless than he had been earlier, poking needlessly at a perfectly made fire, twirling the ancient globe until it creaked in protest.

"Must you do that, Thorn?" Philo's tone was thin and

querulous, and although I sympathized with his complaint—the globe's brass fittings shrieked like chalk across a schoolroom slate—I began to have doubts about casting him in the role of Louise Ramsay's lover. He was perhaps *too* refined, too lacking in manly vigor for his blood to have run much hotter at any age.

"How about a game of backgammon, Philo?"

Then again, few men could match Thornton Ramsay in that respect.

"What's the point, Thorn? You always win."

His expression was dispirited, his voice plaintive, almost petulant . . . no, there was no contest.

Contest? What contest? Whose lover are we choosing here, I asked myself, Louise Ramsay's or Kate Mackenzie's? My head awhirl with confusion, I failed to hear Thornton Ramsay address me.

"Do you think you might descend from those clouds long enough for a game of backgammon, Miss Mackenzie?"

It was a tempting prospect. Although I was sure I was asked only as a last resort, I was good at the game. "Are you prepared to lose to a woman, Mr. Ramsay?"

That stopped his pacing. "I don't know," he said, lifting one eyebrow in mild surprise. "The possibility has never occurred to me."

"That should make our match interesting, then. But not tonight, I fear. I have yet to change rooms as I promised I would."

"Then perhaps I'll pop down to the kennels and engage Harry in a game of checkers. He's good enough to be challenging, yet when he loses he takes it so badly it's rather amusing."

Philo frowned. "I wouldn't have thought either your ego or your pocketbook were that much in need of bolstering."

"That's unworthy of you, Philo," Thornton retorted.

"Tonight I'm more interested in distraction than in victory, and you know perfectly well I never gamble."

Philo grimaced. "Sorry, Thorn; I had forgotten about your mother's problem in that regard, truly I had."

As Thorn grunted his acceptance of the apology, I wondered how many more family skeletons awaited revealment.

"As for distraction," Philo added bitterly, reaching for the decanter of brandy brought in with the coffee, "oblivion's more to the point."

As the slender man left the room with the decanter clutched in his hand, his movements were jerky and unnatural. I was concerned enough to give Thornton Ramsay a meaningful look, but he dismissed my worries.

"There's not enough brandy in it to do Philo more harm than a morning-after headache, and he's not the type to rummage in the pantry for more. I just hope he recovers in time for Louise's arrival," he added with a frown. "We'll all be needing as clear a head as possible for *that.*"

CHAPTER EIGHT

I had brought so few belongings with me, the transferring of them to my new quarters should have taken only a few minutes, but there was a spot on my serge traveling suit, my shoes had need of a polish, and my best white shirtwaist was badly soiled. I would have to consult Mary Rose about the proper washing and ironing of it in the morning.

Still I lingered. I smoothed a ragged fingernail, then polished the silver back of my mother's hand mirror until my reflection in it almost matched that on the front, and in both my frown of indecision was plain to see. "You've dillydallied long enough," I told myself sternly. So saying, I ventured forth into the dark corridor and took the few steps that would bring me to the entrance to Roxelana's suite.

Placing my lamp beside me on the carpet, I grasped the curved brass handles firmly, and when the doors swung softly open, a whoosh of warm air enveloped me in cedarwood and roses. Expecting dank mustiness, I was so surprised by the heady aliveness of the dream-remembered scent, I felt faint with apprehension: what else might have survived my nighttime fantasies? Not knowing which way to turn, I anxiously inclined first one way, then the other, as my ears hearkened to creakings and rustlings in the shadows.

I took a long step back, snatched up the lamp, and advanced defiantly into the darkness with it raised up high, daring I-knew-not-what to reveal itself. As the shadows scuttled back behind drapes and bed curtains, carved wardrobes and gilt-mirrored dressing table, I felt more relieved than foolish to find that the source of the creaking was a parquet floor, the rustling no more than a silk bed curtain stirred by a draught of air I had myself created, and the hiss the homely sound of steam from a radiator turned on, no doubt, by Mary Rose. No snakes lay coiled to strike; no dark-haired woman lay sighing in a seven-year sleep upon the counterpane. There was no living, breathing presence here save mine.

I lit a lamp of baroque design on an inlaid table placed within reach of a graceful, peach satin–upholstered chaise. The warm glow of light through the opalescent shade revealed a riot of cabbage roses painted in a rich array of pinks and golds and apricots. Recovered from my initial shock, I found myself enjoying this luxurious room's assault upon my senses, and I hastened to establish my claim upon it.

The dressing table boasted a set of gold-rimmed silver implements and an array of crystal perfume bottles whose amber-shaded contents tempted me to sniff one of the long, tapered stoppers, but the scent had long since withered away to a bitter residue. No roses here. Then I spied a covered porcelain bowl on a small Boulle cabinet, and a similar one, initially overlooked, behind the rose-shaded lamp. I lifted their pierced covers, revealing the heaped potpourri which awaited only warmth to release

102

anew its scented message. That is why I had dreamed of it, I realized. The sudden change in the weather that night from icy blasts to an unseasonable and humid warmth had sent musky roses wafting under doors to search out my impressionable nose.

Set at ease by this practical explanation for my mysteriously perfumed dream, I found myself humming as I settled in. I replaced the gold-trimmed dresser set with my mother's, which though far less valuable was to my mind of handsomer design, and placed my toilet bag in a well-appointed bathroom almost as large as the room I had just vacated. An amenity rarely found in rural areas, this one not only boasted a small wood-fired boiler for heating water, but was entirely sheathed in marble. I was willing to wager that no seraglio boasted a finer one. Why, the sunken tub was wide and deep enough to sport about in! Quite big enough for two, really. A moment later, as the implications of my conclusion overcame me, I could feel heat suffuse my cheeks as an irrepressible vision of myself engaged in such sport with Thorn Ramsay rose to taunt me.

Unnerved by the path my imaginings were taking—a pathway to damnation, my father would have proclaimed —I hastened to hang away my two day dresses, the russet velvet Thornton Ramsay had admired, my green tweed skirt, lawn shirtwaists, and trusty serge suit. Nothing could be less stimulating to the senses than navy serge, I assured myself wryly.

I opened the rosewood doors of one of the wardrobes and was immediately reminded of Cora's dismissive description of Roxelana's taste. All glitter and gauze, she had said. But what astonishing glitter, and how sumptuous was this gauze! Far from sharing Cora's contempt, I was transported back to my Turkish childhood, when older cousins and serving girls breathlessly rivaled each other's tales of the rumored splendors of the sultan's harem.

Here before me were wonders none of those girls had even begun to imagine. Gossamer silk *chalvar* in limpid shades of amethyst, jade, sapphire, and crimson swayed on padded hangers together with brassieres netted of fine-spun strands of silver and gold, lined with satin. Silk-embroidered vests, cropped short to fit snugly under full breasts, hung above a row of exquisitely tooled slippers of the softest leather, and on the backs of the doors elaborately wrought hooks held barbaric gold-tasseled belts set with rough-cut gemstones and chiffon veils as delicate as a baby's breath and winking with tiny starlike jewels. How could I possibly hang my drab workaday garments in amongst such luxury?

I sighed as I shut away the dazzling array and turned to the other wardrobe, which held clothes designed for everyday use, albeit of the finest materials and workmanship. As I pushed Roxelana's fineries aside to make room for my own few things, I wondered that there was enough money left to maintain the estate at all. Charles Quintus's last mistress appeared to have worn most of his fortune on her pampered back.

What could have persuaded Roxelana to abandon all this? An even more interesting question was how she had persuaded Charles Quintus Ramsay to provide it in the first place. From what I had learned so far, he was an unusually lusty, self-centered man, more interested in sexual conquest than domestic bliss with any one woman.

I recalled the boldly sensual face in the portrait on the stair landing. I pictured that firmly fleshed body swaying in silken garments, those huge dark eyes offering sidelong invitation above one of those jeweled veils. These were the arts of the harem, the practiced craft of a favored concubine, frequently highborn, whose status—and sometimes her very life—depended on her mastery of it.

Could Roxelana's tale be true? Was she the threatened princess she claimed, or the wily whore Cora detested,

Thornton wished dead, and Philo hoped to replace as C.Q.'s heir? I found it hard to condemn her as whole-heartedly as the Ramsays did; in fact, a little bit of me hoped Roxelana would sweep in at the last minute to claim Hawkscliffe and return it to its former and thoroughly vulgar glory.

Perhaps it was this defiant sentiment that prompted me, as I searched for space in the dressing table for my undergarments, to open a pretty little carved box whose contents I would not ordinarily have investigated. Inside, in a soft nest of finely spun wool, was a beautifully crafted pair of *zil,* the little brass finger cymbals Turkish dancers use to accompany their sinuous movements. On impulse I slipped them on, and their clear, pure, ringing tone whisked me back many years and across many miles.

The memory thus evoked was of excited girls, all of them older than my then eight-year-old self, who whispered and giggled together in a room upstairs in my parents' house on the Bosphorus, sent there, no doubt, to keep us out from underfoot. It must have been a wedding, for I recall smirking speculation about the marriage bed, a concept that meant nothing to me at the time.

Halide, the servant girl who was sent up with refreshments, had demonstrated her skill with the cheap, bazaar-grade *zil* she had secreted in her apron pocket, but it was a tall dark girl I had met for the first time that day and never saw again who precipitated the crisis.

The room was very hot, and this girl, this near-woman, appropriated the cymbals and then, after stripping until she was all but naked, proceeded to dance. I can see her still, swaying, her eyes half closed, head thrown back, body undulating like a snake, shocking the other girls, including me—especially me—into wide-eyed, mesmerized silence. The only sounds were the rhythmic bell-like ching of the cymbals and the whispery glide of the dancer's feet on the carpet. Then my father burst in upon us.

It never occurred to me to wonder what had alerted him; I merely assumed he was as omnipotent as the stern God he worshiped. What truly astonished me, what I had forgotten until this moment, was the culprit's flashing-eyed, voluble defiance, followed by her abrupt disappearance from the room, the house, and our lives.

I still find it hard to believe that a little bit of ringing brass could evoke a memory so vividly, but as if to discover how much more could be conjured forth, I struck the little cymbals again and again, faster and more surely until my hips and belly began to respond to the rhythm my fingers coaxed from the *zil* as if animated by the erotic spirit of that daring, long-forgotten girl.

The room grew oppressively hot as I danced on, and with no real consciousness of what I was doing, I shed my restrictive garments one by one and flung them into the cavernous wardrobe. My prim highbuttoned shirtwaist was followed by my brown flannel skirt, neat kid boots, cotton stockings, and even the pins that tamed my hair. How lovely to feel its saffron waves slide free around my shoulders! The pleasure was intensified by the cool lushness of the glorious silk Hereke carpet slithering beneath my bare toes.

All at once I caught sight of myself in the long oval of a pier mirror set at the foot of the wide curtained bed. By chance, it was angled so as to reflect peekaboo glimpses of my barefoot dancing image, clothed only in a simple, ribbon-trimmed white lawn chemise and a petticoat enlivened by a single deep flounce.

As my reflection swayed in and out of sight, I flattered myself that my figure was still trim enough to forgo the suport of a corset, and as I turned to eye myself in profile I decided that my waist, though perhaps not small enough to be spanned by two hands, would meet all but the most exacting standards. Amused by my mirrored expression of satisfied vanity, I threw back my head and laughed, enjoying the shimmer of my hair, more red than gold in the rosy lamplight. Then, urging my cymbal-bedecked fingers to an even faster pace, I abandoned what was left of my usual reserve.

I did not hear Thorn Ramsay enter the room, nor did I know how long he had been standing there watching me, when I caught sight of his image, wavering ghostlike behind mine in the mirror. His face was taut with an emotion I could not identify, yet which made my breath catch in my throat and caused me to raise my hand in a fluttering, uncertain gesture, as if to free the imprisoned inhalation. As he advanced slowly toward me, I was aware only of the sounds of our breathing and his intense, falcon-eyed gaze fixed upon my astonished reflection.

I whirled to confront him, and it was then that I saw the small whip in his hands, not the black intricately braided one of my dreams, but similar enough to make me suddenly, dizzily aware of my dishabille.

"I heard the cymbals," he said. "I couldn't . . . I thought . . ." He shook his dark, shaggy head as if in denial of unimaginable sucpicions. He smiled at me crookedly and gestured with the whip. "It was as if she had crept back from some shrouded netherworld to plague us all."

I had no need to ask to whom he referred. Charles Quintus's last mistress might yet have the last laugh. I stared at the little whip as he absently tap, tap, tapped it into his palm.

He followed my mesmerized gaze, then impudently flipped the fine leather tip under my nose. I thought his slow smile wolfish, one a sultan might bestow on a concubine he was preparing to enjoy. I felt . . . trapped.

"It's merely a precaution," he said as he carelessly twirled and separated the locks of my loosened hair with the supple wand. "When I visit Harry after dark," he added, raising his eyebrows. "For the *dogs*, Kate. Surely

107

you did not . . . could not think . . ." He tossed the offending object behind him, out of my sight.

Betrayed by the foolish fears he had sensed, I turned my head away, embarrassed, but he reached out one finger to notch beneath my quivering chin. "Oh, my poor, dear Kate . . . my sweet little Kate . . . I would never hurt you. . . ."

Gently he nudged up my drooping head, and as his searching green eyes captured mine, his hands drifted down to rest upon my naked shoulders. The sensation of scorching heat as his flesh met mine scattered my thoughts into the rose-scented air. I swayed unresistingly into his demanding arms, nuzzled against his broad chest, delighting in the male smell of him, of leather and wood smoke and cigars. I raised my mouth toward his as eagerly as a dungeoned prisoner seeking light and air. The echo of my father's dire exhortations were drowned out by the hot blood singing in my veins.

"You smell always of violets," he murmured. "Of sweet violets and springtime. . . ." His mouth trailed fire along my cheek, plucked teasingly and deliciously at my lips, and rested on my swelling pulse. I cupped his head in my palm to press it closer, the spring of his dark hair alive against my fingers. His warm breath wafted to my nostrils, bringing with it another scent, one that revived my passion-lulled alarms. It was the scent of whiskey; he reeked of it.

I pulled out of his resisting arms and wiped my mouth with the back of my hand. "Had a tipple or two with Harry, did you? Did he suggest you try to snare the little mouse who had eluded him? Who thinks she's better than she is? Or perhaps I'm just another distraction to see you through the long night before Louise Ramsay arrives to upset everybody's apple cart. *For shame!*"

We stood staring at each other for a long moment in stunned silence. For my part, no sooner had I spoken than

I regretted the self-righteous words whose contemptuous tone echoed unpleasantly even in my own ears. But, as I very soon learned, the harm was already done.

"I am not everybody, Kate Mackenzie," Thorn thundered. "I am my own man—not Harry's, not Louise's, and certainly not yours!"

He reached for his whip and smacked it into his palm. This time I was quite sure he wished it were stinging me.

"I should know by now that for all your lively wit and intelligence, the promise in those dark Eastern eyes of yours wages a losing battle with your pinched Scottish soul. Why, even Mary Rose dares risk more than you! So, now that you have put me in my place, I will leave you to yours."

He nodded stiffly, turned on his booted heel with military precision, and strode to the door. He opened it, then turned back to fix me with a dreadful grin, entirely lacking in mirth, that made me shiver as if possessed by a sudden chill.

"Perhaps Roxelana's bed will warm your pious heart, eh?" His sneering emphasis made it very clear there would be no more warmth for me from Thornton Ramsay, not tonight; perhaps not ever.

CHAPTER NINE

The next morning, just before lunch, Louise Ramsay arrived at Hawkscliffe.

Her conveyance, a rickety estate trap driven by Harry Braunfels, hardly did her justice. It was as if Queen Victoria had been supplied with a stool instead of a throne at her coronation. But her measured descent from the simple carriage was impressive, and as we watched from the terrace she approached us with the majesty and churning power of a Mississippi riverboat, Harry and a slim youth trailing in her wake.

Sensing an audience, she slowed her pace to a regal glide that displayed her elegant traveling costume of black soutache-trimmed plum velveteen to best advantage. The haughty tilt of its modish draped bustle echoed the elevation of her long, straight aristocratic nose, and a smart little plumed bonnet perched atop abundant hair the color of polished mahogany.

Although I judged her age to be on the far side of forty-five, there was not the least shimmer of silver in her auburn coiffure, but whether this was due to an inherited family trait or the artful use of henna it was impossible to say. Her face, slightly doubled chin and all, might have been carved in marble by an ancient Roman hand, and her ample, snugly bodiced embonpoint made my youthful slimness, of which I had been so recently proud, seem woefully inadequate.

Still shaken by my disastrous encounter with Thorn Ramsay the previous evening, I sidled over to close ranks with Philo and Cora, the one looking hollow-eyed and stricken, the other wearing an expression worthy of the grim reaper. It was Thorn who descended to initiate the welcoming courtesies, but Louise soon made it clear she was having none of it.

"A room on the top floor? I never heard of such a thing. It will be much too hot way up there under the roof, and think of the rats scurrying through the attic over my head. It won't do, Thorn; it won't do at all."

Philo winced at the sound of her rich contralto boom of disapproval. Poor Philo. I could not help but sympathize with the price his indulgence in an after-dinner brandy was exacting.

Thorn pointed out that it was, after all, late November, and unlikely to be too hot anywhere in the house. Then, before a contrary objection could be lodged, he hurried on to state that Cora did not tolerate rats at Hawkscliffe.

Louise turned to Cora, whom she had so far ignored. Flashing a set of teeth that looked strong enough to crack walnuts, she bent upon the little woman an unloving smile. "No rats in your attic, Cora? In view of your legendary devotion to duty, I find that hardly surprising, although I could swear we had at least one in residence in the New York house during your tenure there."

To Cora's credit she chose not to rise to the bait.

"Welcome to Hawkscliffe, Mrs. Ramsay," she began untruthfully. "I regret we are unable to provide you with

112

one of the second-floor suites, but Thornton has a long-standing claim upon the one C.Q. occupied, and this young lady is occupying the other. She is here at Philo's invitation," she added in a meaningful tone.

Louise Ramsay's proud head shifted fractionally in my direction, her dark blue eyes beaming astonishment. "This young woman is Philo's guest? How extraordinary!"

Her tone of disbelief caused Philo to draw closer to me, and although he did not go so far as to clasp my hand, the solicitous tilt of his head toward mine conveyed a similar impression.

"I am Katharine Mackenzie, Mrs. Ramsay—you may have known my uncle, Vartan Avakian? I am here at Mr. Ramsay's request to appraise and catalog the Hawkscliffe rug collection," I volunteered.

Louise Ramsay raised her dark arch of eyebrows. "Ah! I knew it must be something like that." Her smug, self-satisfied expression made me wish I had not been so quick to explain myself. "I remember your uncle well, Miss Mackenzie. Such a dear man. He always preferred my husband's taste in rugs to mine, but of course Charles Quintus was paying for them, wasn't he?"

"Perhaps they simply shared a similar taste, Mrs. Ramsay. My uncle spoke admiringly of those rugs to the end of his life, long after all accounts were settled. In fact, it is considered to be the finest collection in America—isn't that so, Philo?"

Philo blinked at my cozy tone and the hand I settled on his arm, but he recovered admirably. "Indeed so, Kate," he replied in kind, and for a moment we were chums again, joined in a common, if as yet undefined, cause.

The elegant woman eyed us suspiciously. "Perhaps then, considering Miss Mackenzie's . . . ah . . . function here, she might be persuaded to relinquish her suite?"

"Really, Mother!" The youth, who until now had been standing by patiently as his elders jousted, shifted uncomfortably from one well-shod foot to the other.

"If the circumstances were ordinary, I would be happy to accommodate you, Mrs. Ramsay," I countered smoothly. "Perhaps you are unaware that the suite in question remains furnished with its former occupant's clothes and . . . adornments? I fear it would prove an unhappy choice for a sensitive woman like yourself."

Mrs. Ramsay's eyes flashed outrage. She was obviously not used to having her wishes challenged. Dismissing me with a withering glance and ignoring Cora and Philo, whom she knew were arrayed against her, she whirled on Thornton.

"Really, Thorn, I would have thought that by now you would have had that . . . that *woman's* things cleared out!"

"She's not dead quite yet, Lulu, not officially, anyway—after all, isn't that why you're here? In any event, I should think it unwise to house Miss Mackenzie on the same floor as this hot-blooded young man. Lance, isn't it?"

"Yes, sir! And very happy to meet you at last, Cousin Thornton," Lance Ramsay replied, obviously delighted to be judged virile and sophisticated enough to have designs on an unmarried young woman several years his elder.

Thornton's ploy, although I resented being made a part of it, worked. As expected, the lioness did not share her cub's delight, and as the hideous suspicion that he might indeed be on the brink of sensual manhood impressed itself upon her doting heart, she uttered a shuddering sigh of resignation.

Harry Braunfels, loaded like a camel and looking quite as disagreeable, sensed a decision had been made. "Can we go up, then? All this talk's getting us nowhere."

"Now, Harry, don't be such a bear," Louise said, playfully tapping his arm with one kid-gloved hand.

I boggled at the sight of Harry Braunfels being treated

114

like a naughty boy—could it be that there once had been, as Thorn had suggested, more than met the eye here?

"The birds expect their fresh meat at midday, if you'll remember," Harry grumbled.

"Ah, yes, the dear birds! Whatever happened to that lovely peregrine you trained for me, Harry? What good times we had. . . ."

As they entered the house together, Louise Ramsay chirping pleasantries to the uncouth, unresponsive groundskeeper, I could not help but admire her resilience. But as she gained the stairs, still engaged in one-sided conversation, I became aware of her blue eyes darting here and there, recording every exotic detail to mull over later, in private and at leisure. Except for a long, icy stare at the portrait of Roxelana, there was no way to guess at her impression of Hawkscliffe: was she envious? Contemptuous? Or was she simply assigning little mental price tags, totting up the treasure so to speak, on her son's behalf?

"Miss Mackenzie?"

It was Lance Ramsay, loitering behind, figurative cap in hand.

"Mr. Ramsay?"

"Oh, do call me Lance, Miss Mackenzie." His smile was dazzling, and just practiced enough to make me suspect he was not quite as callow as I had assumed. "I just wanted to say . . . I love my mother, truly I do, but she does deserve a check now and again." His grin was boyish this time, and more in keeping with his tousled dark hair. "I think she sometimes fancies herself the Dowager Empress of China," he confided.

"Surely she would not go so far as to strangle her adversaries! The Queen of England, perhaps?"

"Too dowdy by half."

115

"The Czarina of all the Russias," I suggested tentatively.

"Don't know the first thing about her."

"Neither do I," I admitted, "but your mother certainly looks grand enough to be a czarina."

"The very image," he agreed solemnly.

"Lance? Lance, do come along!" Louise Ramsay's rich voice spiraling down the staircase held a note of querulousness.

"Her Majesty calls," he whispered. Another dazzling smile and he was off, bounding up the stairs two at a time. "At your service, Your Royal Highestness!" I heard him say to his mother, and somehow it pleased me his impudence was not reserved for conversations held behind her regal back.

A charming boy. His classic features and coloring was obviously his mother's gift to him, but that slim, long-limbed and limber body—I recalled Lance's lighthearted leap up the staircase—betrayed no trace of coarse blood in his veins. No, Harry could claim no credit for him.

"Well, if it isn't our Miss Mackenzie, lost in reverie. If not one Ramsay, then another will do, eh?"

Thorn Ramsay had stolen up behind me, his footsteps muffled in the thick pile of the carpet. I shrank back to escape the magnetic aura of his easy grace. His rough-sculptured features were softened by wind-tousled hair that resisted taming by an impatient brown hand, and his lithe, long-legged body completed the illusion of youthfulness. So like Lance, I mused. *So very like* Lance. . . .

I blinked to keep my dizziness at bay; I could not remember his question. "I beg your pardon?"

"Oh, please spare me your righteousness, Kate!" His drawled delivery emphasized his disdain. "I saw your little tête-à-tête with Louise's boy—the little whispers and

116

flirtatious smiles, gazing after him as if to lure him back to you, yet not fifteen minutes earlier you simpered and made sheep's eyes at my dear cousin. *'Isn't that so, Philo?'*" It was a cruelly accurate caricature. "All you lacked was the lacy fan of a ballroom belle to snap open under his nose."

I stared at him unable to speak. If he had hit me with his brown fists he could not have hurt me more.

He looked at me intently, his green gaze no longer mocking. "Are the Hawkscliffe rugs that important to you, Kate?"

Appalled, I finally found my voice. "Is that what you think of me?" I asked in a disbelieving whisper. "Good Lord in heaven, is that what you *really* think?"

Pierced by my heartfelt cry, Thorn took an unsteady step back and threw his arms wide. "What *am* I to think? That you are genuinely attracted to a mere boy? That Philo's bloodless presence sends your senses reeling? I know better than that, Kate!"

"Do you? Wasn't it you who warned the mere boy's mother of his hot-blooded threat to me? Wasn't it you who said my pious heart betrayed the promise in my eyes?" I was on the offensive now, and determined to press my advantage. "But regardless of whether or not I find the boy charming and Philo gentlemanly in every respect, no rug, not the finest carpet in the world, is worth trading myself for!"

We stood for a long moment, shocked into silence. A muscle worked in Thorn's jaw as he silently ground his teeth, and as I fought to control the heaving of my breast, a tightening in the back of my neck presaged the ache I knew would soon be mounting to my temples.

The sonorous bonging of the dinner bell shattered the tension between us like a flat stone skipped across the surface of a glassy pond. It is one of the triumphs of western civilization that as the rest of the household gathered we were able, without conscious effort, to transform our strained postures into convincing evidence that our interrupted chat was of no consequence, at most a bland passing of time by two persons of disparate age and gender brought together only by circumstance. The same cannot be said for the ensuing conversation at the dinner table which, like the unwary crossing of a mine field, was punctuated with unanticipated explosions.

Louise Ramsay, for example, sallied forth with questions about why Charles Quintus had engaged Thornton to draw the will that had left his entire estate to Roxelana.

"Wasn't that an unusual thing to do, Thorn?"

"Which, Louise? Asking me to draw his will or leaving everything to his mistress?"

Louise laughed and rolled her eyes, as if to convey to the rest of us that it was Thorn who insisted upon being blunt, not she. "Well, both, really. After all, the ink was hardly dry on your degree, and for Charles Quintus to disinherit his own flesh and blood . . . *most* unusual. Why, Theodore Bailey refused to have any part in it, even though Bailey and Fernstrom had always handled the Ramsay family affairs. Something to do with undue influence, I believe."

Thorn looked up at her from the rosy, clove-studded ham he was carving. "Since you seem to already know all the answers, Louise, why ask me?" If he was annoyed, one could not tell it from his agreeable expression or from the precise slices that fell away from his knife.

Trite though it may be, injured innocence is the only term that fairly describes Louise's little shrug and artful widening of blue eyes. "Really, Thorn, I only thought—"

"In the first place, what C.Q. asked me to do was entirely legal; in the second place, I needed the money—more, apparently, than Theo Bailey did at the time. It was not my place to point out to C.Q. his lack of common sense or instruct him in the finer points of family loyalty.

"Besides, if you will remember," he added in a mutter as he deftly transferred the ham slices to the warmed platter Mary Rose held for him, "I was not overburdened with common sense at the time myself, and I had no particular reason to care about a family whose loyalties stopped short of me."

Boom.

Louise Ramsay colored deeply. A palpable hit, but I had no idea of the where or how of it.

The passing of the ham and accompanying vegetables gave time for the smoke to clear. Then, undaunted, Louise sought another target.

"I understand, Philo, that you are seeking a change. Philadelphia's loss will be New York's gain, I'm sure. Your . . . ah . . . professional qualifications are impeccable."

It was very clear to all of us, especially Philo, that other qualifications were decidedly in question.

"How . . . I've told no one . . . where did you . . . ?"

Louise Ramsay's expression as she watched Philo wriggle on the end of the hook she had set in him was not pretty.

"Elizabeth Van Rensselaer has been asked to serve on the Metropolitan's board, Philo. Couldn't be less suited to the sophisticated world of the arts, poor dear, but of course you," Louise leaned toward Philo confidingly, *"you* of all people know how desperate museums of art are for wealthy patrons—especially a new and ambitious undertaking like the Metropolitan—and if there is anything Elizabeth has to recommend her, it's money. Why, she's the veritable pot of gold at the end of the rainbow!"

As Louise chattered on and on, the pace of our eating slowed. When, we all wondered, would Philo be given the coup de grace, and what form would it take?

"Dear Elizabeth and I have known each other forever.

119

She confides in me and asks my advice, and it really is quite a responsibility because here she is, suddenly a person of influence, blessed with no aesthetic sensibility at all, and so very proper, that anything the *least* little bit out of the ordinary . . ."

Louise allowed the sentence to drift off in a way that emphasized it more than if she had shouted. Then she continued, "A classmate of ours is on *your* board, Philo, and you simply wouldn't *believe* their correspondence. Elizabeth insists they share a common interest in maintaining standards, but if you ask me, what they're *really* sharing is nothing more nor less than common gossip . . . Philo? Are you all right?"

Philo had gone quite white. I leaned toward him to urge a sip of water.

"Miss Mackenzie, I do wish you had seen Philo when he was Lance's age," Louise continued relentlessly. "*Such* a romantic-looking young man, my dear. Oh, he is still *très sympathique*, but then, he was a veritable angel. All the prettiest girls set their caps for him, but he would have none of it. When all the other boys were rowing young ladies in the park or playing at football or whatever it is vigorous lads do, Philo could be seen painting on his easel, or watching my late husband painting on his. I sometimes wondered at his patience with you, Philo. Hour after hour . . . I must say I found it puzzling."

Philo, recovered from his earlier distress, eyed her coldly.

"No puzzle that I can see in it, Aunt Louise. I simply knew when to keep my mouth shut."

This time the explosion had originated in an unexpected quarter, and although none of us went so far as to express our satisfaction, Louise Ramsay sensed she was deep in hostile territory. So did her bewildered son, who initiated a hasty retreat.

"Aren't you the director of the Philadelphia Museum, cousin?"

"Yes, Lance."

"So, if they already have a director at the Metropolitan —they do, don't they?—what I mean is . . ." It was clear from young Lance's earnest expression that his confusion, unlike his mother's, was genuine.

Philo smiled. "But you see, I applied to the Metropolitan for a curatorship. It was of course an honor to be appointed director of the Philadelphia, but for several years now I've been anxious to return to my field. There's so much research waiting to be done. Then, too, relief from administrative duties and being situated in New York would allow me more time to—" He paused abruptly. *To manage Hawkscliffe,* is what I am sure he had been about to say; "to pursue other interests," is how he diplomatically concluded. No point in stirring up Louise again.

"Have you always been interested in art?"

"As your mother indicated, ever since I can remember."

"It must be . . . satisfying."

"The study of art? Oh, yes!"

"Well, yes, art of course, but what I meant was the study of anything. To care that much about anything."

The longing in his voice gave us all pause. It is only the very young who can express envy untinged by jealousy or bitterness. Forced thereby to view the preceding petty snipings in the proper perspective, even Louise looked shamefaced.

Thornton cleared his throat. "You're quite right about the satisfaction," he said gruffly, sounding more like an uncle than a cousin. "Philo's profession has its problems, of course, but I daresay he would not trade his study of art to be free of them. I find the law endlessly fascinating despite the attendant disillusionments, and I'm sure Miss

121

Mackenzie prefers the challenge of buying and selling fine carpets to driving around town leaving calling cards in silver salvers."

The compliment—at least I assumed that was what he had intended—caught me unprepared. Startled, I looked across at Thorn to find my assumption confirmed by his admiring green gaze upon me. Feeling a betraying warmth rise in my cheeks, I dropped my head and pretended to find something of enormous interest in the folds of my napkin.

"And what about you, Lance?" It was Philo this time, and from his tone and guarded expression I judged his question anything but casual. "What plans have you for your future?"

As Lance colored and shrugged, his mother reached over to pat his arm reassuringly. "Such a solemn crew!" She laughed musically. "Lance's nose is much too handsome to be applied to your grindstone just yet. There's time enough for him to learn how real and earnest life is."

"One would think work and pleasure were mutually exclusive terms, Lulu," Thorn said. *How nice that his sardonic smile was meant for someone else, for a change!* "But then, I fail to see how satisfaction can be found in an endless round of social duties dictated by a book of etiquette. At least the Ten Commandments originated with God."

There was a gasp and clink of china from Mary Rose, whose instinctive effort to cross herself was frustrated by the dishes she held in both hands.

Louise's mouth pursed. "Are you suggesting we would be better off conducting ourselves like savages?"

"Not at all! I am aware, more than most, I think, of the terrifyingly thin line separating us all—men, women, even young Lance here—from the life of tooth and claw. But for women of your class, who are otherwise largely powerless, the meticulous observance of socially correct behavior too often becomes an obsession. How else can a woman exert influence on her husband's life except through instruction in social arts he hasn't the time to acquire for himself? Sex is essentially the same game, you know—the femme fatale is an otherwise impotent person who has perfected her one strength to an unusual degree."

Cora rose abruptly, her mouth compressed to a thin, disapproving line. "Really, Thorn! I must question the suitability of this . . . this topic at the dinner table."

Louise followed suit, albeit more gracefully. "I'm forced to agree, although in *your* case, Cora, I question the suitability of the topic wherever it may be met. I'll have you know, Miss Mackenzie, that Miss Banks's sterling virtue is an example to us all."

Startled to be addressed in an admonitory tone by a person in no way entitled to do so, I was on the verge of an indignant retort when her next words made it clear I was merely a convenient way station.

"Charles Quintus held her in the highest regard. In fact," she continued, cocking her dark auburn head to one side, "I do believe she is the only woman he unfailingly held at arm's length. Quite a tribute, wouldn't you say?"

I could tell from Cora's expression that she took it for the cruel taunt meant. She departed in outraged silence, and Louise, pleased to have at last hit an intended target, smiled cheerily.

"Speaking of social niceties, I would so enjoy a tour of Hawkscliffe's every little nook and cranny, for belated as our visit is, one never knows—or so they say." Her smile quirked coyly as she looked first at Philo, who paled, then at Thorn, who got up from the table, pulled back her chair, and crooked his arm for her to grasp.

"Come along, then, Lulu, for as they also say, better late than never."

After a moment's hesitation, Lance, too, rose from the table. He looked first at me, then at Philo, opened his mouth as if to speak, then shrugged and trailed out of the room.

Philo, meanwhile, stared after his aunt and his cousin, his face expressionless. Then, as a contralto lilt of laughter floated up to us from the terrace through an open window, his gray eyes narrowed and his mouth twisted and hardened into a sneer that slightly bared his teeth. The very air seemed charged with his hostility. Involuntarily, I shivered, and as I did so the fine hairs on the back of my neck prickled with an uneasiness that underscored the irony of the situation.

When I was thirteen, Hawkscliffe had seemed such a magical place! It never occurred to my young mind then— nor through the years I yearned to visit here—that golden spires could have dangerously sharp points; that fairy castles could be besieged by foes; or that the magic might be black.

CHAPTER TEN

As his aunt's and cousin's voices faded into the distance, Philo turned back to me. If judged solely by the ensuing businesslike exchange the bizarre dialogue in the recently vacated dining room might never have taken place.

"Miss Mackenzie . . . uh . . . Kate? Have you any notion of when you will complete your notes for the rug catalog?"

Philo and I had, it seemed, returned to a first-name basis.

"It's largely done already, except for some small rugs on the top floor—"

"Which are unlikely to be important ones, I imagine."

I decided to let that pass without comment, despite the stirrings of my conscience. "But," I continued, "I will need to check some of my notes against my uncle's journals in New York."

"Hmmm, that will be all right, I guess. The important thing is to have all the work at Hawkscliffe completed before the hearing. There is no way of knowing, you see. . . ." Philo's words trailed off. The corners of his mouth drooped.

"I understand," I said gently. "I assure you I will have everything accomplished in time."

He shook his head slowly. "All we can do then is hope."

"Hope for what, Cousin Philo?" Young Lance, obviously at loose ends, spoke from the doorway.

"Why, that all our wishes come true," Philo answered with a smile.

"So that beggars may ride?"

"Just so. Abandon the sightseeing tour, did you?"

"I wasn't asked to join it. Two's company, and all that sort of thing. Probably just as well. I'm more interested in architecture than Mother is, anyway. My questions would have bored her." He looked expectantly at Philo.

"Then come along with me, Lance," I offered impulsively. "I have work to do on the top floor, and if you'll lend me a hand, you may ask me all the questions you like. I was raised in Turkey, you see, and I have a pretty good idea of what Charles Quintus Ramsay was about when he built Hawkscliffe."

"What a splendid offer," Philo exclaimed. Then, when Lance politely asked him to accompany us, he added, "As you yourself said, two's company," and advised us to run along as if we were children being sent off to play.

As Lance turned to mount the stairs, Philo grasped my arm. His fine gray eyes glistened with gratitude. "Thank you," he whispered. "Your kindness is more than I deserve."

I inclined my head in silent acknowledgment and hurried to join my youthful companion. As we climbed the stairs, exclaiming over the decoration and discussing the Hawkscliffe distortions of the true Ottoman style, I found myself chattering away with a lighthearted fervency quite unlike my usual cautious self.

What fun we had that afternoon! I discovered that

Lance, thanks to his interest in architecture, could turn out quite an accomplished sketch in jig time, so while I recorded the rugs' measurements and structural descriptions in my journals, I set him to making drawings of them on the facing pages.

"I suppose I take after my father," he said, when I complimented him. "Did you know him?"

I was nonplussed. Fortunately, the only answer I wanted to give was also truthful. "No."

"Nor I. I guess he was an odd duck. Of course, he and Mother were divorced, and I've heard that last mistress of his—what was her name again?"

"Roxelana," I supplied in a muffled voice. I was not accustomed to discussing mistresses with anyone, much less with the purported son of the man who'd had them.

"I've heard she was a stunner! She must have been, if he built this place for her. Jolly good place, too."

I swallowed, thinking of Philo and his hopes. "If Hawkscliffe should become yours, Lance . . . what will you do with it?"

"Don't know, really. Never thought about it much, till we actually came, of course." He looked thoughtful and a bit troubled. His visit had apparently presented him with unsettling wonderings and yearnings. Then his face brightened. "Tell you what, though . . . if I lived here I'd buy myself a velvet smoking jacket with brocaded facings—"

"—and tooled leather slippers with turned-up toes," I added, falling in with his new mood.

"Exactly! And a red felt fez with one of those . . . those . . ." He pointed to the top of his dark head and twirled his finger.

"Tassels," I supplied. "A gold tassel falling down over the edge to meet the twirled-up end of your black moustache. Oh! What a fine Terrible Turk you'll make!"

"And I'll sit cross-legged on this prayer rug here," he said, immediately taking up the position, "smoking my whatchamacallit—"

"Hubble-bubble. That's what that water pipe contraption is called, you know."

"'Pon my word," he drawled, eyeing me through an imaginary monocle. "Smoking my hubble-bubble," he continued with a delighted grin, "whilst you, me Turkish delight, dance for me and send my jaded senses reeling."

He looked up at me, his young face alight with expectation, and all at once I was aware of the possibility of my own allure. I whippped a lace-trimmed handkerchief from my pocket and, holding its ends against my temples with my fingers, allowed it to drape below seductively narrowed eyes.

"Lance? Lance, where are you?"

"My God, it's Mother!" Lance scrambled to his feet. Then, suddenly overcome with the sense of being naughty children caught out, we collapsed in a fit of giggles.

"What on earth is going on here?"

Louise Ramsay stood in the doorway, the very picture of a starchy matron. Behind her I glimpsed Thornton Ramsay's frowning face. Too late I became aware of the dust on my skirt and my hair's disarray.

"I was helping Kate—Miss Mackenzie—with her rug catalog. Dashed off a few sketches for her."

"Your son is quite talented, Mrs. Ramsay," I said primly. "You should see to it that he has proper instruction."

Louise Ramsay raised her eyebrows, amazed that a little chit of a tradesperson should presume to instruct her about her son's talent. "May I see, please." It was not a request.

"Of course." I obediently proffered for her inspection the journals Lance had adorned.

128

"Why, he does show promise, doesn't he?" she agreed. "But then blood tells, wouldn't you say so, Thorn?"

Thornton's frown became a scowl. Although relieved that I was not the only cause for his displeasure, I was troubled that Louise Ramsay was apparently determined to establish Lance's claim upon the estate by every means possible, fair or foul.

I squeezed by Thorn, precious journals in hand, to return to my room to freshen up for supper, and as I did so he wiped his thumb across my cheek with a slow, caressing deliberateness that made my breath catch in my throat.

"Just a smudge, Miss Mackenzie. From messing about in the carpets with your young helper, I expect."

I expelled my breath in an angry whuff as his lips quirked in that familiar, altogether disquieting, sardonic grin. *I hate you, Thorn Ramsay*, I silently raged. I hated him, and yet I knew that more than anything else I wanted his lips, those hateful, exciting lips, twisting demandingly again on mine.

I retreated to my room, to Roxelana's exotic domain, as if to a haven, but as I restlessly paced, it began to seem more like a cage. The bars of my cage were ghosts—hers? mine?—dark ghosts from the past that clamored and clashed and yet, oddly, were not as fearsome as the pale ghosts from the colorless future I sensed would be mine if I failed to come to terms with what was happening to me at Hawkscliffe. Wherever I went and whatever I did here presented me with a challenge as sharp as the talons of the hawk I had seen clutching Harry Braunfels' gauntleted wrist.

Except when I was with Lance. I reviewed the easy afternoon I had spent with him. No challenges there . . . unlike Cora, Philo, Harry, or even his mother, Lance accepted me as a person from whom he wanted nothing and expected to be anything other than what I was. And what about Thorn? I stopped my pacing. *Ah, Thorn.*

For all his taunts and sardonic smiles, I knew—and it pleased me to know—that he respected Katherine Mackenzie, carpet connoisseur and rug dealer, and yet, and yet . . . oh, I knew it was foolish, but I also suspected him of stalking me, for reasons that utterly escaped me. What on earth could a man of the world find of more than passing interest in a dark-eyed little wisp of a Scot who smelled of violets, a scent more suited to girls and maiden aunts than femmes fatales?

I strode to the larger of Roxelana's wardrobes and flung open the rosewood doors with such violence that the whispered chorus of its silken contents, set asway, seemed to chide me for my misdirected anger, and a leatherbound volume, dislodged by my vehemence, tumbled from a hitherto unseen shelf, barely missing my head. I picked it up, intending to replace it, but a casual riffle of the beautifully illustrated, minutely detailed pages soon changed my mind.

Enrapt by the astonishing scenes depicted, I made my way to the peach satin-covered chaise. As I slowly turned the book's pages, I'm sure my blushing cheeks rivaled the roses on the shaded lamp at my elbow. It was an erotic book, and in it men and women disported with carefree abandon in a variety of postures my untutored mind could never have imagined. Yes, a *highly* erotic book, and yet. . . . As I leafed through the remaining pages, a radical notion entered my mind: how could anything so obviously enjoyed by its participants be thought sinful?

I closed the book, laid it on the chaise, and began again to pace. A long-forgotten memory struggled to the surface of my consciousness. Something about Halide, the serving girl who had smuggled in the finger cymbals to entertain a roomful of restless girls. A year or two after that incident she was dismissed from my parents' employ and sent off to a forced marriage in the hills of Anatolia. I recalled her pleading to be allowed to stay, but my father refused. "Harlot!" he had thundered. "Your baby will need a father," my mother had explained.

Later Halide and I had cried together, for I was very fond of the pleasure-loving girl who alternately teased and spoiled me.

"He tried to make me say I was sorry I had sinned," she said, referring to my father, "but I'm not. He was so beautiful, my Ahmet. I knew he would not marry me, but he was so beautiful I could not resist him. When I am lying with that dirty old peasant in his cold stone house, I will dream of Ahmet's honey-sweet words and strong young body."

"Confess to Papa," I entreated. "Swear to be good for always and always and maybe he will let you stay."

"Never," she hissed fiercely. "I would do it again . . . and again and again." She smoothed my hair and searched my uncomprehending eyes. "Someday you'll understand, little Katty."

"Do confess, Halide," I sobbed.

"Never!"

Such defiance! Such bravery for naught. Dear, foolish, impetuous Halide. I had not thought of her for years— could it be she had something to teach me now? Perhaps that life devoid of love and the pleasure of loving was no life at all?

I returned to the wardrobe and, standing on tiptoe, just managed to reach the shelf from which the leatherbound volume had fallen. I reached my hand back and felt across the length of the narrow space. My fingers touched first a sheaf of papers and then the hard edges of more books. I teased my discoveries toward the edge of the shelf, eased

131

them down into my arms, and then, seated on the silk prayer rug, sorted carefully through Roxelana's hidden library volumes one by one.

In addition to a variety of erotic drawings, my trove included several books of stories whose sensual language and descriptions reminded me of the fabled princess Scheherazade, who kept the headsman's ax at bay by entertaining her capricious new husband so well that after one thousand and one enchanted nights he finally forgot his purpose. Foolish Prince Schariar! As if any man, even one whose power is God-given and absolute, could prevail against a clever woman's wiles!

I closed the last book of stories reluctantly, wishing either that I had found them sooner, or that my stay at Hawkscliffe would not so soon be ended. I sighed and picked up the last volume. Both the cover and the pages densely written in Arabic reminded me of the stacks of journals kept by my Uncle Vartan over the sixty years of his business life, but there the resemblance abruptly ended. The style of the script was prosaic; the content, anything but. Roxelana, obviously educated to a degree unusual for a Muslim girl, had put her learning to use in an even more unusual way, for this commonplace-looking book was nothing more nor less than a handbook of sexual practices.

At first individually described in numbered sequence, they were later incorporated into little scenes. As I read on, variously amazed and shocked by the variety and ingenuity of Roxelana's playlets, I was once again reminded of the princess whose gift for spinning tales had saved her life. Had I discovered Roxelana's secret? Had Charles Quintus Ramsay been her Schariar, and had Roxelana's flair for erotic fantasy assured her permanence in the bed of her easily bored American prince?

That would also account for her collection of glittering, gauzy garments and leather and jeweled curios. Costumes and props, that's what they were! I understood now why Charles Quintus's will had ignored his family: how could the homely ties of flesh and blood prevail against chains forged from silk and satin and hot, perfumed flesh? Roxelana's clever manipulation of the sexual drive that had fueled the aging artist's enormous talent had, in the end, degraded it to blind, carnal lust.

As Thorn had said, Charles Quintus's last mistress had indeed become his master.

CHAPTER ELEVEN

After supper that evening Louise prowled through the house sowing discord. It was a Saturday; I remember that because there was no mention of sending a carriage into town the next morning to accommodate churchgoers. I was still a practicing Catholic, although I tended to ignore my obligations except when troubled, which heaven knows I had been to one degree or another ever since the moment of my arrival at Hawkscliffe.

Since the hearing to determine the missing heiress's status was scheduled for Monday, I thought Cora might want to go into Hendryk on Sunday to pray under God's roof for divine intervention on her and Philo's behalf. Considering Cora's interest in maintaining the status quo, Louise's performance that evening must have been disheartening in the extreme.

Her first victim was Philo, snared from the backgammon game he was enjoying with Lance. I say "enjoying," because with me as a teasing onlooker shamelessly supplying Philo with hints about strategy, the contest had deteriorated into a rather noisy affair of silly jokes, underhanded ploys, and undignified yelps of triumph and protest. Thorn, who was attempting to read his paper, regarded us frowningly, and when Lance asked him to mediate a particularly outrageous move, he muttered testily that he saw no point in playing games one doesn't intend to win.

"Winning isn't everything, coz," Philo protested with a smile. It was nice to see a little color in his cheeks for a change.

"If Thorn's dear mother had been yours, I doubt you would say that, Philo. Although as I understand it, her problems only began with her losing the games she so blithely entered and invariably lost. Nevertheless, I *am* relieved; it isn't everyone who can be so philosophical whilst standing on the brink, so to speak." Louise's dazzling smile was succeeded by a rounding of her mouth in exaggerated surprise. "But you're so flushed! The excitement of the contest, no doubt. I wouldn't have thought Lance would be challenge enough for you—I'm referring to the game, of course."

The blood that had lent a youthful glow to Philo's face drained away, leaving him pale as milk. He shoved back his chair and rose unsteadily to his feet. As he did so, Louise, who had been bending over him solicitously, grabbed his arm just above the elbow in a grip so tight I could see him wince.

"My dear Philo, you're looking *quite* unwell again. Do let Miss Mackenzie take your place at the board and walk with me out to the terrace. The fresh air will do you a world of good." So saying, she adjusted her fichu of heavy cream lace to cover her shoulders and, in a flurry of lilac silk faille that set the purple bows on her bustle atremble, she all but hauled Philo out of the room.

"Good heavens," I murmured, "I wonder what *that* was all about!"

"I daresay it's her overdeveloped maternal instinct coming to the fore again," Lance offered with an embarrassed half smile. "I can't seem to convince her I'm old enough to take care of myself—you know how mothers are."

"What on earth does she have to protect you against, Lance? You were winning as often as you lost."

"It wasn't backgammon she was concerned about, Kate."

"Well, I hardly think Philo wants Hawkscliffe badly enough to do away with you in front of witnesses!"

The whole thing was idiotic, including finding myself in the position of defending Philo. Although I no longer begrudged his appropriation of my idea about publishing the Hawkscliffe rug catalog, I was not yet kindly enough disposed to act as his champion. I looked at Lance indignantly.

"He *is* a bit of a poof, Kate," he said with a sheepish grin.

I stared at him uncomprehendingly. "A *what?*"

Lance looked about him helplessly, then sent a silent appeal to Thorn, who had long since given up the pretense of reading his paper and was listening unashamedly to our dialogue.

"What my young cousin is trying to tell you, Kate, is that Philo is a homosexual."

Lance turned beet red at Thorn's frank use of a term forbidden in polite society. I nodded gravely and thanked Thornton Ramsay for enlightening me, determined to indicate thereby that the term and the relationships implied did not shock me. As indeed they did not: accustomed from birth to the ways of Eastern societies, which sequester their women, affection displayed openly between men seemed to me neither unusual nor abnormal.

No wonder Louise had looked so astonished when Cora told her I was at Hawkscliffe as Philo's guest! In light of her maliciousness—and despite Thorn's contemptuous interpretation of what he saw as my attempt to worm my way into Philo's affections—I was glad I had acted impulsively to create the illusion of a romantic attachment between us. However, when Philo returned grim-faced and paler than ever from his involuntary stroll with Louise, it was obvious the bluff had been called.

As he walked wordlessly by us toward the hall, Louise could not resist throwing a gracefully fashioned dart at his departing back.

"We are agreed, then? There is no need for dear Elizabeth and the Metropolitan Board—not to mention Flossie Biddle on your board in Philadelphia—to know absolutely everything about everyone in their employ. As I always say, a bit of mystery lends appeal, and I would be the last one to deny your appeal, Philo darling."

The remaining vestige of my grudge against him faded from my mind and heart as Louise smoothed her faultless coif with dainty pats of her beringed white hands and turned back to us with a happy little sigh. "Philo thinks he may stay on in Philadelphia after all. He was quite unaware of some of the . . . nuances at the Metropolitan; someday he'll surely thank me for pointing them out to him, but just now, as you can see . . ." She paused and quirked her mouth in a coy fashion unbecoming to such an imposing woman. "Oh well, none of us likes to see his plans go awry, do we? How did the Scottish poet put it, Miss Mackenzie? 'The best-laid schemes o' mice and men gang aft a-gley. . . .'"

". . . an' lea'e us nought but grief and pain for promis'd joy," I completed expressionlessly, the familiar words dropping like stones from my lips. Confound the woman! She had apparently not only blackmailed Philo out of his expectations, but quoted my father's favorite couplet from Robert Burns to boot. Considering how often Papa had serenely caused my own childish plans to go a-gley, they were lines I could very well have forgone hearing.

Lance looked from me to his mother. His alert uneasiness reminded me of a twitchy-nosed young rabbit testing the morning air, its hippity-hopping ebullience slowed by something not quite right—a fox, perhaps? The dreaded weasel? Whatever Lance sensed, he obviously felt unable to cope. He abruptly yawned.

"Do you mind if we resume our game tomorrow, Kate? All at once I feel most awfully tired." Another yawn was accompanied by an elaborate stretch that drew his mother's reproving attention.

"Really, Lance! Miss Mackenzie will think her company has fatigued you."

"She knows better than that, Mother. It was only her stimulating presence that kept sleep at bay during my game with Cousin Philo."

I burst out laughing. "You make me sound like a bottle of smelling salts, Lance. Go along with you, sleepyhead, but no games tomorrow, mind you. It's going to be work, work, work for us both."

Lance pursed his mouth and raised his eyes heavenward. "On the Lord's Day, Miss Mackenzie? Surely the weary deserve their rest," he protested.

"The weary, yes, but not the wicked," I said briskly.

"Well, I must admit I would rather be thought wicked than weary," Lance conceded with a grin. "Goodnight, sweet Kate! I shall count the hours 'til the morrow and the counting of carpet knots together again. Goodnight, Mother." He kissed his mother's cheek, placidly ignoring her muttered disapproval of his boyishly flirtatious exchange with me. "Goodnight, Cousin Thorn." His long legs took him quickly out of the room. "Goodnight, Miss Banks," we heard him say as he entered the hall.

I rose, planning to follow Lance's example. This war of nerves had nothing to do with me; why should I allow myself to be conscripted into it?

"What have you done to Philo?"

I was too late; Cora had fired the opening shot of another battle.

"Whatever do you mean, Cora?" Louise Ramsay gazed down serenely round-eyed at the little woman whose own eyes had narrowed to angry slits. The sparrow had met her match in this big owl of a woman whose luxurious plumage masked a coldly covetous heart. "He left us about an hour ago . . . to go to the studio and his lonely bed, presumably."

"Your presumption was wrong, Mrs. Ramsay, as has often been the case. Philo is nowhere to be found, and neither is the decanter of brandy I left in the library."

"What do you think, Thorn?" Louise's languid voice betrayed her lack of concern. "Could Philo be wandering about the grounds imbibing false courage? Trying to avoid facing the inevitable? He never was much of a one for reality, as I remember."

"The dogs are real enough, I trust, to keep him off the grounds at night. He'll soon turn up," Thorn began in a quiet tone of tightly controlled anger, but his effort to keep tempers leashed was outflanked by Cora.

"You're a fine one to talk about facing reality, Louise Ramsay! Sashaying in here trying to pass off that boy as C.Q.'s son."

Shrugging disdainfully, Louise glided over to station herself beside Thorn's chair. She turned back slowly to face Cora, her silk gown hissing softly in the sudden silence. "And who among you is to say he is not?"

"C.Q. threw you out because of him!"

"Charles Quintus's name is on the birth certificate."

"He wished to spare you the disgrace!"

"Did he, now."

Louise's dry tone and raised eyebrows alerted me to the fact that C.Q.'s vanity made it probable he had been much more interested in concealing the fact that he had been

140

cuckolded than in protecting Louise's reputation.

"There's nothing about that on the certificate, Cora, only his name," she added with a sly smile. "And it's the name that counts, you know. Isn't that so, Thorn?"

After a long pause, Thorn inclined his shaggy dark head. "In lieu of evidence to the contrary, yes."

His reluctance alerted me to the intriguing possibility that contrary evidence might, in fact, exist. But even if it did, the hearing was, after all, the day after tomorrow. There was hardly time to institute a search. And then it came to me: no wonder Louise had waited so long to press her claim! She knew that a birth certificate presented by a grand lady like herself to a rural judge in a rivertown court was unlikely to be questioned, no matter how vocal the opposition. Proof was proof, especially when registered in a New York City hall of records.

Cora, too angry to be sensitive to nuances, persisted in her attack. "He divorced you! He never even saw the boy, much less publicly acknowledged him."

It was clear from the glitter in Louise's eyes that this time Cora had drawn blood. "It would have cost him nothing to make the gesture *then*, but now the rest of you will have to pay his debt for him. You'll see! After the hearing Monday, Hawkscliffe will be ours, Lance's and mine, and then it's out with the old and in with the new!" Louise's smile had become a sneer of triumph.

Cora advanced on Louise with her little fists clenched and her thin mouth pulled tight in a grimace of rage.

"This was to be my home until I died! C.Q. promised me, he promised. . . ." Cora's voice broke, and her slight, taut figure suddenly drooped. Alarmed, I moved forward, but Thornton forestalled me.

"Enough!" he commanded. "The two of you are only making a bad situation worse."

Louise raised her eyebrows. "Bad, Thorn? From whose point of view? Not mine or Lance's, certainly."

141

"I doubt that young Lance will be happy about depriving Cora of her home."

Louise guiltily averted her gaze, confirming Thorn's suspicion that Lance hadn't been told of all the consequences of his inheriting Hawkscliffe. "She should have known better than to believe Charles Quintus's promises," Louise exclaimed. "He was always ready to promise anything to get what he wanted."

Thorn clasped his hands behind his back, and leaned toward her confidingly. "Ah! So that's where you learned that little trick, Lulu."

Louise pulled abruptly away from him. Gathering her draped lilac silk skirt with one hand she made her haughty way between us, Cora and Thorn on one side, I on the other. At the entrance to the hall she paused, and looked back over her shoulder. "I would suggest, Cora, that you begin packing your bags. Under the circumstances, two weeks' notice is all that I am inclined to give."

After Louise left, Cora began to cry. Thorn moved forward to comfort her, and as he awkwardly patted her shoulder her sobs subsided to mewing sniffles. There was nothing I felt I could do, and when they began talking together in low murmurs, I quietly departed.

Although I was not overly fond of Cora, I had learned to like the formidable Louise even less, and so was disconcerted to stumble upon her in the shadows of the stair landing, studying Roxelana's portrait in the wavering light of a lamp affixed to a wall bracket opposite. Although the effect of the illumination was not as dramatic as that created for me days earlier by flaming wax tapers held aloft in the bronze peacocks' beaks, it was sufficiently arresting to capture Louise's entire attention.

I cleared my throat. She uttered a little shriek of alarm and whirled, wide-eyed, to confront me.

"Miss Mackenzie! You might have spoken, you know. I didn't know who . . . I didn't know what to think."

"I'm sorry," I said stiffly. "I had no idea you were here."

"Did you know her, Miss Mackenzie?"

I was amazed. "Roxelana? Good heavens, no. She disappeared long before I ever came to Hawkscliffe."

"I thought perhaps . . . Thorn tells me you grew up in Turkey."

"Yes, but our lives . . . our paths would never have crossed. For one thing, she's a good deal older than I. That is, I'm not quite sure how old she was when your . . . when Mr. Ramsay painted her portrait, but she would be years older now."

"Mmmm, yes. Yes, of course." Her tone was thoughtful. "She's not beautiful, is she? Not even pretty, really."

"No."

Judging from the look of sullen resignation on her face, there was no need to elaborate on the obvious: Roxelana's unmistakable erotic appeal had nothing to do with conventional ideas of beauty. I had sensed that much even before I'd found her secret journal.

I realized it would be difficult to edge by Louise without touching her, and somehow I was loath to do that. She shifted uneasily, self-consciously, and it then became impossible to get by her at all.

"Miss Mackenzie, what kind of ring is that she's wearing?" Louise tentatively extended one long white finger toward the glowing gold disk, but no sooner had it grazed the painted surface than she snatched it back as if from burning coals.

"A talisman ring. Quite old, probably. The inscriptions are rendered in an archaic script, but most likely they are variations on ancient runes meant to ward off evil."

Louise gave a dismissive sniff. "I might have suspected as much of her. Superstitious as well as coarse."

"In the East, belief in the evil eye is taken seriously

regardless of class or rank, Mrs. Ramsay."

"It doesn't seem to have done *this* one much good, eh?" She flicked a contemptuous glance toward the portrait. "After seven years gone to heaven—or hell—knows-where, she's hardly likely to return to claim Hawkscliffe now."

"Well, now, we won't know that for sure until Monday, will we?" I countered smoothly.

"*We? You* say *we*, Miss Mackenzie?" Panic flared out at me from quickly hooded eyes. "What, pray, have *you* to do with Hawkscliffe or us?"

"Why, nothing, Mrs. Ramsay; I was using 'we' in the editorial sense. A careless choice, nothing more." I deeply regretted arousing a suspicion that I feared would not easily be put to rest.

"Be that as it may, Miss Mackenzie," she said, eyeing me warily, "I have no doubt justice will prevail. Although what we will do with this vulgar monstrosity I can't imagine. Sell it, I suppose."

Imagine dismissing Philo's and Cora's dreams and plans so casually, so heartlessly! I fought to suppress any outward sign of my indignation.

"Lance quite likes Hawkscliffe," I offered lightly. "He rather fancies himself in a velvet smoking jacket relaxing in the library, fire ablaze, brandy in hand."

Louise tensed. The little shop person was turning out to be more than she bargained for. "My son's tastes, unlike his cousin Thorn's, are as yet unformed." She wagged her finger coyly at me, cutting off the protest on my lips, but her playfulness was in deadly earnest. "Oh, I've seen the way you look at him, Miss Mackenzie, but I can assure you Thorn's appetites run more to ripe, juicy pears than tart little green apples. Don't waste your girlish sighs on Thornton Ramsay, my dear; why, you'd be better off with Philo!"

Her voice was the silky purr of a domestic cat that, bored

with the fare provided it, lies in wait to swipe out a well-nourished paw at passing small creatures. Loathsome woman!

"Ah, but surely he has learned by now how fleeting is a pear's perfection, Mrs. Ramsay! No sooner does it reach its glory than rot creeps in to claim the flesh beneath its still unblemished skin." I paused, then added in a musing tone, as if it were a spontaneous afterthought, "But apples, if sensibly kept, endure."

Having demonstrated that even a mouse, if provoked, can use its sharp little teeth to advantage, I was rewarded with the hiss of her indrawn breath. It was only later that I realized I had all but admitted what Louise had implied: Thorn Ramsay had indeed invaded my thoughts and dreams and was even now laying siege to my heart.

CHAPTER TWELVE

My mean little moment of triumph over Louise was short-lived. No more than an hour later, after I had completed my toilette except for the ritual one hundred brush strokes of my hair, I heard a muffled but insistent rapping. Wondering who it could be, I laid down my brush and hurried to the door. When I opened it, my halfhearted greeting died on my lips.

No one impatiently waited at my door to be admitted; rather, I saw first a figure at the other end of the dark corridor, then a spill of light from Thornton Ramsay's suite and a flash of lace-trimmed ecru satin as the door began to close upon a half-whispered exchange of bass and contralto voices. *Louise and Thornton.* My hand froze on the curved brass handle in my hand, and before I could recover my senses, Thorn's door swung out again—he must have caught a fleeting glimpse of me earlier—just wide enough to frame his face. Paring the distance between us, the intensity of his gaze dizzied me until I was ready to drown in its turbulence.

Stumbling back into my room, I pulled the door shut and leaned against it, eyes closed, hands splayed against the cool, carved surface. As I did so, a wholly unfamiliar emotion seized me. My body began to tremble, and as I fought the urge to wail, I felt the bitter taste of bile in the back of my throat.

That woman . . . *that dreadful woman.* My God! She was almost old enough to be his mother, and yet the knowledge of it did nothing to calm me. All I could see was the gleam of satin and lace in Thorn's room; all I could think of was that ripe body in his bed. Tears began to fall, and I dashed them away with angry fists . . . angry, jealous fists. *Jealousy* . . . so that's what it was! But recognition did not stop the monster's mocking taunts. What a poor, helpless, sniveling little wretch I had become: weeping and wringing my hands as I paced; next I would be tearing my hair and moaning of my woes. . . .

I suddenly caught sight of my red, puffy, tear-tracked face in Roxelana's pier mirror. What would *she* have done? Scorned him? Scolded him? Not Roxelana—she was too clever by half for that. I thought of the journals I had read with such guilty fascination. I knew exactly what she would have done—*had* done—with the skills she had refined to an art. Schooling her body to attract his eye and divert his mind, she had, time and time again, driven Charles Quintus to erotic distraction.

I began again to pace. This was not a course I should be considering, not even for a moment; not high-minded Katherine Mackenzie, to whom self-respect was more important than self-indulgence. As I pondered, an old Scottish ballad suddenly skirled through my mind, its words making a mockery of my genteel reservations. *Oh, ye'll tak the high road and I'll tak the low road, and I'll be in Scotland a'fore ye* . . . was I perhaps *too* high-minded? Was I perhaps making too much of a simple flirtatious impulse? I had had no such qualms with young Lance. . . .

Young Lance. Ah! There was the nub of it: Lance was a boy. A handsome boy, a bright, talented, and spirited boy, perhaps more sophisticated than first impressions had led me to believe, but for all that, a boy. He did not tie my tongue in awkward knots, or rouse my temper for no good reason at all, or dizzy me with a single look. It took a man to do that; it took Thornton Ramsay to do that to *me*. Flirtation? The road I was considering taking was lower than that. Seduction was more like it; seduction, pure and simple. Well, simple, anyway, I reflected wryly, though it wouldn't be simple for me; no, not for me. *Think, Kate, think!*

I paused to take stock of my situation. On Monday was the hearing; on Monday I must depart. Even though the disposition of the estate was still uncertain, Philo had told me it would be best if my work were completed by then, and I had no choice but to comply. But once I left Hawkscliffe, once there was no longer any natural reason for my path to cross with Thorn's. . . .

I twisted my hands together in anguished frustration. *Oh! If only there were more time!* But there was not, and I could think of no way but Roxelana's.

Deliberately, I went into the spacious marble-sheathed bathroom and lit the boiler fire to heat water for my bath; deliberately, I walked to the wardrobe, opened it, and sorted through its gauzy contents, garment by garment. Gold? Not enough contrast with my hair. The blue? Too vibrant; it would make me seem more wan than fair. Pink? Insipid. Black? Too obvious. Aquamarine . . . the color of the Aegean Sea in summer. I lifted the padded hanger off the rod and carried it over to the mirror. I held the sheer bouffant pantaloons close against me and watched them sway in rhythm to my tentative movements. I smiled. It suited me, this color. I hastened back and chose a brassiere fashioned from satin of the same limpid hue trimmed with crystal beads and seed pearls. Charming! Then slippers—but, oh dear, they swallowed up my narrow feet; I would have to settle for bare toes, nails buffed and polished.

What else? I tapped my forefinger thoughtfully upon the tip of my nose. Ah yes, the veil. How difficult it was to choose among them! At length, I selected a glittering wisp of silver netting. I held it up experimentally beneath my eyes. Even without kohl darkening the edges of my eyelids, the veil seemed to magnify my eyes and lend them—and me—an air of mystery. I chuckled softly, and the delicately suspended fringe of tiny pearl droplets, stirred by the gentle huff of my breath, quivered seductively. I could almost hear the ching of the brass *zil* I would slip upon my fingers to accompany my dance.

I spread the garments I had chosen upon the counterpane and surveyed them with mounting pleasure as I undressed. I removed my flower-sprigged flannel robe from a hook upon the door. I began to don it, then allowed the homely garment to slip to the floor and stood naked. Naked, yes, but not proudly so; I trembled despite the warmth of the perfumed air.

The unclothed body is the devil's lure, my father was wont to say. *Katherine! Secure your stockings! Katherine! Button up your bodice!* Better I should suffocate in the stifling heat of a Turkish summer than display one untoward inch of my childish flesh to hot male eyes. I folded my pale arms across the gentle thrust of my small breasts and took a deep shuddering breath. *Old habits die hard.*

*　　　*　　　*

I returned to the bathroom to find the boiler popping and hissing. I turned on the ornate faucets and gasped as I esased myself into the filling tub. Truly, there is nothing like a steaming hot bath to ease the body and lull a restless mind! I added a handful of pink crystals from a cut-glass jar on the wide white marble ledge, and whatever remained of my misgivings soon dissolved in the intoxicating rose-scented cloud that soon enveloped me.

I have no idea how much time had passed when, while dreamily toweling the last droplets from my heated skin, I heard a knock at the outer door. I donned my robe, and as I ran my hands over my flyaway, steam-tendriled hair in a fruitless attempt to subdue it, I heard another knock, louder and more peremptory this time.

A deep voice called in a husky whisper, "Kate? Kate, I saw the light under your door. . . ." Thornton Ramsay's voice.

My eyes darted frantically from the door to the filmy garments beckoning me from the big bed. There was no time . . . what could he want? This wasn't at all what I had planned!

"Kate? A moment, please."

I opened the door. His nostrils flared as the warm, perfumed air flowed out into the dark, chill corridor. I drew my robe close about me, for fear that that penetrating green gaze of his could pierce through its homely fabric to the pink, warm body it sheltered.

"I cannot let you in!" To my dismay, my quavering voice was as high and shrill as a schoolgirl's.

He raised his eyebrows, and as I took hold of my scattered wits. I realized his expression was not that of a man intent on midnight dalliance; rather, it was withdrawn, remote. "It was not at all my intent to do so. I merely wished to inform you that Louise Ramsay's visit to my room was not of an . . . amorous nature." He

151

smiled mirthlessly.

Of what nature was it, then, I wondered, but I dared not, *would* not, ask. He wished to *inform* me, did he? Not quite the same as being told or persuaded or assured. "As you are so fond of telling me, Mr. Ramsay, surely this is no concern of mine."

His expression, which had briefly softened as he surveyed my flushed cheeks and tousled hair, became coldly dismissive. "Quite true, but I would prefer the rest of the household not be made aware of it."

"I am not a common gossip, Mr. Ramsay. Neither Louise Ramsay's nor your comings and goings hold any interest for me, and I expect I will have quite forgotten them by morning. So you see, your secrets, whatever they may be, are quite safe with me."

He gave a bark of harsh laughter. "My dear Miss Mackenzie," he began in a jeering return to formal address, "I have more secrets than you will ever know."

His back, as he turned on his heel and strode down the corridor, was as stiff and unyielding as his manner. Somehow, I sensed he had shut me out even before he'd knocked at my door; my childishly defensive manner had merely made it simpler for him.

I eased back into the room and gently clicked the big door shut. Hawkscliffe held so many secrets, most of which, like Thorn's, I would never ever know. I sighed and began to hang away the garments that lay waiting patiently to fulfill a role in a play prematurely cut short.

Once again I felt trapped between my father's implacable authority and the temptation Thornton Ramsay offered. *Offered?* No, that was not true. He had offered me nothing. What drew me to him I had discovered for myself.

152

I suspended the pearly veil beneath my dark eyes and searched their defiant depths. It was like hearing a mouse roar.

The notion made me laugh, a rueful laugh that ended in a quiet sigh. I hung away the veil, tucked in an errant wisp of scarlet silk, and firmly closed the wardrobe door. I had my secrets, too.

CHAPTER THIRTEEN

The next morning found Hawkscliffe submerged in a fog so dense, so seemingly unyielding, it was as if some malevolent spirit had heaped loose bales of dirty cotton against its windows and doors, piling it up around the tiled surface of the masonry and up and up, ever thicker, until even the tarnished spires were wholly enveloped in murky fluff.

The dull ache clutching at my temples sank its claws deeper in the face of weather which could only serve to imprison Hawkscliffe's inhabitants, aggravating an already uneasy association of personalities. Upon descending to the ground floor, I scurried from window to window seeking a promise of sunlight through the shifting misty veils, but the grayness was absolute. I could find no chink that might admit an errant, cheering ray. The conservatory windows, which only yesterday had framed the most splendid view yet of the landscape Charles Quintus Ramsay had so masterfully rendered in oils, were no more revealing than the others. We might as well have been set adrift on an island in space with no past, no future, only an interminably unresolved present.

"Good morning, Kate."

It was Lance. His eyes were still puffed from sleep, a cowlick had escaped his comb, and his coat, misbuttoned, hung askew. He looked, I thought, more like a boy on the brink of adolescence than a young man at the tail end of it.

"What's good about it, Lance? Once can't see beyond the windowpanes, and the air is so heavy I can hardly breathe."

He looked at me owlishly. "My, we are in a grump, aren't we? Actually, it strikes me as a perfect kind of day to spend in a stupefying activity like counting carpet knots."

He stood aside to allow me to precede him into the dining room, then joined me at the sideboard. The usual Hawkscliffe array of breakfast treats, which heretofore I had regarded as an irresistible luxury, failed to tempt my appetite. If anything, the mingled aromas of scrambled eggs, grilled kidneys, and kippers made me queasy.

"May I serve you some of this crisp bacon?"

I irritably waved away the platter thrust beneath my nose. "Dry toast and tea is all I can tolerate this morning."

"Why not stale bread and water? Then you can feel even sorrier for yourself."

I looked up to meet a teasing smile. "Oh, dear, I do sound a bit of a martyr, don't I?"

Lance nodded. "Sackcloth and ashes. Whereas I am the one truly deserving of pity. I haven't gotten up before noon on a Sunday since . . . since . . ." He stared at me, genuinely astonished. "Since I can't remember when, and all to be at your service."

To be at my service. It was an offer not to be underrated. I smiled at Lance gratefully. Judging by the way the tips of his ears reddened, my smile was considerably warmer than intended.

"Tea with your milk, Kate, or lemon?" The red flush invaded his cheeks as his words tangled on his tongue. "What I meant to say was—"

"Thank you, Lance," I returned solemnly. I was determined not to embarrass him further by betraying my amusement. "No milk, no lemon, no sugar."

"A Spartan woman, is our Miss Mackenzie, Lance. Self-indulgence is not her cup of tea."

My heart thudded against my ribs. I did not have to see Thorn Ramsay to suffer the effects of his dark magic. Just the deep, rough sound of his voice was enough to alarm me in a way I did not understand at all.

"You will not have to put up with my Spartan ways much longer, Mr. Ramsay. No more than twenty-four hours, to be precise."

I had turned to address him and was . . . what, exactly? Confounded? At the very least, unprepared for the look of consternation that briefly supplanted his customary guarded expression.

"You surprise me, Miss Mackenzie. I would have thought you would be curious to see how all this turns out." The sweep of his arms encompassed Lance, the room, the fogbound estate—it even appeared to encompass me.

I raised my eyebrows. "You surprise *me* even more, Mr. Ramsay. Surely 'how all this turns out,' as you put it, is even less a concern of mine than all the other matters you have been at pains to chide me about during my stay here at Hawkscliffe."

He smiled. It was a sad smile, and the yearning look I thought I detected in his green eyes, a liquid, longing look quickly suppressed, fair broke my heart.

We stood in tense silence, unable to look away. Out of the corner of my eye I was aware of Lance's glance flicking from one to the other of us as if he sensed something

157

animating our hostile formality, something mysterious beyond his ken and experience, and which, until that moment, had also been beyond mine. All I knew was that I feared if I spoke, if I so much as moved, I might shatter into a thousand pieces.

Thorn smiled again, this time a remote smile suited to a coolly courteous acceptance of my announced departure. "Perhaps one day I shall have an irresistible urge to furnish my study with a Persian rug."

The devil he would! His words were, I was sure, deliberately chosen to convey to me his impression of my place—if any—in his future life.

I cleared my throat. My moment of fragility had passed; I would allow no surface cracks to appear in my armor. "If so," I began smoothly, "I, or one of my assistants, would be pleased to be of service. Avakian's is well respected in the trade, and will be even more so for having catalogued the Hawkscliffe collection."

"Where there's a will there's a way, eh, Miss Mackenzie?"

Considering our present circumstance, it seemed a tactlessly ambiguous choice of words, but a quick glance at Lance reassured me. He seemed more restive than offended. "Are you sufficiently fortified to proceed with the morning's agenda, Lance?"

The boy drew himself up into a quiveringly erect posture, saluted smartly, then, sensing an oddly unequal pull on his coat, looked down and realigned the buttons and holes. "I am now," he said with a sheepish grin. "Will I see you at dinner, Cousin Thorn?"

"No doubt," was the deep-voiced reply. "Assuming, of course, that you survive the tasks set for you by Miss Mackenzie. I warn you, the woman is a worker!"

"That may be, sir, but I would rather slave by Kate's side than loll in the presence of another, lesser maid."

"Good heavens," I admonished as we hurried up the

stairs followed by Thorn Ramsay's hoot of laughter. "You may catch more than you bargained for with honeyed words like that!"

"I might if I were as jolly as cousin Thorn," was his unexpected reply.

I stopped short and looked at him incredulously. "'Jolly' is hardly the word I would choose to describe Thornton Ramsay."

"What *would* you choose, Kate." He looked at me with a hint of both envy and challenge his his eyes. "Whatever it is should express an appeal to women, don't you think?"

Exciting, mysterious, provocative, virile. . . . The adjectives streamed through my mind unbidden. "Well, whatever I chose would apply to you, too, Lance. *Will* apply," I amended hastily as he grinned at me wolfishly, "given a few years of worldly experience. Be that as it may, you're much nicer than your cousin Thorn—promise me you'll remain so!"

Lance accepted my evasion. "Only if you promise you'll wait for me, Kate," he proclaimed, rolling his eyes ridiculously, "for without you my life would be a barren wasteland, joyless and bereft of hope."

It was impossible to resist his boyish hyperbole. We teased and giggled our way up the next flight, and when we reached the final landing a door opened to reveal a somewhat bloodshot and very annoyed eye.

"Why are you up so early, Lancelot, and what are you doing with that young woman?"

"Did I wake you, Mother? Sorry about that! Kate and I have business together."

"Business? What kind of business?" Louise Ramsay's incredulous tone conjured up a vivid image of a bawdy throng of monkeys. The door opened wider, revealing her uncorseted form wrapped in the satin and lace concoction

I had seen flowing into Thorn's room the previous evening.

"Counting knots, Mother."

"Counting *nuts?* I never heard such nonsense in all my life!"

"Knots," Lance repeated patiently. "Carpet knots. Actually," he added hastily, as storm clouds gathered on his mother's face, "Kate will be counting the knots while I finish sketching the carpet designs."

"Well, do try to be quiet about it." She fixed me with a baleful glare. "I do wish, Miss Mackenzie, that you would kindly consider that my son might have more rewarding things to do with his time than assist you with a task you seem to be having trouble accomplishing on your own. I really don't know what Philo could've been thinking of," she added in a mutter meant to be overheard.

The echo of her meanly expressed opinion threw a damper on the rest of the morning, and although we no doubt accomplished more than we might have had lightheartedness prevailed, we hadn't nearly the fun I had counted on seeing me through the forlorn, fogbound day.

Three hours later I rubbed tired, strained eyes as Lance put the finishing touches on a sketch.

"There you go, Kate. The lot of 'em's done, but for the one you're working on, and a rather sorry lot, too, if you ask me. No flowers, no trees, not even a lion pouncing on an antelope like the one in Mother's bedroom at home."

I wrinkled my nose. Probably a late copy of a popular but bloodthirsty theme I disliked even in its original sixteenth-century Herat version.

"As they say, beauty is in the eye of the beholder, Lance. I grant you I've seen prettier rugs, but these archaic designs are so powerful! It's no wonder they were once so prized."

"Prized, Kate?" Lance looked at me askance. "By whom?"

I stared at him. Prized by whom, indeed! Why, only by Holbein and Lotto, who painted lovingly detailed rugs like these beneath the feet of saints, or hung over stone balconies to cushion the elbows of fair maids waiting for their lovers. Even portraits of the artists' patrons often included tables adorned with carpets like these to symbolize a well-supplied purse. Come to think of it, the modern counterparts of these smug, well-fed burghers furnished their parlors with carpets from Avakian's!

I smiled. "All you see is a dusty old rug, Lance, but to me the history of textile design can be read in these rectangles of knotted wool."

Lance looked alarmed. "I can see I'm in the presence of a specialist with an obsession." He wagged a warning finger as I opened my mouth. "No, no, spare me the details! I have a chum like you, Kate. Collects stamps. Gets all excited about a little square of paper missing the thingummies along one side."

"Thingummies?"

"You know, perforations. And if the color's a bit off he's ecstatic." Lance shrugged and smiled winningly. "I dunno, but to me a rug is to walk on, and a stamp takes a letter through the mails."

Just then the dinner bell could be heard ringing in the distance. We gathered our paraphernalia, hastened to our respective rooms to freshen up for the midday meal, and as I tidied my tousled hair I wondered what function a will, specifically Charles Quintus Ramsay's, performed in Lance's young life. No doubt he was content to follow his mother's lead, untroubled by any complications or disappointments his inheritance might present to the lives of others. As far as Lance was concerned, a rug was for walking on, a stamp for posting letters with, and the

161

purpose of C.Q.'s will was to provide him with an exotic residence suitable for the wearing of smoking jackets and smoking a hubblebubble—until, of course, the amusement of it palled and he put Hawkscliffe up for sale. Self-interest, yes, but purely innocent and unthinking. How very young he was!

I entered the dining room a few paces ahead of Lance and Louise, and it was clear from Lance's hangdog look and sidelong glance at me as we took our seats that his mother was displeased with him, largely, I suspected, because of his association with me.

"Such a dispiriting day," Louise Ramsay commented as she frowningly regarded the fog-shrouded windows. The gray light was not quite dim enough to necessitate the lighting of the oil lamps, and the day was too warm for a cheering fire. "Does the sun never shine at Hawkscliffe?"

"A hasty judgment to make on the basis of not quite two days of residence, Louise," Thorn said dryly. "Might I suggest a distracting postprandial visit to the conservatory, or perhaps the library?"

Louise's strong white fingers fidgeted with the tailored velvet bow at the throat of her watered-silk dress, woven in a handsome but untraditional plaid of pale blues, pinks, and ivories. I had not had time to change out of my workaday green tweed skirt, so perhaps it was the contrast between my homely garb and her elegant costume that accounted for my sudden, resentful awareness of her affinity for fabrics that rustled when she moved. No wonder it was so difficult to escape her presence!

"Really, Thorn! One green thing is very like another. The only thing worth looking at in the conservatory is the view. Did you know that C.Q. did that glorious painting of it in his New York studio? He never would tell anyone where he made the sketches."

Thorn turned to Cora. "That platform on the cliff edge that Harry flies his hawks from, Cora—didn't he build that for C.Q.?"

"Good heavens!" I exclaimed, recalling the rickety structure. "You mean he actually sat out there, suspended above that sheer drop, and calmly *sketched?*"

"But he didn't own the property then," Louise said. "Do you suppose he spirited up the materials to build his little aerie without the owner being any the wiser?" She laughed. "Isn't that just like C.Q.! I would like to see it," she added in a tone of grudging admiration. "What do you suppose he paid for this property? A good deal more than he realized on the Catskill lodge, I have no doubt!" Her eyes narrowed. "Imagine him coveting it all those years and then building this gilded cage for a bird who, I was told, flew off to New York every chance she got!"

"Shopping trips, perhaps?" Philo's bland expression didn't fool me for a minute, but Louise rose to the bait.

"A woman doesn't become known as Turkish Delight because of her talent for shopping!" The look of contemptuous outrage she leveled upon him spilled over to include Thorn. "Perhaps your cousin can enlighten us on that score; tell us, Thorn dear, did you ever sample her sweet wares? You know what they say about forbidden fruits!" she added in a grotesque attempt at playfulness.

"I never make the same mistake twice, Lulu." His voice was level and calm, but the look he loosed upon her was as deadly as a poisoned arrow. "Including the soiling of an unloving family's linen."

She blinked and dropped her eyes to stare at her suddenly clenched fingers. After an interminable moment of silence, she forced a bright smile and finished her response—by now a thumping non sequitur—to Thorn's earlier suggestions about how to pass the time. "As for the

163

library, it holds little charm for me. I daresay I have read all the books in it twice over."

Thorn looked up quizzically from the leg of lamb he was carving. Fresh from skirting one conversational abyss, he apparently decided, despite the unlikelihood of her claim, to refrain from voicing his skepticism. "Lance and Miss Mackenzie appear to have passed the morning profitably. Maybe they can suggest a suitable diversion. Sketching, perhaps?"

Thorn's sardonic tone was not lost upon his aunt, whose mouth thinned; she lifted her lips to display a ferocious gleam of teeth. I was uncomfortably reminded of the hunting carpet Lance had mentioned, and when Mary Rose set before me a gold-rimmed plate supplied with a slice of meat oozing pink juices, I felt a lessening of my appetite.

"*Lance* was sketching; I'm not sure exactly what Miss Mackenzie was up to, but whatever it is seems rather elaborate for a straightforward appraisal and cataloguing service."

I was aware of all eyes fastening expectantly upon me.

"The fee was fixed in advance, Mrs. Ramsay; my appraisal and catalog will be more accurately detailed than my competitors could have supplied, if only by virtue of the carpets having been originally purchased from my uncle, who was famous for the completeness of his records. The rugs on the top floor were particular favorites of his, and Lance was kind enough to indulge my whim for a pictorial record of them."

"Are they so valuable then, Miss Mackenzie?"

"Monetarily? At present, no, although I hope someday the historical importance of their designs will be better appreciated by Western art scholars. The catalog of the general collection, which Philo is planning to publish with artistic assistance from Miss Banks, will appeal to a much wider audience."

A predatory gleam appeared in Louise Ramsay's dark blue eyes.

"I would imagine," she began coolly, "that any profit accruing, or that might accrue, to such entreprises rightly belongs to the owner of the property, isn't that so, Thornton?"

"Yes," he admitted. "Unless, of course, one agrees to assign the rights to such profits to others."

Louise dismissed Thorn's amendment with a scornful laugh.

"Mrs. Ramsay, please!" I cried, belatedly aware that in my haste to divert Louise's attention from me I had inadvertently provided her with another target. Even though it was a classic case of the biter being bit, I could take no pleasure in it.

She raised an imperious hand. "There is no more to be said on the matter, Miss Mackenzie, although I must congratulate you and dear Philo for making as much hay as you could while the sun still shone. I assume your scheme also included having first choice of the Hawks-cliffe carpets when they are offered for sale?"

Her dark eyes, fixed upon mine, were bright with malice, but why? Of what dreadful sin was I guilty? Did she, like Cora, associate me with her successor, Roxelana, by virtue of a shared birthplace?

The Greek-marble perfection of Louise Ramsay's strong features seemed more gray than white in the cold, unflattering light that filtered dimly down from the high arched windows, and for the first time I noticed little pouches clinging beneath her eyes like pale leeches, blighting the high arch of her cheekbones and the illusion of youth a kinder light allowed her to maintain. Of course! *That* was what this was all about! It was about youth—mine—and her increasingly bitter loss of it. It was about a mother and a son on the brink of manhood, and—I looked across at Thorn's frowning face—about a woman and her younger lover. He *had* been her lover, I was sure of it now, but he never would again. I could almost feel sorry for her. Almost . . .

"It would be a shame to disperse the Hawkscliffe collection, but should it ever be sold," I said, refusing to acknowledge openly that the decision might be hers, "I would welcome competitive bidding."

"Would you indeed? Your intimate knowledge of them would of course give you the advantage, wouldn't it? What clever young woman you are! So clever, in fact, it has crossed my mind more than once during the hours you have danced attendance on my son to wonder if you are what you claim to be."

I longed to slap the insinuating smile from her face. "No doubt my father's family was unable to come to terms with the thought of a half-Armenian granddaughter in a clan tartan."

My wry tone was rewarded with a smile from Thorn; it gave me the lift I needed to keep my voice strong and steady. Those cursed, uncaring Mackenzies! I wouldn't be caught dead wearing their colors.

"I suppose they must have been notified of my parents' deaths, but even if they had attempted to claim me they would have been no match for an uncle familiar with the ways of Ottoman officialdom."

My matter-of-factness failed to dilute Louise's supply of vitriol. "An interesting story, my dear, one I suppose that grows more convincing with each telling."

"As well it might," Thorn interjected mildly, "for it also happens to be true."

Now it was Thorn Ramsay's turn to claim our undivided attention. For my part, I was too astonished to speak.

"Lord knows how many pockets Vartan Avakian was required to line with baksheesh to get his niece out of Turkey, but once here her future in this country was assured."

Louise raised a skeptical eyebrow. "Come now, Thorn, what chance would an immigrant rug dealer have had against Scottish aristocrats if they chose to contest his claim?"

Thorn hooted. "Do you really imagine a Tammany Hall judge would hand over the niece and ward of a respected and prosperous citizen? Louise, you can't be that naive!"

"What a gallant champion you are, Thorn. I'm sure Miss Mackenzie will think of an appropriate way to reward you for it."

"For heaven's sake, Mother!"

Lance's mortified appeal was acnowledged only by a spit of "Hush!" by his mother. "Kindly remember I am looking after your interests," she added in a harsh whisper.

A stain of deep red mottled Lance's cheeks as he bent his head in silence over his plate. Although disappointed, I understood: he was still a boy in his mother's eyes, and still a minor, dependent on her, in the eyes of the law.

"I suggest you find someone else to savage, Lulu." Thorn's green eyes glittered dangerously, as hard as emeralds. He loosened his cravat and deliberately exposed his neck to her. "Well? What are you waiting for? Isn't my blood tempting enough for you? Surely I need not supply you with a motive!"

Louise drew in her breath. She stood up and threw down her napkin. "What I need is a change of scene. Even the fog is preferable to the continued company of this sorry crew! Lance? Will you accompany me?"

Lance hesitated, then shook his head. His eyes

remained downcast.

"Very well, then. I can do without a sulky boy." Her eyes distributed scorn impartially upon us as she plucked a fringed cloud of rosebud-pink mohair from the back of her chair. "Tomorrow cannot come too soon for *me*." With a sweeping gesture she flung the luxurious shawl around her shoulders and swished in silken grandeur from the room.

Conversation during the remainder of the meal was confined to subdued monosyllables. By the time dessert was served, Agnes's flaky lemon custard tarts could have been made of sand and paste for all the pleasure they gave us.

Lance was the first to excuse himself, and when I asked if he would be joining me later to do the final sketch, he shook his head regretfully.

"I think not, Kate. I'm sorry, truly I am, but Mother seems so dead set against it, and . . ." He shrugged, and I allowed him to escape putting his humiliation into any further words.

"No need to fret, Lance. I can do the last rug myself, if only to justify the art lessons my uncle paid for."

Lance gave me a wan, grateful smile before trudging from the room. The rest of the company soon followed suit.

I sighed. I knew my sketch, even though perhaps more accurate, would lack Lance's verve and style.

"Not much backbone, has he?" a voice breathed behind me. It was Cora.

"He's only eighteen, Miss Banks, and a rather sheltered eighteen at that, it appears. I'm sure he'll learn to assert himself when the time comes."

"I knew more of the ways of the world at his age than

most do at mine," was her bitter comment. "I'm not sure I can spare him the time to learn."

As I nodded and turned away toward the stairs, she plucked at my sleeve. "I have completed only two watercolors. I did the best carpets first, as you suggested, but they are not as I hoped." She held up her arthritic hands and regarded them with sad disbelief. "They took such a time to do," she murmured, then added distractedly, as if to herself, "she can't be allowed to rob us of work already accomplished, can she?"

The little woman drifted away before I could answer, and the appearance of Thorn Ramsay drove all else from my mind.

"You had me investigated," I accused in a furious whisper. "How dare you!"

"What an odd way to thank me for verifying your story. I'll think twice before volunteering as your knight errant in the future; I'm not sure I care for your habit of placing burrs under my saddle."

"How *dare* you," I repeated.

"I had no choice," he repeated flatly. "As I have already told you, I have been beset by claimants to the estate; most were preposterous, but a few, the clever ones, could not be dismissed entirely out of hand, and you could easily have been one of those. Your intelligence has never been in question."

"But I never made any claims!"

"Which is precisely why, in view of your unorthodox arrival here, my suspicions were aroused. Suspicions, I might add, that were lulled when I went to New York last week. I assigned the investigation of your adoption papers to one of my clerks, who reported they were quite in order, and I visited your shop myself. Quite an impressive establishment . . . your employees speak well of you, Miss Avakian."

I flared at the rebuke I sensed. "I find it easier to use my uncle's name professionally. It spares me the tedious explanations required of me on more than one occasion here."

He sighed. "I do wish you would not be so quick to infer criticism where none was intended, Kate. Your decision to use your uncle's name, considering the well-established nature of his business, was the only sensible course under the circumstances."

"Do enlighten me, Mr. Ramsay: to what circumstances do you refer?"

He grinned disarmingly despite my arch tone. "Merely that I imagine the carpet trade is as traditional as its customers are conservative, and unready for a radical locution like Avakian and Daughter, much less Avakian and Mackenzie. Neither has quite the right authentic ring to it, eh?"

I ducked my head to hide my smile, then decided it would be churlish not to at least admit the correctness of his reasoning. "My thinking exactly."

"Well! This must be my red-letter day! I had all but given up our agreeing on anything."

"Except, I trust, that my reason for being at Hawkscliffe is the same as I told you the day I arrived: to appraise and catalog the Hawkscliffe carpet collection—no more, no less."

Thorn Ramsay's eyes darkened as he drew his black brows together in frowning consideration. "Let us say I have no reason at the moment to doubt it."

Hardly a ringing declaration of faith. Caught by his compelling scrutiny, I wondered how I could find so attractive a man who doubted my integrity. Perhaps it was the novelty of it. There was nothing very exciting about being thought a sweet young miss, whereas an adventuress . . .

170

I turned away from him abruptly, wordlessly, and mounted the stairs, determined this time to pass unseeingly by the portrait on the landing. But at the last moment, just before I slid safely by, something tugged my eyes to the right and there she was, her full lips curved in that perpetual knowing smile. Again I could almost hear her husky laughter echoing mockingly along the corridors and issuing seductively from behind closed doors. I recalled my conversation about Roxelana held here on the stair landing with Louise. We had been discussing her age and mine, and I was suddenly struck anew by the realization I was almost the age Roxelana had been when Charles Quintus painted her. Yet as I stared into those varnished eyes, which hinted of depths of experience I could not even imagine, I knew that if I lived to be one hundred, I would never be as old as C.Q. Ramsay's last mistress was in the full bloom of her youth.

CHAPTER FOURTEEN

I closed the door behind me when I entered the top floor storeroom so I could finish my work among the rugs undisturbed. I completed the last sketch in short order, and although it lacked the dash of Lance's gifted hand, it was workmanlike and accurate, which sufficed for the purpose. Slowed by my yawns, the recording of the knot count took longer. Before long the temptation to rest my eyes for just a moment became too much to resist.

I awoke with a crick in my neck, the coarse weave of a bird-patterned Ushak pebbling my cheek and a dull ache in my head. I retrieved the journal that had slipped from my hand and shook my skirt into some sort of order before slipping out into the hall. The house was very still. The doors to Lance's and Louise's rooms were closed, as they had been when I came up, but I could not tell if the rooms were occupied. As I felt too dull either for repartee with Lance or for sparring with Louise, I made my way downstairs as quietly as I could.

Pausing briefly to deposit my notes and sketches in my

room, I was heartened to see through the window a brightening heralding an end to the imprisoning mist. I snatched up a wrap and hurried downstairs in the hopes that a walk through the grounds might refresh me.

As I approached the massively arched front door beyond whose porte cochère stretched a formal *allée* I had not yet explored, the great clock in the court hall struck three. As the deep bonging notes reverberated through the long corridor, the vibrating echoes set in play among the crystal prisms dangling from the chandeliers fell upon my ears like distant mocking laughter.

I whirled. My hands flew up to ward off the sense of a haunting presence, insubstantial yet chilling, that once again proved to have no reality except in my overwrought imagination. I exhaled slowly, and as I looked about me, my senses sharply attuned for any irregularity, all I heard was the loud, montonous, strangely reassuring ticking of the clock.

The ragged shreds of fog that still clung to Hawks-cliffe's walls and spires like the drowning hands of ghosts emphasized rather than softened the .sad neglect I had noted upon my arrival.

I turned my back on the looming mansion and walked down the avenue lined with pin oaks, whose downswept lower branches extended as gracefully as the legs of a Degas ballerina. Lost in thought, I strolled slowly between the curtsying limbs until the sound of approaching voices attracted my attention.

Pausing near a sheltering oak, I spied Cora and Harry Braunfels advancing toward me uphill from the right, deep in conversation. Cora, burdened with a spade and a basket, was wearing stout boots and a coarse enveloping garment of uncertain design, somewhere between an apron and a coat, which made her look more like a dusty-feathered crow than a neat little sparrow. Armed with a pruning hook, she pointed away from me toward a clump of shrubbery in the mid-distance, talking all the while, gradually widening the scope of her gesture in my direction. As she did so, one of the pair of leashed dogs held by Harry raised its head alertly, but before it could become sure enough of my hidden presence to utter a warning growl, I had scurried from trunk to trunk to a rustic gazebo perched atop a knoll marking the end of the avenue.

As I entered the rough structure, no doubt a pleasant enough retreat on a hot summer day, but gloomy now in mid-November, I started at the sight of a lone hunched figure seated on a low built-in bench that encompassed the cobwebbed interior.

"Philo!" I exclaimed as my eyes adjusted to the duskiness of the light in which his fair hair seemed more silver than blond. "I'm sorry to intrude; I had no idea that you—that anyone was here. I came out for a solitary stroll, but Cora and Harry were in the offing, and I had no wish—" I broke off. Although I knew Philo had no great liking for Harry, I sensed a tie between him and Cora that made me sure that if Philo inherited Hawkscliffe, she would remain as housekeeper.

"I understand, Kate. These last two days . . ." He shook his head. "I expect you too have found that considering the poisonous atmosphere pervading Hawkscliffe just now, one's own company is preferable to anyone else's."

I turned to leave. Cora and Harry would have passed by now. "I'm sorry if—"

Philo's long hands reached up in an imploring gesture. "Please! Don't go! I've also found that one's own thoughts lead to nothing but despair. Oh Kate," he blurted burying his head in his hands, "I fear I'm a sorry excuse for a man."

I hastened to his side. "Hush, Philo! There is no call to

175

berate yourself." I sat down beside him and patted his shoulder. "Your aunt has put you in an impossible position."

Philo turned a tearstained face to me. "If I were the only one her threats affected, I could manage—I always have. I am not a greedy man. My needs are of an aesthetic, not material nature, and I am well satisfied by my work. Even Thorn grants me that much. But my dear friend . . . the one I told you about, Kate? The one for whom I wished to order a carpetbag like yours? My friend has tuberculosis, and I thought . . . I hoped if I could bring my . . . friend here to live, up here where the air blows clean and fresh, with Cora to help care for . . . for . . ." He paused, groping awkwardly for a way to avoid the pronoun that might reveal his secret to me, the secret with which Louise Ramsay had threatened to destroy his professional life.

"For *him*," I completed gently.

Philo stared at me, aghast. "You mean you *know*?"

"That your friend is a man? I guessed as much, Philo. Your aunt's insinuations; a word here and there." I shrugged. "It is important only in that it is causing you such distress."

Philo sprang to his feet and began to pace. "I don't understand, Kate. You know this about me, yet you seem to calm . . . so accepting. How can that be? I am a pariah, an unclean thing, to anyone who knows of my . . . depravity." He spat out the word bitterly. "Why aren't you like that?"

I raised my eyebrows at the unexpected note of accusation in his question. "Good heavens, Philo, would you rather I were? You forget I grew up in a world where affection displayed between men is commonplace, and since most of the liaisons are succeeded in due course by marriage and a family they arouse neither censure nor scorn, much less a basis for life-destroying scandal."

176

"Whereas in our so-called civilized society I am compelled to live a life of deceit," Philo exclaimed, "and that, I daresay, is why Louise is here. She's laying claim to the estate not just for the sake of her son, but also to right what she considers to be a wrong done to her. A very old wrong."

I could make neither head nor tail of what he was saying. "Philo, I—"

"The how and why of it are no longer important," Philo continued, ignoring my interruption. "What's done is done. But she shouldn't be allowed to keep us paying for it for the rest of our lives."

The last was said in a fierce whisper, more to himself than to me, yet the words reverberated oddly in my mind. Was it an echo of something said, or merely a reflection of the hostility Louise had provoked in all of us?

Philo continued pacing, head bowed, then stopped abruptly and faced me. "Under the circumstances, it was very generous of you to protest Louise's plan to usurp the Hawkscliffe rug catalog."

"Please, Philo, let it be." It was a subject I was still not comfortable discussing with him. "If the truth be known, I'm not quite sure why I did. Perhaps it's just because Louise is so much easier to dislike than you."

I could tell by Philo's purposeful expression that my attempt at lightness had failed to deflect him.

"No, I must tell you. I couldn't before, but now that you know about Ralph—" He hesitated, then resumed his pacing. "You see, I didn't want the rug catalog just for myself. Even if my plans for Hawkscliffe worked out, we would still need every penny I could lay my hands on. The medical expenses alone . . ." He shook his head. "Ralph has little money of his own, and Cora even less."

"Cora?" I was bewildered. "What has Cora to do with him?"

177

"Why, Ralph is Cora's nephew, Kate. Surely you know about him?" He looked at me with a startled expression, then passed a shaky hand over his head. "Of course you don't," he muttered, answering his own question. "No reason you should, it's just that..." He broke off, hunched his shoulders and threw his arms wide in a gesture of amazement. "It's just that so much has happened during your brief stay here, I feel as if I've known you for years!"

Cora's nephew! The boy in the photograph in her bedroom.

"She doesn't know the nature of our relationship, Kate. She wouldn't understand. Please, you won't..." As Philo again reached his hands out to me imploringly, I suddenly realized how much power he had placed in mine. I had neither sought his confidence nor wanted it, yet once given, I felt obligated to safeguard it.

"Tell her? Of course not! Cora and I are not exactly friends, you know. I can't imagine any circumstance in which I would share such knowledge with her—or with anyone else, for that matter," I added deliberately. I grasped his hands in mine reassuringly, and when he winced I looked down to see that his carefully kept nails were broken, his knuckles and palms scraped and raw. "Philo, your poor hands—"

"It's nothing!" He pulled them away from me. He hesitated, then blurted, "I came upon Harry earlier, in the fog ... in my foolish haste to escape his notice I stumbled and fell."

I could tell that being thought fearful and clumsy was repugnant to him. "Tell me about Ralph," I urged gently.

Philo crossed to one of the rough-arched openings and rested his cheek against the shredding bark of the timbering.

"He wasn't much older than Lance when I met him," he

began quietly. "Convinced of his artistic promise, Cora brought him to me, hoping I might become his mentor—C.Q. was far too self-centered to waste his time encouraging the young. At first I too was excited by his talent, but although Ralph is an excellent and painstaking draftsman, and blessed with an unusually discerning eye, I gradually became aware he was entirely lacking in originality." Philo paused then, turning toward me, he added dryly, "Lord knows I tried to persuade myself otherwise."

Philo began again to pace, his steps quickening and his forlorn air slipping away as he shared his private life with me, an unlikely confidante perhaps, but a needed one.

"He was such an appealing boy, Kate. Quiet, serious, and with absolute faith in my judgment. I hemmed and hawed for as long as I could, and then it came to me! Maybe he could never be a creative artist of the first or even second rank, but his particular talents were ideally suited to restoration work.

"I took him with me to Europe to see at first hand the masterpieces he had seen only in engravings and in shoddy reproductions, and to visit the ateliers of the masters of the restoration arts in Germany and Italy." His face softened, and he seemed in the dimness almost as young as I. "Especially Italy."

I guessed that the Italian golden light and *la dolce vita* had nudged their budding relationship into full flower.

"He stayed on in Europe for several years—it seemed a lifetime to me—to serve his apprenticeship. When he returned, word of his extraordinary skill spread like wildfire through museum and collector circles. He could soon pick and choose among the many commissions offered him. Cora was . . . is very grateful," he said simply, his mouth twisting wryly. "Ralph is now too ill to work, much less for any physical . . ." He paused, then looked

179

directly into my eyes. "She must never know."

Cora must not know. The Philadelphia Museum's board of directors must not know, and especially the straitlaced Elizabeth Van Renssalaer, newly elected to the board of the Metropolitan, must not know. Louise Ramsay had a great deal to answer for.

"So you see, Kate, I may apply for a position at Avakian's after all."

Good Lord, I thought, whatever would I do with him if he did? But this was no time for sober realities. "I think we'd make a capital team, Philo: Mackenzie and Ramsay, purveyors of rugs as fine art."

He smiled at that. I stepped to the archway overlooking the path where I had seen Cora and Harry. Harry was well away, walking back toward his quarters, the two leashed dogs trotting at his heels; Cora was nowhere in sight. I turned back to take my leave of Philo, but his smile had been succeeded by an expression so bleak I decided it would be kinder to depart in silence than to force him to summon a courteous response from the depths of his despair.

A few yards beyond the gazebo I came upon a copse of yew whose branchy reach, untamed by knife and shears, had long outgrown the original ornamental intent of the planting. Rather than retrace my steps, I forced my way through the scraggly clawed tips and emerged, mussed and breathless, face-to-face with Thornton Ramsay. It was hard to say who of us was the most startled: Thorn, I, or the shaggy Akbar by his side whose deep woof of alarm was succeeded shortly by a wag of tail and a softening of the alertness in her deep-set brown eyes.

"It might have been easier if you had stayed with the path, Kate," he said, as he plucked needles of yew from my hair.

"True, but if I had I would have encountered Harry coming up from the kennels. This appears to be a day for walking the dogs," I said as I ruffled Zulu's ears. Her well-muscled posterior vibrated with the quickened tempo of her wagging tail.

"And you appear to have made a friend. I daresay you are the sort of person dogs instinctively trust."

I laughed. "I'm glad Zulu accepts me without question. She may be the only resident of Hawkscliffe who does."

"Come now, Kate, surely you don't include young Lance in your harsh indictment! I'd say he was hopelessly smitten."

"Oh, but I do. Mrs. Ramsay considers me an unsuitable companion, and Lance is a dutiful son." Resentment welled up in me as I recalled the boy's awkward dissassociation from me after dinner. "Considering the uncertainty concerning Lance's paternity, Louise Ramsay is a remarkably bold and determined woman."

"Ah, but haven't you sensed that she wants control of the estate as much for herself as for her son? Why, it's the ultimate revenge! Think of it, Kate—C.Q.'s last mistress may have been able to enslave the old philanderer as Louise was never able to, but here she is, the wife he treated so shabbily, busily positioning herself to enjoy the fruits of her successor's labors. How she relishes the prospect, and how she enjoys rubbing everyone else's nose in it!"

In view of Louise's vanity and pride, both Philo's and Thorn's readings of the matter made more sense than one based solely on the protectiveness of a doting mother. Her self-interest may have been cloaked by her display of maternal concern, but it was the grit of her greed for revenge that had honed those formidable claws of hers to murderous sharpness. Yet I had a strong suspicion I was hearing only part of the story.

I cocked my head to one side. "And you, Mr. Ramsay—are you, like me, merely a disinterested bystander?"

He looked at me warily. A muscle twitched in the long hollow of his cheek. "I'm not sure that is a question I should answer," he murmured finally.

We stared at each other. I recognized the troubled doubts in my own heart, but what was in his? What had been the purpose of Louise's late night visit to his room, if not for the lovemaking he had denied? If he was in fact Lance's father, what use was Louise planning to make of that? His face was as unreadable as his heart. I shook my head at the hopelessness of it all, uttered a few trite parting words, and moved on.

"Don't wander too far afield," he called after me. "It is easier to lose one's way in this murk than one might imagine."

I had already decided to stick to the known path, but I nodded my acknowledgment. I walked slowly up the slope where I had suffered humiliation at Harry Braunfels' hands earlier in the week—it was a route I was unlikely to forget—and as I did so I became aware of a change in the air, a freshening stir and a cooling of the temperature that made me draw my wrap more snugly around me.

Within the next few minutes the fog's cloak had thinned to tatters, and by the time I topped the rise a breeze bounding out of the western hills had sent its gray coattails scurrying for cover in the approaching dusk, revealing the late afternoon sun in all its golden glory. I hastened toward Harry's hawking platform for one more look at the glorious view Charles Quintus had sketched there and masterfully fixed in paint to remind future generations of the wild fastness we had been privileged to know here.

My footsteps slowed, then faltered as I neared the edge. I stopped—thank God I stopped!—long enough to catch my breath and summon the courage to step out upon that aerial wedge of clumsily cobbled planks only to find that my worst fears had become a hideous reality.

Minutes earlier the fog would have masked this danger dangling above the abyss, this sinking ship upon a sea of air. The crude platform sagged at an alarming angle, and its splintered railing swayed gently in the wind that now swirled along the cliff top.

I stood frozen upon the precipice until a sudden gust, which threatened to wrench the platform from the few spikes that remained to moor it, caused me to sink upon my heels in sudden panic. As the broken rail twisted and creaked above me in the wind's embrace, I became aware of a flutter of color clinging to its raw, jagged edge. It was just a little snippet, hardly bigger than a pen wiper, but it had an iridescent sheen that dizzied me with foreboding.

Slowly I inched forward through the roughly grassed coarse gravel. As I again reached the barren edge I fearfully eased my head over the brink. Below me on a small rocky promontory, much too far to reach but close enough to see all too well, a tangle of scrubby oaks clutched a crumpled mass of plaid watered silk. The bone-hard spiky branch ends jagging up every which way through the shimmering stuff called to mind the paintings that depicted in loving, ghastly detail the martyred Saint Sebastian, pierced similarly by arrows.

I looked down numbly for a long moment, then closed my eyes to shut out the pretty effect of sunlight glistening on the folds of fabric fingered by the gusting breeze. But it was no use . . . in my mind's eye I still saw Louise Ramsay sweeping imperiously out of the dining room, the fringes of her soft shawl bobbing above her bustle to the staccato tempo of her angry heels, her pastel plaid skirt billowing behind her.

I heard a thin, piercing call above me. A sudden swoop

of shadow blotted out the play of sun on silk. Shot through with shock and terror, I gasped as a large hawk descended upon the scraggle of oaks and began to inspect fastidiously with outstretched neck and probing beak Louise's oddly askew red shawl. I watched in horror as the bird transferred its perch to the crimson wool. All I could think of was how cold she would be if it carried her shawl away in its talons.

A surge of hot anger gave me the courage to rise. Distracted by my screams and waving arms, the huge bird soared effortlessly away, lifted by the winds rushing up the cliff face into the limitless blue of the darkening sky.

Help. We needed help, Louise and I.

As I ran headlong down the slope in search of Thorn, I recalled with sudden, dreadful clarity that the luxurious cloud of mohair Louise had flung around her shoulders had been pink, not red. A pink as pale as pearls.

I intercepted Thorn on the path to the kennels. Harry had already returned to his quarters there, and as soon as I had blurted out my sorry news, Thorn ran ahead to alert him. By the time I arrived to assist in the rescue preparations, Thorn had already coiled a length of rope around his shoulders, while a scowling Harry, forced to abandon his tumbler of whiskey, backed a stout, sleepy pony between the shafts of a small wicker go-cart.

"No need for all this rush," the groundsman grumbled. "The hawk the girlie described would be a red-tail, indulging its curiosity. Carrion's no treat to that breed of bird. Now if missy here had seen crows feeding—"

"For God's sake, Harry!" Thorn exploded, cutting short the groundsman's chillingly brutal observations. "Wait for us here, Kate," Thorn commanded. "There is no need to alert the others yet."

"I'm coming with you! We don't know yet if she is—she may need my help," I concluded falteringly, trying to deny the awful truth of the red—*so much red!*—cloaking the plaid silk. I drew in a shuddering breath, then met Thorn's stern, inquiring gaze directly. What he saw must have reassured him.

"Come along, then." He swung me up into the back of the little cart along with an armload of hastily gathered horse blankets, and we jounced wordlessly up to the top of the cliff.

Thorn securely knotted one end of his rope around the axle of the pony cart, and while Harry held the stolid pony, he let himself down over the precipice in a smooth, practiced motion. I peered down to see him land lightly on the protruding island of rock among the sparse, stunted oaks. As he gently freed Louise from their stubby clutch, her head lolled at an angle that left little doubt that her most precious possession, her life, was lost beyond recall.

I lifted my eyes beyond the somber tableau to the glittering river and the hills rolling away serenely to the west, set aglow by the slanting copper light of the setting sun. A majestic scene, upon which Louise's cruel passing had left no mark.

The pony snorted and tossed his shaggy head as the weight on the rope, doubled now, telegraphed its pull to the shafts secured to his harness. I looked away as Thorn cradled Louise's body with blankets in the little cart meant for picnics and carefree jaunts. It seemed a frivolous choice for a hearse.

As we walked, Thorn and I, behind the cart toward the house, a sudden gust caught the horse blanket thrown loosely over her, tugging her silk skirt back above legs plumper and ankles thicker than I was sure she would have cared to have so baldly revealed. I called to Harry to halt.

Gently I tucked in the errant folds of coarse wool, whose pungent odor vied with the rusty smell of blood. Harry looked back at me over his thick, hunched shoulders.

"She's past caring for that, missy," he said, baring his yellowed teeth in a wet gummy smile. "Took Mr. Death to bring her ladyship down off her high horse, didn't it?"

He laughed then, and the jeering, unfeeling sound of it made me turn to Thorn for reassurance.

"Was it so foolish of me? She was so proud . . . so very proud."

He lifted his bowed head to look at me gravely. "Not foolish at all." He slid a comforting arm around my shoulders and drew me close. You are as good as you are brave and bonny, Kate Mackenzie."

We trudged on in the gathering dusk, made companions by tragedy. The warmth of his encircling arm reminded me of my first glimpse of Hawkscliffe as I stood side by side with Uncle Vartan on the deck of the Mary Powell, straining to follow the path of his pointing finger. As we approached the many-spired mansion now, with dread in our hearts, I realized sadly this might well be my last sight of it.

CHAPTER FIFTEEN

I could not stay at Hawkscliffe, of course. Once I had recovered from the numbing shock of discovering Louise's broken body, I realized I had no more place in that distressed household than at the hearing, delayed now by events, that would determine who would inherit C.Q. Ramsay's estate. I had informed Thorn Ramsay I would be leaving in twenty-four hours, and, albeit in tragically altered circumstances, I did just that.

That I was able to escape so soon was due largely to Mary Rose and Agnes. Summoned from the kitchen by Thorn, they wordlessly viewed Louise's gray waxen pallor, compared it with my trembling exhaustion, and decided, with but a single knowing glance between them, that their duty lay first with life. Accordingly, despite Lance's grief-stricken pleas, they bundled me off to bed before attending to his mother's bloodied corpse.

Those stalwart women! Coarse in speech and dress, they lacked all the finer social graces, but it was their stubby, reddened fingers, unsuited for crooking elegantly over teacups, that gently sponged the chill from my body, their stout arms that supported me when representatives of the local constabulary, alerted by Harry, demanded I join the others in the parlor.

The method of interrogation employed by these simple country policemen, unnerved by a violent death among the gentry as well as unequipped by training for its proper investigation, consisted largely of bluster. If the occasion had not been so melancholy, their strutting and posturing might have seemed comical.

At length, intimidated by Thorn's gruff insistence that I had suffered enough for one day, the sergeant in charge reluctantly agreed to consider accepting my written statement in lieu of my appearance at an admittedly pro forma inquest to be held the next week. "But no promises, mind you!" he called after me as I mounted the stairs to return to my bedroom to prepare it.

"Miss Mackenzie has better things to do than cool her heels in this gloomy house so's to answer again the questions you've already put to her, Joe Bollocks!"

Agnes's tone of familiarity and belligerent posture, with fists planted firmly on ample hips, noticeably flustered the pompous little man when he tramped upstairs an hour later to pass judgment on my statement. She was quick to press her advantage. "Why, she has a business to attend to in New York City!"

Mary Rose, lent courage by Agnes's scornful treatment of this minion of the law whose character flaws, she later told me, were a fruitful source for town gossip, chimed in. "An *important* business, Sergeant! Miss Mackenzie has her own shop, she does, filled top to bottom with priceless carpets from the Orient. Isn't that right, miss?"

Fearing this immoderate claim might have an effect opposite from that intended, I smiled wanly and assured the harried officer of my sincere desire to do whatever the law required of me.

"Well then, miss," he began in an expansive tone, obviously placated by my submissive manner, "since you are all agreed it was death by misadventure, there's no reason you shouldn't be allowed to attend to your business. You *do* agree, miss?"

Alerted by a sudden sharpening of his tone, I looked up from the paper on which I was completing my statement as rapidly as legibility would allow, and nodded.

"And you maintain you did not know the deceased's state of mind at the time?"

I hesitated fractionally before answering. I knew Louise Ramsay was greedy and overbearing and unkind; I knew she was angry—very angry—the last time I saw her alive, but how could I possibly claim, based on our brief if unpleasant acquaintance, to have known her state of mind?

"I hardly knew the woman, Sergeant Bollocks," I stated firmly.

Hours later, as the train to New York City clickety-clacked its way south alongside the broad silver ribbon of river, I pondered Sergeant Bollocks's final question. I may not have known Louise's state of mind, but I knew she was a fighter.

I closed my eyes and leaned my head against a window frame greasy with coal dust.

You all agreed it was death by misadventure, Sergeant Bollocks had said. He had talked of accident, hinted at suicide, yet the possibility of murder was never so much as mentioned.

I recalled Philo's raw knuckles and abraded palms, kept carefully concealed and unremarked within his pockets throughout the interrogation. He had suffered the injuries, he had told me, in an attempt to escape Harry's attention—but couldn't they as well have resulted from an unexpected encounter with the woman who threatened all he held dear?

I remembered Zulu's snarling lunge through the shrubbery the day I arrived, and my unthinking scramble up the wall to escape her—could Thorn have anticipated a similar reaction from Louise? Could he have seen her making her way along the unfamiliar path, nearing the precipice . . . *the confounded woman! Such a trial to all of us!* That huge gray shaggy beast, bounding out of the mist, would have seemed a veritable hound from hell!

Might Harry have crossed Louise's path on the cliff top and, having misinterpreted her chatty friendliness on arrival as readiness to accept his advances, grown angry when she refused? Had he slyly edged her out onto the platform and then, failing to frighten her into submission, sent her plummeting to her death in a fit of frustrated rage?

Then there was Cora. It was Cora who had suggested Louise might have been searching for C.Q.'s sketch site for the monumental painting she so admired. If Louise had been less fearless, Cora had told the police, she would never have stepped out upon the platform, certainly not without inspecting it. "But Mrs. Ramsay," she added, "was nothing if not fearless."

Her admiring tone had made it sound like a compliment, but out of the corner of my eye I saw a feral smile quiver fleetingly on Cora's thin lips.

I shuddered then, remembering the gardening tools I had seen Cora carrying and the wiry strength she could have employed to undermine the platform's frail hold upon the edge of the cliff, grim purpose dulling the pain in her arthritic fingers.

Nobody inquired about any possible motives for Louise having been assisted in her headlong plunge from the platform, and nobody volunteered any. They were all kept hidden, secret, protected from the outside world. . . .

In short, we closed ranks after Louise's death much as we had immediately before her arrival at Hawkscliffe. Misadventure? Perhaps . . . but how, in all that murk, had a woman unfamiliar with Hawkscliffe found the particular site she was seeking? And why would she then, fearless or not, step out upon a precariously perched platform to view a scene shrouded in fog, a scene which had not been revealed in all its vast golden glory until *after* she had fallen?

It made no sense; it made no sense at all.

What made even less sense was my profound feeling of loss. It had nothing to do with Louise, of course, or with Hawkscliffe's grand spired folly of a house—not even the wonderful rugs contained there. No, what shone in my memory and haunted my heart was the fire in Thorn Ramsay's green eyes and the proud spirit animating his careless grace. I ached to feel again the comforting warmth of his encircling arm, to experiene the exciting pressure of his demanding mouth on mine. I would have welcomed even his baseless suspicions and the contemptuous withdrawal which had seared me on more than one occasion.

Our parting had been brief, practical, cool: *Did I feel strong enough to leave? At what time would I need a conveyance to take me to the train?* I was thanked for my forebearance; I was told I would be informed when I could return to complete the rug catalog. Nothing was said one way or the other about my notes and Lance's sketches, so I had packed them along with my belongings, trying not to feel guilty about my sense of triumph.

I kissed Mary Rose and Agnes goodbye; Lance kissed me. Philo took both my hands in his and wished me a quietly fervent *au revoir,* but Cora had more pressing things to do than bid farewell to a houseguest who had been unexpected and unwelcome in the first place. Thorn, after offering me a hand into the carriage, gave me a brooding look from under dark brows and nodded curtly. No words were exchanged between us; for my part, I could think of nothing appropriate to say.

I looked back once as Harry clucked up the horse, but Thorn had already turned dismissively away, his head bent toward Lance as he attended to something the boy was saying. As they disappeared together into the house, I realized with dull anguish that I was once again an outsider, no more than a watchful onlooker of events that, as Thornton Ramsay had so often reminded me, were no concern of mine.

Damn Louise Ramsay! To think it took her death to accomplish what all her carefully calculated disparagements of me had not! I continued to brood upon this irony, a bitter envoi indeed, until we arrived, in a great chuff of steam, at Grand Central Depot.

Mariam, my housekeeper and faithful companion, held me away at arm's length after our initial hug of greeting.

"Miss Kate! You look as if you came home on a coal barge!"

I turned to the tall, oak-framed hall mirror as Mariam relieved me of my wrap and bags. A broad smear of greasy soot, transferred from the train's window frame to my cheek, had smudged across to the tip of my nose and down to my jawline. No wonder the cabdriver hailed by my porter had looked at me askance.

When I returned downstairs after a wash-up and a welcome change of clothes. Mariam apologized for the meagerness of the larder.

"If only I had known you were coming," she explained as she set before me a bowl of hot, thick bean soup and a basket of crusty bread. "I only have a bit of lamb and some carrots—"

192

"Anything you prepare for supper will be delicious, Mariam," I said, cutting short her menu recital. "I'm sorry I didn't send word I was coming, but . . ." I paused, wondering how much need be said. "There was a sudden death in the Ramsay family."

Mariam's momentary look of sorrow, dictated by convention, even for someone known only by name, was followed by a contrite gasp. "Sweet Lady Mary, I almost forgot. Krikor has been after me and *after* me about when you were expected home. Something about a Mr. Marquand and a carpet?"

Krikor Jorian, who had succeeded his uncle as assistant manager of Avakian's as I had succeeded mine as owner and manager, was not given to unnecessary agitation. If Mr. Lawrence Aloysius Marquand was the cause of it, I thought as I hastily tied on a bonnet, I had better learn why without delay.

"If you have no time to rest after your journey, at least take the time to put on your bonnet properly," Mariam reprimanded me as she tugged the silk and feathered confection into place on my upswept hair.

"Haven't got it," I replied breathlessly as I dashed out the door, down the brownstone steps that fronted on busy Madison Avenue, and around the corner of Twenty-Seventh Street to an even busier Fifth Avenue.

The rich, familiar odor of carpets old and new, a homely mingling of wool, wood smoke, and camel dung, greeted me as I entered the shop that had become my second home. A jangle of brass bells suspended on the back of the door heralded my arrival, and I was soon engulfed by an excited babble of Armenian in the Stamboul dialect that had been my first language, much to my learned father's despair.

"Miss Kate!" cried a tall, dark young man with a luxuriant black moustache. "At last you have come!"

"What is this about Mr. Marquand? What carpet could be causing him—and you—such distress?"

"No carpet that he has purchased from Avakian's, I assure you, Miss Kate. No, it is the palace carpet he wishes to buy for his ballroom."

His *ballroom*? Surely Krikor had misunderstood. "No one could want a carpet for a ballroom—"

"Excuse me, Miss Kate, but Mr. Marquand wants one. "You see," he continued, "the youngest Miss Marquand—"

"Daisy? The one with the squint?"

"And the squeaky voice. She is going to be married. She wanted a spring wedding, but Mr. Marquand, I think, does not wish for that much time to pass."

"Sensible man," I commented approvingly. "Squints and squeaks have but a fleeting charm."

"Just so," Krikor agreed. "That being the case, he plans to bring springtime to Fifth Avenue in December, and he wishes to have a garden carpet underfoot for the reception. Then, before the dancing begins, the carpet will be rolled up and concealed behind a row of potted flowering trees."

"I see. It will have to be a newish rug, of course; the old ones are too narrow. Let's see, now, I remember seeing just the thing about two years ago—a palace-sized carpet. We won't sell Mr. Marquand the carpet, Krikor; we'll *lend* it to him. Here's what we're going to do. . . ."

Lawrence Marquand was delighted when I told him that not only was it unnecessary for him to buy the carpet he wanted; I would not even charge him a fee for the service of providing it.

"Consider it a wedding present," I said, happily anticipating the order for the rugs needed to furnish the house being built for the young couple. "Just think! A spring wedding in December! It is much too lovely a concept to involve an exchange of money."

Mr. Marquand was not fooled for a minute by my expansive gesture, but he appreciated my style. A man does not become enormously wealthy by disdaining the saving

194

of small expenses, and I would not prosper if I begrudged providing an opportunity for these minor but satisfying exercises in thrift.

As day succeeded day with still no summons to return to complete my work, the exotic mansion and the strange events that had occurred there took on a fabled quality, like my long-ago glimpse of Hawkscliffe's spires from the deck of the *Mary Powell*.

The only reality left to me, the lodestar of my otherwise busy life of commerce, was the vivid, pulsing memory of the green fire in Thorn Ramsay's eyes, kindled by something he found in my own. At one moment I bitterly regretted that blaze of ardor; the next, my blood ran hot at the thought of it.

What had he seen there? I searched my mirrored image not once but many times, searching in vain for an answer. My eyes were large, to be sure, and dark as Turkish coffee, but otherwise unremarkable. What promise lurked there, unrecognized by me, to dispel his suspicions—fleetingly, alas!—and ease the mocking smile from his lips?

Foolish questions . . . the lengthening silence rebuked my yearning, questing thoughts, telling me more eloquently than words that those sparks of desire had guttered out to lifeless ashes, as cold and gray as the November days fast drawing to a close.

CHAPTER SIXTEEN

December was almost upon us, and the urban scurry associated with readying wardrobes and houses for the winter social season forcefully reminded me that I had better things to do than fret about a man I might never see again.

I had new stock to check against invoices, and orders to dispatch to Avakian's agents in Turkey and Persia. I also had my fall reminder letters to write.

The hands on my office clock read three before I was able to turn my attention to the orders, and I had barely begun the first draft when Krikor appeared in the doorway.

"Miss Kate? There's a young man out front asking for you."

"Oh, dear, will you take care of it for me, please? It's probably just another salesman."

"I don't think so. Salesmen usually have a smile on their faces; this one . . . I think it's a personal matter," he added solemnly.

"Good Heavens, Krikor!" I said in mock alarm. "An unsmiling young man here on personal business? That sounds ominous indeed."

I swept through the kilim portieres that separated the showroom from the office and stock area and moved briskly toward the tall, slim, oddly familiar figure that stood, turned away from me, looking out of one of the display windows that faced on the avenue.

"You wished to see me?" I inquired cheerily.

The young man turned. It was Lance Ramsay.

"Lance! How are you? It's wonderful to see you, but whatever brings you here?"

Lance removed his kid gloves one finger at a time and fussed with the cuffs of his immaculately tailored chesterfield before answering. His dark eyes, scrutinizing me through a disdainful sweep of lashes, were indeed unsmiling.

"To New York City or to Avakian's, Kate?" A wave of his arms encompassed the showroom furnished with brass, copper, and carved wood ornaments which complemented the exotic effect of the glossy rugs hung upon the walls, draped upon racks, and artfully strewn across the drugget-carpeted floor. "I *am* impressed," he continued in a sardonic tone remarkably like his Uncle Thorn's. "It is no wonder you would do whatever you could to preserve what, I am sure, is a most profitable enterprise."

I fought to keep from gaping. What on earth could have happened to transform my sweet, lighthearted companion into this . . . this *popinjay?*

"But to answer your question, I have come to New York to see Mother's—that is, *my* lawyers about my mother's estate, and to Avakian's to deliver a message to you from my Uncle Thorn. He asked me to tell you that the hearing postponed by—" Lance broke off abruptly, and the sudden tears that filled his eyes moved me to step impulsively toward him.

"Lance, *do* sit down," I gently urged, indicating the low cushioned couches provided for customers.

He stepped back from me, and ignoring my invitation, doggedly continued. "The hearing to determine who will inherit Hawkscliffe has been rescheduled for December fifth. It would be appreciated if you could return to complete your commission at Hawkscliffe before that date. May we assume that will be possible?"

I all but snorted at this mincing locution. "May we assume," indeed! It would be difficult—there was the delivery of Lawrence Marquand's palace carpet to arrange, among other urgent matters—but I would do it. "And how is your jolly Uncle Thorn?" I asked, deliberately delaying my answer.

Lance looked discomfited by the sarcastic edge to my question. "He's fine, Kate . . . he's been very kind. They all have been, really, but especially . . ." His voice drifted off uncertainly as he sensed the change in my mood. He cleared his throat. "We've . . . I've been wondering about those rugs on the top floor. The drawings I did of them— as well as your notes about them—seem to be missing."

I could hardly believe my ears. I had wondered why Lance had come to deliver a message that could as well have been conveyed by one of Thorn's clerks. Why, he was as bad as Philo!

"I have them, Lance."

"Well, I really don't think—"

"You *offered* to make those sketches for me, Lance—you had nothing better to do, you said—and my notes about those particular rugs are unrelated to the work I was commissioned to do, aside from certain technical information I have already incorporated into the catalog."

"But if you will remember, my mother—"

"I remember your mother's words very well, but she had

199

no authority, legal or moral, to dictate to what use your sketches or my notes should be put, and as far as I am concerned her death has not altered the situation."

Lance's jaw set in a stubborn line so uncharacteristic of his former, devil-may-care nature I began to suspect that someone had deftly played upon the boy's postmortem guilt about his innocent defiance of his mother on my account.

"If you wish me to return your gift of sketches," I continued deliberately, "I will do so, but the request must be yours and yours alone; I will not honor one reaching from the grave."

Lance's eyes widened with shock. I had determined to be forthright, but perhaps I had gone too far, thus inadvertently accomplishing exactly what had been intended. Once Lance's puppyish affection for me was allayed and the rug catalog completed, all my ties with Hawkscliffe would be severed. But whose purpose would be served? Cora's? It was not difficult to imagine her bidding good riddance to my bad rubbish, unable to separate me in her mind from Roxelana, the interloper who had robbed her of the chance to extend her domain from Charles Quintus Ramsay's home to the man himself.

Or perhaps Philo had come to regret how much he had revealed about himself to me in the gazebo. If so, he would be strongly motivated to discourage any lasting relationships between me and his family. Since the Ramsays and I did not move in the same social or professional circles, I would then largely cease to be a threat once I had completed my mission at Hawkscliffe.

And then there was Thorn, whose suspicions of my motives had never been very far from his mind. Could he be trying to protect his nephew from the sly manipulations of an adventuress for whom Thorn himself had felt desire? And how much more protective might he be if

200

Lance was, in fact, his son?

"Well, Kate? What shall I tell my uncle?"

I preferred his frowning impatience to his earlier pomposity. "When will you and your uncles be arriving?" I had no wish to see any more of them than necessary.

"The hearing is scheduled for two in the afternoon at the Hendryk courthouse; we plan to go up together that morning."

I nodded. "Then I will arrive the preceding day to collect Cora's watercolors so I may write the appropriate explanatory notes for them. I also wish to resurvey every room against my final draft of the catalog."

"Just in case an overlooked rug should be lurking under the fern fronds in the conservatory?"

"Exactly!" I said, responding eagerly to this welcome flash of the old Lance. I needn't have bothered.

Averting his eyes from mine, he ducked his head and muttered, "Well, then, I guess I'll be going, Kate." He shuffled indecisively, rocking from toe to heel, as if unable to make a clean break of it.

"Goodbye," I returned succinctly, unwilling to prolong this painful leavetaking.

I offered neither my hand nor the cheek he had kissed upon my departure from Hawkscliffe, but as he reached for the doorknob, I called after him impulsively. "Lance, wait! I do not want you to leave thinking me unmindful of your feelings about your mother. I know you loved her, and it was right that you should. But if I have learned anything in the few more years I have lived than you, it is that we need not unfailingly admire those we love, nor is it necessary that they always be worthy of our respect. In fact, if love were not so blind, I fear few of us would be loved at all."

Lance looked at me for a long time, soberly, thoughtfully, but I could not tell at all what he was thinking; and

201

when he left it was without a word or backward glance. I remained staring after him, numbed by a profound sense of loss, my eyes following in mindless fascination the slowly diminishing arc of the plait of bells swaying on the back of the door.

"Are you still working on your orders, Miss Kate?"

I jumped at the sound of Krikor's voice, which pulled me out of a reverie set far from my office, swathed now in the shadows of approaching night. I stared up at the dimly lit clock on the wall. Two hours had ticked by since Lance's disturbing visit.

I sighed. "I can't think where the time has gone. Now this will have to wait until tomorrow, and we have Mrs. Wentworth bringing her husband in at eleven to look at that Kashan for their parlor. If only that woman wouldn't prattle on so about her spaniels. . . ." I sighed again. "Oh, well, if it weren't for those ill-trained dogs of hers, she wouldn't have to keep buying rugs."

Krikor looked confused. "Mrs. Wentworth is coming tomorrow morning? I thought Yervant Keyishian had arrived in New York and was taking you to lunch tomorrow."

"He is. They are." I threw up my hands at the impossibility of the situation I had gotten us into. "Tell you what, Krikor, I'll leave the Wentworths to you."

"Miss Kate? Is anything wrong? All this week, especially today, you seem . . . distracted."

I summoned up a smile, shook my head, and blamed my advancing years. Looking relieved, Krikor laughed at that, probably deciding it all had something to do with being female.

I don't know what Mariam thought was the cause for my distraction, but I managed to hurt her feelings because of it.

"What do you wish me to prepare for your Thanksgiving dinner, Miss Katherine?"

I looked at her blankly.

"It's the day after tomorrow," she said stiffly.

"I know that, Mariam, but I'm spending the holiday with the Hagopians as usual. Surely I told you."

Mariam stared at me, her mouth a curve of woe. *I hadn't told her.* I stared back at her, aghast. I knew how much she looked forward to spending Thanksgiving in the Bronx countryside with her niece's lively family.

"We'll send a messenger up in the morning, Mariam . . . at my expense. And I'll hire a carriage to take you up there on Thursday in style. I'll even lend you that lavender bonnet you so admire," I offered magnanimously, for it was my favorite bonnet, too. "Now am I forgiven?"

Mariam beamed. "Oh, yes, Miss Kate!" She bustled off to prepare my supper, then, pausing at the door, she turned to look back at me thoughtfully. "Perhaps we should have more fish."

Whether seafood actually has the salutary effect ascribed to it, I do not know, but the oysters served at the Hagopians', nestled in beds of crushed ice, pleased my palate enormously.

"My sons got them yesterday at the Fulton Market," Salome Hagopian said, smiling fondly at the two strapping young men, Armen and Aram, seated across the table from me. Square of head, broad of shoulder, with identically set dark eyes and coarse black hair combed similarly straight back from wide, slanting foreheads, they always gave me trouble; I could hardly tell them apart.

"And the honey and nuts for Uncle Yervant's baklava," chimed in little red-headed Anouk, a blazing poppy in this

203

family of black tulips. The title of uncle given to Yervant Keyishian was, in fact, honorary. A distant relative of the Hagopians, he had been my uncle's oldest friend and most trusted agent. This was his first visit to Amreica, and I was delighted when I learned he had been invited to share this traditional holiday with us.

"Let us give thanks to God not only for a good harvest!" I said.

"And our thanks for prosperous business," added Leymel Hagopian."

"And the blessing of good friends," said his wife.

We toasted the occasion solemnly with rich, dark homemade red wine, and then, as an excuse to drink more of it as quickly as possible, toasted each other and anything else we could think of that was remotely appropriate.

After dinner I prowled restlessly through the big house, unwilling to suffer the pipe and cigar smoke generated by the menfolk in Leymel's study "discussing business"—the term used by men to lend dignity to an exchange of trade gossip—although I had been courteously, if not enthusiastically, invited to do so.

I turned back with a resigned sigh toward the kitchen, where the women were helping the servants put away the mountains of leftovers, but I had nothing to add to the chatter about food and fashion, and the rather piggy face of Zaruki Hagopian Sassouni's new baby, delivered like a sultan's treasure into my awkward arms, failed to charm.

I would love my own child, I thought as I tried to rock away the baby's scowl of discontent. It was no use; the child began to squawk. Zaruki hastened to rescue her small son, and cradled the flailing infant lovingly, cooed endearments into its tiny, unheeding ears.

Yes, I told myself again, as I retreated toward the front parlor, I *would* love my own. For if, as I had told Lance, love is blind, then maternal love is the most blind of all, I concluded as the squalling sound of Zaruki's baby pursued me down the hall. Why else would a mother put up with all that noise?

But without a man to love enough to make a home for and bear his children, how would I ever know for sure?

I could find no ready answer. I entered the ornately furnished parlor and sank down upon a horsehair sofa whose shiny surface was as unyielding as my despair. It was there that Yervant Keyishian found me.

"Ah! Katherine! I thought I caught a glimpse of your pretty dress as I passed by."

Pleased, I smoothed my skirt of soft green Russian cashmere. "Do you really like it?" I asked shyly as I drew aside the overskirt of silk striped in autumnal shades of crimson, gold, and plum to make room for him to sit beside me. "I seldom have an opportunity to shop." In fact, it was only the previous week that I had dashed over to Arnold Constable and found this costume, expensive but ready-made, requiring only a few adjustments. "I fear it is rather plain."

"Not at all! It suits you admirably and sets off your coloring to perfection, as does your jewelry. If you ask me," he continued in a confidential whisper, "it is only plain girls who require to be decked out like a candy box."

Unused to compliments, I blushed and fingered the simple but elegant gold and emerald brooch on the fine ecru lace of my collar. "Uncle Vartan gave me this and the matching earrings for my twenty-first birthday," I volunteered. "Oh, I do miss him so!" I blurted.

Yervant slid a stout arm around my hunched shoulders. "Come now, my girl! Save your tears for the living! Are there no young men vying for the opportunity to give you pretty things? No special man that makes your heart beat faster?"

"There is one," I admitted. "But he has no eyes for me." As if beckoned by my words, recollections of Thorn's green eyes flashed through my mind: now the dark, brooding shade of hemlock; then brilliant emerald, a reflection of the cold fire animating their depths; and finally, fleetingly, a green as soft as brookside moss in spring.

"Perhaps someday—"

I shook my head. "No. Not him. Not ever."

"You are still young, Katherine! There will be others for you, many others, men who have the wit to recognize a jewel when they see one. Why, if I were just a few years younger myself . . ." Yervant eyed me roguishly. "What do you think, eh? Thirty years younger? Thirty-five?"

We smiled at each other.

"Oh, well, in *that* case, I'd say yes so fast it would make your gray head spin," I teased. "In the meantime, while you're searching for that elusive fountain of youth, I'll have the shop to occupy my time. By the way, did I tell you . . ."

Yervant allowed me to chatter away. He shook his head over the late hours I kept in order to finish the Hawkscliffe catalog and expressed his disappointment at being unable to see it before it was delivered. "A collection to be proud of, that one," he said.

Yesterday, at the shop and during lunch at the Fifth Avenue Hotel, our conversation had been impersonal, about the bales of rugs en route by steamer, and orders yet to fill—the special orders I saved for him, as my uncle always had. We had talked, too, of the centuries-old Anatolian rugs—the very ones Lance had sketched for me.

"Tell me, Katherine," Yervant said to me now, "that book you told me about yesterday, the one you plan on

206

writing about those early rugs—you will send me a copy?"

"Of course! However, it won't be *my* book, you know. If published at all, it will bear Uncle Vartan's name, in tribute to his lifelong dedication to the weaving tradition."

Yervant Keyishian gripped my hands tightly and nodded his head several times. "Just so, just so," he said in a gruff voice whe he was finally able to speak. "It is no wonder he loved you like a daughter, Katherine *Baji*. More, much more, than he ever loved his own."

I laughed. "But I *was* his own daughter, Uncle Yervant. He adopted me, you know."

"Yes, yes, but I mean his daughter by blood. That ungrateful girl, Araxie . . . a wild, cruel, greedy girl, that one, not a drop of filial loyalty in her. I remember the time she traded the silver jewelry her parents could barely afford to buy for her, one by one, out of the pitiful sum left them each year after the terrible taxes levied by the Turks. How she wheedled and sulked to get those pretty trinkets! Traded all of them for one old Ottoman bauble, can you imagine? Magic, she called it. Hah!" Contempt dredged from the past transformed his deep, kindly voice into a harsh growl. "What an insult to a devout household! I ask you, what kind of daughter . . ."

Uncle Yervant's flood of words trailed off into confusion at the sight of my deathly pale and uncomprehending face. His forehead creased in an anxious frown as he tried to make sense of a distress so deep it robbed me of words to express it.

"You didn't know?" he whispered at length. "Oh, my dear child! I assumed . . . I had no idea . . ."

A daughter? Uncle Vartan had a daughter I never knew about? Impossible! "What happened to her, this Araxie? Where is she now?" I stared at Yervant accusingly, as if he were somehow responsible for the shattering effect of this unwelcome revelation.

He reached out and awkwardly patted my hand. "I'm so very sorry, Katherine, if I had had any idea . . . But," he sighed, "to answer your question, I don't know where Araxie is or what happened to her. She went away to school, I know, somewhere on the Bosphorus. She was a clever girl, and Vartan hoped the academic discipline might help her settle down." He shrugged. "At the time I had worrisome family responsibilities of my own, so Vartan traveled our old routes alone. Later he never spoke of Araxie, and I was reluctant to pry. She may have died in the same outbreak of the plague that took your Aunt Vosky."

He looked at me and snapped his fingers. "But you did meet her once, Katherine. I remember Vartan telling me about a big celebration at your house, a wedding, I think, and something happened, something Araxie did, that so shocked and angered your father he told your uncle's family to leave. Imagine denying hospitality to your wife's only brother!" Yervant's voice shook as he recounted this outrage. "Poor Vartan, he was so humiliated! It was after that—now I remember!—that she was sent away to school."

Something that had shocked and angered my father? I smiled wryly and shook my head. Almost anything could and did arouse his ire, from his students' inattention at lessons to my championing of our wayward servant girl Halide. Dear Halide! How good she had been to me, and how nourishing her high spirits as she laughed and sang and twirled me around in little dances of her own making. I doubted that her banishment from the excitement and temptations of Stamboul to the barren Anatolian hills with a man she didn't love allowed much opportunity for dancing. . . .

Dancing . . .

All at once the connection became clear. Of course! I saw

208

again that roomful of giggling, chattering girls reduced to awestruck silence by the half-naked, ebony-haired dancer who boldly defied my father and was thunderously banished from our midst. That girl must have been Uncle Vartan's daughter, I realized in wonder. That voluptuous stranger . . . who undulated so thrillingly to the sensuous rhythms she struck from Halide's *zil* twinkling on her fingers, was his daughter. And my cousin . . . Araxie.

CHAPTER SEVENTEEN

The Friday and Saturday after Thanksgiving were busy days at the shop, and the lack of time for reflection allowed me to pretend, once the initial shock of discovery had passed, that Yervant's revelation about Araxie Avakian was of academic interest only.

The Wentworths had purchased, Krikor smugly informed me, not only the Kashan I suggested he show them to replace the damaged carpet in their parlor, but a very fine Ravar Kerman for their bedroom. It seemed a spaniel puppy had amused himself with a silk Hereke prayer rug that never should have been on the floor in the first place.

In truth, although the rug's chewed edges and fringe were unsightly, the repairs presented no particular difficulties except for the time it would take to execute them properly, which was too long for the impatient Wentworths. Roused to indignation by their casual dismissal of this exquisite piece, Krikor offered an absurdly low trade-in price meant to shame them; instead, to his amazement, it was readily accepted.

"A splendid day's work, my friend!" I said, as I made a note of the handsome commission to be included in Krikor's next paycheck. "Two very profitable sales, and since I have a customer waiting for a silk prayer rug of the quality of that Hereke, there's another one in the offing."

All in all, the events of the holiday weekend had provided me ample reason for giving thanks. On Sunday, confined to the house by a cold, freezing rain that varnished the sidewalks, I found that commercial success was not in itself sufficient to buoy my spirits.

I roamed through the house restlessly, seeking a task that would engage my entire attention. It was no use. Lacking diversion, my mind returned like a homing pigeon to the puzzle of a cousin I never knew I had.

Dear Uncle Vartan! How I missed the pungent smell of his tobacco and the stories he would tell as we sat together in front of the fire in his study on days like these. So many stories, *wonderful* stories, yet not a single hint *ever* about his daughter Araxie.

How could this be? If it had been my father, I could understand. What was it Yervant had said? "Imagine denying hospitality to your wife's only brother!"

I shivered. Once again I thanked the kind fate that had delivered me to the United States and Uncle Vartan's protection. But knowing Uncle Vartan as I did, having experienced firsthand his warmth and kindness and strong sense of paternal obligation, I was unable to comprehend how he, of all people, could have denied his own daughter.

The hows and whys of it tugged unceasingly at my consciousness. The afternoon nap I had hoped would provide escape from my churning thoughts proved impossible. I retreated finally to Uncle Vartan's study to look for the notes he had made years before about the very old Anatolian rugs Lance had sketched for me.

I had postponed sorting through Uncle Vartan's personal papers time and time again, perhaps because when I was still torn by grief, I had unconsciously avoided examining too closely anything Uncle Vartan might have wished to keep private. Just the sight of his dear, funny, curlicued script could bring tears to my eyes.

I found the first set of rug notes I was seeking almost at once, but the second and third—I knew there were three because of the scribbled list of contents attached to the first book—eluded me. I finally discovered them lying side by side on top of a small, finely worked donkey bag in a box that had been shoved to the rear of the cupboard under the desk top.

I picked up the little bag and found it surprisingly heavy. Curious, I untied the fastenings and found inside a journal. Like the others, it was covered in black, pebbled leather—as were Roxelana's at Hawkscliffe, I recalled—but it was much thicker. Knotted around it was a stout linen cord, and under the cord was an envelope addressed to me.

I turned the heavy, creamy, oddly lumpy square over and around, looking, I guess, for something to give me some clue to its contents, something to prepare me for this unexpected message beyond the grave. There was nothing.

I began to ease open the sealed flap, but trembling made my fingers awkward and clumsy. Fearing I would tear the contents, I reached for the dragon-shaped brass letter knife on the scarred green leather desk top and slit open the envelope with its long, pointed tail. The sound of the ripping parchment was startlingly loud.

I upended the envelope. A single folded sheet and a

213

small, silk-wrapped object slid into my hand. Dutifully I began to read, expecting the usual insulating stiltedness of written communications, but as my eyes sped over the closely penned lines, I could almost hear Uncle Vartan speaking to me, here in this room where he had so often regaled me with tales of his exciting, adventurous past.

Happy tales, they had been. This was not one of them.

Katherine, my dear daughter, it began. *If you have somehow learned of Araxie, you must read this journal; should the name mean nothing to you, then I beg you to destroy it, as it would only distress you.*

If, knowing of Araxie, you read my diary, it will answer many of the questions you are sure to have. One question it may not answer, but which I want to answer for you now, is the extent of my feeling for you, daughter of my heart.

Knowing something of your relationship with your own father, it is possible that during these last few years you may have mistaken my love for you for mere appreciation—which is indeed great!—of your ability and intelligence. Nothing could be further from the truth, dear child! You have brought me more joy and happiness than you can possibly know. A reading of the pages of my journal may help you understand why that is so.

I may not be here for you much longer. The dizzy spells that sent me to the doctor last week are more serious than I allowed you to believe, and the least effort—no more carrying of carpets for me!—brings pain. But you are well provided for: I saw to that five years ago for reasons you will soon learn.

I hope it will not be necessary for you to read this, dear child, but if you do, please never forget that I love you very, very much.

First I unwrapped the small parcel enclosed with the letter. I gasped as the layers of fine silk fell away to disclose an evil-eye amulet exquisitely crafted of crystal, jet, and lapis lazuli. It was unlike any I had ever seen, and I examined it at length before returning it to its soft nest. I had no idea of its signifiance, if any. Could this be Araxie's "old Ottoman bauble" that Yervant Keyishian had spoken of so scornfully? I could only hope I would learn the truth of it in the course of reading Uncle Vartan's journal.

I untied the linen cord slowly, apprehensively. Never had that old saw "Ignorance is bliss" seemed more apt. Yet the first section of the diary, a lyrical account of Vartan and Vosky Avakian's early married life, was anything but a tale of woe. The Arabic in which it was written lent a sensuous flavor to the flowery phrases.

I hurried through those pages, unwilling to intrude any more than necessary upon this intensely personal description of what can only be termed a romantic idyll. They lived near Erzurum at that time, in a village west of Mount Ararat on the Silk Road, the busy trade route stretching from Europe into Asia. Uncle Vartan's shrewd head for business and good eye for the carpets he acquired as he traveled around the countryside—including Van, where he met Yervant Keyishian—allowed him to prosper. Then, after an anxious wait, came the event for which the young couple, now in their late twenties, had been planning and industriously saving. A beautiful black-haired daughter was born.

Araxie was their first, and despite their prayers, their only child. She was an ailing child when young; lacking a houseful of children upon whom to distribute their largesse of love, her parents lavished it all upon this pale, huge-eyed, fretful mite. There were many references to new remedies tried, and the cosseting and little gifts

215

intended to console the listless girl left their mark.

By the time of her tenth birthday, Araxie had outgrown her frailty, but not her parents' habit of indulgence. My uncle was acting as an agent for European rug buyers by then, and the family had moved west to Constantinople and taken a small house in the Stamboul district. Araxie's birthday was made the occasion for a modest family gathering, including my parents, and to my surprise, me.

. . . we could afford only one of the silver bracelets Araxie had set her heart on, but it was the prettier of the two, and the other was promised for Christmas. She wouldn't hear of it, and began to scream and pummel her heels. Such a fuss she made! Poor Vosky was mortified.

My dear sister tried to overlook it, but not John Mackenzie. He gave little Araxie a withering look, saying her behavior set a bad example for his own daughter. A hard man, that Mackenzie. He has turned my gentle sister into a plodding donkey. There is not a spark of spirit left in her.

I sighed, closed the journal, and went out to the kitchen to prepare myself a cup of tea. The seeds of estrangement between the two families had, it seemed, been sown long before the final break in our *yali* on the Bosphorus. It made Uncle Vartan's rescue of me all the more remarkable, I reflected as I returned to the study with my tea.

As I continued reading, it became clear that my uncle had more sense of the obligation due one's family than his daughter had in her body—a body that as it voluptuously matured, presented her anxious parents with a whole new set of problems.

. . . she has been seen near the Dolmabahce Palace again. How she manages to get there I do not know, nor am I sure I want to know. The wicked girl says she would

216

like nothing better than to be an odalisque, the most beautiful and accomplished of all the concubines in the Imperial Harem. Vosky is sure she is teasing us, but there is a look in Araxie's eye that frightens me. Even John Mackenzie has never looked so coldly determined to have his way.

Imagine! Our daughter in an Ottoman harem! What a disgrace for a Christian family! Even the Turks are unhappy about the Sultan's revival and expansion of the harem; in fact, it is rumored that the cost of supporting it and Abdul Aziz's other luxuries is the principal reason we are so heavily taxed.

My Araxie is beautiful enough to catch the Sultan's eye and she sets her restless mind to only those studies that would fit her for his Europeanized court. Her French and English are better than mine now, and she sings and plays her zither like an angel. I must admit, too, that when it is to her advantage, her manners are faultless, although when crossed she is, God help me, like a spawn of the devil himself. . . .

Poor Uncle Vartan. His journal continued in this vein, anguish alternating with the anger of frustration, as his daughter pursued her willful way. In addition to unexplained absences, there were the notes and flowers and little gifts brazenly delivered to their door. Finally, there was the episode of the Ottoman talisman that had so shocked Yervant Keyishian.

Even I was shocked to learn she had purchased it in the Corand Bazaar. True, I had prowled the bazaar myself in search of my evil-eye charms, but no one paid any attention to children there, as long as they weren't caught stealing. But for a proper young lady to venture unescorted into those rude, crowded passageways was unheard of.

I recalled my father's fury when he discovered that

217

Halide, who was only a servant girl, had sought out the excitement to be found under the arches there. It was no wonder Uncle Vartan confided to his diary his fear that his daughter had exchanged more than her jewelry for the costly amulet she insisted had once belonged to Sultan Mehmet the Conqueror, given by him to honor his favorite among the palace women. *From that day on,* he wrote, *although she dared not flaunt it openly under my roof, she kept it with her always, tucked in a pocket or suspended on a ribbon around her neck.*

Like my uncle, I doubted the truth of the story. What mattered, however, was not that Araxie believed it, but that she had no qualms about trading the tokens of her parents' loving generosity to gain a symbol of imperial debauchery.

Had she, too, become debauched, as her father feared? Debauched in fancy, I suspected, if not in fact. I closed my eyes and leaned back in Uncle Vartan's huge, worn leather chair, too disheartened to read any more that evening.

As I put away the journal, I was reminded again of Roxelana's journal at Hawkscliffe. I felt a warm, tingling flush as I recalled the explicit little sketches that accompanied her notes and descriptions.

Is every woman an odalisque at heart?

Wasn't that Philo's rhetorical inquiry my first evening at Hawkscliffe, after recounting Roxelana's deliberate rout of Thorn's former fiancée?

Certainly not I, I had thought indignantly at the time, offended by Thorn's dark scowl and grunt of what I had taken to be agreement. But now I was not quite so sure . . . perhaps it was merely a matter of degree—or should I say intent?

The memory of myself swaying in a shimmer of silk came unbidden to my mind. Deliberately swaying and humming, in front of a pier mirror that reflected, approaching from behind me, Thorn's unruly dark hair and glittering green eyes. . . . That was different, I told myself. *That was very different!*

But if so, why did I lie awake until well after the clock struck twelve, wondering at my need to assure myself of such an obvious certainty?

CHAPTER EIGHTEEN

The next morning dawned cold and clear, the streets and sidewalks aglitter from Sunday's freezing rain. I was taking the train to Hendryk the next day, so I delayed leaving for the shop long enough to assemble the few garments I would take on my trip to Hawkscliffe, for which a tidy appearance was more appropriate than a fashionable one. On impulse, I included the cashmere and silk dress Yervant Keyishian had admired, just in case. . . .

What with one thing and another, I did not leave the house until eleven. By then the ice had melted from underfoot, and although the air was still cold enough to puff the exhalations of pedestrians and horses into frosty clouds, I was able to set a smart enough pace to bring me breathless to the door of the shop by quarter past the hour. Even so, I arrived later than our first customer of the day.

"Miss Avakian! I could not resist popping in to see the

prize you offered me."

A small, dapper man sprang up from his seat on the carpet-covered divan provided for clients and crowded in upon me, the fleshy droop of his eyelids and the confidential whisper of his cultured tenor voice making our meeting seem conspiratorial. For a moment I was at a loss. I blinked, glided half a step back, and focused on the unnatural glossiness of the golden-haired head inclining toward mine. Surely it couldn't be . . . but it was. Duncan Meriwether! No wonder I was confused. That head had been largely bald the last time I had seen it.

"Mr. Meriwether," I returned gravely, offering my hand. "How very nice to see you! I regret to say, however, that the Hereke is unavailable for inspection."

Experience had taught us never to show a customer a damaged rug—in this case, the Wentworths' spaniel-chewed silk rug—if it could be avoided. The memory of the damage, no matter how expertly repaired, invariably diluted the new owner's pleasure.

"I have entrusted it," I continued, "to the most accomplished craftsman in our employ, and he has taken it home so he may ply his magic undisturbed."

Although my glib excuse was, in fact, true, I found myself falling into the arch mode that men like Duncan Meriwether seem to expect of womenfolk. An artist more competent than gifted, he had been introduced to Oriental rugs by Charles Quintus Ramsay, much his senior in age as well as talent. They used to drop in together for chats and occasional purchases at Avakian's, which at that time was a short stroll from the Studio Building on West Tenth Street.

Rumor had it that in the old days he allowed his studio to be used for C.Q.'s extracurricular activities; in return, clients of C.Q.'s seeking an oil suitable for hanging over the sideboard were referred to Duncan

222

Meriwether. I used to think the story scurrilous; knowing what I did now about the late artist, it seemed highly probable.

"Drat! I had been so looking forward to savoring my new acquisition. It's been a long time since I've been tempted; as it is, I shall have to sacrifice another treasure to make room for it, and I do love all my rugs!" He moved ever closer, his hushed voice more appropriate to a church than a business establishment. "Do you think I could have it by Christmas? As a special present to myself?" I had to strain to hear his whispered importuning. "Do say I may, Miss Avakian!"

After Charles Quintus Ramsay's death, Duncan Meriwether rarely came to the shop, but I knew my uncle had enjoyed Duncan Meriwether's youthful enthusiasm, and his long-standing desire for a reasonably priced Hereke had stayed in my mind. I thought him a rather silly man—his blatantly artificial hairpiece was proof of that—but there was no harm in him, and since he was independently wealthy, his notion of a reasonable price did not have to be taken too seriously.

"It all depends on the matching of the silk, Mr. Meriwether. It must be exactly right. The quality, the color—"

He raised his hands. "Say no more, my dear. I will curb my impatience. But you see, I have this enduring memory of the Hereke I saw at Hawkscliffe—"

"At *Hawkscliffe?*" My suppressed laughter was routed by surprise—which, I realized immediately, was unwarranted. He was an old friend of C.Q. Ramsay's; he had abetted his escapades; nothing was more likely than his having been a visitor at Hawkscliffe.

"You know the Hawkscliffe collection, Miss Avakian? Ah, of course you do! Your estimable uncle assembled it, after all, and didn't someone say you had been selected to do the cataloguing? I can't for the life of me remember who . . . I never much cared for the place. Magnificent site, of course but the house itself . . . And things do have a way of happening there, don't they? That woman of C.Q.'s runs off never to be heard of again; C.Q. suffers a fatal stroke; and just last month Louise Ramsay falls to her death—"

"The only Hereke I remember," I said, cutting short his morbid recital, "was in Roxelana's suite. Could that—"

"Yes, yes, that's the one! An exquisite piece! She appropriated it for herself. It hung in the stairwell for all to enjoy until it was displaced by C.Q.'s portrait of her." He frowned. "Dreadful female . . . much younger than C.Q., you know, but somehow she never seemed . . . *young*." The hushed voice drifted away like an echo. "There was something ageless and . . . *nasty* about her. My poor niece!"

His blurted phrase seemed at first a non sequitur; then it clicked into place like a piece in a jigsaw puzzle. Meriwether . . . of course! Eloise Meriwether was the name of Thorn's fiancée. His *former* fiancée.

"Your niece . . . she was engaged to be married to Thornton Ramsay, I believe. Didn't something happen at Hawkscliffe? Wasn't there—" I stopped abruptly and clapped my hand to my mouth. "Forgive me, Mr. Meriwether, I do not mean to pry; it is certainly no concern of mine. . . ."

No concern of yours, Miss Mackenzie. I would never forget the dark sound of Thorn Ramsay's deep, rough voice. I closed my eyes.

Duncan Meriwether had other ideas. He pressed me to accompany him back to the divan. Evidently, this opportunity to confide a story long unshared was too tempting to pass up.

"They had been living at Hawkscliffe for about two years," he began. "The landscaping had been largely completed by then, and that lovely pink marble fountain had finally arrived from Turkey for the courtyard herb garden. No house is ever entirely finished, of course, but C.Q decided it was time for a party. Not just any party—the conventional housewarming had been held long before—but a costume party designed to show off Roxelana as much as the estate he had created for her.

"The theme was the Ottoman Imperial Court, and the effects were splendid! There were colorful paper lanterns aglow in the trees. Large turtles, gotten from heaven knows where, wandered the grounds with candles on their backs. I've often wondered what happened to the poor creatures."

"I know a little about the historical precedent," I said. "Sultan Ahmed III's turtles, loosed each year during his Tulip Fêtes in the seventeenth century, were kept caged between times and treated like royal pets."

"But this was a one-time affair!"

I shrugged. "Soup, then."

Unable to decide whether or not I was joking, Duncan Meriwether fell silent; then, after a moment's reflection, he nodded. "Yes! Exactly her style. *Soup*." He shuddered elaborately before continuing. "Pretty little tented pavilions had been put up here and there, some for the gorgeously costumed musicians; others for the food.

"Oh, the food, Miss Avakian!" He paused to pat the little bulge of his stomach. "Pastries filled with meats and cheeses, charcoal-broiled lamb, eggplant mashed with garlic, tomatoes dressed with olive oil and herbs, and flaky confections with pistachios and wild honey—it was a feast to remember."

The costumes assembled by the guests were, he told me,

225

inauthentic, but given the number of artists in the throng, the effect must have been, well, artistic. Roxelana, on the other hand, was a vision straight out of the imperial harem.

"Only her dark, plummy eyes could be seen. She was draped head to toe in silks which glowed like jewels against the milky whiteness of her skin. I've never seen skin quite like hers. It was a warm night, and later, when she danced . . . but I'm getting ahead of myself.

"I remember how surprised I was when Eloise and Thorn arrived in conventional evening dress. Eloise was barely out of her teens, but even so, she was unusually shy and unsophisticated. She didn't remember the invitation's saying anything about a costume party; in fact, they had assumed it was a small family gathering to celebrate their engagement. Roxelana pressed upon her an ensemble from her own wardrobe. How fetching she looked! And how dashing Thorn looked in the red fez C.Q. plopped down upon his dark curls.

"It was an exciting evening, Miss Avakian, I won't deny it. The cooling champagne punch released us from our inhibitions. Even dear Eloise sparkled that night. Swathed in the luscious chiffon lent her by Roxelana, she seemed a veritable woodland sprite as her toes twinkled across the close-mown grass to the insistent rhythms of the palm-stroked drums.

"Thorn was obviously pleased with her—not that she danced well, mind you, but it was unlike her even to try. He joined her in their own version of a courtship dance: pairing and parting, circling, twining. It was very moving, and Roxelana very soon had had enough of it.

"Insinuating herself into the space created for them by the laughing, clapping onlookers, the twosome became a threesome. Roxelana didn't dance, she writhed; she didn't twinkle, she smoldered. It was an unequal contest, Miss Avakian," he concluded sorrowfully.

"And one an innocent young girl never had a chance of winning."

"Are you implying my niece's humiliation was planned?"

"One way or another, yes."

"How could you know that?"

"I'm a woman: I've seen Roxelana's portrait," I reminded him. *And I've read her notebooks*, I thought.

He shook his head as if to clear it of this unpleasant notion. "As I said, it was a warm night. Earlier Roxelana had discarded her encumbering veils; all that remained was a hip-slung billow of transparent silk and a cropped, beaded bandeau-like vest that barely contained her."

Mr. Meriwether got to his feet. He began to pace and threw his quickened words over his shoulder at me. It was almost as if he wished not to be held responsible for them.

"The sheen of her moist skin, Miss Avakian, that milky white skin, had the pulsing glow of fine pearls. I remember her throwing back her head and bending her body until that loosened cloud of ebony hair brushed the grass at her heels. By this time, you see, the music had taken possession of her, and she vibrated, mouth slack, eyes half closed, in a tight circle with Thorn at its center, shamelessly offering herself to him. . . ."

He paused and swallowed hard, his eyes averted. "C.Q. was furious! As for Thorn, during those few . . . *wanton* moments, Eloise ceased to exist, just as surely as if she'd never been born. It took just those few moments to destroy any possibility of her ever meeting his expectations—which was probably all for the best."

He resumed his seat beside me on the bench. "I took

my niece home that very night. I never returned to Hawkscliffe, and I never forgave Roxelana, but I never suspected her actions might have been deliberate." He shook his head. "How cruel," he whispered. "How very cruel."

"I did see Roxelana again, though," he added un-expectedly. "Late one night at the Hoffman House bar."

I felt a stab of shock. Loiuse had mentioned gossip about Roxelana's so-called shopping trips into the city— had this been one of them?

"I had gone there with a group of friends. A woman was screaming and cursing—the shrill voice was what caught my attention—and it was Roxelana, engaged in a donneybrook with a coarse-looking, heavyset chap. Didn't know him—none of us did—but standing close to her side, talking earnestly down into her angry face, was Thornton Ramsay. They left together. It was two in the morning, Miss Avakian," he added meaningfully, lest I miss his implication.

"Mr. Meriwether, I am aware . . ." I hesitated, then decided that enough confidences had been exchanged for one day. "I'm pleased we were finally able to find a Hereke of the quality a discriminating eye like yours deserves," I said, rising to my feet. "You may be assured I will do all I can to speed its restoration so that Santa Claus may bring it down your chimney Christmas morning."

"Oh, Miss Avakian!" he said smilingly as he pressed my hand good-bye. "Think of the soot!"

Soot was the last thing on my mind as I packed my portmanteau that evening, although my thoughts were black enough. Thorn Ramsay and his uncle's wife; Thorn and his uncle's last mistress. It wasn't a pretty picture.

He seemed to have as little family loyalty as my cousin Araxie.

I paused before sliding tissue paper into the folds of my pretty new cashmere and silk dress. *What is the point?* I wondered, yet I not only packed it, I also slipped in the suede pouch containing the brooch and earrings Uncle Vartan had given me.

The people we love aren't always worthy of our respect, I heard myself telling Lance. Advice is always so easy to give, I told myself. I wondered in what light Araxie had seen Uncle Vartan's well-meant advice to her.

I was too restless to sleep, so there was nothing to do but to take up my uncle's journal again, although I had had my fill of tales of willful, selfish females for one day.

The next section repeated in greater detail what Yervant had already told me: the wedding at our *yali*, and the entertainment devised by a roomful of bored girls. Considering the lasting harm it had done, there seemed little to choose between Araxie's dance and Roxelana's at Hawkscliffe.

Araxie had been placed in a school, but not only because of the rift she had created in the family, I learned. Ottoman taxation had become increasingly oppressive. The Hagopians had already emigrated to America and occasionally commissioned Uncle Vartan to find them special pieces.

One day he received a letter from Charles Quintus Ramsay, who saw no point in paying an intermediary for a service he could acquire on his own. Uncle Vartan refused. Bypass his old friend, Lemyel? That wasn't the way he did business!

Charles Quintus, who at the moment was not only awash in the money his fame had brought him but suffused with the white hot avidity of the beginning collector, then proposed that Uncle Vartan come to America, at C.Q.'s expense, to explore the possibility of opening his own shop in New York with C.Q. as his backer. It was Uncle Vartan's golden opportunity! Lemyel Hagopian, when consulted, assured my uncle he was not at all sorry to see the last of a customer who had treated his wife, Salomé, with altogether too much familiarity.

The die was cast. Aunt Vosky moved back to Erzurum temporarily until Uncle Vartan could establish himself; Araxie was enrolled in a boarding school. The next year my uncle made two trips to Turkey: the first to buy rugs; the second to mourn at the grave of his beloved wife, the victim of an outbreak of plague that had ravaged the local population. No one knew where Araxie was. She had been sent for to care for her mother, but when it became apparent her mother was dying, she fled. She did not return to school. All that was left of her was the crystal evil-eye amulet, found under her mother's deathbed, that had somehow escaped her. *For shame!* her father wrote. And he cursed her name.

The amulet enclosed in the envelope addressed to me had been Araxie's! I got out of bed and fetched it from my lingerie case, where I had temporarily lodged it, and once more unfolded its silk wrappings. This must be her Ottoman treasure. It was very old and very beautiful, but not worth—*nothing* was worth—the pain it had caused. I would add its glitter to the keepsakes in my carved box as a forceful reminder of what Uncle Vartan had told me so many years ago: you will find, dear child, that faith and courage and loyalty serve better to ward off evil than lifeless, glassy objects ever can.

As far as I could tell, the rest of the journal was an account of his years here in America. The section that remained to intrigue me was the so-called smuggling of Roxelana from the harem on the Bosphorus to the estate high above the Hudson.

On impulse I closed the book, took it with me up to my room, and packed it in my bag. I would save it for tomorrow night at Hawkscliffe. Perhaps when my work was completed there I could throw Cora's malicious version of my uncle's role in Roxelana's saga back at her. He had suffered quite enough.

CHAPTER NINETEEN

I found Harry Braunfels waiting for me at the Hendryk station. It was not a pleasant surprise.

"Thorn told me you were coming. Told me not to keep you waiting," he added.

We eyed each other warily.

"This all you got, then?" he sneered, as he carelessly slung my bag into the back of the dusty trap. I clutched my portfolio protectively, resisting similar treatment of the painstakingly transcribed pages within. "Not planning on doing much sashaying around in furbelows, I reckon."

When did I ever, I wondered as I eyed him coldly. "I'm here on business, Harry; I suggest you mind yours."

"Monkey business," he muttered under his breath, and before I could remonstrate, he flicked the horse with his whip. "Giddap, Sassafras!"

The nervy little chestnut mare leapt away from the platform at a pace too fast for comfort, and the pounding I took as we rattled up the long, winding road to Hawks-cliffe ensured my silence. The sparkling blue of the morning was smudged now with the cloud scales of a mackerel sky, and the spanking breeze had become a steady, raw blow from the northeast.

"You look a mite windblown, missy," Harry pronounced with satisfaction as he pulled the horse to a haunch-buckling halt under the porte cochere.

Mary Rose, who must have been watching for us, ran out to meet me. "Ooh, Miss Kate," she said, as I all but tumbled off the seat. Planting the heels of her hands on her hips, she turned to Harry indignantly. "I saw you whipping up over the rise like a whirlwind! What could you be thinking of? You're such a roughneck, Harry!"

"Not always, Mary Rose."

Harry's voice was suddenly so softly compliant I stopped fussing with my bonnet, which had jiggled all askew, and regarded him in amazement. He looked almost . . . human.

"Oh, Harry, go on with you!"

And Mary Rose was blushing. *What on earth?* Was this an example of Harry's way with the ladies that Thorn had mentioned? I had found it impossible to believe then; I still found it hard, but seeing is believing . . .

"Tell me, Harry," I said on impulse, "have you ever been in the Hoffman House bar, in New York?"

His eyes shifted. "In New York? Not likely, missy! I can get me a tumbler of whiskey closer than that."

As a denial it wasn't very convincing, but I allowed Mary Rose to shepherd me inside.

"I'll take your bag upstairs, miss. Agnes has a kettle boiling on the stove and a tray all set and waiting. You look as if you could use a nice cup of tea about now."

"I can indeed," I replied gratefully.

Mary Rose lifted her black cambric skirt to mount the stairs, then turned back. "Miss Kate? What was that about a bar in New York? You know, with Harry just now?"

"Oh, just that someone thought he might have seen him there . . . but that was years ago. It's nothing, Mary Rose. I don't know why I asked."

And I didn't. There must have been many coarse-looking, heavyset men in the Hoffman House over the years. No reason to think it had been Harry who Duncan Meriwether had seen brawling with Roxelana that night; none at all. The only thing certain was that Thorn had been there, and that he'd left with his uncle's mistress at two in the morning.

Reassured, Mary Rose smiled and mounted the stairs.

"Am I to be in the suite, Mary Rose?" I called after her.

"Oh, yes, miss . . . Mr. Thornton said you was."

Somehow, the way she put it hinted at disagreement—with Cora, probably. Now that there was no longer any purpose served in my being there, I suspect she would have liked to put me back in my former room—in my place, as it were.

Where *was* Cora, I wondered as I looked about me. I shivered. The house seemed dark and cold and unwelcoming. No lights had been lit yet, though the afternoon was half over. Oh, well, Agnes's teakettle was waiting for me in the kitchen . . .

I was halfway down the dim hall when a figure glided out of the library. It stopped soundlessly a few feet in front of me, its dusky, indistinct clothing seemingly fashioned of shadows, like an apparition. My indrawn breath became a quavering gasp of alarm.

"Good heavens, Miss Mackenzie!" the ghost cried. It

was Cora.

I exhaled slowly and smiled weakly. "Miss Banks, forgive me. I wasn't expecting you—"

"You weren't? How odd. I thought that was one of the purposes of your visit."

"Of course I was expecting to meet with you, but not so unexpectedly . . . the hall is so dark, you see."

"Yes, to be sure," she said as she reached up to set a globe in the hallway alight. "I forget you are not as familiar with Hawkscliffe as you would like to be. Also, I'm sure you have more important things on your mind than meeting with me. I have laid a fire in the library—I shall wait my turn for you there."

I clutched nervously at my skirt as she scuttled from side to side along the wide corridor lighting lights, all the while spewing forth her genteel hostility, telling me, for example, that it was wasteful to heat the entire house when no one was in residence. No one that *mattered*, was the implication. She reminded me of a little spider, a venomous little brown recluse.

My spiteful thoughts made me feel better. "I was just going to the kitchen for a cup of tea, Miss Banks. May I bring you one?"

Her refusal was expected. I nodded, and as I resumed my walk to the kitchen, I wondered about the change in Cora. She had never liked me; I knew she distrusted me. But it had always been expressed in a prickly, taut, high-pitched sort of way. Now she seemed to . . . to *relish* it more, to savor her meanness . . . as Louise had. It seemed . . . oh, it was silly of me, I know, but it almost seemed as if Louise's malicious spirit had found a new—not home, home was too cozy a concept—a new place of residence. Just pushed Cora to one side and set up housekeeping. I could almost see those dark blue eyes peering out through the shutters of Cora's wrenlike brown ones.

Self-confidence, *that's* what it was, I suddenly realized. I stopped short in front of the kitchen door. Somewhere, somehow, Cora had acquired the confidence that comes only with security.

Had she contrived that sense of safety? It wasn't hard to imagine her planning to lure Louise Ramsay to that foggy, fatal hilltop; it was harder to see Louise following docilely in her footsteps.

Misadventure. Once more I pondered the notion, twisting it, stretching it, leaving no angle unexamined. It was, of course, possible, and much, *much* less unnerving to contemplate than the alternative.

Even so, my puzzlement remained unresolved: If Cora hoped to stay at Hawkscliffe and secure it as a haven for her seriously ailing nephew, she still had another obstacle to contend with . . . unless Lance had dropped his claim to the estate. Had he? Had he and Philo and Cora come to some sort of accommodation? Or was Cora's new confidence based on nothing to do with Hawkscliffe at all, something I knew nothing about?

It is none of your concern, Kate, I scolded myself, and pushed open the kitchen door.

Agnes shooed me out and up to my room to freshen up. Mary Rose would take my tray to the library in fifteen minutes. When I protested that Cora was waiting impatiently for me. Agnes sniffed. "She's not the guest, miss," she said, shrewdly assessing my anxious expression, *"you* are!"

The cook's down-to-earth sense of place emboldened me to mount the stairs with a sure step, and to use with a clear conscience the time she had allowed me to repair the damage done by Harry's hell-for-leather delivery. Not that Cora Banks cared how I looked, but I could do without her

237

tight-lipped appraisal. Also, I must confess it, I was looking forward to sampling again the suite's rose-and-musk-scented ambience, to see if it was as sybaritic as I remembered.

It was, down to the last luxurious detail, except that the air lacked sufficient warmth to coax forth more than a hint of potpourri's fragrance.

"Will they do, Miss Mackenzie? I know it's hard to judge color in this light; if only you had been able to come earlier . . ."

Cora had spread her watercolors out on the library table. She was right; the light was both distorting and inadequate. I faulted myself for not taking that into consideration, and admitted as much.

". . . but the execution is quite wonderful!" And it was. Not as good as she had been at her best, but for this purpose, accuracy of detail was more important than the finish. "And look! You were able to do eight! We were expecting only five. Philo will be so pleased."

Cora's grateful, proud smile transformed her. She might not like me, but she was able to separate her personal feelings from a professional undertaking like this. It was not easy to do, and in my experience, harder for women than for men. Had I judged her too harshly?

"I soaked my hands in hot water," she said, "ten minutes at a time. It helped."

But only temporarily; her knobbed fingers, as she shuffled through the drawings, reminded me of scuttling crabs.

We chatted a little longer; I promised to review her portfolio in the morning light, although I had no doubt it would pass muster, and then I made my excuses.

"I must make a final round of every room in the house to be sure I haven't overlooked anything, as well as write the captions for your pictures. Since there are more

238

than expected, it will take me longer to do than I had planned."

She stiffened. "I'm sorry if I've made your task more difficult. I only—"

"No, no, no! I merely wished to explain why I cannot continue our conversation. As for your sketches, the more than merrier!"

The minute the words were out of my mouth, I feared she might interpret them as a veiled rebuke for having completed only eight. To my relief, she chose to take them in the spirit intended.

"Perhaps, then, you would perfer to have a supper tray in your room?"

The thought of being relieved of making small talk with Cora Banks throughout an entire meal made me giddy with relief. "How very considerate of you, Miss Banks! May I instead stay here in the library? It is warmer here; the light is better, and the seating more conducive to concentration.

"I will see to it. Will six o'clock suit you?"

I smiled and nodded, then a thought struck me. "Miss Banks, do you happen to know what time the Ramsays plan to arrive in Hendryk tomorrow?"

"On the noon train."

"There is a train leaving for New York at half past twelve; do you think I might ride down with Harry?"

She looked puzzled. "You do not plan to stay?"

"I think not. All I need to do is give the completed portfolio to Philo. I can do that as easily on the station platform as here." It would be hard enough seeing Thorn at all; no point in prolonging the ordeal.

Miss Banks' eyes gleamed with delight. She would be rid of me even sooner than she had dared hope.

"We will see that you make your train," she said, her fervent tone implying she would carry me down herself piggy-back if need be. "Goodnight, Miss Mackenzie!"

The lilt in her voice was almost enough to make me change my plans. But, unsettling as it is to know that one's farewell will earn another's hallelujah, I also knew that staying on would bring me nothing but heartache.

The captions flowed effortlessly from my pen—I had, after all, already done the research—and by eight o'clock, despite time out to enjoy the savory beef pot pie Mary Rose brought me, I had copied them neatly on separate sheets of paper and clipped them to the margins of Cora's watercolors.

The survey of the house would take at least another hour, and yet I kept finding little things to do to postpone my penetration of the soundless shadows: retying the portfolio closure; burnishing the point of the pen I had already cleaned; returning my tray to the kitchen. Even the kitchen was deserted now, Mary Rose and Agnes having retired to their quarters.

Except for the wide corridor Cora had lighted earlier, the big house lay in darkness. The lamp I had brought with me from the library flickered in the drafts created by my opening and closing of doors. The dining room was cold and dank and smelled of damp ashes. The only carpet in the room, the Heriz under the table, bore no evidence of the water spilled upon it during that dreadful dinner my first night in this house. The incident could be traced now only in memory, and probably only in mine.

I retreated to the studio. The colors of the small, finely woven Caucasians leapt into glowing life as I paused at each one, lamp in hand. As I turned to leave, the arc of light swept across the huge landscape on the easel.

I recalled standing on this same spot, exchanging words of praise with Philo for Charles Quintus Ramsay's masterful rendering of the view from Hawkscliffe's highest point. At the time it seemed to me the ultimate proof of C.Q.'s conviction that the contemplation of God in nature was the proper function of the artist; all I could see when I looked at it now was death.

I returned to the corridor. Its arched alcoves, providing quiet nooks for reading or private conversations, held no surprises, nor did I find any rugs lurking unsuspected under the fern fronds in the conservatory.

Oh, Lance, I thought despairingly as I recalled his only lighthearted words to me during his strained visit in New York. *Who could have turned you against me?* If he were with me now—the old Lance, not the new stranger—his merry laugh would have chased away the gloom, and we might have played hide-and-seek among the shadows.

The great clock struck nine, robbed of its resonance by the lengths of heavy, dark red plainweave drawn across windows and French doors against the approaching winter's cold. I made a brief foray into the sitting room—there was a backgammon game, half-played, upon the table there—and took a turn through the rococo chinoiserie of the east parlor before turning back into the court hall.

The kilims behind the bronze peacocks had long since been measured and noted, as had the bags and trappings crowding the large space beyond. Their dark shapes, draped as they were on racks and small tables, seemed like slumbering animals. I half expected to see half-slitted golden eyes contemplating me hungrily from here and there among the furry piles. I would expect no protection from the blue-and-white-eyed amulets staring glassily from around the necks of the stone Hittite lions. They had failed Roxelana and Louise; why should I expect any more benevolent treatment?

I had overlooked nothing. All rooms, all corridors, all nooks and crannies were accounted for. I closed my notebook and started up the stairs, past the crossed lances and brassy shields, past the unsettling portrait that this time, thanks to my resolute shading of the lamp in my hand, remained masked in shadow.

As I gained the second floor landing, I paused, then looked back downstairs over my shoulder, not knowing quite why I did so. Nothing had changed as far as I could tell—nothing material, that is. Nothing lay in wait but an abandoned game of backgammon. Yet everything as I remembered it had subtly altered, become alien in the way familiar scenes do in dreams. *I never much cared for the place,* Duncan Meriwether had said; I, on the other hand, had, but now I sensed a similar sense of—what was it, unease? Distaste? Because of all that happened during my previous stay? Or had I, myself, changed during the two weeks between my visits?

Had it really been only two weeks? It seemed a lifetime . . .

I glanced involuntarily toward the suite at the other end of the hall . . . Thorn's suite. I walked slowly down the hall, lamp held high, and knocked—a formality—at the closed door. The bronze doorknob looked almost too large for my slender palm to encompass, but it turned smoothly, disengaging the latch with a soft click. I entered.

The room was as I remembered it, although at night the somber effect of walls and windows covered alike in dark red brocade approached the funereal. I found the empty stillness unbearably depressing. As I turned to leave, silver-backed brushes winked at me from the top of the bureau. *Were they Thorn's?* I crossed the room, picked one up, and plucked a few dark, springy hairs from the coarse bristles. They felt alive in my hand, welcome symbols of vitality in this cold tomb of a house. There was a handkerchief next to the brush, slightly dusty, seemingly forgotten. Without conscious thought, I wrapped the hairs in the white linen and thrust it into my pocket.

What do you intend to do with your prize? I asked myself mockingly. *Squirrel it away in your box of amulets with other forbidden treasures?* Heat rose in my cheeks. I pulled the handkerchief out again, scattering its contents. *Keepsakes are for silly schoolgirls.* I smoothed out the wrinkles and placed the refolded white square back on the bureau.

I turned again, and as I passed the magnificent rosewood sleigh bed, worthy of a Napoleon, I couldn't resist tracing the smooth, glowing cyma curve of the footboard with my forefinger. What rousing rides Charles Quintus must have enjoyed here with Roxelana! I pictured Thorn's lean muscularity against the creamy linen sheets, and then, next to his darkness, my pale red hair, pale body . . . I hurried out and closed the door firmly behind me. *Silly, foolish schoolgirl!*

It was eleven o'clock before I settled into bed with the third of Uncle Vartan's journals. I had finished it by midnight, but as I heard the last of the twelve deep notes striking faintly from below, I knew that despite my fatigue I would not sleep that night.

His last journal, which recounted the events of Uncle Vartan's life after he came to America, was written in English, signaling, perhaps, a break with his painful past. Business success had not been long in coming, for although his sponsor, Charles Quintus Ramsay, always expected first choice, at a preferred price, of the rugs my

243

uncle acquired, he introduced him to his free-spending friends and clients.

Many words were devoted to my uncle's impression of Charles Quintus Ramsay, a man whose company he enjoyed but about whom he had few illusions: he was vain, selfish, and self-indulgent, and Uncle Vartan deplored his taste for very young women hardly more than girls.

He wrote about Louise and Cora, whose dislike for him he reciprocated. Louise, he wrote, was overbearing; Cora made no effort to hide her low opinion of rug dealers. Thorn Ramsay was, to my surprise, his favorite among the young people he met at Hawkscliffe. *Not as respectful of his elders as he might be,* he wrote of him, which did not surprise me, *but a young man whose handshake I trust.* He continued to grieve for Vosky, but he never mentioned Araxie.

As drowsiness weighted my eyelids, I scanned the pages more and more rapidly, seeking the account of C.Q.'s journey to Turkey and his return with Roxelana, hoping to exonerate my uncle of complicity in the incident, or at least of the penny-dreadful intrigue of which Cora had accused him. At last I found it.

Leaving Charles Quintus on his own in Constantinople, Uncle Vartan had traveled with some misgivings to the East to look at rugs Yervant had assembled since his last visit. When he returned, he found his worst fears had been realized. The aging artist, whose waning popularity had rendered him vulnerable for the first time in his life, announced he had met the most exciting girl in the world at a reception for foreign notables at the Dolmabahce Palace.

She was a true Ottoman beauty, he had boasted; aristocratic in speech and manner, but endowed by Allah with the milk-white skin and dark, velvety, insinuating eyes of an odalisque. Uncle Vartan's suggestion that she might in fact be just that was dismissed out of hand.

Charles Quintus was convinced she was the princess she claimed to be, her hand promised in marriage to a man she had never seen but known to be old, dissolute, and diseased. The Sultana Mother had urged the union for political purposes; the girl feared for her life if she resisted. The infatuated artist, in thrall to the romanticism of moonlight rendezvous at the palace gardens—he on one side of the elaborate fence, she on the other—had promised to save her. "I must, Vartan! And you must help me find a way!"

Uncle Vartan was appalled. His friend had taken leave of his senses. An attempt to abduct a woman from the imperial palace would be considered an offense against the sultan himself, and punishable by death.

It was no use. By then the sweet thrill of soft fingers curled around his on gilded bars had been succeeded by earthier pleasures indulged in a ride with his lady-love along the Bosphorous. Charles Quintus remained adamant.

I placed my finger in the journal to mark the pages and leaned back with a sigh against the pillows. Whatever the actual course of their conversations, C.Q.'s bullying tactics finally wore Uncle Vartan down. He agreed to meet with the aging lover's incomparable Roxelana.

It was a clever ruse: as Roxelana's carriage wound its way up to the Yíldíz Palace gardens, the veiled occupant, attracted by a beautiful rug slung across a ragged old man's bent shoulders, commanded her driver to stop. She pulled aside the curtain to inspect the rug and exchanged whispered words that had nothing to do with the price of carpets.

Except for one unforeseen detail, all went exactly as had been planned. When my uncle returned from the meeting and informed Charles Quintus that the abduction, though hazardous, was feasible, the aged Lothario was too overjoyed to notice his accomplice's grim expression and unusual pallor.

Grim? Pale? He must have been, for when I determined to confirm for myself what had shattered his peace of mind on that long-ago afternoon, those were the words that best described my own reflection in the pier mirror as I reached down to the foot of the bed for my challis robe.

The fire had burned to a listless glow, and my unprotected toes—I had forgotten to bring slippers—seemed to shrivel in against the cold, which became more pronounced as I moved into the hall. The lamp's warm glow of light was an illusion my light wrap, clutched close, failed to sustain.

The big house, quiet earlier, creaked and groaned as its wooden skeleton adjusted uneasily to the frosty blanket of winter enfolding Hawkscliffe's ramparts and binding with icy lace the edges of the dark waters gliding far below. The wide stair rail slid greasily under my nervous palm as I edged slowly down the carpeted steps. The springy wool prickled the soles of my bare feet like a scurry of insects frantically escaping my nocturnal prowling. I pulled my feet high, first one, then the other, from their imagined shattered antennae and splintered chitinous casings. Shuddering, I hurried down to the landing.

I paused to catch my breath, then turned the wick up, spreading light where I had avoided casting it earlier, when I ascended. As if beckoned by its searching, flickering fingers, C.Q.'s portrait of his last mistress glided out of the shadows. The uneven ridges of paint, caught in the lamplight's net, sped dancing rivulets of illumination into the huge dark eyes, curving along the full red mouth and glinting across the ancient runes inscribed upon the huge golden disk adorning the plump, milk-white hand

246

resting on her breast.

I swallowed hard. I tried to deny it, but I knew my uncle had written the truth; he was too honest with himself to do otherwise. The unforeseen detail that had broken my uncle's heart for a second time and crumbled his defenses was the sight of this gold ring glittering on the finger that had pulled aside the sun-drenched curtain of a carriage paused below the gates of the Yildíz Palace.

This was the bauble exchanged for a lifetime's gifts of silver trinkets. It was this Ottoman ring for which the tokens of parental love had been scorned, not the crystal amulet lost beneath a dying mother's bed. *This* was the magic talisman so prized, and this woman known as Roxelana was my cousin, Araxie Avakian.

CHAPTER TWENTY

My hunch that Cora would be no more anxious than I for our paths to cross the following morning proved to be blessedly accurate. I had enough on my mind without coming face-to-face with the person whose dark suspicions about the part my uncle had played in Roxelana's abduction had proved, to my deep distress, to be more right than wrong.

According to my uncle's journal, it was true that Roxelana's life had been threatened. Not, however, by the Sultana Mother, as she had claimed, but by Abdul Aziz's wife, who was murderously jealous of the calculating concubine who had caught the sultan's jaded eye. Roxelana had shrewdly guessed that if the aging wife were to be made aware of the planned abduction of her young rival, she would do nothing to thwart the scheme. A whisper here and there was all it took to ensure a diversion of the guards' attention on the appointed night.

Heady with success, it never occurred to Charles Quintus

that his daring rescue was, in fact, a deliverance. It was an irony Uncle Vartan kept to himself. The girl was his daughter; he owed it to her mother, his darling Vosky, to ensure her protection. He knew C.Q. would reject his high born Turkish beauty if he thought he had been deceived.

His daughter. As I walked down the hall to the dining room, my mind still balked at the thought of Araxie and Roxelana being one and the same—his daughter, my cousin. I wasn't sure I cared for that. I cared even less for the sudden realization that, by virtue of Uncle Vartan's adoption of me, she was also my sister.

I paused in the doorway, *My sister?* Feeling suddenly faint, I moved falteringly toward the sideboard and gripped the edge of it with trembling fingers.

"Miss Kate!" It was Mary Rose, bringing in a pot of tea. She deposited her burden on the damask-covered table, heedless of the hot amber liquid sloshing from the spout, and hurried to my side. She pulled out a chair and assisted me into it.

The fragrant steam rising from the cup of tea she forced into my fingers revived me. I sipped gratefully. "Mary Rose to the rescue again," I said.

My smile seemed to reassure her; she filled a plate with eggs, bacon, and toast for me before returning to the kitchen. Alone once more, fortified by the hot, nourishing fare, I grappled with the revelation that had dizzied me: I had learned the previous night that Uncle Vartan had disinherited Araxie in my favor when she disappeared from Hawkscliffe. He wanted no chance of her arriving after his death on my doorstep to snatch the fruits of her father's and my labors. That was also why he had adopted me; he wanted my inheritance to be doubly secure. What he had not known was that Araxie, as Roxelana, was the sole heir to Hawkscliffe.

Once more I examined my reasoning. It was simple and

irrefutable: if Araxie was my uncle's daughter, and if I was Uncle Vartan's daughter by legal adoption, then I was not only Araxie's cousin by blood, but her sister, her closest living relative and her legal heir.

It was true I had no birth certificate to substantiate my uncle's blood relationship to Araxie; what I did have, however, was a significant exchange of letters between father and daughter after she was established at Hawkscliffe. Such sad, dreadful letters! I had found them clipped inside the back cover of Uncle Vartan's journal, mute evidence that, resisting the natural impulse to hurl them into the fire, he had anticipated a possible future need for them.

His foresight would be rewarded this very day, at two o'clock in the Hendryk Courthouse. When Roxelana, a.k.a. Araxie Avakian, was pronounced legally dead, no claim to Hawkscliffe would have more force than mine. *None of my concern, Thorn Ramsay?* I'd soon learn if he was as honorable a man as my Uncle Vartan had judged him.

I consulted my lapel watch: ten o'clock. There was no time to consult a lawyer, of course. I would just have to do the best I could on my own. I added the journals and letters to the personal belongings I had not yet unpacked and left them together with the portfolio next to the wardrobe now filled to overflowing and hardly able to accommodate a capacious carpet bag.

I told Mary Rose and Agnes I would be returning later in the day and would appreciate the suite being left undisturbed, but I decided not to inform Cora of my change in plans. Prudence persuaded me to let this particular sleeping dog lie. Then, when Harry pulled up in front of the house promptly at eleven, he didn't even

251

bother to inquire about my bags—I'm sure he couldn't have cared less about what was to become of them—or of me, for that matter.

The clouds had spread into a seamless gray sheet, the sun a puddle of white glowing through it. The wind had dropped and the temperature with it.

"Going to snow, missy . . . I can smell it. Those pretty shoes of yours'll be ruint." He seemed pleased at the prospect.

I had changed into the Thanksgiving costume I had brought, which included the bronze kid shoes I was wearing, but I wasn't sure why. To give me courage? To, as Thorn Ramsay had once said, put the starch back in my spine? Lord knows I needed it. I wasn't happy about the prospect of facing down the three Ramsay men, but one thing I did not lack courage about were my convictions.

If I had learned nothing else during the course of the events at Hawkscliffe it was that no one, not even the least selfish of us, can escape entirely the claims of self-interest: the Ramsays—all of them, from Charles Quintus to Lance—Cora, certainly Araxie. Even my father.

Poor Papa! His own world was so dominated by a dread of sin it became his sole mission in life to deliver others from his self-defined view of it. Once I realized this, the crippling burden of sin he had laid upon my frail shoulders slipped away.

Freed at last to decide for myself the kind of life I wanted, I discovered to my bemused surprise that my choice had already largely been made. The shop granted me more independence than most women ever dreamed of, and the rugs I traded in meant much more to me than mere articles of commerce.

Always seek the advantage, Uncle Vartan used to say. In my case, at this stage of my career, the Hawkscliffe collection was my precious advantage: I wanted to publish the catalog under *my* name; I wanted the disposition of the collection to be *my* decision. As for the rest of the estate . . . that remained to be seen.

I saw Thorn before he saw me. He stood facing away from me, at ease, hands clasped loosly behind his back, his tall figure silhouetted against the pale sunlight shining ever more weakly, as if through frosted glass. He turned.

"Kate!" he cried. The smile on his face as he strode forward to meet me delighted my heart. "How lovely you are."

I was pleased I had taken the time to change; I was even more pleased when I realized my pretty dress was concealed by my long, fur-edged caped coat. How very nice—how *heavenly*—to be thought lovely by the only man whose opinion mattered to me.

He grasped my arms in his strong hands and pulled me to him. I tipped my face up to meet his. A sigh parted my expectant lips as my eyelids drifted down in silent acquiescence to the demand I saw in the glittering green depths of his eyes.

"Kate! I didn't expect to see you here!"

Philo's exclamation wrenched me out of the clouds and back to the grimy Hendryk railroad platform, upon which the second of the Ramsay men had just stepped out from the station house. Thorn's urgent embrace softened to a comradely hug, one of his arms relaxing into a friendly slide around my shoulders before releasing me altogether.

"Were you able to complete the catalog?"

I raised my eyebrows. First things first, eh, Philo?

"Oh, yes," I answered coolly. "It's at Hawkscliffe. Along with Cora's eight watercolor illustrations."

"Eight, you say? Why that's splendid! Absolutely splendid."

"And the little carpetbag you ordered for your friend? It's not quite finished, but will be shortly . . . by Christmas, surely. Where would you like it delivered?"

"Oh, Kate! How good of you! Let's see . . . to the Metropolitan, I think. They offered me the curatorship I applied for, but my living arrangements are still . . . undecided."

Oh, dear, I thought. They may remain undecided for longer than you expect, Philo.

"Hullo, Kate."

His greeting perfunctory, a wary Lance made three.

I nodded and opened my mouth to speak, but the shriek of the whistle announcing the imminent arrival of the train to New York made me clap my hands over my ears. We stood, shrugging helplessly, as the locomotive roared up to the platform in a great whuff of steam. Considering the unwelcome tidings I was about to deliver to the three men surrounding me, I was grateful for a few moments of enforced speechlessness in which to gather my forces.

"Missy! Your train!" It was Harry, looming up out of the steam like an evil jinni loosed from a lamp. "You'll miss your train."

"It's all right, Harry," I shouted back at him. "I intended to."

Harry stared at me. Then, as the train lurched forward and chuffed its way south to New York, he hunched his shoulders and threw out his arms. "Women!" he growled.

As he roughly pushed back through the Ramsay men to resume his lounging posture against the station freight wagon, I saw Philo surreptitiously consult his watch and look questioningly at his cousin.

"Will you be our guest at lunch, Kate?" Thorn asked. "As you know, we have an appointment at the courthouse at two, but your company would allow us to pass the intervening time much more enjoyably, and then we can

254

all return together to Hawkscliffe.

"You do not expect anyone else, then?"

"Who else would we ..." Sardonic appreciation rapidly succeeded his earnest, inquiring gaze. "Oh, of course," he drawled. "No, we do not expect anyone. According to the locals Harry canvased, no one in the least out of the ordinary has arrived recently by boat, train, or carriage."

"Or shanks' mare?" I inquired dryly.

Thorn turned to his cousin, who had been listening to our conversation with growing agitation. "What do you think, Philo? Might Roxelana have arrived on foot?" He threw back his shaggy head and gave a shout of laughter. "Hardly likely, Kate!"

Judging from Philo's pained expression, he failed to share Thorn's amusement. In truth, Thorn's high spirits puzzled me as well. Did he know something the others of us did not? Something that convinced him the chance of his uncle's last mistress arriving to claim her inheritance was not only remote, but impossible? Or was it simply the joyous imminence of being relieved of seven years' sole responsibility for an estate that had proved a costly burden?

"It's twenty minutes to one, Thorn," Philo complained, "and it's growing colder. Can't we continue this indoors?"

"Yes, let's do!" Lance agreed, rubbing his hands and stamping his feet.

I hung back. How could I be their guest at lunch, knowing what I did? Since meeting the Ramsays, there had been too many disquieting scenes at table; I had no wish to become the catalyst for yet another. Just the thought of it roiled my insides.

Thorn crooked his arm to me and smiled invitingly. "*Avanti*, Kate!"

I hesitated. If only there were some way to preserve that smile, that caressing look in his eyes. If only . . .

"Please," I said. "Stay a moment longer. There is something you . . . something *all* of you must know."

My words were not sufficiently arresting in themselves; there must have been something else, in my voice or posture, that caused all three to stop, to look, to attentively listen. Even Harry roused himself to cock an ear in our direction.

"It is something I began to learn about only in the last few days, but didn't fully understand—understand all the implications, that is—until a few hours ago at Hawkscliffe."

Thorn's warm smile faded. He drew his dark brows down. "Why do I have the feeling," he muttered, "that I am about to learn you are not simply a person from Porlock after all?" His question was not addressed to me so much as the thin cold air above and beyond me. In effect, he had already turned his back on me.

Stung, I drew myself up as tall as I could, and clasped my gloved hands tightly. "I have just learned that I . . ." The story was so long, so complicated, and even to me so unlikely that I faltered, unable to decide where to begin, how to soften the blow and yet secure what was legally mine.

Oh, get on with it, Kate. His neck is strong enough to bear another albatross! Say it and get it over with. I took a deep breath. "Roxelana is . . . was . . . my sister."

Philo blanched. "Her sister? Her *sister?* What is she saying, Thorn? What does it mean?"

"What it means, dear coz, if true, is that our Miss Mackenzie may have just snatched Hawkscliffe right out from under your and Lance's eager noses. If true," he repeated ominously.

"Mother was right about her . . ." Lance said in a flat tone.

So it was Louise who had sown the seeds of his distrust

256

of me, seeds nourished by grief and guilt.

Harry let loose a hoot of raucous laughter that made all of us start. "Prissy missy is Roxy's sister? Who would've believed it!"

Thorn wheeled to face him. "Harry, be so kind as to inform the hotel dining room we'll be a little late, and while you're at it, arrange for the delivery of the new furnace. *Now,* if you please!" he added commandingly as Harry shuffled back and forth, obviously reluctant to absent himself from such an interesting scene.

"No need to air the family linen in public," he added in low-pitched warning, as Harry took his slouching leave. "He has a point, though, has our Harry. Who indeed would believe it?" His question was blandly rhetorical; his green eyes, oddly lusterless now, held no expression at all. Was he angry? Disappointed? I could not tell. I sensed the guarded, alert focus of a big cat waiting to pounce.

"I have proof."

"I have no doubt of it, Miss Mackenzie." His voice was a deep, smooth purr of unconcern.

Unsettled, I plunged into the story despite my better judgment. What I had to say was more suited to a judge's chambers than the hostile audience assembled on this gritty stage.

"It seems that my uncle Vartan had a daughter, Araxie. She was a wild girl. She caused her parents much pain, and in the end she deserted her dying mother while my uncle was in New York establishing the business for which Charles Quintus Ramsay provided the financial backing."

Thorn and Philo exchanged astonished glances. Had they not known this? "His generous advances have long since been paid back," I blurted defensively. "With interest. I have—"

"Proof," Thorn supplied with a grin that unsettled me

257

futher. "I have no doubt of *that* either, Miss Mackenzie. But do continue," he added. "We are, I can assure you, all ears." Philo and Lance, tight-lipped and grim, nodded their agreement.

I dropped my eyes. I knew this would not be easy, but . . . I took a deep breath. "Uncle Vartan never heard from Araxie, never spoke of her, never saw her again until C.Q. insisted he help him abduct a princess from the sultan's palace. Uncle Vartan was appalled when he discovered that C.Q.'s Roxelana was his daughter Araxie! He wanted nothing to do with her or her deception, but what choice did he have? She had earned the murderous enmity of the sultan's chief wife—how could he abandon his own flesh and blood when C.Q. offered sanctuary, even marriage?"

"But he adopted you!" Philo broke in. "Why would he do that when he had his own daughter back?"

. "Because he broke with Araxie a second and final time. She became pregnant—"

"How could you know this?" Thorn, visibly shaken, asked in a hoarse whisper.

"Because she wrote her father demanding money to pay for ridding herself of the unwanted child. She refused the obvious alternatives, and my uncle was sure C.Q. would turn her out if he had so much as a hint of her betrayal. He knew what had happened to . . . to another of C.Q.'s women in similar circumstances." I amended my sentence just in time; it was not my place to acquaint Lance with the rumors about his paternity. "So he supplied the necessary funds—blood money, he termed it. Later, after taking me under his roof and into his heart, he wrote her he would tell Charles Quintus everything if such a thing ever happened again.

I laughed bitterly. "And his threat worked. Apparently it had never occurred to Araxie that her father would sacrifice C.Q.'s patronage to salvage his honor.

"First, he manufactured a quarrel with C.Q. to remove himself from Araxie's orbit. Then, when she disappeared, he adopted me, not as a way of laying claim to C.Q.'s estate—he had no idea Araxie was C.Q.'s heir—but to protect *his* estate for me should she reappear after his death!"

My concluding words floated away on the frosty air. Philo and Lance seemed numbed—more, I reckoned, by my narrative than the cold.

"A fascinating tale, eh, chaps?" Thorn had regained his earlier nonchalance; the momentary tremor of alarm evoked by my mention of Roxelana's pregnancy might never have occurred. "But I fear you lack one essential item, Kate." My given name was pronounced not with affection, but condescension.

"I have detailed journals," I protested. "Letters—"

"As I said before, I have no doubt of it. But have you a death certificate for Araxie Avakian, a.k.a. Roxelana?"

I was astounded. "Of course not! Isn't that what today's hearing is supposed to accomplish?"

"Oh yes, but you see, Roxelana disappeared *before* C.Q. died, so today's hearing will establish her death as of that date, in lieu of evidence to the contrary. That done, C.Q. will be found to have died intestate, in accord with the will I drew up for him, and which, by the way, has long since been accepted by the surrogate court. Then, as I explained to these worthy, long-suffering gentlemen on our way up, it will require another court proceeding to determine who of C.Q.'s kin is entitled to what."

He smiled at me. I could sense his mental muscles tensing, preparing for his spring. "Any questions? Is it all quite clear to you so far?"

I shook my head, unable to speak, undone by his exaggerated teasing considerateness.

259

"Good! Then you will understand—perhaps you already have, clever girl that you are—that unless you can prove Roxelana died *after* C.Q., your claim is entirely without merit."

The snow Harry had predicted began to fall. One large lazy flake, then two, settled upon my lowered lashes. I felt the touch of Thorn's finger as he reached out to gently dislodge them. Flinching, I looked up to meet an earnestly regretful green gaze denied by a satisfied grin. He had reservations about me from the beginning: how gratifying to prove oneself such a shrewd judge of character!

"Ah! Here's Harry back from his errands. He'll take you up to fetch your bags in time for the four o'clock train, but mind you leave the Hawkscliffe rug collection portfolio," he added with a cruelly playful wag of his finger. "I should hate to be forced to bring charges of theft against you. Goodbye, Miss Mackenzie. May you have a safe journey home."

The three men walked away from me without a backward glance, Thorn pausing only long enough to discuss with Harry the installation of the new furnace, which would be carted up that afternoon before the snow made the delivery of such freight too difficult.

How ironic, I thought, that the only leavening element at this dreadful moment was the realization that Cora had had a legitimate reason for rationing the use of Hawkscliff's heating system.

We rode in silence, Harry and I, the wheels of our carriage tracing narrow gray ribbons in the snow that had only just begun to cling to the graveled surface of the turnpike.

Shortly after we passed through the looming stands of rhododendron flanking the entrance to Hawkscliffe, he spoke to me over his shoulder.

"So you're Roxy's sister. Except for the eyes, there's not a smidgen of likeness."

"The eyes! Of course! Imagine Harry spotting it. That explained my unnerving sense of déjà vu whenever I glanced at her portrait: it was the Avakian eyes—brother, sister, daughters, and cousins. "Adopted sister," I corrected tersely. "We were only cousins by blood."

"She fancied me, missy," he blurted unexpectedly. "Oh, she fancied a lot of fellows, that I know, but those last two years, it was me she smiled on . . . and more," he added, lest his insinuation had escaped me.

Charles Quintus must have found about them, I guessed. She hadn't run *to* her lover, but away from him, away from the unlikely man whose embraces had cost her the cozy nest she had so carefully feathered. But if that were the case, how had Harry escaped his employer's wrath?

"C.Q. never guessed about us," Harry said, as if he had read my thoughts. "He couldn't imagine his fancy woman taking up with a rough sort like me. The old fool! It was her getting in the family way what did it . . . that and Cora."

"I would've married her," he said, turning to glare at me, daring me to express disbelief. "But she'd have none of it. Happy enough to share my bed, but not my name." he muttered. "Thought herself too fine for that."

Poor Harry. No wonder my disdainful attitude had riled him. Apparently Roxelana had never told him she was C.Q.'s heir, an enviable prospect that marriage to anyone, much less Harry, would have destroyed. She had shrewdly let him think her objections were based on sensibility rather than future gain: she didn't want to risk his blackmailing her into a permanent liaison.

"But what had Cora to do with you and Roxelana?"

"I thought she might know what to do."

"You asked *Cora* to help *Roxelana?*"

"You don't know how Roxy could be, Missy. She was beside herself, after me and *after* me to do something, an' it was a woman kind of thing an' Cora and me got along pretty good . . ." Harry broke off and raised his arms helplessly, the resulting tug on the reins causing the little chestnut to shy and toss her head in protest. I could almost feel sorry for him.

"So Cora told Charles Quintus, and he threw Roxelana out, and no one has seen her since," I pronounced flatly, bleakly anticipating the neatly uncoiling chain of events, hoping my uncle, to whom honor meant everything, never realized how unlikely it was his stern warnings would curb his wayward daughter's excesses.

She had ended up just as he most dreaded: banished and penniless. C.Q. may not have found her in the stews of Stamboul, as Cora luridly supposed, but she had probably ended up as badly. Once past the first flush of youth, it's a short walk from the Broadway dance houses to the pavements between Canal and Bleecker.

Harry, who had been distracted by the fidgety mare, turned back to me. "You have it pretty well figgered out, Missy. 'Cept I did see Roxy again. Only once, for a little bit, after the old man died."

I could hardly believe my ears. "You saw Roxelana after Charles Quintus died?" I asked as calmly as I could. "You're sure of that, Harry?"

"Course I'm sure. The place was in such an uproar an' all. Thorn and Philo was here and Cora at sixes and sevens." He grinned complacently. "Yep, Roxy came trailing back. My guess is, Missy, that with C.Q. dead she decided maybe she'd have me after all. But I'd changed my mind by then."

My guess was that Roxelana had come for her inheritance, not Harry, but I decided to leave him his small illusion.

"So you sent her on her way?"

He shrugged. "You could say that. When I told her the vultures had gathered, she went steaming up to the house—to try and collect the valuables he give her, I guess—and she must have met one of 'em along the way, 'cause I heard her screaming and carryin' on." He shook his massive head. "She could really give a person what-for, missy."

"And that was the last you saw of her?"

"The very last. None of 'em ever said anything about her to me, and I wasn't about to say anything to them. Especially Cora. I was still mad at Cora for crossing us. After a while, though," he added thoughtfully, "I was sort of glad she did, if you know what I mean."

I nodded. Roxelana, whose favors had once been an unexpected benefit, had become a shrewish liability. "But didn't you wonder what happened to her?"

Harry looked at me in amazement. "I guess they took her back with 'em, missy. Philo had come up from the city in a fancy new rig—never occured to him how bad the dust would be, what with the dry spell we'd been having." Harry's shoulders shook with glee. "That yeller head of his was as gray as Father Time's . . . Come by train ever since."

Interpreting my silence as reproof, he added, "It wasn't my place to inquire." The expression that accompanied this genteel disclaimer of responsibility for his lover's fate was a caricature of affronted dignity. Harry Braunfels' code did not include offering a woman a second chance.

Harry pulled up in front of the house, remaining stolidly seated as I scrambled out of the springy carriage. The snow was falling faster now, in smaller flakes, and

263

although Hawkscliffe's new white cloak disguised the evidence of decay, it seemed to me now a looming ghost seeking redress for the years of neglect. I shuddered and hurried inside.

Harry's astonishing news had changed the complexion of my situation altogether. Assuming Harry's story could be confirmed, I was not only back in the race but once again ahead of the pack. This time, however, I would take my story to a lawyer and deal with the Ramsays from a safe emotional remove. Thorn's dismissal of me as an adventuress had robbed that role of the enticing excitement I had once fantasized; the reality of being thought unscrupulous brought nothing but pain. I would rather he had shouted at me, struck me even, anything but that calm, cold contempt.

But if Thorn had been cold, the house at least was warm, a tribute to the status of the Ramsay men in Cora's scheme of things: apparently she had decided that since the old furnace's days were numbered they might as well make the most of it.

I unbuttoned my coat with a relieved sigh and consulted my lapel watch. My relief was short-lived. One-thirty! Within the hour Harry would return to take me to the train, then pick up the Ramsays at the courthouse they must be entering just about now, and bring them back up to Hawkscliffe. Time was of the essence!

I hurried up to the suite, only to find it colder than ever. There was no longer the slightest trace of the potpourri's scent. I retrieved my bag from where I had left it next to the wardrobe and hurriedly exchanged my damp bronze shoes for my stouter traveling boots. I didn't have time to pull on woolen hose over my thin silk stockings, so I thrust the pair I had brought into my pocket, thinking to change them on the train.

I hated to leave my bag unguarded downstairs. I was

sure my jewelry was safe, but I dared not take the chance of curious eyes perusing Uncle Vartan's journals and letters, so I locked it, strapped it, and pinned the key inside my other pocket. Bag in hand, portfolio tucked under my arm, I hastened down the staircase. *I must speak with Cora before leaving.*

Mary Rose and Agnes, wreathed in steam and the homely odors of pot roast and baking bread, distractedly directed me to Cora's cottage. I asked Mary Rose to tell Philo the catalog portfolio was on his desk, and before she could dutifully finish repeating my instructions, I had pushed through the kitchen door and swept through the main corridor, depositing my bag at the door before retracing my steps via the studio and Philo's desk to the courtyard that opened out above the sloping path to Cora's cottage.

I gave but a cursory glance at the pink marble fountain imprisoned by the icy spikes of dried herb stalks. It seemed out of place in this suddenly arctic setting, like so much else at Hawkscliffe. The tall yew hedge which softened the steepness of the slope below me, seemed transformed by its snowy cloak into a huddle of white formless creatures. I hastened silently by lest they turn and snarl and rake me in to store against the long winter ahead.

The only unchanging element was Cora Banks.

"Well, Miss Mackenzie, you didn't leave after all. My, you are full of surprises."

I didn't care for her smile, or rather what passed for one, but then, I never had.

"May I come in, Miss Banks? I have something to ask you before I leave. Harry is taking me down for the four o'clock train."

She raised her sparse eyebrows, but before she could wonder aloud why she had not been informed that the twelve o'clock departure had been advanced to four, there was a clattering commotion outside that drew us both to the window. Cora lifted her drab skirt—had she nothing in her wardrobe other than blue-gray and rusty brown?—and wiped the fogged panes with the edge of it.

"What on earth—"

A large, clumsy cart had begun to slide off the roadway onto the slope, but a great cracking of whips and pushing from behind and mouthing of oaths soon enabled it to resume its plodding journey to the big house.

"I expect it's the new furnace," I explained. "Thorn thought . . . they thought it best it be delivered before the storm worsened."

"Better still if it had been delivered before the storm started. I am a great believer in foresight, Miss Mackenzie, aren't you?"

The mocking glint in her small brown eyes reminded me to take care; this woman had already thrown her lot in with Philo.

"Please, Miss Banks, I haven't much time. An old friend of Charles Quintus's—Duncan Meriwether?—stopped in at Avakian's last week and mentioned a rug, a silk Turkish prayer rug, that used to hang on the wall in the stairwell, where the protrait is now, and I wondered if, when Roxelana returned to Hawkscliffe after Mr. Ramsay's death, she took it away with her." I had stretched the truth in a way my father would not have condoned, but in this case my ends, I decided, justified the means.

Cora stared at me. She might have been a wax figure.

"Harry thought she might," I added in an apologetic tone, hoping to provoke some response.

"I remember Mr. Meriwether. And the rug in question is among my illustrations for the catalog. It is in the suite you have so lately occupied—how could it have escaped your notice?"

"Oh, *that* rug! I should have—"

"Harry told you Roxelana came back? After C.Q.'s death?"

Ah! The bait *was* taken, after all. I could sense her marking time to collect her wits.

"He told me that, among other things. It is hard to believe they were . . . that he was the man responsible for . . ." I shrugged. "It's hard to believe."

"Harry is a foolish, stupid man! He never should have told you that."

"It's untrue, then? He said he heard her quarreling with someone after she left his quarters. He thought it might have been you."

Please say yes, I silently implored. All I need is corroboration, a second witness—is that too much to ask?

Cora's eyes flicked from side to side, like a little brown rat trying to escape a corner. But why? She knew nothing of my relationship to Roxelana; did her loyalty to Charles Quintus Ramsay extend to protecting his image seven long years after his death? Did she really think anyone still cared if his mistress had betrayed him with his grounds-keeper?

The shrill whinnying of a horse close by made us both jump. The freight cart had already departed, and the deepening snow had muffled the hoofbeats heralding this new arrival.

Cora hurried to the window. "Merciful heavens! It's Thornton Ramsay!" she reported. "You must leave at once, Miss Mackenzie!"

"But it can't be," I protested, joining her at the window. "Harry was going to pick up the three of them at . . ."

My words drifted into disbelieving silence. She was right . . . there was no mistaking Thorn's tall, erect posture as he calmed the horse he must have hired from a Hendryk stable. He was hatless, and the snow starring his thick, dark curls gave him the look of a Norse god. Why

267

was he here? What urgent errand could account for his unexpected arrival? Hope leaped up in my heart, but Cora's fierce clutch forestalled my move toward the door.

"No, Miss Mackenzie! I beg you to let him pass by!"

"But why, Miss Banks? What are you trying to tell me?"

She shook her head wildly from side to side, seemingly unable to speak.

Dazed with shock, I gripped her thin shoulders and tried to shake an explanation from her. "Dear heaven, woman, I must know!"

The words poured out of her then, and as I listened, dread washed over my soul. It was Thorn who had been Roxelana's lover, she said. Thorn who had gotten her pregnant, just as he had Louise. It was Thorn that Harry had overheard Roxelana berating, and Thorn—she was sure of it—who had last seen her alive.

"But Harry said—"

"Harry is a drunkard and a braggart. He was merely a straw man, easily used."

Roxelana had left the Hoffman House with Thorn at two in the morning, Duncan Meriwether had told me. Had the rough, heavyset man she had quarreled with there been Harry?

My head was spinning. I couldn't make sense of what Cora was saying. As the flood of words spilled forth, my mind struggled back against its rushing flow to fasten on the phrase that had all but drowned me in dread: it was Thorn, she said, who had last seen Roxelana alive.

"Are you saying he killed her, Miss Banks?" My voice was harsh, my grip on her shoulders rough. "Is that what you're implying? But what motive did he have? He had no claim on C.Q.'s estate!"

Cora's gush of words ceased. The shoulders under my hands tensed.

"His motives have nothing to do with Hawkscliffe, Miss

Mackenzie; they have to do with power: the power of men over women."

My hands relaxed their grip and slipped away.

"Thornton Ramsay has never been able to dominate the women that most attracted him. Roxelana cost him Eloise; Louise, his pride. And their pregnancies . . . Lord only knows what guilty price he paid for those!

"I've seen you look at him, hoping you could coax some warmth from those green eyes. Foolish girl! He is cold as a snake at heart, and as deadly; a man consumed by rage and frustration, Miss Mackenzie, and the roots run deep: his mother—what a charmer she was!—was a gambler. Soon after Thorn started to practice law, which at first was modestly self-supporting at best, his stepfather washed his hands of her. Until she died five years ago, Thorn was never out of debt because of his responsibility for hers. He grabbed at the fees Charles Quintus's estate offered him— you heard him admit as much yourself!"

Cora's hands had fastened on my wrists, and as I looked into her eyes I sensed a link deeper than friendship, stronger than blood: two women against their age-old adversaries, men. Foremost among them for me now was no longer my father but Thornton Ramsay, the man I thought I loved.

My very first day at Hawkscliffe, as Zuleika and I trailed across the terrace in his wake, I suspected even then that our silent docility fulfilled his requirements for females of whatever species. The few brief, wonderful moments since—his grudging admiration, his warm touch, his searing kiss—seemed more the stuff of fantasy than memory when compared with his cold, quiet, deliberately contemptuous dismissal of me at the Hendryk station.

Fear replaced my lingering sense of humiliation, clutching me, distorting the rational pattern of my thoughts. Thorn knew by now I was not docile: and unlike

269

Cora, he knew the threat I posed to the orderly disposition of C.Q.'s estate. He could not take the chance of my asking questions whose answers he was unsure of. He did not know if anyone else had seen Roxelana at Hawkscliffe after C.Q.'s death, or if so, the long dormant realization of the full significance of her return awaited only my prodding to unfurl into the light of day. The answers were seven years buried; his inexplicable return could only mean he intended them to remain so.

I returned Cora's intense gaze. I had to trust her; there was no one else. "Help me, Miss Banks. Tell me what I should do."

CHAPTER TWENTY-ONE

My plea for help was rewarded with a thin-lipped smile and a curious little bob of the head, as if a decision had been made and secretly acknowledged.

She's going to refuse me, I thought helplessly. She's going to—

"Come along, then," Cora at length commanded. "I'll take you to Harry. I'll tell Thorn that Harry . . . I'll say he tried to take advantage of you, and you chose to ride down on the freight wagon."

I nodded. Thorn would accept that, but . . . "Won't Thorn find us there? Or pass us on the way? He'll—"

Cora cut off my panic-stricken babble with a brusque gesture. "I know a shortcut through the spruce grove." She tossed a wooly hooded cape around her shoulders. "From the end of it we can see the stables, Harry's quarters, and the roadway to the main house. We'll simply shelter there until we see Thorn well away on it."

She beckoned me through the pantry to a small door that opened out upon a long, narrow fenced service area masked further by a planting of mountain laurel extending beyond the high palings. As we neared the end of the evergreen shrubbery, I stopped short.

"My bag! I left my bag just inside the main entrance. Thorn will know I'm still here."

Cora whirled, her skirt carving a shallow arc in the snow. "How could you be so—" She broke off, compressing her mouth grimly.

Stupid. That was what she meant to say. *How could you be so stupid, so careless*—but at the time I left my bag there, how could I know?

"I'll take care of it," she said. "Just follow the grade behind the house and up the other side to the spruces. Wait for me there. You can't miss it," she added, waving me impatiently ahead.

I hesitated, loath to relinquish the bag containing Uncle Vartan's journals and his last precious gift.

"I'll send your bag on to you, Miss Mackenzie. You needn't fear for your little emeralds!"

I resented her sneering dismissal of my anxiety about my belongings; I had, however, locked and strapped my bag, and besides, what choice had I?

I recognized the grove of Norway spruce as the one below the precarious cliffside path I had scrambled up to Hawkscliffe's summit and my first meeting with Harry. Few flakes of snow had escaped capture by the long, darkly feathered branches, but enough to blaze the trails crisscrossing the dark maze. On my first visit, I had been aware only of the path illumined by the rays of the setting sun.

I stamped my rapidly numbing feet, regretting I had not warmed them before changing out of my bronze slippers. I hoped we didn't have much further to go.

"Not much further," Cora said when I posed the question to her as she rejoined me. "But don't worry, Thorn won't find your bag," she added, mistaking the reason for my anxious query. "Nobody will."

Why did I fail to find that reassuring? And why, as we debouched from the grove into an unsuspected declivity, did I have a sense of unease? The slope above the other side of the widening gulf must, I was sure, rise to the rough meadow that lay below the stables. How would we cross to it, and where was the shelter Cora had promised?

"Miss Banks, are you sure this is the right path?"

Cora turned. "Oh, yes, Miss Mackenzie, quite sure. Hawkscliffe is my home, you see; I know it well." She smiled serenely before resuming her steady progress, heedless of the snow that, lacking convenient branches to lodge upon, swirled ankle deep around our plodding steps.

"Miss Banks!" I exclaimed a moment later as she halted before a pile of stone that looked crudely cut, almost as if quarried. "Miss Banks," I repeated more calmly, "I've been thinking, as we walked, about your situation, and it seems to me that if—"

"If what, Miss Mackenzie? She smiled again, then continued without waiting for my answer. "If Louise's son had no more claim than mine?"

I stared at her uncomprehendingly.

"My son, Ralph, Kate—you don't mind if I call you Kate, do you?" She stepped closer. "This is a secret I'm telling you," she confided in a stage whisper, "a secret no one else knows. Formality has no place in secrets, does it?"

My mind worked furiousy. *Ralph . . . Philo's Ralph? The boy whose hand she held in the photograph?* "But I thought Ralph was your nephew . . . didn't you tell me his parents were lost in a fire?"

"And so they were. You see, they could have no children of their own. 'It will all work out for the best,' my sister said. *The best!*" Years of frustration and heartache and rage spewed forth in that agonized cry. "Charming Johnny! How I cried when he went off to war; how I

273

mourned his death until my sister learned he had sneaked back and married a prosperous dairy farmer's daughter somewhere upstate. Hah!" she snorted, "Can you see Johnny milking a cow?"

I began edging away, but her hand shot out and clutched my sleeve. "Well, can you?"

I recalled the soldier boy grinning cockily from the faded daguerrotype in her bedroom. "No, Miss Banks, I—"

"Cora," she corrected, shaking my arm like a terrier. "We have no secrets, Kate!"

"No, Cora," I agreed placatingly. "Not Johnny."

"Of course not! But after he milked the farmer and his daughter dry he'd have gone on his merry way, leaving them just as he left my Ralph and me. I couldn't raise my child alone, not without letting the whole world know he was a bastard! First my sister, then foster homes . . . I've waited a long time to have him at home with me, in a home I've *earned*. . . . But no one cares about *that;* no one ever did. Not Charles Quintus, or Louise or Thornton or—"

"Philo cares!" I exclaimed. "That was what I was trying to say. If—"

But Cora was too involved in her own nightmare. "'If, if, if,'" she mocked me. "Don't you understand yet, Kate? All the ifs and might-have-beens are blocked by Louise's bastard son and that Turkish whore's sister!"

I should have been prepared, but I wasn't. Cora's other hand shot out, and she pushed with every ounce of her wiry strength. Even then I might have saved myself, but my toes were by then too numb to grip and help sustain my uncertain balance on the slippery path.

I felt myself falling, plummeting backward through the dense, shrubby growth that masked the edge of the pit I had been insufficiently aware of. Before darkness cloaked my consciousness, I remember thinking of emeralds:

Thorn's eyes, and the modest stones set in gold Cora could not have known about unless she had searched through the bag where I had placed Uncle Vartan's journals for safekeeping.

I could not have been unconscious for long. The snow on the pile of brush that broke my fall bore evidence of disturbance hardly blurred by the steady fall of snow. I scooted cautiously off my twiggy cushion and slowly rose to my feet. My head ached, but except for a twinge in a shoulder and a tear in my coat, I was remarkably undamaged.

I recalled Thorn speaking of Cora's periodic attacks on the Hawkscliffe shrubbery: the brush piled thickly about me would account for fifteen years of diligence. If, however, I had fallen a foot or two more to the left or right, their uneven distribution among the tumble of stone would have resulted in much more serious injury—or worse.

The thought sent bitter bile into my throat. Yet considering the desperate plight in which I found myself, I bleakly wondered if the latter fate might not, in the end, have served me better.

Panic dizzied me. "Thorn!" I shouted, "help me!" My voice, shrill and thin with fear, was unlikely to carry far, but I persisted. "Harry! Please! Someone!" I even called for Cora; then, realizing she would be more likely to hurl a rock upon my head than render assistance, sanity at last prevailed. I saved my waning energy to take stock of my situation.

The roughly square excavation containing me was not large . . . no more than twenty or so feet on a side, I reckoned. Nor was it particularly deep. Perhaps twelve feet at the highest point—except at the rear, where the slope rose steeply above it. But it might as well have been a confidences now instead of kisses.

Thorn confessed how bitterly betrayed he had felt when Louise, after seducing him, had sent him on his way with a sneering review of his fumbling inexperience echoing in his ears. "She was a stunner, Kate; I could hardly believe my good fortune, and I was much too full of myself to question the right or wrong of it."

He shook his shaggy head. "From start to humiliating finish within a week. After it was over I felt weak, sick. I think that's why Eloise's childlike air so appealed to me, Kate. My injured pride couldn't risk another failure, yet I fretted at the celibacy her fears imposed upon me. She resisted all our efforts—mine and her parents'—to set a date for our wedding, yet she demanded constant attention. I was at a loss, completely frustrated—I think that's why Roxelana's mischief-making at the Hawkscliffe fete had such a startling and unanticipated effect: on me, on Eloise, on everyone who witnessed it."

"I'm surprised Louise didn't use her wiles on someone older, more worldly."

"But all she was after was revenge, Kate. She wanted to see if she could attract boys as young as the girls C.Q. habitually debauched. Besides, an older man, one of their set, might have proved hard to discourage once her purpose was achieved."

"Poor Philo was her first choice. He was older, and seemed both more sophisticated and more malleable than his raffish young cousin. But he was unable to rise to the occasion—I think it was then he realized he was . . . different."

So that was the great wrong Philo thought he had done Louise, I realized. How *furious* she must have been!

"Didn't it occur to Louise that she might become pregnant?"

Thorn shrugged. "She never had. I suppose she assumed it was her fault, not my uncle's. Once her hundred, for the walls were stone—as was the floor—and sliced as cleanly as if by a giant's shovel. What saved it from being a drowning pool was a narrow cleft at the downslope end, a natural outlet in the living rock which afforded rainwater and snowmelt an exit.

This must be a quarry, I realized, a small local quarry which had supplied the stone blocks for the mansion's foundation and for the wall I had clambered up my first day at Hawkscliffe. If I had managed it then, I reasoned, why not now? Granted, this wall was higher—*much higher*—but surely saving my life provided more of a spur than a snarling dog!

Time was of the essence. The light, though adequate, could not last much longer—an hour at most. I wobbled toward the lowest section of the wall, my feet numb with cold. Then I remembered the woolen stockings I had thrust into my pocket when I changed my shoes. I reached into my pocket and drew forth a crumpled mass of warm, dry wool, more gladsome to my eyes than a sultan's treasury.

Using a block of stone for a stool, I unbuttoned my boots, stripped the damp hose from my chilled legs, and rubbed my waxy toes with the flannel lining of my coat. As soon as I felt the prickle and pain of blood prodded grudgingly into circulation, I pulled on the warm stockings, tugged on my boots, and confronted the challenge.

Close inspection revealed the sheer gray granite face as less seamless than I had at first thought. I spied here an offset ridge, there a crack, and near the top a stunted evergreen twisting up toward the sky, its gnarled limbs splotched with scanty whorls of densely set needles. Its blind struggle to survive inspired me: those ridges might be wide enough for toes, those cracks deep enough for fingers. I would inch my way up, pushing and hauling from ledge to crevice to the rugged hemlock dwarf whose stout main stem, curling back across the broken edge of my granite cage, would provide me the final, crucial hand-hold to escape.

I set my little fur-trimmed bonnet firmly on my head and retied its broad grosgrain ribbon, the better to protect earlobes already aching from the cold. I eyed my new kid gloves regretfully. They would be ruined, of course, but I dared not attempt the climb bare-handed. I took a deep breath. Wedging my toes upon a narrow offset about fifteen inches above the brush-littered stone floor, I blindly explored with my right hand for a chink, which when finally found stretched my reach to its limit. I pulled myself up, ignoring the sibilant stutter of tearing silk. My pretty new dress could be added to the price of escape.

My dangling foot searched for the next stone rung, found it, and together with a higher handhold, propelled me up another hard-won stretch. And so it went, wider ledges alternating with blade-thin uneven ones, and generous hidey-hole crevices with cracks hardly wide enough to admit the tips of my fingers, until the nearness of the stunted hemlock told me I had gained a height I feared looking down to assess.

My breathing labored and shallow, I flailed wildly for the twisted trunk spiraling out of the cleft above me. The rash effort caused my foot to slip, and my cry of alarm was followed by a spill of snow dislodged from above. *Could it be Thorn?* Dear heaven, let it be! I knew now that his villainy was a wicked creation of Cora's.

"Help!" I cried hoarsely. "Please, oh, please help me!"

I looked up to meet two pairs of yellow eyes. The dogs! My heart pounded fearfully as one of the black-snouted muzzles rippled back in a snarl. I felt hot breath on my outstretched hand, and as I strained to grasp for my salvation, the dog lunged forward, huge paws braced on the broken edge of granite, and snapped viciously at my fingers.

I reached up desperately, heedless of the slashing teeth,

but my hand closed around a trailing branch instead of the stout limb I had blindly sought. The crackle of splitting fibers told me it had given way.

Down I plunged once more. When I recovered consciousness for the second time, I felt a trickle of warmth slid down my cheek. My elegant gloves reduced to tatters, I pressed my exposed fingers to my temple, wincing from the pain caused by the light pressure of their tips. They came away wet with blood.

I lay back, my strength drained by defeat. The falling snow melting and mingling with my blood and tears brought the taste of rust and salt to my trembling, parched lips. The light had begun to fade. Once darkness fell, the cold would slip under my blanket of snow to strum a seductive lullaby upon my languid limbs. My fate would be sealed.

And so would Lance's.

Cora was a woman possessed: with no one to warn him of his danger, she would soon find a way to solve the problem he posed, as she had done—I was sure now—for his mother before him.

Poor sweet, sulky Lance. I could not bear the thought of his bright promise imprisoned in a stone tomb! Well, then, my conscience entreated me, if you don't make the effort to free *yourself*, what of the boy?

Indeed yes, what of the boy!

I lifted my head, groaning as pain stabbed at my temple. The bleeding had stopped, though; and so had my tears. Slowly, I rose to my feet. Except for the gash on my head and the sorry state of my fingers, my situation seemed much the same as before—until I took a tentative step, crying out as my knee all but collapsed beneath me.

I stared up at the little tree; its gnarled stem both beckoned and mocked me. The height I had earlier estimated at twelve feet loomed above me, as distant now as the peak of Mount Ararat. I limped toward the wall.

The ledges and crevices I had negotiated only minutes before seemed as treacherous as an ice field. *If only there were some way to start highter up . . .*

I stumbled against a block of stone half-covered in snow. Of course! Here, scattered all around me, were a giant's building blocks. But it would take, I realized after laboriously hauling the smallest fragments into place, a giant's strength to move them.

Despite this bitter disappointment, my spirits began to rise. I was determined to attack the problem as fiercely as Cora had the shrubbery whose severed branches covered the quarry floor, in some places as high as haystacks.

That was the answer . . . not stone but brush. Managable armfuls of brush stacked carefully like cordwood, one bundle atop and across another, until . . .

I set to work, praying the light would hold. As stack followed stack, my staircase, a bizarre openwork structure, began to take shape. How could I think it capable of taking me up within reach of that decades-anchored tree? Undaunted, I labored on. What choice had I?

I came upon a heap of stouter branches with curiously rounded ends, too short for my purpose. I reached down to throw them aside and became entangled in a length of dark stuff, like the goat hair Baluch weavers use to bind the edges of their rugs. Thin, long black goat hair . . .

I gagged and frantically scraped the hair from my fingers. Not goat hair, but human—and the mottled, oddly shaped bits of wood were human bones.

I crouched to examine my dreadful find. I flicked some leaves from around a grinning skull and found some shreds of cloth. A silver purse frame lay near a bony hand, the rotted remnants of its pouch still harboring a few beads in bright colors—white, blue, red and a luminous patch of yellow . . . yet somehow the yellow didn't look like beads . . . it looked more like . . . I prodded the tattered bits to one side. There it was! Yellow, but shiny . . . almost like gold. . . .

I stumbled back, both hands pressed across my mouth. Yes, it was gold . . . a flat gold disk on a finger no longer plump nor white, that I had last seen curved upon the painted breast of Charles Quintus Ramsay's last mistress.

First Roxelana, then Louise, now me, and next . . . the need to warn Lance—to stop Cora!—was more urgent than ever. The light, I prayed, let the sky hold the light a little longer! I hastily scattered branches over Roxelana's brushy grave; then, ignoring my throbbing knee, and with a lightly balanced step I would not have thought myself capable of, I scrambled up my insubstantial staircase as if those hellish hounds were snapping at my heels.

I stretched up on tiptoe from the final stony ledge. This time, first one hand than the other closed firmly around the ancient trunk. As I slowly, painfully levered myself over the edge to land on my back in a shower of snow upon the path, I became aware of a pair of eyes glowing hotly above me out of the gloom. This time the growl was too low to distinguish above the thudding of my heart. I had tried; I had *really* tried, I thought, as a profound weariness overcame me. I closed my eyes.

I felt dampness on my face—a curious, warm sort of dampness, and then a spot of cold nudging at my neck, poking at my crushed bonnet. It was as if . . . no, not as if, it *was* a tongue, a warm, wet, wonderful tongue!

"Zulu!" I cried. "Oh, Zulu!"

At the sound of my voice, the big dog gave me a final nudge with her nose and plodded off.

"No, Zulu, wait!"

She stopped, turned, and eyed me reproachfully over her massive shoulder. *Come along, then,* she seemed to be saying. *I know it's my job to herd you home, but do come along!*

And so I stumbled back, trudging through snowdrifts that clutched at my coat like the blind beggers of Stamboul, weighing me down, slowing my progress. The spruce grove proved easier going, but the darkness destroyed my sense of direction, and only the gently swaying bulk of Zulu's posterior kept me from straying off on the paths that glimmered whitely among the hulking trees.

At last we gained the slope below the terrace. Narrow rays of light piercing through chinks in the sitting room's curtained French windows traced shining patterns upon the unbroken surface of the snow. I wondered nonsensically if the game abandoned on the table there would ever be played out. *Not by me . . .* my strength was almost gone. *No, not by me. . . .*

Suddenly one of the long curtains was swept aside. A man stood there, tall and still, staring out at the falling snow. It could have been Philo, but somehow I sensed it was Thorn. The strong beam of light released from the room by his motion was like a lighthouse beacon. With Zulu as my sturdy tow, I followed waveringly in her wake toward safe harbor.

Zulu barked once, twice, deep-throated, like the roar of a distant cannon. I heard the clickety-clack of lock and handles being opened and twisted. The long, windowed door opened shudderingly, the glass rattling in its panes.

"Why, it's Zulu!" I heard Thorn exclaim, his deep voice warm with pleased surprise. My savior ambled through the door in a swirl of snow. "Look here, Harry, the old girl's not lost after all."

"Where you been, Zu?" Harry asked roughly, but I sensed his relief. "Pasha et your dinner . . . serves you right," he added gruffly.

"You know I don't like those dogs in the house!"

The window, forgotten, had creaked slowly closed, but not enough to mute the high, thin, grating voice: Cora's voice. I felt the hairs rise on the back of my neck.

I moved forward to the accompaniment of a muffled chorus of male protest.

"Just this once, Cora . . ." "The poor creature's paws are clogged with snow . . ." "Not a smidge of harm in'er, Cora . . ." Then, commandingly: "She stays, Cora!" That was Thorn.

I paused just outside the door, which was still ajar. They were all there, assembled as if for a curtain call, a company ignorant of its audience of one. As I watched, Cora nodded stiffly in reluctant acquiescence and moved through the room proffering sherry from a gleaming silver tray. Her rusty brown dress—the hem of the gray-blue must be wet through from the snow—contrasted starkly with the room's warm, mellow colors. The high polish of the brass fireplace fixtures was a credit to Mary Rose; the firelight coaxed reflections from the softly patinated surface of the Kirman carpet. I hadn't remembered the room being so inviting.

As Cora offered an aperitif to each man in turn, it seemed to me she revolved the tray, ever so slightly, so as to ensure his choice. One glass, set somewhat apart from the others, remained until last. She smiled as she presented it to Lance, a smile so sweet, so tender, so . . . *gratified,* I felt a prickle of unease. Had she smiled thus as she led Lance's mother up the rarely used cliffside path to the sketching platform she had earlier undermined? Had Cora, banking on Louise's expressed curiosity about it, sought her out in the fog and offered to take her there, knowing that the haughty, self-centered woman would have considered such an offer her due? I could almost hear her panting as she scrambled, red-faced from the effort, commanding Cora to slow her pace. Yes, Cora would have smiled then just as she was smiling now, knowing Louise would soon

282

be breathless unto eternity. . . .

Cora does not tolerate rats under her roof, I suddenly recalled Thorn saying to Louise. On a country estate, the only way the absence of rats could be assured was through the frequent use of poison. There would be quantities of it, easily at hand.

I flung the door wide. "Lance, I beg of you!" I cried, gripping the window frame with my gashed fingers, oblivious to the pain. "Do not take that glass!"

Every head whipped toward me, faces contorted by surprise, figures rigid with shock. It was a scene I will take with me to my grave.

Lance's fingers, caught in a plucking motion by my cry, sprang apart, sending the glass tumbling through the air in a shower of honey-colored spirits. Simultaneously the tray slipped out of Cora's hands, bounced off the carpet, and landed off-center on the tile floor, where it oscillated seemingly endlessly, its reverberating clangs shattering our eardrums.

She stood unmoving, a wooden carving with rooted feet, like something out of a dreadful, mythic past. Only her small eyes, fixed on mine, seemed alive. I saw there a hot flicker of emotions: hate, envy, hopelessness, but most of all, madness.

CHAPTER TWENTY-TWO

"Kate! My God! What has happened to you!"

Thorn rushed to my side, swept me up into his arms, and carried me to the wing chair in front of the fire.

"Philo, your sherry!" he commanded tersely as he untied the ribbons of my ruined bonnet, easing it from the clotted blood on my temple with a touch as soft as feathers. *"The sherry, coz!"*

Philo, who had been looking dazedly at the glass in his hand as if wondering how it had arrived there, blinked and rushed to do his cousin's bidding. He placed the rim against my lips.

"It will do you good, Kate," Philo murmured.

The sweet liquid trailed fire down my throat, clearing my dizzied senses. I cried out as Thorn chafed my waxen fingers. He turned them over, revealing the raw, abraded skin.

"Oh, my poor darling," he crooned, as he pressed them to his warm cheek. "I thought you would be in New York by now; instead, you were here all the time, lost in the snow, with only a dog to see you safely home." He unbuttoned my coat and asked Harry to fetch Mary Rose from the kitchen. "Tell her to bring a bowl of warm water and a washrag," he called after him.

"Cora," he began sternly, as he knelt by my side to remove my sodden boots, "I thought you told me—"

"They keep popping up, you see," Cora interrupted in a conversational tone. She had revolved to face my chair—was there no escaping the madness in her eyes?

Thorn looked nonplussed. He had no idea yet what he was dealing with. "Cora?"

"Johnny took me to the fair, to the shooting gallery. He said it would be fun; I could win straw flowers for my bonnet, or a dolly for my . . .

"He showed me how to notch the gun against my shoulder"—she raised an imaginary rifle— "and aim"—one eye closed in a squint— "and shoot the little tin soldiers revolving on the big wheel. They were just like Johnny, only dressed in gray instead of Union blue," she explained earnestly, "and when I hit them they were supposed to clang down and I would win my prize. But no matter how hard I tried, they kept popping up and popping up. . . ."

"I told Johnny it wasn't fair," she said indignantly. "He said my little pings didn't count; I had to hit them square. 'It's only a game, little goose,' he said with that smile of his . . . oh, how I miss Johnny's smile. . . ."

The cousins exchanged alarmed looks. Philo stepped forward and held out his hand. "Come along, Cora. There's been enough excitement for one day . . . wouldn't you like to rest before dinner?"

Cora frowned and backed away. "It wasn't a game, though. He promised me a home—did I tell you that, Kate? So did Charles Quintus, but they kept popping up to take it away from me: Roxelana and Louise and Lance and Thornton. . . ."

She turned to me with a sly smile. "I lied to you a little about Thorn, but it wasn't as big a lie as yours. Oh no! Not as big as yours!"

She started toward me, her upraised fingers contorted into claws.

Thorn swept me tight against his chest. "For God's sake—somebody restrain her!"

Philo and Lance sprang forward, one on either side of her, and seized her arms.

She struggled fiercely for a moment; then, breathing hard, inclined her head in mute surrender. She allowed herself to be led across the room, but resisted her captors briefly at the doorway.

"It wasn't my fault, you know." She stood erect, and her words, pronounced more with regret than self-pity, were addressed to us all, including Harry and Mary Rose who had entered only a moment before.

"I went to Charles Quintus and told him of his whore's betrayal, and he was grateful, as well he should have been. 'Thank you, Cora, no one cares anymore but you.' Those were his very words. And he promised that whatever happened to Hawkscliffe, my little house would always be mine. *Always,* he said. But I should have known," she added in a hushed tone of self-recrimination. "After twenty-four years of C.Q.'s selfishness, I really should have known.

"He grew to miss her, you see—no one else could warm his bed as well as *she.* He accused me of jealous meddling: he said I envied Roxelana's beauty and coveted her place in his life. He said *I* was the traitor, not she, and he told me to leave Hawkscliffe. He told me to clear out and never come back!"

Poor Cora. Her neediness, by its very urgency, had in the end clogged and blocked its satisfaction, but how, I wondered, could she have been expected to see that? Instead, the injustice of her mentor's dismissal had eaten away at her like acid, drop by soul-destroying drop, until there was nothing left but a thin veneer of sanity.

"I couldn't leave then and there, could I? There were the servants to think of, belongings to pack . . . He hadn't been well, you see. All those years of self-indulgence: the liquor consumed, and the quantities of food! I told him he'd pay for it some day,didn't I, Mary Rose?"

Mary Rose, who had been a mere child at the time, nodded a frightened assent: better to fib than provoke her fury.

"I was in the courtyard, clipping some lavender for a keepsake and roses for the house—a last service, don't you know," she added with a deprecating little moue. "The roses were glorious that summer despite the dryness, remember, Philo? I had cut no more than a dozen stems when I heard an odd, muffled sort of cry from the studio. I ignored it, of course: what had I to do with him any longer?"

Cora paused, her neat sparrow's head cocked reflectively to one side. "He came reeling out upon the flagstones, arms revolving like paddlewheels, making this funny, choking noise. Then he fell, just like the little tin soldiers. How Johnny would have smiled! But it didn't keep Roxelana from coming back, and after her came Louise, and after Louise, Kate. . . . They just kept popping up and popping up. . . ."

She searched Philo's appalled face as if seeking his forgiveness for her failure to complete her self-assigned task, then bowed her head, indicating her willingness to leave. Harry, who had taken Lance's place, looked as if he wished he were anywhere else: old friends had no business turning into lunatics.

"But what of my uncle, Cora?" Thorn blurted, asking the question in all our minds. "Didn't you send for a doctor?"

Cora raised her eyebrows. "But there was no need, you

288

see. By stepping carefully around him, I was able to fill my basket—did I mention how unusually fragrant the damask roses were that year? By the time I found enough suitable vases and made my arrangements, minding the thorns as I always do, by the time I had done all *that*, well," she shrugged, "he was dead, of course."

Cora smiled proudly, like an obedient child who has delivered her assigned recitation flawlessly. This time no one delayed her leave taking.

"Oh, Miss Kate, your poor head!" Mary Rose said as she joined Thorn at my side. She gently sponged my temple with a washrag. "I'm afraid the water's cooled off, sir," she added with an apologetic look at Thorn. "What with the excitement and all . . ."

"She tried to kill me," I heard myself saying. "She said *you* were the one to be afraid of, and she led me to the quarry and she pushed me in. I tried to climb out, but Pasha—"

"Hush, my darling, hush now. . . ."

I could feel tears prick my eyes and spill down my cheeks. "Hush," Thorn continued murmuring as he tenderly brushed away my tears with his lips.

But I couldn't hush. "Pasha frightened me and I lost my grip and I fell back down, but I couldn't stay there, could I? Not down there with Roxelana's bones . . ." I shuddered at the memory of the long, dark strands of hair clinging damply to my fingers. "My poor uncle was spared that, at least." The words tumbled out; there was no stopping their disjointed flow. "And after me there was Lance; she told me so, Thorn! I couldn't let her hurt Lance, could I?"

"Have we any sleeping powders, Mary Rose?"

"I have some right here," Philio replied upon re-entering the room. "Agnes is helping Harry with Cora," he explained in answer to the question in Thorn's eyes.

"They've put her in that spare room between Mary Rose and Agnes; I thought a strong sleeping draught would keep her calm until morning."

"But Thorn," I said urgently up into his face. His eyes were as warm and green as summer. "Roxelana—"

"That, too, can wait till morning. For now, it's up to bed with you. Mary Rose, will you please warm some milk to mix the powders in?"

Once again he swept me up into his arms. He carried me down the hall and up the stairs, his slow, steady pace lulling me to the edge of sleep, where reality and dreams, vying for the same space, drift one into the other. By the time Mary Rose arrived with the glass of milk, Thorn had already undressed me and tucked the satin-covered down coverlet into a cozy nest around me.

"I've seen a woman's body before," I heard him say, as if from a great distance, as he coaxed me to drink.

"I've no doubt of it, sir!" was her flustered reply, and the deep chuckle that followed was the last sound I heard before sleep overtook me.

I woke in fright during the night from a dream that crumbled into meaningless fragments as I opened my eyes. All that remained was the terrifying sense of falling, as if from a great height.

My head ached; my knee throbbed, but the warmth that pervaded me from head to toe filled me with joyful wonder, although at first I could not imagine why. I sat up and looked curiously around me. These walls were not stone, and the dim light I perceived was not the cold, gray light of a snowy aftrnoon, but the warm pink of roses.

Cedarwood and roses . . . the warmth had once again coaxed forth the potpourri's heady scent; as for the light . . . I looked towards the richly upholstered chaise. The rose-painted lamp shed its mellow glow upon a figure sprawled in sleep. Thorn's long legs trailed off the end of the small settee; his dark, shaggy head, propped by one of the pillows from my bed, had slid awkwardly to one side ensuring, I realized with tender distress, a stiff neck by morning. Then, reassured by Thorn's stalwart presence, I slid gratefully back into sleep.

When I next awoke, sunlight dappled the gauzy bed curtain and the walls beyond. I turned my head to find Mary Rose's anxious blue eyes inches from my own. We both blinked.

"Oh, Miss Kate! You were sleeping as if . . . I was beginning to wonder if you would ever . . ."

Poor Mary Rose! She seemed unable to avoid an image of death. "Good morning, Mary Rose," I said,

"But that's just it, Miss Kate! It's after noon, and Mr. Thorn wondered if you were hungry."

Hungry? Famished was more like it. Except for a dim memory of something warm and milky and gritty, I hadn't eaten in over twenty-four hours.

"Tell Mr. Thorn I could eat the proverbial horse."

"Tell him yourself," Thorn said, entering the room with a tray well supplied with breakfast treats and, joy of joys, a steaming pot of tea. "Agnes said to tell you she baked these flaky twists especially for you—something nutty, I believe—"

"Pecan, sir," Mary Rose supplied.

"Just so. Pecan swirled with maple syrup, still warm, of course. And look here, Kate, a whole orange! Nothing like being on the right side of the cook."

Mary Rose giggled, bobbed a curtsy, and left, closing the door discreetly behind her.

"Do you think I might have a good-morning kiss before—"

He was too late. I had defiantly popped a bit of pecan

291

twist into my mouth, and a few buttery flakes of it were subsequently snared from my lips by Thorn's warm greeting.

"I still don't understand, Thorn," I said a few thoroughly kissed moments later. "I know now it wasn't villainy that brought you back early to Hawkscliffe yesterday, but what did? What could have been more important than the hearing at the courthouse?"

Thorn rose from his perch on the bed. He walked to the window and stood with his hands clasped loosely behind his back. He was dressed casually in country fashion today; the rough tweeds and polished, well-worn boots suited his tall, spare, muscular figure and dark good looks. He turned to me, and fingered his chin, then threw his arms wide.

"Conscience, Kate. Guilt. Regret. All that and more. You were so brave at the station. This little bit of a thing facing down three—four, counting Harry—insensitive *nincompoops!* As if we all didn't know you well enough by then to be sure you were telling the truth."

"I knew the truth would be hard to accept, Thorn," I said quietly, trying to make it easier for this proud man.

"Hard, yes, but not impossible!" He ran one hand over his dark curls. "You see, Kate, it isn't easy for a man to admit a woman might have more integrity than he. Especially this man. Louise, and then Roxelana— But that's beside the point," he exclaimed, breaking off his own explanation. "There are no excuses for the shabby way I treated you. None.

"I watched as you pulled yourself up into the carriage. You looked so frail, so forlorn, so . . . *abandoned,* yet so purely lovely . . . I knew right then that life without you was not worth living, but I had to put my own life in order before I could think of persuading you to share yours. It was time to tell a few truths of my own: to you, of course— that's why I rode alone up to Hawkscliffe, intending to intercept you—but for starters, to Lance."

"To Lance?"

"Lance is my son, Kate. That's why Louise came to my room the night before she . . . She threatened to expose me as an unprincipled seducer, and I couldn't . . . my friends and my clients could accept an illigitimate son, but a son as a result of my seduction of my aunt? It smacks of incest, you see—not a very savory notion, Kate."

Your seduction of *Louise*? Good heavens, Thorn, you couldn't have been more than eighteen—certainly she was the aggressor! And how could there be incest with no blood tie between you?"

"After so many years, Kate, who would bother to work out the arithmetic, much less the relationship? No, no, I can accept dislike, but sniggering contempt? It was much easier to heap contempt upon *you*."

"But what about Philo's claim on the estate?"

Thorn shrugged. "I told you I had no valid excuses. I knew Philo coveted Hawkscliffe, but I couldn't see that he would suffer much if it went to Lance instead."

What about Ralph's suffering? I wondered, thinking of Philo's plan for his sick friend—but Thorn didn't know about Philo and Ralph, I realized, nor did I know how sympathetic he would be if he had.

"Philo and I have never been close," he added. "Besides, there was always the chance Roxelana would turn up, wasn't there? Until she was declared dead, the question of who would actually be declared the principle heir remained safely academic. Poor Philo! The prize one truth gave him back has been taken away again with another."

"Did I tell you it was Harry who told me Roxelana returned after Charles Quintus's death? It seems they were lovers. He thought she was coming back to him and that as her sister, I might be interested to know that."

"Good old Harry," Thorn muttered. "He has the sensitivity of a warthog."

I smiled ruefully. "It never occured to Harry that the timing of her return had any significance. She came back, he said, and then he overheard her arguing with someone—it could have been you or Philo or Cora, he said. He neither knew or cared what happened after that."

"My, what hornets you stirred up! You know only too well the way Cora chose to soothe her stings; as for me, Lance and I have established a cordial, if somewhat tentative, relationship, and Philo has bowed to the inevitable."

"My bag!" I exclaimed. "All my papers are in my bag, Thorn! Cora hid it, and unless I can find it, Philo need not bow to anything at all."

Thorn hit his forehead with his palm. "Damn me for a fool! It all seemed such a fait accompli I forgot to tell you: Philo found your bag pried open next to the furnace. Apparently last evening's little post-dinner sherry party interrupted Cora's plan to stoke the furnace's appetite. It's in here, somewhere, Kate," he muttered, "Mary Rose put it away for you—"

"Philo found my bag open . . . my uncle's journals? And he didn't . . . ?"

"I don't think it ever crossed his mind, Kate."

"Thank God for sherry," I said, thinking how close my bag had come to being destroyed. Then, as what Thorn had told me made connection with other bits and pieces, I came to a startling conclusion. I looked up at him. "Lance's sherry wasn't poisoned, was it? I thought when I saw that smile of quiet triumph on Cora's face. . . ." I broke off with a shudder.

Thorn sat down again beside me and hugged me close. "No, it wasn't. Cora knew by then that I had acknowledged Lance as my son, so Philo was the clear victor. That smile you saw was in celebration of *your* removal from the field, not Lance's."

"What will happen to her, Thorn?"

Thorn refilled my cup with tea before answering. "It already has, Kate. She's dead."

I couldn't believe my ears. *"What?* How could that have happened?"

"The snow stopped by daybreak; we all thought it best to remove Cora from Hawkscliffe for proper treatment as soon as possible. Harry hitched that nervy little chestnut to the cutter—he said the pony wouldn't go in snow—and Cora seemed calm enough. She was still a bit groggy from the powders she was given last night, and Agnes told me she gave her two more packets with her morning tea, just in case.

"I guess the cold must have revived her. Just as they rounded that curve above the pond, Cora grabbed for the reins. The mare shied and sidestepped up the slope, all but turning the cutter over. Harry was thrown out, and the sudden, unbalancing removal of his weight sent the horse in a panicky plunge straight into the pond, cutter and Cora and all. The mare is none the worse for her icy dunking; Cora, however, drowned."

"I can't say I'm sorry," I said after a brief silence.

"Nor I, my love," he murmured against my cheek. "Nor I." He turned my hand over, exposing the bruised and tender flesh. The quick pulse springing from his fingers throbbed like a whisper against my listening palm.

"Cora's accident is the reason why Philo went into the cellar," Thorn continued soberly. "Lance and I went down with Harry to summon the police; as far as they're concerned, her death was an accident, pure and simple. We saw no point in . . . *complicating* the situation."

Misadventure, that's what they'll call it, I mused. *Just like Louise, only this time it's the truth.*

"Since Philo was the only one left to deal with the furnace, I told him he was responsible for keeping the house warm enough for you. By now I expect he is wondering how many sacrifices he should be expected to make for you, but he rallied like the gentleman he is."

I nodded wordlessly. Philo deserved more than a kind word as a reward. I had some serious thinking to do.

"I will send Mary Rose up later to draw you a hot bath," Thorn said as he lifted the tray away, "but first, you have another visitor waiting to see you."

"A visitor, now?" I yawned. A hot bath sounded much more appealing.

"It's Lance, Kate. He has something for you, and I really think . . . See him, Kate; it's important to him."

"Oh . . . all right, then."

Lance sidled in, nodding as Thorn warned him not to overstay his welcome. He had a large covered basket slung over one arm.

"Well, Lance. You look a bit like Little Red Riding Hood."

Lance's anxious expression was succeeded by a grin. "Except that you're a lot prettier than a grandmother would be. Kate . . ." He cleared his throat. "That day in your shop? What I said . . . my behavior . . . I'm sorry, Kate. You were right about Mother, you know. The more I thought about what she said about you, and what you said about her—"

I threw up my hands, cutting short his painful apology. "Grief does strange things to people. After my uncle died, I was suspicious of all his old friends in the trade, sure that their smallest kindnesses were done for some venal purpose. Time proved us both wrong, Lance; all I want is for us to be friends again. Now, tell me what you have in that mysterious basket."

"There weren't any flowers to be had, and I couldn't see giving you any of what passes for gifts in Hendryk: souvenir trinkets for the riverboat trade, mostly—cheap pillows stuffed with balsam, and crude, lumpish carvings of bears—you know the sort of thing. Then, as we were passing a butcher shop—"

"A sausage, Lance? Have you brought me a spicy sausage or, let me guess, a jar of pickled pigs' feet to keep me on my toes?"

Lance laughed. "Oh, Kate! I *am* glad we're friends again. I just hope you won't eat this little fellow for supper."

Lance folded back the basket's lid, and out popped the orange and white head of the fluffiest kitten I had ever seen.

Mee-eww, it cried, then plopped out upon the comforter, wobbled up the hills and valleys created by my body, and curled in a purring, furry crescent beneath my chin.

"Oh, Lance," I breathed.

"D'you like him? 'Cause if you don't—"

"Like him? I *adore* him! I'll call him . . . I know, I'll call him 'Muhibbi'—that means 'beloved friend.'" I gently stroked the tiny creature. "'Hibby' for short."

"'Beloved friend.' That's nice, Kate."

"And so are you." I yawned again. "Thank you, Lance, but I'm afraid—"

"Not another word. I'll leave you two chums to get to know one another better. Any messages?"

"Please ask Mary Rose to wake me for a bath at four, and if Philo could join me in the library at half past five, I would be most grateful."

"Downstairs? Are you sure that's wise?"

"Both wise and necessary. Don't fret, Lance; a hot bath will soothe away what remains of my aches and pains—what I need most at this point is a nourishing meal. Tell Agnes—and Thorn—I'll be down for dinner."

My bath was sheer heaven. Mary Rose agreed that the swelling around my knee had subsided remarkably, and the balm she gently applied to my hands soothed the tenderness to an insignificant prickle.

"Whatever shall I wear?" I cried. It amused me to find I was not exempt from my sex's small vanities. "You know, Mary Rose, after Eve ate the apple, I expect that's the first thing she said to Adam."

Mary Rose giggled. "I mended the pretty silk and cashmere dress you were wearing, Miss Kate. It won't bear close inspection, but the men won't notice." She opened the nearest wardrobe. The few garments I'd brought with me swung freely in the ample space; beneath them stood my bag. "I put that big black book and your jewelry bag back inside, just as I found them," Mary Rose said, correctly interpreting my anxious expression.

She lifted out my Thanksgiving dress. "I stitched it here, where it tore under the arm, and I sponged the hem and back of the skirt. Your lovely coat is ruined, but this—"

"It will do very well, Mary Rose, thank you," I said distractedly, "but what has happened to Roxelana's clothes?" The Paris dresses and tailormade walking suits and riding habits that yesterday had left no room for my bag were gone. Their padded hangars, now hanging askew, were all that remained.

"I found them in the dustbin this morning, miss. Miss Banks must have bundled them in, for I never did—never *would*, not without a by-your-leave. I was thinking to take them home with me—the styles are out of fashion now, but my mum's clever with a needle, and those fabrics would make up into something grand for me and my sisters, but—"

"Take them with my blessing, Mary Rose," I said, realizing that it was my permission she now required.

I had counted on Cora's profound sense of her elevated station to stay her hand from such menial chores as turning out a room. I should have known she could not resist the impulse to rid Hawkscliffe of Roxelana's traces even before the Ramsays returned to pronounce her legally dead.

She had emptied the wardrobe and found my bag beside it—which tipped her to my intended return—and Uncle Vartan's journals inside. The scene played itself out in my mind's eye: first, a curious look at an incomprehensible page or two, then the concluding section in English—how could she resist reading it?—and finally the brooding return to her cottage to bide her time. What an astonishing stroke of good fortune my unexpected arrival there must have seemed!

And no wonder the suite, lukewarm when I arrived from New York, had been so frigid when I returned to change my shoes. Her sense of duty had not allowed her to waste the faulty furnace's heat on a room she had no intention of my reoccupying that fateful day.

Philo entered the library with the rug catalog portfolio under his arm. His braid-edged lounge suit, snowy shirt, and silk foulard Ascot tie indicated his desire to treat our interview seriously. The firelight flickering across the steadier glow from the table lamps made it difficult to read his expression. The brief, light clasp of his hand was noncommittal.

"How lovely you look this evening, Kate. Those colors become you, and how nice to see the color back in your cheeks!"

"Artificially aided, I confess. Roxelana's dressing table is well supplied with intriguing powders and pastes. I couldn't resist a bit of experimentation."

"Successful experimentation."

"Thank you, Philo. Please do sit down. I see you have brought the catalog with you; we can discuss that later."

Philo chose one of a pair of armchairs placed at an angle

299

near the large fireplace. He crossed one blue-tweed-covered knee over the other and regarded me with wary expectancy.

"Thorn tells me that when you found my open bag next to the furnace, the thought of hurling it into the flames, together with my uncle's papers, never crossed your mind."

Philo looked away from me into the fire. "Thorn said that? Oh my." He shifted uncomfortably and recrossed his legs. "Oh my," he repeated in a faint voice.

"It would have crossed *my* mind, Philo."

Philo's face whipped back, his expression startled. My composure must have reassured him, for he allowed a sheepish grin to take shape.

I reached over to tap his knee. "It's more to your credit to have resisted temptation than not to have experienced it, you know.

"But enough of *that.* I'm a fortunate woman, Philo. I enjoy rugs and the selling of them, and I'm told I have a head for business. But it takes time to establish a reputation in my trade, especially for a woman, and I have competitors eagerly awaiting my slightest misstep. In short, I haven't the need for Charles Quintus Ramsay's estate, nor sufficient time to devote to Hawkscliffe's dire needs."

Philo's polished shoe had ceased its nervous swinging. His attention was absolute. The only sound was our breathing and the crackle of the fire.

"It is my intention, Philo, to turn Hawkscliffe into a private museum, and dedicate the funds from the estate, as well as any the museum may generate, to its maintenance.

"What I wished to see *you* about, what I am *hoping*, is that you and your friend Ralph—forgive me, I do not know his surname—"

"Watkins, Ralph Watkins." He sounded dazed.

300

"That you and Ralph Watkins will agree to become the curators. I realize Mr. Watkins is not very strong now, but at least he could remain in residence to keep a watchful eye on things. Perhaps in time—"

Philo got to his feet and leaned over my chair, his hands clenching the arms on either side of me. "You're serious about this, Kate? This is not some ghastly joke?"

I looked up into his eyes. "I never joke about business, Philo. This is not a one-way street, you know. I wish to preserve Hawkscliffe not only as a gallery for your uncle's paintings, but to display the superb rugs my uncle chose for him. I can accomplish that only with the help of knowledgeable people, people I can trust."

I rose and whirled, my hands upraised. "This should have been yours, Philo, don't you think I know that? You love Hawkscliffe; my only pleasure in it lies in securing Vartan Avakian's fame, via the Hawkscliffe collection, as the peerless connossieur I knew him to be."

We smiled at each other. "Well, what do you say, Philo?"

Philo grasped my hand so warmly I had to bite my lip to keep from crying out. "Done and done, Kate!"

He held me at arm's length, his gray eyes dancing with delight and admiration. "This time I *am* going to kiss you—and Thorn can go to the devil!" He bussed my cheeks soundly in turn.

"Speaking of your cousin, shall we join him and Lance? Tell them the news?" I linked my arm in his.

"Let's do!" he exclaimed. We turned to leave. I had asked Agnes to chill a couple of bottles of champagne; it would be a while before I could enjoy a glass of sherry.

"Kate, we're forgetting the catalog—what are your plans for that?"

"The proceeds to Hawkscliffe, posthumous credit to Cora for her watercolors . . ." My voice faltered; Philo patted my arm reassuringly. "But *my* name," I continued firmly, "and mine alone, on the cover."

Philo leaned close. "Think of the business it will bring," he whispered.

"Oh, I have, Philo, indeed I have." I grinned up at him. "You have the makings of a rug dealer after all, my friend."

CHAPTER TWENTY-THREE

The dinner that followed the announcement of my plans for Hawkscliffe turned out to be something of an occasion, thanks to Mary Rose.

A cover of heavy cream-colored lace had been placed on top of the usual damask cloth, and a luxuriant sprawl of evergreen sprays sparked with red-berried black alder stems graced the center of the table.

"Rushing the season a bit, aren't we, Mary Rose?" commented Philo, a hint of reproach in his voice.

"Only three weeks, sir," Mary Rose replied with quiet dignity. "I thought it might be nice to make things a bit festive, in honor of Miss Kate and Mr. Lance still being here."

Clearly, she meant more than our just being here at Hawkscliffe.

"A capital idea!" Thorn exclaimed; then, as Mary Rose served us with no trace of her former harried air, he murmured, "What a difference a day makes, eh, Kate?"

Indeed it did. As I told Philo later, while sipping our

coffee in the sitting room, we had the nucleus of his staff already in residence.

"Mary Rose as housekeeper?"

"I think so, and she has a houseful of sisters in Hendryk any of whom might be taken on to fill her present position."

"You have no concerns about nepotism?" Thorn asked idly.

"Elder sisters are notorious taskmasters," I answered. The silence that followed charged my words with unintended irony. The only person Roxelana had mastered was Charles Quintus. "Or so I have been told," I added dryly

"Do you think I might visit, Cousin Philo?" Lance asked. "Hawkscliffe is such a jolly place—even jollier now that I won't have any responsibility for it."

Thorn and I exchanged amused glances.

"I'd like that, Lance. I might even put your talents to good use. I have some ideas for announcements, posters for the steamers, that sort of thing."

Lance rolled his expressive eyes. "And here I thought I would be purely ornamental . . ."

He allowed his words to trail off into a theatrical sigh, which caused Zulu to raise her massive head in vague alarm. Her continued presence in the house now assured, she preempted the space in front of every fireplace, depending on where the company assembled. I had considered taking the huge dog back to New York with me, but the thought of Mariam's indignation dissuaded me. Even a kitten was sure to provoke complaint.

I reached down to ruffle Zulu's ears and was rewarded with a lazy, thundering thump of her feathered tail that caused us all to smile.

How nice this was, I thought, feeling relaxed for the first time since crossing Hawkscliffe's threshold those many weeks ago. How pervasive Cora's pinched and bitter spirit had been! The chains of tension forged in the heat of Cora's rage had crippled our sensibilities far more than any imagined sound of Roxelana's ghostly laughter.

My expression must have been as pensive as my thoughts, for Thorn reached out to clasp my hand warmly. The light in his eyes reflected the glow in my heart. I wished I could hold this moment forever, as if preserved in amber. Thorn's gentle words, his fond embraces and his kisses—I dared not think them more than the natural, emotional response of a strong male to a female in distress. Before long, I would return to my world and he to his. In the meantime . . .

"It's snowing again," Lance said from the window. "Anyone for backgammon?"

"Don't forget we promised to help Harry install the new furnace tomorrow," Philo reminded his relatives. "I suggest we retire early and store up our strength."

I burst out laughing. "Good heavens, Philo! The lengths householding is driving you to! Are you sure you do not wish to change your mind?"

"Not a bit of it, Kate! I'm just discovering what varied talents I possess. Who knows but that boiler tending will prove to be chief among them?"

I was awakened in the night by a skritchity-scratching I could not at first identify. I lighted the lamp by my bed. Elfin footprints trailed palely out of the bathroom and across the green silk of the prayer rug. *What on earth . . .*

Hibby scrambled up the counterpane, his tiny orange paws powdered with gray. Clever kitten! He had already discovered the ash-filled pan I had placed under the basin.

Everyone was learning new tricks, I mused as I got out of bed and tossed my robe around me. The room was warm, I had slept most of the day. Perhaps I could put the hours until dawn to good use.

I wondered if Cora had emptied the other wardrobe too. *Please not*, I prayed, surprised by my fervency. They were only gaudy costumes, after all. I swung open the doors.

The silken garments billowed out, a kaleidoscope of color, the paste jewels studding the brassieres and veils and embroidered vests sparkling like the genuine article. Trickery, yes, but magic lay in it.

I recalled the drawings on the wardrobe shelf above me, and Roxelana's erotic playlets recorded in journals whose homely black-pebbled leather exterior was identical to Uncle Vartan's, confirming the wisdom of not trying to tell a book by its cover.

I lifted one down and took it with me back to the bed, where I perched and turned the pages slowly, ignoring Hibby's stalking of my fingers.

My breathing shallowed as I read the detailed stage directions and traced the tangled limbs of the roughly sketched figures that accompanied them. Was this possible? I wondered, staring at one particularly complicated pairing. Would one want to attempt it even if it were?

I put the book aside. The room seemed stifling. I shed my wrap and crossed restlessly to Roxelana's dressing table. I took out the carved box containing the *zil* and slipped them on my fingers. Their clear, pure, brassy ring caused Hibby's tiny ears to prick.

This is me, Katherine Mackenzie, not Roxelana; these are my tricks, not hers, and Charles Quintus Ramsay no longer sleeps in that bed at the end of the corridor.

The kitten's bright eyes followed the increasingly bold and sensuous movement of my hands and arms. *Roxelana may have been C.Q.'s last lover, but tonight Thorn Ramsay will be my first.*

Thorn had left the doors to both suites ajar and the corridor dimly lighted, in case I awoke in pain or fright during the night. I stole barefoot down the long hall, each step a soft tinkle of silver as the azure silk *chalvar* I had first chosen weeks before whispered against the exquisitely worked anklets I had found in amongst the ostentatious glitter in Roxelana's jewelry case.

The heavy door slid open, then drifted closed with a protesting groan. I heard a sigh and the sound of bedcovers tossing. I slid my hand down the sleek curve of the rosewood bed, imagining it the muscular curve of Thorn's long thigh against my longing palm.

Coals glowed red behind the elaborately scrolled firescreen; a guttering flame flared up, throwing spears of hot light into the shadows. I slid the *zil* onto my fingers and began to dance.

"Who . . . what . . . ?" Thorn's words, slurred with sleep, could hardly be heard under the rhythmic bell-like ching of the cymbals. I undulated provocatively before his astonished eyes. I had chosen not to wear a veil.

"Kate?" His voice was incredulous. "Kate, is that you?"

"Today I was Kate, and tomorrow I will be again, but tonight I am your slave, your concubine, your oda-lisque. . . ." I whirled away from him, my hair billowing like a cloud, burnished by firelight.

All at once I became aware of Thorn standing tall beside me. His hands reached out, and as he urged me gently toward his bed, my fingers stilled their provocative dance. Only the echo of the *zil's* brassy chime accompanied my willing surrender. I sank down, as softly pliant as the ivory linen sheets that received me.

"What is it you want of me, Kate?" he asked.

"As much . . . or as little . . . as you wish to allow me. One night—"

He placed a long finger against my lips. "Not enough," he said. "Always, or not at all."

Always. I closed my eyes, unable to breathe, afraid I might shatter this wonderous dream. "Always, then," I murmured, opening my eyes to an even more wonderous reality. "Oh, yes, my darling, always . . ."

He knelt over me and removed my gossamer pantaloons, my beaded vest and brassiere with a swift, caressing deftness that thrilled me. As each garment slipped to the floor, I felt softer, rounder, smoother, more purely female than I had ever thought possible. The violet scent I had stroked across my skin breathed forth, springlike, denying the wintery reality of the season.

As he bared my body to his questing fingers I was no longer Kate Mackenzie or Kate Avakian: the mysteries he was about to teach me were inaccessible through bookish learning or rug lore. Here, in this bed I had freely sought, I was Thorn's Kate, and I felt magnifed by his desire.

My head lifted up, then fell back to receive his kiss upon my throat. My breasts felt as full as peonies, their buds aching to blossom. My mouth eagerly accepted his, my untutored tongue a hummingbird darting in to sup his honey-sweetness.

Shyly my hands explored the unfamiliar map of his body. Roughness and sleekness informed my curious palms, and I boldly claimed the hot column of flesh that rose from the delta of his thighs.

Instinctively I arched my back and opened my body to his gentle thrust, a moment of pain soon lost in the glory of our union.

The snow, a soft whisper against the windowpanes, continued to fall. "A perfect night for a sleigh ride," Thorn whispered as he glided down my snowy flanks and explored my hills and valleys. "My beautiful ice maiden," he groaned. But again and again I melted in his hot embrace.

Even the hottest flames subside. Dawn found us still entwined, as befits new lovers, but our mouths exchanged condition could no longer be concealed, I think she rather enjoyed throwing it up to him, especially when she realized he would never publicly admit he had either been cockolded or was unable to father a child. In fact, until Roxelana came along, the situation suited her very well. She had her independence, her respectability, but how she envied the favors C.Q. showered on your cousin!"

I looked pained.

"Well, she was, you know."

"Tell me, Thorn, what of Roxelana's pregnancy? You seemed shocked I knew of it, and Cora implied . . ."

Thorn gave me one of his old sardonic sidelong glances. "I can imagine what Cora implied. The truth is, I was deeply in debt, thanks to my mother's gambling, and I foresaw nothing but years of scrimping ahead of me. That's why I drew up C.Q.'s bizarre will. His health was failing, and I anticipated the fees my executorship would bring me. But it all depended upon Roxelana remaining his heir. Her adventures were common gossip by then—if they reached his ears, I knew C.Q. might destroy his will and wash his hands of me for not warning him against drawing it in the first place. That was the kind of man he was, Kate.

"Friends told me she'd been seen at the Hoffman House with an unsavory-looking character—her taste ran to ruffians. I intercepted them, threatened her lover with an entirely illegal bluff, and bundled Roxelana out by the scruff of her neck. She told me she was pregnant. It was hard to convince her C.Q. would turn her out, but that's when she must have bullied Vartan into supplying funds for an abortion. According to what Harry told you, she sowed her wild oats closer to home after that. When the next crisis inevitably occured, C.Q. died before he could decide *what* he wanted to do about his will, and I was free—or so I thought."

He laughed. "By the time *we* met, my practice had

310

grown and my debts were finally paid, no thanks to C.Q.'s estate. The last thing I needed was Hawkscliffe hanging like a millstone around my neck."

Millstone and albatrosses . . .

"Thorn?"

"Hmm-mm . . ." His fingers began to trace lazy patterns on the tender inner surface of my thighs.

"Thorn, my plans for Hawkscliffe—you're sure you approve?"

"Approve? My darling, I'm ecstatic! Let Philo cope with balky furnaces and cracked tiles. All we have to do is decide whose house we'll live in after we're married, yours or mine."

"Thorn? Did you and Roxelana ever . . ."

Thorn shifted above me and cradled my face between his hands. "No, Kate—never. She had nothing I wanted, and lacked everything I did. She had no honor—" he kissed one of my eyelids, "—and no pride," he kissed the other. "God knows, Louise was greedy: but Roxelana was truly monstrous."

"Thorn?"

He groaned, and addressed the gold fleur-de-lis above my head. "Will the woman never stop talking?"

"Did you say 'after we're married'?"

"Yes, Kate."

I smiled up into his eyes and found I had nothing further to say.

EPILOGUE

I sold my dear house to Krikor, my shop manager, for a price well below its market value. I knew my profit would be realized in the peace of mind his loyal supervision of the business would afford me when I was distracted by maternal duties.

Thorn's spacious townhouse fronting on Gramercy Park has proved the perfect place to raise an active little boy. Vartan—the name was Thorn's suggestion—turned three just last week. His babble of Armenian—courtesy of Mariam, who delights in being his nursemaid—bemuses his father, but as I keep reminding him, think how useful it will be someday in the business!

Lance makes his home with us—when he is home at all, that is. He is a student in the new school of architecture at Columbia University, and his professors tell us he shows considerable promise. Thorn wishes he took life a bit more seriously, but I enjoy his nonsense, and little Vartan adores him.

Philo and Ralph are well settled in at Hawkscliffe. A

ride up to the fabled mansion via charabanc has become quite the thing to cap off a day's outing on the river, and Philo has developed a flair for theatrics in his weekend role as tour conductor. The ladies, he reports, relish their titillating peek at Roxelana's suite and wardrobe; the menfolk are content to ogle her portrait and dig each others' ribs. Philo did, however, draw the line at Lance's scheme to enliven the tour by engaging a girlfriend of his to model the harem costumes. Smacked of the carnival, Philo said. Thorn, who had insisted I take the azure ensemble—and one of violet-toned gray as well—solemnly agreed.

The tours have been modestly profitable, but the Hawkscliffe rug catalog earned nothing but prestige, the printing and binding costs having proved shocking. Charles Quintus's estate continues to be the major source of the funds supporting Hawkscliffe, recently augmented by a handsome sum thanks to Ralph Watkins's discerning eye.

Ralph, whose real parentage is a secret I have shared with no one, not even my darling husband, has prospered in the clear, cool air above the Hudson, enough to resume his work on a limited basis. While cleaning C.Q.'s canvases, he kept being drawn to the begrimed forgeries C.Q. had acquired in Europe and hung as a private joke in the dining room.

Although Philo cautioned him not to waste his energy on dross, his absence over a fortnight's time to attend to a press of curatorial business at the Metropolitan left time hanging heavy on the younger man's hands. When Philo returned, three of the ten fakes were revealed to have been overpainted on older, much finer works. Needless to say, I lost no time giving my permission to consign them to auction at Duveen's in London, where the winning bids totalled well into six figures.

This windfall allowed us to hire another groundsman, a

young, energetic, sober fellow whose healthy good looks and kind heart soon won Mary Rose's heart. Whether or not Harry Braunfels' was broken in the process I neither know nor much care. I suspect that by now his heart is too pickled to do more than bend.

The young people are living in Cora's cottage. Mary Rose—who has developed into a splendid housekeeper—has brought the second of her sisters up from Hendryk as nursemaid for their expected baby, but until Agnes retires I anticipate no need for a third.

Thorn and I rarely visit Hawkscliffe. We are busy with our family, our work, and our social life in town, and although Thorn and Philo are on good terms now, they are too unlike ever to become good friends. I brought almost nothing away with me: the wisps of silk chiffon and brocade I mentioned; the very old Turkish village rugs from the top floor—my scholarly monograph on them is almost ready for publication, and the brass *zil*. Its pure ringing sound can be heard now and again from behind our closed doors.

The crystal evil-eye amulet—the one Uncle Vartan enclosed in his last letter to me?—lies in the box with the others I collected so long ago in Constantinople. The Ottoman gold ring was buried with Roxelana's bones, removed from the quarry the spring following the snowy December day I found them. They rest in a hidden hollow under a stone marked with her true name, Araxie Avakian: no more, but in deference to my uncle's reverence for family, no less. The only cries that mourn her passing are those of the migrating hawks that gave her splendid folly its name.

FIERY ROMANCE

CALIFORNIA CARESS   (2771, $3.75)
by Rebecca Sinclair

Hope Bennett was determined to save her brother's life. And if that meant paying notorious gunslinger Drake Frazier to take his place in a fight, she'd barter her last gold nugget. But Hope soon discovered she'd have to give the handsome rattlesnake more than riches if she wanted his help. His improper demands infuriated her; even as she luxuriated in the tantalizing heat of his embrace, she refused to yield to her desires.

ARIZONA CAPTIVE   (2718, $3.75)
by Laree Bryant

Logan Powers had always taken his role as a lady-killer very seriously and no woman was going to change that. Not even the breathtakingly beautiful Callie Nolan with her luxuriant black hair and startling blue eyes. Logan might have considered a lusty romp with her but it was apparent she was a lady, through and through. Hard as he tried, Logan couldn't resist wanting to take her warm slender body in his arms and hold her close to his heart forever.

DECEPTION'S EMBRACE   (2720, $3.75)
by Jeanne Hansen

Terrified heiress Katrina Montgomery fled Memphis with what little she could carry and headed west, hiding in a freight car. By the time she reached Kansas City, she was feeling almost safe . . . until the handsomest man she'd ever seen entered the car and swept her into his embrace. She didn't know who he was or why he refused to let her go, but when she gazed into his eyes, she somehow knew she could trust him with her life . . . and her heart.

Available wherever paperbacks are sold, or order direct from the Publisher. Send cover price plus 50¢ per copy for mailing and handling to Zebra Books, Dept. 2896, 475 Park Avenue South, New York, N.Y. 10016. Residents of New York, New Jersey and Pennsylvania must include sales tax. DO NOT SEND CASH.

ROMANTIC GEMS
BY F. ROSANNE BITTNER

HEART'S SURRENDER (2945, $4.50)
Beautiful Andrea Sanders was frightened to be living so
close to the Cherokee—and terrified by turbulent passions
the handsome Indian warrior, Adam, aroused within her!

PRAIRIE EMBRACE (2035, $3.95)
Katie Russell kept reminding herself that her savage Indian
captor was beneath her contempt—but deep inside she
longed to yield to his passionate caress!

ARIZONA ECSTASY (2810, $4.50)
Lovely Lisa Powers hated the Indian who captured her, but
as time passed in the arid Southwest, she began to turn to
him first for survival, then for love!

HISTORICAL ROMANCES BY VICTORIA THOMPSON

BOLD TEXAS EMBRACE (2835, $4.50)
Art teacher Catherine Eaton could hardly believe how stubborn
Sam Connors was! Even though the rancher's young stepbrother
was an exceptionally talented painter, Sam forbade Catherine to
instruct him, fearing that art would make a sissy out of him.
Spunky and determined, the blond schoolmarm confronted the
muleheaded cowboy . . . only to find that he was as handsome as
he was hard-headed and as desirable as he was dictatorial. Before
long she had nearly forgotten what she'd come for, as Sam's
brash, breathless embrace drove from her mind all thought of
anything save wanting him . . .

TEXAS BLONDE (2183, $3.95)
When dashing Josh Logan resuced her from death by exposure,
petite Felicity Morrow realized she'd never survive rugged frontier
life without a man by her side. And when she gazed at the Texas
rancher's lean hard frame and strong rippling muscles, the determined beauty decided he was the one for her. To reach her goal,
feisty Felicity pretended to be meek and mild: the only kind of gal
Josh proclaimed he'd wed. But after she'd won his hand, the blue-
eyed temptress swore she'd quit playing his game—and still win
his heart!

ANGEL HEART (2426, $3.95)
Ever since Angelica's father died, Harlan Snyder had been an-
gling to get his hands on her ranch, the Diamond R. And now,
just when she had an important government contract to fulfill,
she couldn't find a single cowhand to hire on—all because of Snyder's threats. It was only a matter of time before she lost the
ranch. . . . That is, until the legendary gunfighter Kid Collins
turned up on her doorstep, badly wounded. Angelica assessed his
firmly muscled physique and stared into his startling blue eyes.
Beneath all that blood and dirt he was the handsomest man she
had ever seen, and the one person who could help her beat Snyder
at his own game—if the price were not too high. . . .

*Available wherever paperbacks are sold, or order direct from the
Publisher. Send cover price plus 50¢ per copy for mailing and
handling to Zebra Books, Dept. 2896, 475 Park Avenue South,
New York, N.Y. 10016. Residents of New York, New Jersey and
Pennsylvania must include sales tax. DO NOT SEND CASH.*

HISTORICAL ROMANCES BY EMMA MERRITT

RESTLESS FLAMES (2203, $3.95)

Having lost her husband six months before, determined Brenna Allen couldn't afford to lose her freight company, too. Outfitted as wagon captain with revolver, knife and whip, the single-minded beauty relentlessly drove her caravan, desperate to reach Santa Fe. Then she crossed paths with insolent Logan Mac-Dougald. The taciturn Texas Ranger was as primitive as the surrounding Comanche Territory, and he didn't hesitate to let the tantalizing trail boss know what he wanted from her. Yet despite her outrage with his brazen ways, jet-haired Brenna couldn't suppress the scorching passions surging through her . . . and suddenly she never wanted this trip to end!

COMANCHE BRIDE (2549, $3.95)

When stunning Dr. Zoe Randolph headed to Mexico to halt a cholera epidemic, she didn't think twice about traversing Comanche territory . . . until a band of bloodthirsty savages attacked her caravan. The gorgeous physician was furious that her mission had been interrupted, but nothing compared to the rage she felt on meeting the barbaric warrior who made her his slave. Determined to return to civilization, the ivory-skinned blonde decided to make a woman's ultimate sacrifice to gain her freedom — and never admit that deep down inside she burned to be loved by the handsome brute!

SWEET, WILD LOVE (2834, $4.50)

It was hard enough for Eleanor Hunt to get men to take her seriously in sophisticated Chicago — it was going to be impossible in Blissful, Kansas! These cowboys couldn't believe she was a real attorney, here to try a cattle rustling case. They just looked her up and down and grinned. Especially that Bradley Smith. The man worked for her father and he still had the audacity to stare at her with those lust-filled green eyes. Every time she turned around, he was trying to trap her in his strong embrace.